I0768739

WHEN
STORMS
RUIN

A REALM OF ISTMERE NOVEL

BOOK TWO

MICHELLE FROHMAN

1st edition 2024 published by Acorn Hill Press LLC

ISBN: 979-8-9883045-3-1 (e-book)

ISBN: 979-8-9883045-4-8 (paperback)

ISBN: 979-8-9883045-5-5 (hardback)

Cover design by MerryBookRound

Editing by EJL Editing

Map by Cartographybird Maps

Formatting by Michelle Frohman

Art by Alice Maria Power

www.michellefrohmanauthor.com

Author Note

This story explores themes that may be troubling to some readers. For a full list of content warnings please visit www.michellefrohmanauthor.com

For Grammy—
Who will undoubtedly be shocked by the themes in this book,
but without whom I wouldn't have been able to follow my dreams.

THE MYRENE SEA
MYRENE
THE REALM OF
ISTMERE
MAPPED
IN THE PRESENT AGE
DRAKELLIA
SIRALETH
SIRALETH
PORTAL
SIRALE
DOCKS

THE STONE
PALACE
AKRA
PRINS
DRAGON'S
HOLLOW
THE
SHADOW
PRINS
PORTAL
PRINS
DOCKYARDS
DRAGON'S
WAY
THE SIRAWAY SEA

Pronunciation Guide

Characters

Alastir: A-luh-STIR
Araneoch: ARE-uh-nay-awk
Kotova: Kuh-TOE-vuh
Kolya: KOHL-ya
Noctani: KNOCK-tahn-ee
Saanvi: SAHN-vee

Places

Akra: A-KR-uh
Istmere: IST-mear
Prins: Prin-Z
Siraleth: SEAR-uh-leth

PROLOGUE

Akra, Istmere
18 Years Ago

It was beginning to feel as if this baby would *never* come. Annelise had been pushing for *hours*, possibly days. Her body was growing weak, her resolve deteriorating rapidly. Her first child had come into this world easily, in a mere matter of hours. This labor felt like an eternity. The contractions were coming faster and faster, but this child had no plans to join this realm any time soon.

The midwives were beginning to worry. They had already called for the king. He traveled back from Siraleth with haste, but they still weren't sure if he would make it in time. Annelise was a fighting spirit, and she would not give up easily. The bedsheets were soaked with sweat and blood, Annelise crying out as she tried her hardest to *push, and push, and push.*

The midwives had done everything they could to turn the baby, but to no avail. Their last hope was that the Stormshade witch would arrive in time. That she could sneak through the hidden passageways in the stone castle to help bring this baby into the world. She was a renowned midwife with long-forgotten birthing spells, but she was also a Stormshade. If she was caught, she would be killed. She was the queen's last hope for survival.

Annelise had hidden her own nature well. Everyone in the castle, including the midwives, thought her to be a Shade. Even her husband, The Dark King Osiris, didn't suspect her true nature. That she was of the same lineage as the witch they had sent for. That she, herself, was a *Stormshade.*

She prayed night and day that the king's child would be a Shade. Or, mother bless us, a Nightshade, but Annelise feared the worst. This child was a fight from the very beginning, and Annelise knew only a Stormshade would fight *this* hard. Would be *this* stubborn and strong-willed, even before birth.

Annelise released a guttural scream as she gripped the headboard, a wave of pain threatening to take her under. A fresh swell of blood poured forth, and Annelise shook her head back and forth violently. *No.* She wouldn't lose this fight. She would save this child. *Her child.*

A knock on the door sounded, and the midwives hurried to open it. Whether they hoped it was the Stormshade witch they had sent for or The Dark King, they weren't sure. A woman spilled into the room in a frenzy of cloak and chaos, tossing her stark white hair out of her face and kneeling at Annelise's bedside.

"How long?" The woman asked, her teeth gritted, her gaze on Annelise.

They exchanged a glance between them, unsure of how much time had already passed.

"Almost a day and a half, if we had to hazard a guess," one of the nurses replied, bowing her head so as to not make eye contact with the Stormshade.

"*Fools*," the witch spat, "you should have called me right away."

She quickly got to work, mixing a concoction of herbs and spices into a bowl and crushing it into a fine powder with the pestle. She poured the milled powder into a short glass and waved her hand over it, a spell spilling forth from her lips. The glass filled with liquid and turned a dark, murky color.

"Drink," she instructed, thrusting the glass at Annelise.

The witch took a Bloodstone Jasper, a dark green stone spattered with red, and strung it around Annelise's neck.

Annelise met her gaze, a question in her eyes.

"This is the only way," the Stormshade healer confirmed with a finite nod of her head.

Annelise brought the murky brew to her lips and threw the strange liquid back in one gulp, cringing at the bitter, poisonous taste.

"Good. Now we have to turn her."

The healer laid her hand on Annelise's swollen belly, words pouring forth, her eyes closed in concentration.

"Aqua, Terra, Ignis et Aer, da mihi rem pulcherrimam."

The words were a hushed whisper.

"Chant with me, witch." The healer's words were a sharp command.

Annelise did as she was told, chanting with the Stormshade witch, her hand clasping her stomach. She squeezed her eyes shut against the sharp stab of pain.

"*Aqua, Terra, Ignis et Aer, da mihi rem pulcherrimam.*"

"*Aqua, Terra, Ignis et Aer, da mihi rem pulcherrimam.*"

"*Aqua, Terra, Ignis et Aer, da mihi rem pulcherrimam.*"

Annelise could feel the movement as the child turned, and she smiled through the sweat and tears that stained her cheeks. A hysterical laugh bubbled forth from her lips.

"Now *push*," the healer commanded, moving to the base of the bed to deliver the stubborn child.

The midwives remained on the outskirts of the room, letting the Stormshade witch take over. Only magic could save this child now.

Annelise gave the last of her strength, of her energy, *and pushed and pushed and pushed.* With a cry, the newborn entered the world, and the relief in the room was palpable. Annelise had lost a lot of blood, and her vision began to blur from the poisonous mixture she had taken. Birthing spells were dangerous, indeed.

"Take the child!" The Stormshade healer's voice lashed out, a harsh command as one of the midwives scurried forwards to wrap the child in a muslin cloth in her arms. She rocked the baby back and forth, cooing to it softly to soothe its cries.

The Stormshade witch hovered over Annelise as her eyes rolled back into her head, nearing unconsciousness. The healer clasped the Bloodstone in her palm and reached into her cloak to take out a small dagger. She cut her palm, the blood pouring forth to cover the Bloodstone greedily. The witch moved the Bloodstone to her other fist, where she clasped it tightly. Her bloody hand moved to smear bright red across Annelise's forehead.

"This is blood magic!" One of the midwives cried out, clutching her chest with a shaking hand.

"This is forbidden!" Another of the maids called out, backing towards the door.

The Stormshade healer turned towards them, her eyes endless black pits, swirling with bright red blood.

"*Hushhhh,*" she hissed, her eyes falling on each of them before turning back towards Annelise.

Her spell had turned darker now, more sinister. The energy in the room had plummeted, all the magic focused within the spell the Stormshade witch spoke. A few of the candles lining the windowsill snuffed out, and a chill crept into the air. She spoke the same words, over and over, and after a few moments, Annelise's eyes popped back open.

She took a deep breath, choking on the residual poison that coated her tongue.

"You will be fine now," the Stormshade witch assured her.

Her eyes had transformed back to their plain, unremarkable hazel. The blood spell was complete. The healer grabbed a cloth and wiped the blood from Annelise's forehead, the only evidence that remained of the dark magic.

She had saved the queen with blood magic...but at what cost?

The witch turned to the child, still in the maid's arms. She pressed her thumb to the child's forehead, a shocked gasp escaping her lips as her eyes turned milky white. Annelise had feared the worst, and the expression on the witch before her only confirmed those suspicions.

"*A Stormshade*," she hissed, "a girl."

She had *seen*. The witch before her was far more powerful than she had initially thought. She turned towards Annelise, her white hair falling over her shoulder, worry in her eyes. "Keep her *safe*. No matter the cost. *She will be the key*. Without her, there will never be an end to the strife that plagues this realm."

Annelise had already suspected. Alastir had all but seen it, but the healer's confirmation of the child's destiny made her chest tighten painfully. How would she keep a Stormshade child safe from the king himself? Even if she was his only child?

"The king has arrived!" A voice called from the hallway.

Annelise could hear the floorboards creaking, the servants rushing about.

"You must go, *now*," one of the midwives spoke as she led the Stormshade witch to a hidden passageway. She pulled a tapestry in the queen's bedroom to the side, revealing a small stone door.

"Thank you," Annelise called out, her voice strangled.

The Stormshade healer turned once, glancing from Annelise to the child, then disappeared through the stone door and down the corridor beyond without a word.

"Give her to me," Annelise commanded, her arms outstretched.

The midwife hurriedly brought the child forth, placing the babe in her waiting arms.

"What will you name her, your majesty?" The midwife asked, using a wet towel to clean Annelise off and make her presentable for their king.

Annelise's lips curled into a soft smile.

"Diana," she answered, her eyes never leaving the face of the child held firmly within her embrace.

The child struggled and cried out, but she was with her mother, and she was safe. For now.

Heavy footsteps sounded down the corridor, and Annelise dreaded what she knew would come next. There was no way for her to hide the child's true nature from Osiris, she only prayed that he would forgive her. That he wouldn't hurt them. There had been no time to find a cloaking spell to mask the child's magic as she had done to herself, and they were out of time. She only had a few fleeting moments alone with her child before the king burst into the room, his Nightshade guards flanking him on either side.

"Annelise?" The unspoken question held so much tenderness in it as the king met her eyes and spoke.

"I am fine. The child is fine." Annelise's voice shook as she spoke.

"I heard the birth was...difficult." Osiris moved forwards, towards the bed.

"Quite," Annelise confirmed with a nod of her head, swallowing hard. She bit back the surge of bile that climbed the back of her throat.

"Let me see." Osiris sat at the edge of the bed.

"A daughter," Annelise spoke as she turned Diana ever so slightly towards Osiris.

He reached out, caressing the child's cheek with the back of his calloused hand.

"She is beautiful, like her mother." He almost smiled. *Almost.* "You lied to me."

"What do you speak of, Osiris?" Annelise feigned innocence, and a deathly calm settled over The Dark King.

"*Stormshade,*" the king spat the word as if it were a curse, his gaze turning cold.

"Osiris?" Annelise's voice sounded small in her own ears.

The midwives fled the room, fearing what might come next. They didn't want to be caught in the crossfire, or worse, punished themselves.

Annelise and Osiris were alone with the child.

"Only a Stormshade witch could bear another Stormshade," he hissed, standing from the bed.

"Osiris, she has your glacial blue eyes," Annelise pleaded.

"And *your* magic," he seethed. "How could you do this to me? How could you betray me this way?"

"I love you, Osiris. This is *our* child. I bear no ill intent."

"That is no child of mine." Osiris stormed towards the door and paused with his hand on the knob, gripping it so tightly it began to crack under his palm.

"What will you do?" Annelise asked, gripping Diana tight and holding her against her chest. A hot tear spilled down her cheek, catching in the soft muslin of the baby's cloth.

"You will leave The Stone City," Osiris replied, swallowing hard. His eyes were on the floorboards before him.

"Leave?" Annelise whispered, not understanding.

"I will not sentence you to death, Anna. I am not the monster you think me to be," he replied coldly.

"I don't think you a monster at all, Osiris. This changes *nothing*. We can still be together," Annelise replied desperately, her voice ragged and raw.

"*No*. You will leave The Stone City, and you will never come back. I will not kill you, but I will not help you either. Take whatever you can carry and leave. Tonight."

"All of this over *my magic*?" Annelise asked, rising to her feet with Diana in her arms. Her legs felt weak beneath her. She wasn't sure how far they could carry her tonight. "You cast me out because I have *the wrong type of magic*? And what of your daughter? Why this blind hatred? You are better than this, Osiris."

"The king has spoken. If you do not leave tonight, I cannot protect you." His eyes met Annelise's for a fleeting moment before they returned to the floor. He pressed them closed, struggling against the inner turmoil he waged war against.

Was that what he was trying to do? Protect her? Did he think the people of Istmere would rise against her if they found out what she truly was?

"We can fix this. Together. As a family." Annelise's words fell on deaf ears. Osiris opened his eyes and turned the knob, wrenching the door open.

"*Tonight,*" he insisted.

Annelise felt helpless. How could she take her newborn daughter and flee? Where would she go? How could she muster the strength? Hot tears trailed down her cheeks as she coughed back a sob that threatened to choke her.

Annelise had fallen in love with Osiris, despite *everything*. Despite his reputation. Despite his appetite for violence. Despite what she knew would happen if he ever found out her true identity. He was soft and tender. He was kind...but he was stubborn. And he was short-sighted.

Annelise bit back a cry as she called a midwife forth, and the girl came sprinting down the hallway. She passed Diana to the woman as she hastily packed a bag with only the bare necessities. She changed out of her bloody nightgown and donned a thick woolen cape, strapping the pack and her weapons across her back.

"Where will you go, your majesty?" the midwife asked, bowing her head as Annelise moved forwards. She took Diana into her arms, wrapping her tightly in another warm bundle of linens.

"I'm not sure," Annelise answered honestly, wrapping Diana firmly into her arms. "Will you do me a favor, Odette?"

"Of course, your majesty," the maid answered immediately, her eyes wide.

"Tell no one of the child. Not your closest friend. Not your family. No one. And tell the other midwives and maids the same."

"Of course, your majesty. We will keep the child a secret."

"Thank you, Odette. You have been a loyal friend." Annelise gave the nursemaid a soft smile before starting down the darkened corridor of the castle.

She made her way to the first floor of the palace unnoticed and slipped out a side door that led to a steep set of stairs. Annelise descended the stairs with great care, cautious not to jostle the newborn fastened to her chest.

There was only one place Annelise could think to go. To the white cottage in the countryside of Siraleth. The one with the tree swing that hung from the old willow out back.

To Zion and Donika.

Annelise reached the bottom of the steps and started across the dark field, hurriedly rushing towards the tree line before she was spotted by the guards or the archers.

Her strawberry blonde hair billowed out behind her as she fled The Stone Palace, Diana wrapped in a bundle, pressed tightly to her chest.

This night would be her secret to keep.

1

Akra, Istmere
Present Day

Time is a funny thing…it passes in fits and starts, or sometimes, it passes all at once. For me, time felt infinite. How many days had passed? How many weeks or months had been eaten away by the passing of time since I had been locked in the Stormvault? Time was intangible, but it was also reliable in its passing. No matter how many times I scraped my dirty fingernails against the packed dirt floor of this cell, or paced the iron bars back and forth, time would pass.

The sound of the rats chewing away at the stale scraps of bread had me turning my head in the dim light of the cell, searching the darkness for Tess. I was faintly able to make out her sleeping form slumped against the cold concrete wall.

She was weak.

Too weak to bring the stale bread to her mouth to keep her strength up. Her clothes hung limply from her frame, her natural curves reduced to the hard angles of skin and bone.

I stalked towards the back of the cell, shooing the rats away and gathering the bread back onto the tray at Tess' feet. The hollows in my own skin were more prominent than I'd ever thought possible, but I was not broken.

Not yet.

Each day I ate the stale and rotten food the Nightshade guards of Donika's army brought us, and each day my anger and determination grew. The sensation of my magic swelling up inside of me was all but a forgotten memory at this point. I couldn't remember the last time I had even been able to touch it. To sense its warmth under my skin.

But I was ready to call on it when the time came.

Because the time *would* come.

I had no idea how long we had been held captive in the Stormvault, but if I had to hazard a guess, I would say it may have only been weeks. Long enough for our clothes to fit loosely on our frames and for our skin to degrade to a lifeless pallor. Long enough for the dirt to cake under my fingernails thickly enough that it was merely second nature. Long enough to mourn the loss of my magic behind these iron bars. To forget what the sun felt like against my pale skin.

But not long enough to break me.

Tess stirred in her sleep, and I joined her on the floor of the cell, winding my arm through hers to hold her while she slept. To keep her warm. Nights in the Stormvault without windows and only concrete to surround us were cold and endless.

The rat scurried away now that I had removed the bread from its grasp. I felt—not for the first time—envious that it could crawl right through the space between the iron bars. If our food source continued to become more and more scarce, the thought might truly become a possibility for us. It had been a long time since Puck had been able to sneak down and bring us anything. We had to settle for whatever generosity Donika felt to bestow upon us.

I hadn't seen Nik since that first day. The day I had seen him kissing Donika, and he had crawled down to the Stormvault to beg for my forgiveness. To profess he would do *anything* to gain my trust back. That everything he felt was real.

He hadn't fooled me.

His absence was no surprise despite the skip my heart did each time the iron door to the Stormvault creaked open. Each time Donika brought us to the throne room to play with our minds or torture our bodies, his absence was a weight deep in my core.

How could he simply...disappear?

The fact that Puck had stopped his covert visits had me convinced *something* was coming. Donika must be tiring of her endless torture of us for the location of the Grimoire. Tess couldn't give her anything, of course. I was the only one who knew its location.

A humorless laugh bubbled to my lips at the thought of it tucked away in my dresser drawer, not so expertly hidden beneath my underwear. How had she not sent her soldiers after it? It wouldn't be that hard to find if they ransacked my family home. Was there a reason she hadn't visited the human realm herself?

A bitter taste filled my mouth at the thought of Donika inside my home in the mortal realm. The unassuming stone house set at the base of the mountain where my practical, stubborn human mother raised me and my brother. I would never know my birth mother or father...Donika had seen to that.

The first few weeks locked in the Stormvault had my thoughts spinning about my Kotova lineage. I had always felt out of place in the human realm. I had always had a side of me that was drawn to the magic of this earth, and my mother had always dismissed it or downplayed it. Had she known who I truly was? That I was the heir to the throne of Istmere?

I was the daughter of Osiris, The Dark King who sat the throne of Istmere for decades. I was the daughter of Annelise, a brave and powerful Stormshade who would do *anything* for her children. I was the sister of Donika, the selfish and evil Black Heart.

I wasn't Diana Barnes anymore.

I was Diana Kotova, lost heir to the throne, and I would stop at *nothing* to take down my sister. She had taken *everything* from me, and I would allow her to take *nothing* else.

Including my throne.

The taste of vengeance kept me going. It kept me from breaking, deep, deep, down in the cells of the Stormvault.

The iron door at the end of the long corridor squeaked open and the sound of a single set of footsteps filled my ears as Tess stirred beside me. I gave her a gentle shake, and she opened her eyes slightly, enough to see a tall man holding a lantern come into view.

It wasn't someone I recognized, and I was sure he had never been down to the Stormvault before. His black hair was shorn against his head, and his bronze skin shone beneath the glow of the lantern. It took a few moments for my eyes to adjust to the brightness.

"Do you know who I am?" the stranger called out. His stance was wide, his expression skeptical as his eyes bounced back and forth between us.

"Should I?" I called back, my voice hoarse from disuse.

He took a step forwards and pressed his face against the bars to get a better look at us through the darkness. I wasn't sure what he saw, but his eyes widened infinitesimally before he masked his expression once more.

"I am Zion. You have heard of me?" The question sounded rhetorical as he took a step back, his jaw set.

I had heard many of the Nightshade guards and soldiers mention a man named Zion. Fletcher had threatened to call a man named Zion as if he was in charge, back in the mortal realm. What was he doing here? Was this Donika's last ditch effort to get us to turn over the grimoire?

"I have," I replied curtly, setting my own jaw in return.

I would not be intimidated by one of Donika's men. I had cried many tears in the privacy of darkness this cell offered, but I vowed I would be strong in the face of the adversaries I met here in Akra.

I would not flinch.

"Do you know who I am?" he asked, his voice insinuated he already knew the answer to this question.

"Should I?" I repeated, my chin held high.

"I am Donika's father," Zion breathed, lowering the lantern to the ground to better illuminate the cell.

That was...unexpected.

I met Zion's gaze with renewed interest. This was the man that Annelise left to raise Donika on his own, or that was the story Donika told, at least. She had only returned to Zion when Osiris, The Dark King, had found out she was a Stormshade and banished her from The Stone City.

The man before me was distinctly *not* on our side, I decided. I immediately raised my guard. Tess was silent beside me, but I could sense the same resolution in the set of her shoulders and the stern expression she faced Zion with.

"What do you want with us?" I asked, uncomfortable under his heavy gaze.

"As you've already guessed, Donika sent me. You are running out of time. I advise you to give her what she wants, and fast. She grows tired of your games."

"*My* games?" I asked, incredulous. I moved to my feet and brushed the dirt off the back of my weathered pants as I moved towards the front of the cell. "We are nothing but Donika's play-things. Her prisoners. She is the one playing games with us. If she sent you to torture us, I'm sorry to tell you the effort will be wasted."

"I cannot do any worse to you than Donika can herself. I simply came to deliver a warning. Donika gets what she wants, and she wants your family grimoire. I suggest you give it to her," Zion replied, meeting my cold stare through the iron bars.

"I will take your *suggestion* under advisement," I seethed. "You are her father, and I am sure the apple does not fall far from the tree."

Zion swallowed hard before answering. "I loved your mother once."

"And look where that got you," I snapped back, grabbing the iron bars as I drew closer. Zion took a step back.

"You have your mother's resilience, I see." Zion's eyes flashed with a long-forgotten memory as an expression of familiarity crossed over his face. It was as if he was seeing a ghost.

"My mother, who I will never get to meet because of *your daughter*. How can you defend her?" Did Zion seriously think I would simply hand over the grimoire after everything Donika had put us through? Because of the mention of a mother I never even knew? "I will never give Donika the grimoire. Whatever it is you have planned for us...give us your worst. You will have to kill me to get it."

Zion laughed, the sound echoing off the cold concrete walls. I felt Tess' warm presence join me, her hand against the small of my back. "That can be arranged. It's as I thought...you are utterly and completely useless to her." Zion gave us a cold sneer as he bent to pick up the lantern. "Two days. I suggest you be ready."

Ready for what, exactly?

As I was about to open my mouth to ask, Zion turned without another word. I watched as he retreated down the corridor, taking every ounce of light with him.

"What did he mean 'be ready.' Be ready for what?" Tess asked, voicing my own thoughts.

"I'm not sure, Tess." I swallowed hard as I met her gaze in the darkness. I was so, so tired. I couldn't ignore the feeling in my gut that things were about to change, for better or for worse. "I do know one thing for certain...something is coming."

2

I hadn't expected another visit for days after Zion left, so I was surprised when a batch of Nightshade guards descended the Stormvault steps the following day. They carried with them ash shackles that they bound us with, dragging us up the three steep flights to the throne room.

We were unceremoniously deposited onto the cold marble floor and kneed in the back until we dropped to our hands and knees before the throne.

Donika was nowhere to be seen.

A quick glance at the windows that lined the extravagant room let us know that it was nighttime in Akra. Whether it was early or late, I had no idea. The guards quickly retreated, leaving the large double doors unlocked in their wake. I inhaled deeply and leaned back on my heels.

We may have been taken out of the Stormvault to be questioned and tortured, but I appreciated any moment of fresh, clean air outside of that damp, dark cell. They hadn't drugged us this time, which meant Donika wanted to talk. I had a nagging pit in the bottom of my stomach about Zion's visit.

Two days.

What was going to happen in two days? Our execution?

Tess took a deep breath beside me and met my eyes. I wasn't sure she could take another round of torture. The scars on our skin from Donika's shadow magic were sure to be permanent at this point, never giving us a chance to heal before dragging us back out of our cells for another round.

The door creaked open behind us, and my heart jumped into my throat as I turned my head. Despite his betrayal, despite his absence, I still found myself hoping it was Nik.

I swallowed back that hope as Donika's wolf form slunk into the throne room, her white coat stark against the dark night that surrounded us. Her face was covered in a blood red sigil that I couldn't decipher the meaning of. I had memorized its curving lines and sharp angles to search my grimoire for its translation.

That is, if I ever saw it again.

I was sure it was something to do with black magic, or even blood magic. The sigil *did* resemble freshly painted blood, with dripping lines that trickled over her eyelids and down her muzzle.

She slunk towards the throne, her black wolves close on her heels. Her closest guards hadn't left her side these past few weeks. As she ascended the stone steps to the dais, she slowly transformed into the beautiful nightmare that plagued my every waking thought. Her blue and white hair cascaded down her back in thick curls as she parted the black satin dress she wore and sat, her black eyes meeting mine. A chill ran down my spine as her lips curved into a wicked grin. Those eyes were always deeply unnerving. They were as dark as obsidian, and endless.

Donika let a heavy pause fill the room as her guards encircled her throne, her eyes never leaving mine. Before she even spoke a word, her shadows crept out from her perfectly painted red fingernails, snaking across the floor towards me.

For a moment I was relieved that she hadn't gone for Tess—worried that she wouldn't be able to handle one more lashing—before the pain engulfed me.

I cried out, falling forwards. With my hands bound, I had nothing to catch myself with, and my head cracked against the marble floor before I curled onto my side. The pain of Donika's shadows was all-encompassing, as if hot knives or razor blades pressed against my skin. My eyes remained open, but I saw nothing but the darkness of her shadows surrounding me.

My breath strangled in my throat as I tried to fill my lungs with air, but all I tasted was smoke and ash. Donika's shadows were a million needles pricking my skin all at once, but piercing deep. I imagined the depths of hell weren't even this dark and painful. Tess reached for me in the darkness and I cried out again, warning her away. I would sooner pass out from the pain than let Donika break me.

A sinister laugh filled my ears as Donika's shadow serpents retreated, leaving me panting and glistening with sweat on the checkered floor. Tess grabbed my arm to help pull me back to my knees. I coughed as the fresh air of the throne room stung my lungs, and I spit out a mouthful of saliva that tasted of bile and blood.

I met Donika's eyes with my chin held high. I wasn't sure I could take much more of her torture myself, but I hadn't hit my breaking point.

Not yet.

"It's good to see you, Diana. How was your visit with my father?" she asked, tapping a pointed fingernail against her cheek thoughtfully.

I didn't reply. I simply fixed her with a cold stare. The taste of blood filled my mouth once more. I felt it trickle down my chin, unable to wipe my face clean with my hands still bound. I rubbed my bloodied chin against my dirt-stained shoulder before fixing my glare on Donika once more.

"No progress? As I'm sure he told you, I grow tired of you. If you insist on holding out, I don't have a use for you any longer. Or Tess. Think carefully, your decision not only condemns *you* but also those you care about."

"Why haven't you gone to search for it yourself?" I asked, cocking my head to the side. "If the grimoire is so important to you, why don't you go find it? Instead, you sit here on your false throne with your sniveling soldiers at your feet. It certainly can't be that hard to find. I *am* merely a worthless little Stormshade, after all."

Something flashed in Donika's lifeless eyes, something like fear. Had I guessed correctly? Was Donika not able to visit the mortal realm herself?

"If I don't have the grimoire by week's end, you have decided your own fate," Donika sneered. She uncrossed her legs and descended the stone steps towards me. "After all, if you are dead, the grimoire has to pick another Kotova. *There aren't many left.*"

My blood ran cold in my veins as her words settled in, but I set my jaw as she approached me. "When is week's end, pray tell? You have us locked in a windowless dungeon, and I've simply lost track of time," I replied coldly.

"Two days," she spit out, her shadows snaking out to take hold of my chin and turn it upwards, forcing my eyes towards her.

I was on my knees before her, blood trickling down my chin, my breaths coming shallow. I feared the damage her shadows were doing to me each time they attacked me, and if I would ever be able to fully recover from them. Zion *had* been warning us, then. Donika would only give us two more days before she executed us.

Nik had to have some inkling of where I could have hidden the grimoire. Why hadn't he found it and brought it to her himself? Had she done something to him? Or had she sent him back to the mortal realm to search for it himself?

"I'll admit, you're equally as stubborn as our mother." Donika smiled, but it never reached her lifeless eyes.

How dare she speak of our mother, the mother I would never meet.

The mother she killed.

I fought her shadows to turn my chin down and rain blood-soaked spit down onto her satin dress, specks of it flying against her perfectly manicured feet. Donika did not hesitate. She backhanded me so forcefully my head turned sharply and a cry left my lips, blood splattering Tess' shirt.

I was stunned into silence, my cheek stinging as blood flowed from my open mouth to drip onto the floor. Oh, how I craved my magic at this moment. Just a touch of it to send Donika flying back against her precious throne. I met her eyes with a deathly stillness as she threw her head back and laughed.

"Why don't you unshackle me and see if you're still laughing," I suggested.

"Little Stormshade, I've been practicing magic since I was born. You have been practicing magic for months. In *no* realm would you be able to stand against me," she replied.

"Then why don't you let me try?" I smiled, revealing my blood-stained teeth.

Donika was thoughtful as she peered down at me. She had expected to break me by now. She underestimated my will, my thirst for vengeance. I only had two days left to figure out how to manipulate my way out of the Stormvault, or Tess and I were dead.

"Wouldn't you rather run home to your mortal mother and leave this all behind you?" Donika asked with a shake of her head.

Even if I was willing to part with the grimoire, I would *never* give it to her now. Not after she revealed she was my sister. That she ruined any chance I had of meeting my birth mother. After she tortured Tess and me endlessly. Starved us. She hadn't even scratched the surface of my willfulness.

"And leave you to my throne?" I asked with a wicked smile.

"It was never *your* throne," Donika spat, raising her hand again to strike. This time I flinched back, the sting on my cheek still fresh.

"Stop!" Tess called out, halting Donika as she swung towards me.

"The little mouse finally found her voice." Donika laughed, turning towards Tess with her raised hand.

"Do. Not. Touch. Her." My voice was cold and foreign in my own ears.

I could take Donika's questions and her abuse, but I wouldn't let her do the same to Tess.

"Or what?" Donika replied, turning her attention back towards me. "You are *my* prisoner. I will do with you both as I please."

It was the same conversation, over and over again. How many times had Donika brought us to the throne room to torture us, and how many times had we stood fast against her?

"I've given you a lot to think about," Donika started, brushing her hair over her shoulder. "Think long and hard, Diana. I know you'll make the right choice...in the end."

Donika's gaze flicked towards the open doorway and the soldiers standing there advanced, hauling us up by our arms and dragging us from the room.

I glanced over my shoulder to see Donika standing in the middle of the throne room, encircled by her army of black wolves, standing in a pool of my blood.

3

The blood that had coated the throne room floor had me thinking about what options we may have left. I wasn't able to touch my magic through the bars of the cell, or with the shackles on, but what about blood magic? Did blood magic surpass the ash and iron that was dampening my magic and stopping me from reaching out to it? I didn't know anything about blood magic, but we were running out of options. Puck and Nik hadn't returned, and it had been a whole day since we had any visitors at all, including Donika's soldiers. I assumed Donika was going to starve us until weeks end to ensure we 'made the right decision.'

Tess and I were weak, and I feared that even if an opportunity to escape presented itself, we wouldn't have the strength or speed to make it out. I wasn't sure I would have the strength to reach out to my magic, even if we weren't bound with ash shackles outside of this prison. We were out of time, and we were out of options...unless I could figure out a way to tap into black magic or blood magic, like Donika. Was it worth the price of my soul? To keep the grimoire from Donika and save Tess and my family?

If it came to that...it had to be.

My mind was racing trying to remember all the spells from my grimoire. Some of them I hadn't understood, but I had never spoken Latin before. The opening spell had come to me in my time of need, as if it was a long-forgotten memory. As if I had known it once, but was spelled to forget. I rest my head against the back wall of the cell as I was lost to my own thoughts. With each passing moment we were running out of time. I wasn't sure how much time was left to our last day, but I was certain it was coming to an end.

I once again found myself wondering how much time had passed since we arrived in Akra. My mother and Jake must have been going crazy searching for us...and Tess' parents, too. In the solitude of the dark cell, I let myself grieve my choice not to tell them where we were going. I hoped they would not be searching for us for an eternity. I wanted them to find closure.

A hot tear rolled down my cheek as I fought against my desperation. I felt utterly and completely helpless. Tess rested her head against my shoulder with a deep sigh as she squeezed my leg. I needed to figure out a way to save Tess, if nothing else. Even if it cost me my own life.

At first, I had tried giving Donika false locations to search, but that had made her angrier than ever. Her torture was particularly cruel in the weeks following. I would give anything to sleep in a soft bed, or to take a hot shower.

The tears traveled through the grime and blood caked to my skin, surely leaving stains across my cheeks. It had been too long since I had seen my own reflection, and I was certain the one that would stare back at me now would be a stranger, anyway. I was so deep in my own thoughts, racking my brain to remember a spell from the grimoire, that I hadn't even heard the Stormvault door creak open.

A lantern came into view and I hoped to see Puck or Nik, but it was Zion whose face shone beneath the glow of the lamp.

"What are you doing here?" I called out, wiping my tears with the back of my dirt-smeared hand. Tess perked up beside me.

"As I told you, there isn't much time left. I figured you would be needing this," Zion replied as he nodded towards the tray in his hand.

I hadn't even noticed it. He unlocked the cell and placed the tray on the dirt floor before closing and locking it once more. He took a step back as I reached for the tray and dragged it towards us.

Stale bread and stew.

Tess and I began to devour it as if we had never been given such a decadent meal. It had been weeks since we had anything more than stale bread in our stomachs. As I brought a piece of the bread dipped in stew to my mouth I paused, my eyes meeting Zion's.

"I wouldn't poison you," he said, guessing my thoughts. "I wouldn't deny Donika her last few hours with you."

"Then why bring us food?" I asked as I shoved the wet piece of bread into my mouth and savored the taste of the gravy and meat.

Zion didn't answer, he simply watched us eat in silence, studying us in the glow of the lantern.

"You aren't as evil as she is if you brought us this food. Is there a small piece of you that wants to let us out?" Tess asked, swallowing a hard piece of bread.

Zion was thoughtful before he answered. "Even if I did, you would never make it past her guards."

His answer gave me pause.

He hadn't said no.

Did Zion want to...help us? Is that why he brought us this food? He had warned us that we were running out of time, but I had thought that was simply his warning from Donika.

What if it was something else?

"You want to help us?" I asked, confused.

"I didn't say that," he replied, but his voice wasn't cold and his eyes were warm as they met mine.

He appeared...different from our last interaction.

"Does Donika know you are here?" I asked around a mouthful of the brown stew.

"No."

I couldn't decipher his expression in the low light, but I thought he appeared regretful. He had gone against Donika's orders to bring us this food. Was he feeling guilty that we only had hours left? Or was this about my mother? Whatever it was, I was grateful for the meal.

Even if it was our last.

"Thank you," I said as we finished off the plate of food and slid the tray back towards the front of the cell. Zion quietly unlocked it and took the tray, removing any evidence that anyone had been here.

"Three hours. Be ready." He turned towards the Stormvault door, but I called out after him.

"Three hours for what? What do we need to be ready for?" I asked, "I thought we had another half a day, at least."

"You do," he replied, turning to meet my eyes.

I couldn't decipher the meaning behind his gaze, or the fact that when he turned back around towards the door, the corner of his mouth lifted into a smile.

"Then what does that mean?" Tess asked urgently as Zion walked away once more.

"Three hours. Be ready," he repeated the words, calling over his shoulder without turning back. He quickly disappeared down the long, dark corridor, leaving nothing but silence in his wake.

4

Zion had come down to the Stormvault to warn us, but what was he warning us about, exactly? Did Donika plan to cut our deadline short? Whatever she had in store for us, I would be ready. I couldn't tell how much time had passed as Tess and I sat in the darkness, awaiting our sentence. I would give anything to know what day it was. What time. The waiting was the worst part.

Had an hour passed already? Two?

Tess held my hand in the darkness and gave it a squeeze. "Do you think Donika is done with us? That they will drag us back to the throne room to execute us?" she asked, uncertain.

Her voice sounded brittle and weak. Tess hadn't fared as well in the Stormvault as I had. She didn't have a thirst for retribution driving her. She didn't crave vengeance the way I did. Tess hated Donika, but my anger...my anger was personal.

"I'm not sure," I replied, giving her hand a squeeze in return. "Whatever it is, we will face it together," I told her resolutely.

My stomach felt hollow at the thought that we had run out of time, despite being full with the only real meal we had been given in weeks. These could be our last moments together, and we hadn't seen Puck or Nik in weeks.

Where were they? What was keeping them away?

They had promised to come up with a plan to break us out of the Stormvault, but Nik had never even come back at all. Puck had returned a few times over the following weeks, but his visits had stopped some time ago. Had they given up? Had they left Akra entirely? Left us to our fate with Donika?

"Do you think there's any chance Nik or Puck will come back?" she asked hopefully, voicing my thoughts once more.

Even after everything, despite how weak she had gotten, she still had hope. I admired that about Tess...but I wasn't so certain. I was more cynical by nature.

"I'm not sure," I answered honestly.

A part of me wished to see them again, even if it was one last time. There was so much left unsaid, so many emotions still warring within me. Nik's absence was another betrayal in itself. Had Donika found out he visited us in the Stormvault, and he had been forced to stay away? Or did he simply not care, and all of those pretty words were simply lies?

A large part of me despised him to my very core, that he could touch me and kiss me, then betray me within the same breath. But there was a piece of me, no matter how small, that yearned for him to come down to see us.

One last time.

Zion's words ran through my head on an endless loop. He had said we hadn't yet met our deadline...so what was coming? Why had he been kind to us and brought us food? His words had been a warning, but without knowing what was coming...we had no way to prepare.

Was Zion on our side?

Tess and I both startled as the door to the Stormvault creaked open at the end of the long corridor. Had it been three hours already? I expected to see Zion making his way towards our cell, but the sound of multiple sets of footsteps echoed through the chamber.

Was this it? Was our time up?

I swallowed hard and turned to Tess, grabbing her hand in the darkness as the light of a lantern slowly illuminated our cell. I squeezed her hand tightly, vowing not to let go even if they had to tear us apart.

If this was the end, Tess and I were in this together.

Always.

When a figure came into view, their face was obscured by the cover of their hood. A black face covering sat barely over their nose leaving only their eyes exposed. Green eyes met mine in the low light, then fell on Tess before rushing forwards, pulling the mask down.

"Puck," Tess breathed, scrambling to her feet beside me.

I rose as well, cautiously remaining at the back of the cell. It had been weeks since we had seen Puck. What was he doing here? Had Zion sent him?

Tess grabbed Puck's forearm through the bars of the cell as a tear ran down her cheek. She softly wiped it away, a humorless laugh escaping her.

"Where have you been?" she asked, gripping Puck tightly.

He gave a firm shake of his head. "We don't have time for that, we have to go. *Now.*"

Puck turned, and for the first time we saw another figure standing behind him, obscured by his broad frame. Before us stood an older woman with freckled cheeks and rosy, golden hair that appeared to have been dipped in copper. Her unruly curls flowed down her back to her hips. She handed Puck a set of keys and he fumbled with them, unsure of which one would open the cell door. It appeared to be a master set of some sort, each key almost identical. Had they stolen it off one of the Nightshade soldiers, or did the keys belong to this woman?

She was dressed as if she were a servant, her white shirt crinkled and dirty, her brown shift dress that she wore atop it plain and falling to her ankles. But her eyes were alight, bright and blue beneath the glow of the lantern.

Who was this woman?

Another pair of footsteps approached the front of the cell and my breath caught in my throat as he came into view. His nose and mouth were covered by the same black mask, but I would recognize those piercing blue eyes anywhere.

I swallowed hard as our eyes met, and Nik gripped the bars of the cell with both hands, knuckles turning white. His eyes traveled down my body, and when they locked with mine again, his expression was one that would haunt me until my end of days.

He hadn't known.

It was clear in his expression he hadn't known the torture Donika had subjected us to. That she had been starving us. Burning us with her shadow magic. A hot tear escaped and spilled down his cheek, catching in the fabric of the black mask.

"Diana—" Nik started, his raw voice cracked as he shook his head back and forth.

He pulled the mask down to reveal his face.

It appeared as if he hadn't slept in days, dark circles ringing his eyes. His face was gaunt, his skin pale. He looked like a ghost. Apparently he hadn't fared much better in The Stone City, despite not being held prisoner in the Stormvault as we had been.

I caught myself, setting my jaw and crossing my arms over my chest under his gaze. I would not appear weak. It was Nik who had left me to this fate, after all. I hadn't seen him since that first day.

Puck continued to fumble with the keys and Nik never took his eyes off me, a pleading expression in his sorrow-filled gaze. He wiped away another tear as it escaped, silently slipping down his cheek. If this was our only chance at a jailbreak, I would take it, but that didn't mean I trusted them.

Tess shot me a glance over her shoulder, her expression unreadable as the lock finally clicked and the door swung open with a loud screech. Puck winced, his eyes searching the corridor as if the sound might have drawn unwanted attention from nearby guards.

"We don't have any time for pleasantries or apologies, we have to move," Puck instructed, ushering us out into the corridor.

I followed without hesitation, anxious to be out of this cell. Whatever they had planned...it better be good. I couldn't imagine escaping this castle when it was crawling with Donika's guards.

As soon as I stepped over the threshold of the cell, I expected to feel my magic surging forth, free of the iron bars and ash shackles for the first time in weeks.

But what I felt was *nothing*.

No magic sparking at my fingertips, no warmth in my core where I had once felt the magic reside. Absolutely nothing.

I didn't have time to think on it further. Maybe it had simply been such a long time since I had reached my magic. Maybe I would need to learn how to grasp it all over again.

Puck ushered us down the hallway, Nik silent on our heels with the nameless woman following closely behind. Nik and Puck both pulled the black masks back over their faces, leaving only their eyes exposed once more. They both had swords and daggers strapped to them, prepared to fight any guards we might encounter.

We ascended the steep stone staircase as quickly as we could, Tess and I greatly weakened by the time we had spent locked in our cell. When we reached the top of the staircase, we burst through another thick, wooden door. The corridor beyond was dimly lit with torches hanging against the wall, softly illuminating the path before us.

Puck led the way down the corridor, up another set of stairs. We weren't approaching the main level, were we? I wanted to avoid being seen or catching the eye of one of Donika's guards at all costs. Once the alarm was sounded, there would be no going back. We either made it out alive, or we were dead. I was surprised to find that there weren't any guards manning the door at the top of the staircase. Had Puck and Nik disposed of them?

When we reached the top of the second staircase, we were right below the main floor of the palace, the staircase opening up into an unoccupied antechamber of sorts.

A flash of movement caught in the corner of my eye, and I turned quickly, raising my arm to shield myself despite having no weapons.

I had *thought* the antechamber was unoccupied...but a guard stood by the main door, his arms uncrossing as he moved towards us. His hand reached for his sword as he pulled it free of its scabbard.

Nik was fast, but so was the guard. Nik lurched forwards, pushing us back towards the staircase and away from the guard. His sword sliced forwards, but the guard was able to back out of the way. The blade barely skimmed the material of his tunic, opening a slice in the fabric.

The guard swung his sword with all his might, Nik narrowly avoiding it by twisting out of the way. He kicked the guard in the back of the legs as he passed and the large Shade fell to his knees, his sword swiping out in front of him as he fell. Nik was able to escape the edge of his blade, maneuvering behind him. He cracked him over the head with the butt of his sword so hard he fell to the stone floor with a grunt. He remained there, motionless.

Puck helped Nik grab the guard's arms, pulling him into the shadowed corner of the alcove. We hadn't had to kill him, and a wave of relief washed over me. He would wake up with a wicked headache, but he *would* wake up. They might be Donika's men, but I didn't revel in the idea of killing anyone.

Except for the ones who tortured us...*those* deaths I would revel in.

Puck backed away, wiping sweat from his brow from the effort. The guard was easily twice the size of either of them.

"This way," Puck whispered softly, guiding us past multiple sets of doors and another staircase that led up to the main level. "Quickly."

Nik still hadn't spoken, his presence a heavy silence at my back as we scurried through the twists and turns of the corridors. We were moving quickly now, passing down an empty hallway unseen. Before we could reach the end Puck stopped suddenly, resting his hand against the stone wall. He brought a finger to his lips to quiet us, and I felt the urge to gulp down air to catch my breath. I held it as best I could, Puck quietly putting his ear to the wall and feeling around for something between the stones.

What was he doing?

He found whatever stone he had been searching for and pulled, the stone swinging away from us like a hidden doorway. Now that I studied it closer, that's *exactly* what it was. There were hidden passageways in the castle. We passed through the doorway into darkness, the only thing illuminating the dirt path before us the lantern that Puck clung to with a gloved hand.

"Liss will have to take it from here." Puck quietly closed the door behind us and handed the lantern off to the woman.

She grabbed it in her dainty hand and moved forwards, as if she knew these pathways by heart. Had she grown up in the castle? Had she discovered these pathways in her time here?

"Watch your step," she called out, speaking for the first time.

She descended the steps nimbly, waiting for us to catch up once she reached the bottom. The corridors here were damp and dark with packed dirt floors. They were narrow, twisting this way and that. I wasn't sure how she had any idea which direction we were going. I could see another lantern up ahead and she quickened her steps, moving ahead of us.

I had so many questions, but no time to ask them as we tried to escape The Stone Palace with our lives. How had they gotten rid of Donika's guards? How did they know this woman, Liss? How had they discovered the pathways out of the castle?

My questions would have to wait, and I swallowed them back as I trailed after Tess ahead of me. My hand traced along the damp stone walls to steady my steps. I was exhausted down to my bones. I had known when the time came for an escape I would need my strength, but I had no idea how quickly I would weaken and tire. I struggled to push onward as we entered another wide antechamber, a familiar face greeting us.

"Zion..." his name fell from my lips on an exhale as I doubled over, trying to catch my breath.

"There were no guards, as promised," Liss told him, giving him a quick hug in greeting.

How did Liss and Zion know each other? Were they allies? I knew deep down that Zion had to have been the mastermind behind this escape. But...why? He was Donika's father...what did he gain from helping us?

"Thank you, Zion," Puck said, clasping his hands in his.

"We don't have much time," Zion replied, his deep voice filling the small, circular room. "Donika will notice any minute that her guards have been...misplaced. She will suspect you right away."

Misplaced? What was that supposed to mean?

"This is where we part." Zion swallowed hard, grasping Liss' shoulder and giving it a tight squeeze. "I will join you when I can, but I have to keep up the charade a while longer. Long enough for you to make it out of Akra and join the resistance."

"I understand. Be safe, Zion. I will be indebted to you forever." Liss' voice was soft as she spoke.

Was she being held prisoner here as well?

Zion gave her a soft smile before standing aside and opening the door behind him, revealing yet another stairwell that led down. How many more staircases were there? I wasn't sure I would be strong enough to make it out of the castle at this rate, let alone Akra. What if Donika and her army caught up to us? I didn't have the strength in me to run.

Zion passed two heavy packs to Puck and Nik, and they took them silently, strapping them across their backs. I glanced at Nik, but he wouldn't meet my gaze across the chamber. We passed through the arched doorway, and it began to shut behind us.

I glanced behind me, and the last image before the door closed entirely was the soft smile on Zion's face as he watched us go.

5

We descended the final staircase, and I could feel a cold draft in the hallway below. It was much wider than those we had passed through previously on our journey out of the castle. As we continued on, I could see that the mouth of this corridor opened onto a patch of grass, the stars glistening in the night sky beyond. A tear spilled down my cheek as we crossed the threshold, and the night air surrounded me as if it were a warm embrace. We continued to walk in silence, but I glanced back at the castle one last time.

The mouth of the hallway was, in actuality, a cave entrance with an iron gate hanging over it. The opening was hidden among the rock face that led straight upward in jagged cuts before reaching the castle that rest atop it. We traveled away from the palace across an empty grass field towards the woods beyond.

How much further would we have to walk tonight? My eyes met Tess' in the darkness, Liss having left her lantern at the mouth of the cave, snuffing out the flame. We didn't want to draw any attention now that we were outside the castle walls.

The expression on Tess' face said the same thing I was thinking, her eyes wide. We were weak, and traveling this far had already been physically taxing on the both of us. We hadn't walked more than the width of the iron cell for the past few weeks, or however long our captivity had lasted. Every time we went to the throne room, we had either been drugged and carried or dragged.

Liss lead the way into the thick, dense forest without glancing back. Even without a pack, the heaviness of my own body was a great weight to carry. I trailed after Tess with Puck and Nik on my heels, feeling our way through the thicket by the glow of the moon.

We walked for another hour, at least, before we stopped at an outcropping of rocks.

"We rest here for the night," Liss broke the silence when she spoke, a cold chill running up my spine.

The blooming of the trees and the lack of snow meant it was likely spring by now. We had been locked in the Stormvault longer than I thought. Nik and Puck unpacked blankets from their packs, creating a spot for us to lay down beneath the stars.

"No fire, it will draw too much attention. Liss' spell will keep us hidden from any soldiers that come searching for us, but it will only hide *us*, not the fire," Puck explained as he settled down onto one of the blankets.

We would have to sleep close together to keep warm without a fire. Tess reluctantly laid beside Puck and let out a soft groan as her muscles got to rest for the first time in hours.

Liss was busy with her border protection spell, her back turned to us as she waived her arms in the air and her lips moved in a silent spell. Nik laid on the edge of the blankets and finally met my eyes in the darkness.

I needed to rest, but the thought of lying next to Nik made my stomach turn sour. I was grateful they had broken us out of the Stormvault and snuck us out of the castle, but I wasn't ready to let my guard down.

"You can't stand there all night," Nik spoke softly for the first time, and the sound of his voice threatened to undo me. It was both gentle and cutting at the same time. The emotions he drew from me were completely opposite one another.

I rubbed my hands along my arms trying to warm myself as my eyes narrowed. I hated him. *Hated him.* He was the reason for *all* of this, but it was my own fault that the sound of his voice could still send a shiver coursing down my spine. Heat rushed to my cheeks, and I swore under my breath, cursing my body for betraying me. I was thankful for the cover of darkness what would hide it.

"Says who?" I replied, crossing my arms over my chest in defiance.

A ghost of a smile crossed his lips at my response, as if he hadn't expected me to still fight him. To push back. I might have been tortured and starved, but the fire never left me. *Not once.* Donika would not break me.

"Diana, you need to rest. I promi—" I cut a cold glare at him as he spoke.

I didn't want to hear any more of his empty promises. He swallowed, his eyes moving to his hands which were woven tightly together in his lap. He paused before his next words came. "We have a lot of ground to cover tomorrow, and you'll need your strength."

I had no choice. I knew he was right, despite not wanting to admit it. I reluctantly curled up next to Tess on the blanket, staying as far away from Nik as possible. Liss finished her spell and joined us on the blankets, curling up on her side. I didn't know her, but I hoped we could trust her. That we could trust Zion. That we weren't being led into another trap.

I held Tess close to my side to keep warm, and she let out an exhausted sigh against me. I had to admit, it felt incredible to touch something as soft as a blanket for the first time in weeks, despite the ground being cold and hard. With Tess wrapped in my arms sleep took me quickly, and I slipped into familiar nightmares of the Stormvault, and Donika's cold, dead eyes.

I woke to someone shaking my shoulder vigorously, my eyes straining against the dawn kissed sky. No more than a few hours could have passed since we had fallen asleep, and the quick respite hadn't been nearly enough to soothe my sore muscles.

"We need to go, *now.*" A harsh whisper sounded against my ear.

My eyes popped open and took in our surroundings with a sleepy gaze. Puck and Tess were hurriedly packing the blankets back into the pack, and Liss was on her feet, anxiously biting her lip.

"They're on our trail," she explained, motioning for me to hurry.

Puck grabbed the blanket as soon as I made it to my feet and hastily stuffed it into his pack.

"Ten Nightshade soldiers, maybe more. Only about ten minutes behind us. My spell must have worn off in the night, it's quite complex and takes a lot of energy. I don't have the magic left to reinforce it, we need to move."

I nodded in understanding as I steeled myself for the brisk pace we would need to maintain to evade them.

"Are you ready?" Nik asked, his voice close enough to me that I flinched away.

I couldn't meet his gaze, I only nodded in return and moved to join Liss. She had begun to pave our way through the forest once more.

"We have two options," Liss spoke, but didn't turn to see if we were close on her heels. "You either run back to Silver Oaks and pretend none of this ever happened, where Donika and her soldiers will simply capture you again. Or hurt your family. Or option two...you join the resistance. As Zion wanted."

I had been thinking about what I would do if I ever got out of the Stormvault, and I already knew the answer deep in my bones. Once I was introduced to this world of magic and to Istmere, there was no turning back.

Liss glanced back and met my eyes, recognizing the resolve there. She nodded once before moving faster towards whatever our destination was, Tess and I struggling to keep up. Tess gave my shoulder a tight squeeze in reassurance. She would fight this battle with me, no matter the outcome. We had to stop Donika and save the innocent witches she was killing. We needed to free Istmere from the tyrant who had ruled with a heavy hand this past decade, valuing nothing but herself and her own magic.

I was the daughter of the last King of Istmere. Donika murdered him, making me the rightful heir to the throne. I would stop at nothing to see her demise.

My breathing came sharp, and my legs stung as I pushed on with Nik at my heels. I knew he could easily keep up with Liss, but he stayed back to ensure I kept up with the punishing pace she had set.

"Where are we going, exactly?" I asked, my breath coming in short puffs.

"Prins. There is a resistance growing there, with healthy numbers. Saanvi sent word of their location and where to meet them," Nik replied.

How far away was Prins from Akra? When I had traveled here initially I had been knocked out for most of the journey and couldn't remember. I prayed it wasn't far, and that Donika's Nightshade soldiers lost our trail.

With a pang, I realized I hadn't felt my magic once since escaping the Stormvault, and I was too weak to try to pull on it now. Would it come back on its own? A trickle of dread spilled down my throat as I thought about the torture Donika had put us through, the poisons she had made us drink.

Could she have given me something to erase my magic? Or steal it?

Movement in the brush to my right caught my attention and before I could call out in warning Nik had moved forwards, pushing my body behind his as he unsheathed the sword from his scabbard. A memory surged forth, and I realized it was the same sword he had used when we had trained in the meadow in the mortal realm.

With a shock, I realized that had been *months* ago. I swallowed hard as we stopped. Tess and I were motionless, pressed between Nik and Puck. Liss closed her eyes and her lips moved with a hushed incantation. Was she trying to hide us from them?

The eerie silence of the forest was broken by a ball of grey fur breaking through the tree line, jaws snapping as it aimed right for Nik's throat. He had been ready, parrying quickly and throwing the large grey wolf to the ground. A guttural growl escaped him as he slashed his sword downward, the grey wolf jumping out of the way barely in time to avoid losing a limb.

Nik's shadows slithered out around him, casting the forest in darkness. Through the shadows I could make out Puck unsheathing his Katana as another wolf emerged from the woods, its murky brown fur standing on edge. It peeled its lips back in a fierce snarl as it surged forth.

I didn't have the energy to fight, but I grabbed a dagger sticking out of the top of Nik's pack so that I was at least armed. The brush behind us was rustling, and I turned to find Liss locked in battle with a black panther, its sleek coat glistening in the light of dawn. The sun had started to rise and cast a soft pink glow across the battle. My eyes bounced back and forth, covering Tess with my dagger held tightly in my grip should another soldier break into the clearing.

Nik's sword was swiped from his hand with a clatter and a grunt as it went soaring into the woods. The grey wolf had him pinned to the ground, snapping its teeth at his face mere inches away. In the blink of an eye Nik was pushing against the neck of the wolf with his very mortal, very human hands, and then suddenly they were no longer human at all. Nik transformed into a sleek black wolf, rolling out from under the grey with speed and grace. He leaped out of the way as Puck swept his Katana in an arc, slicing through the rough fur and flesh of the grey wolf.

It let out a curdled yelp as it fell to the ground, panting and whimpering. Nik lunged forwards to finish it off, grabbing its throat with his immense jaws and giving it one quick snap. Puck had finished off the brown wolf and he joined Liss, quickly dispatching the panther. Realizing it was outnumbered, it retreated into the woods.

"Don't let him get away! He will bring our location straight to the other soldiers!" Puck called out.

The panther was fast, but Nik was faster. He caught up to the panther in merely a few short strides as he knocked it to the ground, Puck running close on their heels. Before Puck could reach them I heard a strangled cry, and a spray of blood coated the surrounding trees. Nik had used his teeth to tear its throat out.

I turned to Tess, squeezing her arm to make sure she was ok. She met my eyes and nodded. Puck jogged back towards us, his brow covered in sweat and his unruly mess of curls matted to his forehead.

"The others will be close behind, we've got to move," he said, grabbing his fallen pack and strapping it onto his back.

Nik joined us with his fallen sword back in his hand. His cheek was stained with fresh blood and his shirt was ripped at the collar. He sheathed the sword and grabbed his pack.

"Ready for battle, firecracker?" The ghost of a smile crossed his lips for the second time since we had entered the forest as he nodded towards the dagger still held within my grasp.

The nickname felt like a knife to my heart. Instead of replying with a witty quip I swallowed hard, casting my eyes aside. I looked anywhere but at him.

"I know you aren't going to like this..." he started, trying to meet my gaze.

"Then don't say it," I snapped, glaring at him.

"But we need to move faster than you and Tess are able," he continued on anyway, his chest rising and falling with rapid breaths. He was still winded from the scuffle with the Nightshade soldiers. "I need to carry you. I can move twice as fast, even with you in my arms."

"Out of the question," I replied through gritted teeth.

I would have to set a better pace, I would need to push myself harder. I couldn't let him carry me. *I couldn't.* I hadn't realized I was shaking my head back and forth furiously until my gaze met his.

"Diana, we need to. We need to get away from the soldiers, out of their domain," Tess said as she moved towards me, giving my hand a gentle squeeze.

As I met her eyes, I could see the pain in them, that she knew how much this cost me. That under any other circumstance she would stand by my side and insist, but that we were running out of time. We couldn't afford to be thrown back into the Stormvault again. Donika would never let us leave with our lives a second time.

My eyes were on my feet again as I nodded softly. Nik didn't give me a chance to change my mind, he grabbed the back of my knees and scooped me up into his arms.

"Hold on to my neck," he ordered, not meeting my eyes.

His breath fanned across my face and the faint scent of coffee and cinnamon sent a searing hot flash down to my core. I bit my lip hard, hard enough to draw blood, as I delicately wrapped my arms around him. I squeezed my eyes shut as I felt his skin, hot against mine due to the ripped collar of his shirt.

"Tighter," he instructed, clearing his throat.

I gripped tight, and we were off, Liss jogging ahead of us with her sword in hand, Puck following on our heels with Tess in his arms. We were moving much faster now, and Nik barely broke a sweat as we jogged through the forest and over fallen tree branches with the weight of me in his arms. I had to remind myself the weight was much less than it had been a few months ago.

Before he had betrayed me.

Tears stung the back of my eyes, threatening to fall. I swallowed them back down, closing my eyes tight once more. I would not cry in his arms. *I would not.*

I hoped we would reach Prins soon, as in, within the next ten minutes, because I wasn't sure how much more of this I could take. I could feel every breath Nik took as his ribcage expanded beneath me, his arms gripping tightly around me. I wanted nothing more than to bury my face in his neck, and I cursed myself for even thinking it.

I watched Tess over Nik's shoulder and the sympathy in her eyes was clear. I gripped tighter, digging my nails into Nik's shoulder. His breath came shorter, but he said nothing. He simply kept running close on Liss' heels as we sped through the forest.

As we ran, I could sense the surrounding atmosphere changing. I heard the faint chirping of birds and the rush of water in the distance. I hadn't realized it, but the forest in Akra had been completely devoid of wildlife. Utterly silent. The trees were greener here, lusher and more vibrant. Even the landscape had been oppressed in Akra. We must have crossed over into Prins at some point.

A small black shadow shot out of the brush and joined Nik, running at his feet. It was a black cat with a sparkling green emerald hanging from its collar.

It was Saanvi.

She meowed once before shooting forwards and joining Liss, running ahead of her. She must be leading the way to the encampment where we would find the resistance.

After a few more minutes of running, I could finally see stone buildings through the trees and hear the bustling of carriages on the cobblestone streets. I let out a sigh of relief. We weren't safe yet, but at least we were back in familiar territory.

As we reached the edge of the forest, we slowed to a walk and Nik set me back on my feet, clearing his throat and averting his eyes. He adjusted the collar of his shirt and joined Liss and Saanvi without saying a word.

I waited for Puck and Tess to join us and then we continued on, walking down the cobblestone streets as if we hadn't barely escaped Donika and her prison in Akra. We kept our eyes glued down to avoid any curious gazes, and we walked briskly.

We passed The Giddy Griddle and I could almost hear Tess' mouth watering at the smell of simmering sausages and buttery pancakes. It had been months since we had eaten anything of substance, not counting the strange grey stew and stale bread they would bring us when they were feeling generous. We turned towards the charm shop we had visited once, climbing the steep hill to the more secluded part of town.

As we made our way back down the hill on the opposite side, we turned sharply right into a dense formation of buildings built so closely together it only left narrow alleyways between them. This part of the city could only be traveled on foot.

I wasn't sure what I had been expecting, surely not a welcome sign that said, *The Resistance,* but what we found was certainly not it. We squeezed through an alleyway narrow enough that we could only pass single file before finding Saanvi stopped and laying her hand against the stone wall. She unveiled a hidden door set into the wall with a whispered spell. The door opened inward, and we all shuffled inside. We were met with a blast of warmth from a fireplace situated right inside the entrance to the strange, hidden building.

The room we entered was narrow and filled with people, a bar top running the length of the left wall with stools filled with Shades of all kinds. But this wasn't a bar...it was well hidden, and spell protected.

This was a safe house.

The room fell silent with only hushed whispers and chairs scraping against the hardwood floor filling the silence. All eyes turned towards me as the bartender slung a white dish towel across his shoulder and approached. His blue eyes quickly flitted towards Liss before meeting mine, and without hesitation he knelt before me. He bowed his head before lifting his chin and meeting my gaze once more.

"Our true queen has returned."

6

The stranger kneeling before me set off a chain reaction across the room. Witches dropped from their bar stools to kneel on the floor before me. A crowd formed around me, witches on their knees with their heads bent. Tess came up behind me, squeezing my arm, a smile in her gaze. Tears stung the back of my eyes, but I blinked them away.

I had no idea there were witches in Istmere who knew who I was before *I* even did. That Osiris had a daughter, the true heir to the throne.

"Allow me to introduce myself," the stranger spoke, reaching out to clasp my hand in his. His eyes were a soft blue with faint wrinkle lines creasing his skin, his hair a salt and pepper grey. "My name is Isaac. We have been waiting for you for a long time, Diana."

"How do you know who I am?" My voice sounded small in my own ears.

Isaac stood and the rest of the room followed, all eyes still glued on us.

"We all know who you are." Isaac smiled down at me, his eyes traveling over our group. "The resistance has been waiting for the daughter of Osiris to come forward for over a decade. We always knew you were out there, and that your time would come."

I could sense a familiar energy emanating from Isaac, one I recognized from my own magic.

"Are you—" I started, my gaze meeting his, my breath caught in my throat.

"A Stormshade? Yes. Not many here are, but there are a few of us that lingered in Istmere after the war. Constantly moving to avoid Donika's watchful eye. This isn't all of us, this is only one safe house of many. The resistance has healthy numbers. I think you will be pleased. We have a council that leads us in your stead. Liss and I are only two of the members who have done work in your name in your absence. We strive to bring freedom to the Shades in Istmere, to end the oppressive rule of the Black Heart."

My mouth fell open, so many questions at the tip of my tongue. I had vowed to take back what was mine, to burn Donika's empire to the ground, but I hadn't realized there were *so many* Shades ready to fight with me. So many people whose lives would be in my hands.

Isaac was a Stormshade, the first one I had ever met. I knew there had to be others like me out there, but I never imagined one standing here before me. I had unanswered questions about my magic, but Liss interrupted before I could begin to ask them.

"Diana needs her rest. We have had a long journey from Akra. She will need to build her strength before we can discuss any strategy. Donika was not kind to her in the Stormvault," Liss said as she parted the crowd, nodding for us to follow.

Isaac nodded with a soft smile, allowing us to pass. As we walked towards the back of the room, all eyes remained trained on us, whispers following our trail. There, in the back of the long room, we found a narrow staircase that led upwards towards a second level. This wasn't any sort of establishment I had ever seen before. It appeared to have once been a house that had been modified to suit the needs of the resistance.

The first floor had a bar top with seating, but it also had a kitchen with a long island covered in beakers and vials of colorful liquids and potions. The windows were covered in cobwebs, cream candles melting onto the windowsills. Feathers, crystals, and ink pots were scattered across a number of surfaces about the room.

We followed the staircase upwards, the long hallway branching off in two directions. The doors were old and worn, painted a chambray blue, the paint chipping off from years of use. Despite its odd setup, it was warm and inviting. Liss led us into a large room with a fireplace and couches. It was set up as a common room, with doorways branching off to separate bedrooms and washrooms around the main space.

"I'll leave you to it," Liss said as she moved towards the door. "I will have fresh clothes and food brought up for you."

She slipped through the door and disappeared down the hallway, leaving Tess and me alone with Puck and Nik for the first time.

The sight of the chaise lounge pushed in front of the fireplace made my head feel very, very heavy. I had known I had been tired, but now that we had time to rest, the fatigue settled deep into my bones. I imagined Tess felt the same. I wasn't sure what I wanted to do first...bathe, sleep, or eat. Those things were such a luxury to us now, ones we hadn't been able to indulge in for quite some time.

"How long?" I asked, my voice a husky whisper.

"How long, what?" Puck asked, throwing himself down on the leather couch and propping his feet up on the ottoman.

"How long were we in the Stormvault? What month is it?" I asked, turning towards Nik.

He held my gaze but said nothing. An awkward silence fell, and I wasn't going to be the first one to break it. I had asked a question, and I expected an answer. Puck swallowed hard, glancing once at Nikolai before answering.

"It's the end of April..."

I bit my lip hard to stop the tears that threatened to fall, blinking rapidly. I tilted my head to swallow them back.

Three months.

We had been locked in the Stormvault for three months. What was my mom thinking? That I had simply *disappeared*? I would need to get to her as soon as possible, to explain everything that had happened. Once she knew I was safe, knew what had happened, I needed to confront her about the secrets she had been keeping. I needed to ask her about my true lineage, and if she had known all this time.

But not like this. I couldn't let her see me like this.

"I'm going to wash up," I announced, moving towards one of the bedrooms with an adjacent washroom and slamming the door behind me.

I sat at the edge of the claw-foot tub and, now that I was alone, released the tears I had been holding back all day. I stifled my sobs with the back of my hand, the tears running down my cheeks to soak through my dirt-stained shirt.

I was strong and unbreakable...but I was human. The events of the past few months came rushing back, threatening to consume me in a swell of emotion. I was unbelievably thankful to be safe, but I was also unbelievably angry that Nik had put me in this position in the first place.

I ran the hot water and filled the bathroom with steam as I shirked out of my dirty clothes, kicking them aside. I never wanted to see them again. I wiped the tears from my cheeks, grabbing a washcloth and soap from the shelf and slowly lowering myself into the tub.

The sensation of hot water against my skin was the most incredibly decadent thing I had ever experienced. I took the washcloth in my hand and gently scrubbed my filthy skin as the tears continued to fall. I desperately wanted to see my mother again, but with that realization came the fact that the other realm wasn't my home anymore. I felt as if I was grieving my old life and my time in the Stormvault all at once. My emotions were all over the place, and I was utterly *exhausted.*

It wasn't long before the bathwater turned brown with dirt and blood, and I had to drain the tub only to refill it again. I washed my hair and scrubbed my skin clean, but I still didn't feel any better. I didn't think I would until Donika was dealt with. As soon as I was well enough to travel, I needed to return to the other realm to handle things with my mother and retrieve the grimoire. I needed to know what was in that book of shadows that Donika was willing to kill me in order to get.

I wanted to wash away all the anger, all the sadness and betrayal, but all I accomplished was scrubbing my skin until it was pink and raw. There was no dirt under my fingernails for the first time in months, and I emerged from the bath smelling of vanilla and lavender.

I wrapped myself in a fresh bath robe, a pang running through me at the memory of the last time I had put on a robe. We had been at Eight Bells, and Nik had his hands all over me. His mouth. I bit back a scream of frustration as I stared at my reflection in the cracked mirror.

My once brilliant blue eyes were dull and sunken, surrounded by dark purple bags. My cheeks were hollow. I had lost the natural roundness of my face. My auburn hair was dull and lifeless despite it being freshly washed. I gripped the sink with both hands and hung my head, biting my lip to distract myself from the emotions twisting inside of me.

Would I ever feel normal again? Would I ever quench these emotions running rampant through my mind? I dreaded returning to the common room in a robe, but I also refused to touch the dirt-stained clothes I had worn in the Stormvault ever again.

I reluctantly gripped the door handle, steeling myself with a deep breath. When I returned to the common room, Tess was freshly bathed as well, wrapped in the same white robe. She was curled up on the couch with a plate in her hands.

"You have to try this, Diana," she said around a mouthful of food. She brought the chicken leg to her mouth despite not having swallowed the bite she was currently chewing. Nik and Puck were nowhere to be seen.

"They went down to the first floor, to speak with Isaac and Liss," Tess said as she saw my eyes search the room.

I exhaled a sigh of relief. I felt, for the first time since leaving the Stormvault, as if I could truly relax without the sense that I was being watched. As if my every action was being scrutinized. I was a leader to these people...but I didn't feel like much of a leader at all right now, let alone a queen.

There was a spread of food laid out across the ottoman. Juicy and brined chicken legs, mashed potatoes, fresh vegetables, and bread. I cringed away from the bread, pushing it away, though I was sure it wasn't stale like what they had fed us back in Akra. The smell had my mouth watering immediately and I dove in, the chicken bursting with flavor I had long forgotten. My eyes lit up and Tess let out a soft laugh.

"This feast is fit for a queen." She winked as she took another bite.

"Don't remind me," I groaned, propping my feet up and sitting back with my plate.

"There are two bedrooms, one for us and one for the boys," she announced, reloading her plate with food.

I was relieved at this. Despite having not been alone in the last three months, I didn't *want* to be alone. Not tonight. I wanted to stay with Tess.

"And Nik and Puck will be staying with us?" I asked, "with the resistance?"

Tess nodded. "They are with the cause. They're friendly with Isaac from what I've gathered before I went to wash up, and with Liss. She was an important factor in our prison break, apparently. She has lived in the castle for a long time. They befriended her months ago."

"Did they say anything else?" I asked around a mouthful of potatoes.

"No." She shook her head gently. "We will regroup with Isaac and Liss once we have rested and gotten a full meal in our bellies."

"That shouldn't be hard. This is the best chicken I have ever had in my life," I said around a mouthful of food.

"Are you sure you aren't only saying that because we have been locked in a prison since January?" Tess asked with a shake of her head and a roll of her eyes.

My eyes met hers, a laugh in them. I appreciated her sarcasm, and I was glad we could joke about it, despite how fresh and angry my emotions were, warring inside of me.

As we finished our meal, my eyes grew heavy. I was bloated with the amount of food we had consumed. I was glad that the boys hadn't returned and we could go straight to bed.

I wasn't ready to face them again.

Part of me wanted to rake my fingernails down Nik's face, the other part of me wanted to thank him for risking his life to get us free of Donika. He betrayed her, and there was no going back for him now. He would be hunted as fiercely as I was. I was glad that the safe house was spelled, but I was still unsure if it was enough to keep us safe from Donika's spies.

Tess led me towards one of the bedrooms, and a wave of exhaustion rolled over me as I spotted the comfortable-looking bed. The room was small and cozy, with a cast iron bed pushed into the corner of the room against two large windows that overlooked the cobblestone streets below. Lit candles were scattered across the floor, and a lush, dark carpet covered the space. I crawled into the bed first and closed the blinds tightly against the light of day. The room was plunged into darkness except for the soft glow of the flickering candles.

Tess climbed in after me and we pulled the lush blankets over us.

"I have to explain things to my parents," Tess said as she turned towards me in the dark.

"I know." I swallowed hard. "I need to confront my mother. And retrieve the grimoire. But I need a few days to eat and rest."

Tess nodded, grabbing my hand beneath the blankets. Her skin was cold and dry against mine.

"We will plan to go back next week, then," she replied resolutely.

"But I *am* coming back here. You don't have to come with me, if you don't want to. But Istmere is my home now. This is where I belong. This entire life was taken from me, and I am not going to give it up now. I need to see an end to Donika's reign, and I don't expect you to join me."

"Are you serious?" Tess' expression was furious in the darkness. "How many times do we have to go through this?"

"Through what?" I asked, confused.

"I'm with you, no matter what," she said sternly. "If your home is in Istmere, then my home is in Istmere. If you are going to defeat Donika, so am I."

I couldn't believe how lucky I was—to find a friend like Tess. She was fierce and loyal. Funny and witty. She was stubborn, just like me.

A hot tear streamed down my face, and I wiped it away quickly. This was a tear of happiness. A tear of thankfulness. I couldn't imagine what I had ever done to deserve a friend as steadfast as Tess.

"Have I ever told you that you're the best?" I asked quietly, a small smile on my face.

"All the time, babe. And don't you forget it." Tess laughed as she fell back against the pillows. "Now get some rest before we have to deal with all of this." She waved her hand in the air vigorously to mimic 'all of this' and I let out a soft laugh.

"Thank you, Tess."

I gave her shoulder a squeeze before closing my eyes. Sleep took me quickly, but it wasn't the empty, hollow sleep I had hoped for. I had felt this sensation once before, and immediately recognized it.

I was dream walking.

7

I was pulled into a familiar scene that made my blood turn cold. I was on my hands and knees on the checkered marble tile of Donika's throne room. I froze, unsure if anyone could see me or not. Hadn't Tyr been able to sense me in the dream when I had taken the grimoire from the laboratory? Was that because he, too, was a dream walker?

Donika sat on her throne with her enormous black wolves at her side. Her face was devoid of all emotion, her endless black eyes fixed on the people before her. I stood slowly, not wanting to draw any attention. No one in the room had noticed my presence yet. Was it possible they didn't know I was here?

A group of people knelt before her, huddled together. Their eyes were wild with fear, their clothes stained with blood and dirt. I recognized one of them as a Nightshade guard who had been posted outside our cell for weeks in the Stormvault. The other faces were strangers to me, but they didn't appear to be soldiers.

They were dressed as civilians.

Donika stood, slowly descending the stairs of the dais. Her black stilettos clacking against the tile floor were the only deafening sound reverberating through the silence. Nightshade soldiers lined the walls of the room, one stationed at each window. I watched in silence as Donika approached the Nightshade guard I recognized, using her shadows to turn his chin up to face her.

"Do you deny the charges that have been brought against you today?" she seethed, her shadows leaving a black trail against the man's skin.

He shrunk back, as if her shadows stung him. Burned him. As they had to us. He tried to cast his eyes downward, afraid to meet her cold glare. Another Nightshade soldier stepped forwards with a long, black whip in his hands. He lashed out quickly, once. The Nightshade soldier screamed, and I stepped forwards, my arm outstretched, before I caught myself.

No eyes moved in my direction.

They couldn't see me here.

I might be dreaming, but the scene before me was all too real. Somehow, I knew that this was unfolding in real time back in The Stone Palace.

"Did you help those spineless little worms escape the castle?" Donika hissed, her shadows wrapping around the Nightshade's face tightly enough that he couldn't breathe, his hands clutching at his throat until the skin there began to purple.

"What was that?" Donika laughed, tossing back her blue and white hair.

The man struggled harder, trying in earnest to answer her through the suffocating shadows that encased him. Donika re-

tracted her shadows all at once and the man fell to his hands and knees, gasping for air.

"I swear to you, My Queen. I had nothing to do with their escape," the man spat, unable to catch his breath.

"Donika, I tire of this questioning." A voice sounded from the doorway and my head turned to see Zion standing there in his black leathers, a broadsword at his hip.

"If you won't answer my question, I have no further use for you," Donika spoke with a cold threat.

"As I said, my grace. I have answered you. I had nothing to do with the Stormshade's escape." The guard's jaw quivered as his eyes met Donika's, knowing what he would find there.

There would be no mercy for him.

"Pity," Donika sneered as her shadows encased the man once more.

This time, they did not let up. Her shadows encircled the Nightshade guard until all I could see was darkness, the shadows traveling up his nose, down his throat. In only a few moments, the Nightshade guard fell in a heap to the floor before Donika as she turned away, towards the larger group of Shades gathered in the throne room. Blood trickled from the guard's eyes and nose onto the floor, his gaze empty.

Lifeless.

"And what of you lot?" she asked as she moved forwards. "I've heard murmurings of a resistance, and you have all been accused of partaking in such treason. Are you so unhappy in Istmere that you would support the rise of Stormshades? That you would betray your crown?" she asked.

The men and women before her remained huddled together, holding onto one another, their faces downcast. I didn't recognize any of them. My gaze shot back to Zion, who wore an unrecognizable grin.

What was he playing at? Was he simply playing his part for Donika? He had orchestrated our escape. How could he sit by and watch Donika torture and murder innocents?

Donika used her shadows to turn the head of the man closest to her. "Speak."

He opened his mouth, but no words came forth. He shook his head violently, as if trying to speak, his hand clawing at his throat.

"Cat got your tongue?" Donika laughed, crossing her arms over her chest.

"My Queen, we have nothing to do with the resistance. We are loyal to you, and you alone," another woman spoke from the crowd.

Donika's gaze turned, her expression cold.

"Was I speaking to you?" she asked, her shadows slithering out, suffocating the woman in a matter of moments.

I staggered forwards and knelt by the woman's side, my hand across her throat to check for a pulse, but she was already gone. I closed my eyes and inhaled deeply. I wanted, desperately, to intervene, but I was alone in this dream. I hadn't touched or felt my magic in months, and I wasn't sure I even could *affect this reality from my dreaming state.*

"Zion, can you hear me?" My voice sounded small...far away. "Zion! You need to do something!" My voice was cracked and desperate.

Zion blinked hard, once, as if maybe he had heard me, but his face remained unchanged.

"Zion, if you can hear me, you need to do something. She is going to kill these innocent people! You cannot stand by!" my voice was hoarse from screaming.

Zion remained unchanged.

"If you all plan to lie to your queen as Sir Bansent did, you will suffer the same fate." Donika spoke with a smile on her face.

She was enjoying this. She was an insufferable monster, and I couldn't watch.

I needed to wake up.

I tried to concentrate on my sleeping form back in my room in Prins, but I still felt the pull to this dream too loudly. I closed my eyes and shook my head back and forth, desperate to sever the link.

Donika's shadows crawled out of her fingertips and surrounded the crowd of people. Their screams were soft at first, quickly growing into a suffocating cacophony of pain.

"Stop!" I screamed, clawing at the sides of my face with my nails. "Please, make it stop!"

My cries went unanswered. When Donika's shadows retreated, my eyes fell on the pile of dead bodies, pools of blood gathering on the marble floor. Their lifeless eyes stared back at me.

"You monster*!" I cried, moving forwards.*

Would Donika feel it if I threw her to the floor along with her innocent victims? Would she feel my boot on her neck as I pressed down, crushing her windpipe...

I woke with a start, shooting up in bed. My hair was plastered to the back of my neck, a fine sheen of sweat coating my arms and chest. I was back in my room in Prins, the bedsheets tangled around my waist. It wasn't Tess who sat beside me on the bed, but Nik. I immediately recoiled, hitting the glass window behind me with enough force that I thought it might shatter, cracking my head against it painfully. I winced, but the glass did not break.

"Diana, it's ok. It was just a dream." Nik's voice came out as a hushed whisper in the darkness of the room.

Where was Tess? How long had I been asleep? My eyes darted to the doorway wildly, calculating if I could make it around him and out of the room without him catching me. But if Nik had wanted to hurt me, he already would have. What was he doing here?

"What did you see?" he asked, his eyes a glimmering blue in the light of the flickering candles.

"How do you know I saw anything?" I asked tersely.

Nik's eyes moved to my shaking hands, and he paused before answering. "You were screaming."

A shudder ran through me.

Despite the sweat coating my skin, I was freezing cold. I pulled the blankets against my chest, digging my fingers into the material.

Should I tell him what I saw? I wasn't fool enough to think he could be trusted, but he *had* helped me escape Donika's prison. There was nothing for him to gain from that. He forever fell from Donika's good graces when he made the decision to help me and Tess. Whatever his motivations were, he was no longer on her side of this war. That much was abundantly clear.

I stayed curled in the corner of the bed against the windows, as far from him as I could get. I pulled the mess of blankets up to my shoulders to cover my bare skin despite the sweat.

"Where is Tess?" I asked defensively.

"Downstairs with Puck, having her eighth meal of the day. You've been asleep a long time," he replied.

"How long, exactly?"

I was scared to know the answer. The dream felt as if only moments had passed, but my legs were sore as if from disuse, and my hair was mussed beyond simply tangling.

"Three days," he answered softly.

For the first time, I noticed the trays stacked by the side of the bed with food that had been brought up. I hadn't been awake to eat them.

I had lost so much time to the Stormvault, I hated the idea of losing even more time to unconsciousness. I know I needed to rest, to regain my strength, but I had already lost three months of my life. I didn't want to lose a moment more.

"Diana, you have nothing to be ashamed of. You need to rest. To heal. You endured so much in Akra, and it was my fault—"

"Don't," I cut him off, my hand out as if I could physically stop his words. "Just...don't. Please. I can't hear it right now."

Nik swallowed hard, his gaze falling to his lap. "I understand."

I waited to see if he would leave, but he remained on Tess' side of the bed, his leg curled beneath him. There were bags under his eyes still, as if he hadn't slept at all since we had arrived at the safe house.

Did his actions haunt him, the way they haunted me?

Finally, his voice broke the silence, and it sent a shiver down my spine. I cursed myself for responding to him at all, involuntary or not.

"Will you tell me what you saw? Why you were screaming?"

I didn't trust him.

I didn't forgive him.

But I...needed him.

He was one of the few people who could understand my dream walking and help me make sense of what I had seen, of what was happening to me.

"I was sucked into a dream," I started. "I didn't want to. I tried to wake up, but I couldn't. I was in Donika's throne room, and she was torturing innocent people. Zion was there, and he did *nothing.*"

I leaned my head back against the window, closing my eyes as I remembered the horrific screams, the pools of blood.

"What did she do?" he asked. His voice was a soft whisper, as if he were trying to calm a scared animal.

"She killed them. All of them. She accused a Nightshade guard of aiding us in our escape and she murdered him first. Then she murdered an entire group of innocent people. They stood accused of being a part of the resistance. I didn't recognize any of them, but I will never forget their screams. The blood on the throne room floor. Their lifeless eyes glaring back at me. There was nothing I could do to stop her. This is my fault. They are dead because I escaped—"

"*Never* be sorry for escaping that hell." Nik's voice was ragged in the darkness as he moved closer to me on the bed. "Never. Do you hear me?"

I swallowed hard. It felt impossible to be thankful that I had escaped when those people *never* would. They would never see their families again. They would never go home. I bit my lip hard as tears stung the back of my eyes and my fist curled around the blankets.

"Her actions are not your fault. Do you understand? You do not need to carry this guilt. You did not kill those people."

He reached out and clasped my hand that was fisted in the blankets, and I let him. He squeezed it, and I squeezed back.

A hot tear spilled down my cheek and I moved to wipe it away with my other hand. Nik reached out and grabbed that hand as well, his eyes on mine.

"You are allowed to be scared. You are allowed to be upset. You are allowed to grieve. You are allowed to feel *everything* you are feeling right now. You don't need to hide from me," his voice was a velvety soft whisper.

A humorless laugh escaped my lips as I shook my head back and forth. I had promised myself I would never let him see me cry.

He pulled me to him and despite a voice in my head telling me this was a very, *very* bad idea, I buried my face in his neck, and I wept. I shed a tear for every person Donika had ever killed. For every day I spent locked in the Stormvault. For every lie I told myself to get through those days. I fisted his shirt in my hands and pulled him closer, and he wrapped his arm around me tightly, his other hand wound in my hair.

He rocked me back and forth as I cried, my tears soaking through his shirt. My breaths came in short, shuddering sobs as I let go of every emotion I had been holding in since escaping, every emotion I was trying to mask as anger. I would let these emotions go until I couldn't cry anymore. I would let them fall from my eyes in fat wet droplets, and I would never look back.

Donika wasn't only murdering Stormshades, she was murdering innocents. Shades who had done no wrong against her. Dark magic be damned, I would find a way to finish her dark rule once and for all.

This war would end in blood, but it wouldn't be mine.

8

When I woke again, I was alone. The candles had burned out hours ago and left hardened pools of wax across the hardwood. There was a groggy memory of having broken down in front of Nik nagging at the back of my mind. Of letting him hold me as I broke down. He shouldn't be the one I turned to when I needed to put the pieces back together, but I had.

I pulled the window shade open and could see that the sun was up, but I had no idea what day it was. The narrow alleyway beneath the safe house was empty, and I could see the main street from here.

From the outside, this building appeared to have no windows or doors. It was a powerful and impressive glamour that hid the safe house from those outside the resistance.

My stomach gave a low growl, and I pushed the tangled bedsheets aside to go find Tess. Isaac and Liss had made sure we were provided with everything we had need of. There was plenty of food, soaps for bathing, and fresh clothes.

I shimmied into a pair of jeans that were fitting better and better each day. Tess and I were already starting to fill out. It wouldn't be long now before I could begin training with my magic and a dagger in earnest.

When I glanced in the mirror, I could see the roundness of my face returning, the harsh lines of my cheekbones disappearing. My hair was taking on a more vibrant auburn glow, but I still hadn't touched my magic. If we were to travel back to Siraleth successfully to access the portal to the mortal realm, I would need to keep my magical signature on lock down until we returned. It was all too easy for Donika's guards to track me if I reeked of storm magic.

I grabbed a plain white t-shirt from the dresser and threw it on, finding the common room outside my door empty. Tess must be downstairs, inhaling more pancakes. I had delivered on my promise to get her a giant short stack as soon as we escaped Akra. Then another, and another. Tess had likely eaten more pancakes in the last week than I had in my entire life.

I took the narrow staircase down to the first floor, which was much less crowded than it had been the first day we arrived. Isaac was behind the kitchen island, a towel strung over his shoulder as he mixed up a huge bowl of batter. Tess and Liss were perched on the island stools. I joined them, pulling one out for myself and giving Tess a smile.

"Are you ready to go back today?" I asked, grabbing a fork and a flapjack from the stack before me, "to the mortal realm?"

"I sure am," Tess said around a mouthful of pancakes and syrup. "I am one hundred percent dreading the inevitable confrontation with my parents, but also looking forward to having it over with."

"My thoughts exactly," I replied, digging in.

The buttery cinnamon pancakes melted on my tongue.

"Isaac, are your pancakes better than The Giddy Griddle?"

He turned, his face covered in streaks of flour, a smile so wide it crinkled the skin around his eyes. "I don't think so, but now that you're staying in Istmere, you can be the judge of that yourself."

"That's true," I replied, nodding thoughtfully. "But not until we put an end to this war."

"Then you might be waiting a long time," Isaac replied, his expression turning somber. "We don't yet have the power, or the numbers. You think we haven't marched on Akra before? Donika's power is *unparalleled.*"

"But Donika doesn't have the Kotova grimoire," I pointed out.

"True," Isaac conceded, "but let's hope you've got something in there that can take her down. Otherwise, we need to bide our time. Grow our numbers. Stay hidden. Train your storm magic so you can learn how to wield it."

"I don't want to live in fear." I bit my lip as Tess met my eyes.

"We will find a spell. We have to. There's a reason Donika was willing to maim and kill to get her hands on that grimoire," Tess reminded me.

Liss was uncharacteristically silent beside her.

"Speaking of the grimoire, where are the boys? They said they would escort us back to the portal in Siraleth today," I asked.

"Something about running to the charm shop in Dragon's Hollow?" Isaac replied as he turned back to the stove with a spatula in hand.

"Alastir's," Tess and I replied in unison.

What would they need at the charm shop? Were they getting more glamours? The last time we had gone to that particular charm shop, Tyr had seen me in Istmere and gone straight back to Donika to tell her of our location.

"They should be back any minute," Liss said, speaking for the first time. "Is Saanvi going with you? To get you across The Shadow?"

"I'm not sure," I replied.

To be honest, I had completely forgotten we needed a guide to get us to the other side.

"I know the way," Liss replied around her last mouthful of pancakes. "Grab your bags and we will go find your troublemakers."

"They're not *my* troublemakers," I replied, my voice coming out sharper than I intended.

Liss gave me an understanding half-smile before nodding and trailing off to grab her pack.

Tess packed us a light overnight bag, and we met up with Nik and Puck in Dragon's Hollow. We found them huddled together, right down the street from Alastir's. They appeared awfully suspicious, but I decided not to mention it. If I could get through this day with one less argument, I would be all the happier.

Liss led the way towards The Shadow, and we followed closely behind. I was half expecting her to turn into a little black cat as Saanvi had, but her entirely human form led us down the steep staircase into a narrow alleyway.

This was a different route than we had taken our first time through The Shadow, and I was hoping it was equally fast. I doubted any of Donika's Nightshade soldiers would be searching for us down here, but in The Shadow, there were other dangers we needed to be worried about.

We wound through the dark, empty streets in the darkness provided by the tarps and sheet coverings hanging above. They obscured the sun from setting its rays upon The Shadow. A few people walked the streets among us, and we cast our eyes downward, avoiding their gazes. We passed one particularly unruly pub which was filled with shouts and the clinking of glasses, and curiosity almost got the better of me. I felt Tess close on my heels and I pushed onward, my eyes downcast.

Liss glanced over her shoulder to ensure we were still following close, then picked up the pace down another dark alleyway. I dreaded having to pass through The Shadow again tomorrow on our way back. The energy here was dark and palpable, raising the gooseflesh on my skin and the hair on the back of my neck. A loud pop sent us down the alley faster, not turning back to see what the commotion was about.

As we were about to turn the corner to the staircase that would lead us up, I saw a familiar figure out of the corner of my eye. I turned to look, and as I did, the figure disappeared. I stopped in my tracks, a trickle of anxiety racing up my spine.

I could have *sworn* I had seen Tyr at the end of this short stretch of road, disappearing towards a pub at the end of the street.

"What are you doing?" Tess hissed, "keep moving!"

"I thought I saw Tyr, right there," I told her, pointing towards the end of the road where the cobblestone met the cinderblock wall that encased The Shadow.

"Where?" she asked, "I don't see anything."

"He was *right* there," I insisted.

The only way he could have disappeared is if he ducked into the pub entrance at the end of the alley.

"What is going on ladies?" Puck whispered, wrapping his arms around us both to shield us.

We had drawn the eyes of a few passersby, but I turned towards him, shirking his arm off my shoulder.

"I saw Tyr. I know I did," I told him resolutely, indicating the spot down the alley where his form had disappeared.

"That's all well and good, love, but we have to be on the move. Even *if* Tyr was in The Shadow, we aren't exactly in the place for a confrontation right now, are we? Besides, we don't want him reporting back to Donika...again. Look at the mess that got us in."

I gave Puck a cross look, but realized he was right. Even if I *had* seen Tyr, what would we do with him? We couldn't detain him, and I wasn't about to kill him. He would simply go running back to Donika...again. I nodded at Puck, allowing him to push us onwards, towards the staircase that would lead us up. We needed to get back to the other realm and meet up at the safe house tomorrow without being seen. Confronting Tyr wasn't exactly keeping a low profile.

We followed the staircase up and Liss and Nik were impatiently waiting at the top, arms crossed.

"Care to fill us in on what took you so long?" Nik asked, his gaze searing into Puck. "I trusted you to bring up the rear."

"Relax, brother. Diana only thought she caught a glimpse of our boy Tyr, that's all."

"She *what*?" he asked through his teeth, his voice taught. "What did you see?"

He turned towards me, his eyes heated. The expression on his face told me he had half a mind to climb back down into The Shadow and set the pub on fire, innocents be damned.

"I thought I saw Tyr, but it was out of the corner of my eye. When I turned to see, he was gone."

"I'll deal with Tyr, you guys go on ahead," Nik replied, moving towards the staircase again.

"No chance," Puck said, placing his hand against Nik's chest as he moved to pass. "We still have quite a way to go before Siraleth, remember? And what do you plan to do, kill everyone in that pub?"

"If that's what it takes."

A muscle feathered in Nik's jaw as he glared at Puck's hand against his chest.

"*Think* for once, will you?" Puck gave Nik a slight push. "Donika's spies are everywhere. We can't risk her finding Diana's location...again."

Nik swallowed hard, his gaze darting from the staircase back to Puck. Finally, he nodded, his eyes landing on me.

"I'm sure we'll see him again," he said resolutely as he rejoined us. "And I won't waste a second opportunity."

"I'm sure," Puck replied, rolling his eyes at Nik's back.

Tess let out a soft giggle which made Puck's smile grow even wider. It was my turn to roll my eyes at them as I turned to rejoin Liss.

The journey through this part of Prins to the portal was much shorter than the first leg of our journey. Before I knew it, we were passing through the two stone pillars that reached into the sky so high they disappeared into the clouds. We crossed over the glamour and onto the empty plains that would lead to Siraleth, and the portal back to the mortal realm.

By the time we reached the portal I was out of breath, resting my hands on my knees and trying my hardest to fill my lungs with air. Despite the skin spells I had gotten from Liss to accelerate the healing process, I still wasn't back at my full strength.

I cringed internally as I had to grab Nik's hand to travel through the portal. If we weren't physically connected, there was a chance we would end up stuck in the in-between, not fully in Istmere or the mortal realm. I didn't want to feel his skin against mine, or for him to get the wrong idea after I had let my guard down in front of him the other night. After I had broken down in his arms.

It felt strange to be back in the mortal realm after having spent so much time in Istmere. The sun was setting on a beautiful spring day, the meadow filled with purple and white flowers. I was surprised to find that the car was exactly where we had left it months ago, at the end of the long, curving dirt path that lead to the portal.

We all squeezed inside, it was a tighter fit with the addition of Liss. She asked that we drop her off downtown before heading back home, and I didn't blame her for wanting to be as far from the conversation I was about to have with my mother as possible. Nik and Puck had a few things to gather before returning to Istmere. We dropped Tess off first, and I gave her an encouraging smile as she closed the door, a slight shake in her hands.

This wouldn't be fun for either of us.

When Nik and Puck dropped me at the curb, a lump formed in my throat that I couldn't swallow. The lights were off on the porch of the old stone house, but my mom's red SUV was parked in the driveway. The only light turned on was in the kitchen, the sun having recently set.

"Whatever she has to say, just listen. Maybe she has a good reason for keeping you in the dark," Nik suggested as I rest my hand on the door handle.

I didn't need, nor want his words of encouragement. I hoped he didn't think we were on better terms now. I knew I would regret it the moment he had left my room that day. I never should have let him see me like that. I met his eyes in the rearview mirror with a cold glare before getting out and slamming the door.

I steeled myself as I took the path to the front door.

I wasn't sure what I was even going to say at this point. Where did she think I was these last few months? Did she report me missing and start a police investigation? One thing I knew for certain, I had to tell her about my magic, and I had to tell her that I was going back to Istmere. After finding out who I truly was...my place was no longer here, in this realm.

I tried the doorknob first, but it was locked. I swallowed hard and raised my first to knock, but the door swung open before my closed fist could make contact. My mother stood in the open doorway, her blonde hair pulled back in a messy bun. Her red eyes were rimmed with purple circles evident of many sleepless nights.

She paused, as if she couldn't believe I was truly here, before sweeping me into her arms. She might not be my birth mother, but this was the woman that raised me. The woman who sacrificed *everything* so I could have the best life growing up. A hot tear trailed down my cheek as she held me, soft sobs escaping her. My arms came around her to pull her close, suddenly not wanting to ever let her go.

My questions about my lineage could wait.

For a moment it was as if I had never left. That my life still consisted of homework and college planning and annoying my little brother. Not escaping an evil queen, putting an end to a decades old war, and reclaiming my place as the rightful heir to the throne of another realm.

My entire life had turned upside down in merely a few months.

She held me at arm's length to inspect me, shuffling her glasses back up onto her nose and wiping at her tears.

Her voice was small when she finally spoke. "Is it really you?"

"Hi, Mom."

9

Jake had been excited to see me, but we had sent him upstairs when we curled up by the fireplace to talk, a mug of hot chocolate in my hands. This conversation wasn't for his ears.

Waffles, the fat orange tabby, had wasted no time curling up on my lap by the fire, and I vowed I would come back for him once Istmere was safe.

We sat in silence for several long moments, the only sound the crackle of the fire in the grate. I wasn't sure where to even begin, there were so many questions lingering in the back of my mind. I wanted to hear her side of the story, but I was also scared to hear it.

This conversation would change everything between us.

She had always written off my more fantastical side, calling me a daydreamer and never taking me too seriously. I had always been drawn to the paranormal...and now I knew why. I couldn't help but feel hurt that she had known this entire time, but instead of being honest with me had made me think I was crazy.

"I don't want you to hate me," my mother admitted, tilting her head back to fight the tears that threatened to fall.

"I could never hate you," I told her honestly. "But I need to know how we got here."

She hadn't called the police or filed a missing person's report, she had known exactly where Tess and I had gone when we disappeared those months ago.

And so had Tess' parents.

It felt as if I were being betrayed all over again, to admit that she knew about magic and Istmere and had kept it from me. I had suspected that this was the case, but the confirmation stung deeply.

She let out a humorless laugh as she took a sip from her mug, anxiously picking at the skin on her fingernail.

We were the same in that way.

I fidgeted with the blanket in my lap, wondering if I should ask my questions first, but then she began to speak.

"It was a long time ago that I met Annelise in New York. She had come to this realm, and we were fast friends," she spoke softly, meeting my gaze with an expression I couldn't read.

"You were friends with my birth mother?" I asked, surprised.

Somehow, in my mind, I had thought I had simply appeared on their doorstep, not that she had known my mother at all. That they had been friends.

"Yes. I hadn't believed her...at first. About the magic. But she showed me and...I couldn't deny what was before my own eyes. She went to college here in the mortal realm, before she had either you or your sister."

She knew about Donika, too. She's had these answers all along. I bit the inside of my cheek to ease the emotional sting that threatened to consume me as she continued.

"She returned to the other realm after college, and we didn't speak for a long time. After I married your father, we had settled down and bought a house. One morning we heard a knock on the door, and despite not telling her where I had moved, she had found me. She was wild with fright...and you were bundled in her arms," she said, wiping away a tear that fell with the back of her hand.

Tears strung the back of my own eyes, but I tried my hardest to bite them back.

I needed to hear this.

"She told me you weren't safe in the other realm. There was a war, between the Nightshades and the Stormshades, and she was caught in the middle. Because of your magic...because of who you are...she had to hide you. A seer had foretold your future, and you were the key. They key to saving Istmere. She needed to keep you safe at all costs. She told me she couldn't think of anyone else she would rather raise her daughter. I miss her terribly." More tears fell in earnest now and my mother stifled a sob as she buried her face in her hands.

"So...she left me with you." It came out more as a statement than a question. I had known as much, Donika had told me this part of the story.

"Yes, she left you with me. To raise you. She was supposed to come back for you."

"But she never did. Because she died," I bit out. "Did dad know?"

My mother paused before answering. "Yes, your father knew. Annelise didn't want that life for you. She didn't want you to be raised in Istmere, with such violence and strife. She thought she could change your fate by bringing you here, raising you as a mortal. She wanted you to be *safe*."

"Lot of good that did," I scoffed, my eyes on the crackling fire.

"I could see that your magic was awakening, despite all we did to conceal it. Anna spelled you before she left, to bury your magic. Hide it. She warned me that it would wear off, that one day it would need to be spelled again, to reinforce it. But she was gone."

"Why didn't you tell me?" I asked, my voice strangled.

If I had known about Donika, if I had known about my magic, everything might have been different.

"She didn't want me to. She wanted you to have a *normal* life, a mortal life," she replied.

"Do you have any idea what I went through? Discovering my magic on my own, thinking I was going completely insane?"

"Diana, I'm sorry. I made a mistake. When your dad passed away, I didn't know how to handle your magic unearthing itself. I was raising you and Jake on my own. Annelise told me to come here, to Silver Oaks, if the spell ever began to wear off. She told me there were other witches here who could help."

"She got that part right, at least. This place is crawling with them," I admitted with a sigh. I pinched the bridge of my nose with my fingers. "We were going to move to Silver Oaks even if dad never passed away?"

"Yes. I wish things were different. I wish she had come back for you. I wish she had lived. I wish the spell hadn't worn off, and I wish I knew how to help you when it did."

My mom shook her head, her gaze focused on her hands buried in her lap. "I made a lot of mistakes, and I am not proud of the decisions I made. I am merely a mortal. I know it isn't an excuse...but I didn't know how to help you through your awakening."

"Did you know about Tess? About her parents?" I asked.

"Yes, I knew. They were Annelise's friends, but they had a Shade child of their own to raise. She thought you would be safer with me, across the country. Tess' parents were adamant about keeping this from the both of you as well, I couldn't turn to them to ask for their help with magic."

"But you *did* bring me to Silver Oaks..." I trailed off.

If the spell had stuck, I never would have met Tess. If my birth mother had it her way, I never would have known I was a witch. I never would have known about my magic. I know she was trying to protect me, to keep me out of this war, but by doing so she was also hiding my true identity from me.

"Yes, I brought you here. Your magic began awakening right before your dad passed. I could see the change in you right away." She met my gaze from across the room.

"But you let me think I was crazy. You told me I was imagining it, that I was only a daydreamer, and I was getting carried away." My voice came out harsher than I intended.

"I never wanted you to think you were crazy. Diana, I didn't know what to do in her absence. I knew how to raise a teenager, but I had no clue how to raise a *witch*. I also needed to keep your magic shielded from your brother. I didn't want him tangled up in this, asking questions I couldn't answer."

Jake. Because he was mortal, too. He was their birth child.

My mother stood, the blanket on her lap falling to her feet as she crossed the room to me. She sat next to me on the couch, her leg resting against my own as she spoke. "Will you ever be able to forgive me?"

How would our relationship have been different if she had been honest with me? Had told me the moment she saw my magic manifesting? Instead of pretending it wasn't happening and leaving me to figure it out all on my own.

I swallowed hard, meeting her gaze.

"Of course, I forgive you," I replied, grasping her hand in mine and squeezing it.

A tear escaped, and I quickly moved to wipe it away. I had shed too many tears this last week.

"I know that I can't tell you what to do, but I want you to be careful. There is a reason Annelise didn't want you anywhere near this war, that she didn't want this life for you," she said.

"So, you knew where I was all this time?" I asked, turning towards her and propping my foot up on the ottoman.

"Tess' parents went searching for you. They went to Istmere. They heard rumblings of a Stormshade being caught in

Prins. You have no idea what it has been like these past few months, not knowing if you were ok, and not being able to go after you. A mortal cannot enter Istmere."

I hadn't known that, not that I would have wanted her to come searching for me, anyway. I wanted her here, safe.

"Did anyone come searching for something while I was gone? Did anyone ask questions?" I asked.

"There was one man, he said he was a teacher at your school. He was asking for a book that you had borrowed that you might have left here? But I couldn't find anything like that. I came home one night to the house completely ransacked, but nobody was here. It has been quiet ever since," she told me.

Fletcher. It had to be Fletcher, searching for the book of shadows. But how had my mom not seen it? I hadn't hidden it well...if they had ransacked the house wouldn't it already be in their possession? As soon as this conversation was finished, I would go up and search for it. I needed to bring it back to Istmere with me, assuming it was still here. There had to be a spell in there I could use, and I needed to know why Donika wanted it so badly.

Was it possible the grimoire had...glamoured itself? Nik had said it was almost sentient in a way. I wondered if it had known people were searching for it...and it had stayed hidden on purpose.

"To recap...my mother dropped me on your doorstep to raise a witchling and told you to bring me to Silver Oaks if my magic ever awakened. Tess' parents are both witches and all of you hid it from us this entire time. And you were friends with my mother before her death. Anything I'm missing?" I laughed, breathless.

"I think that sums it up," she replied, giving my hand a gentle squeeze. "This doesn't change anything...you are and always will be my daughter."

"I know that," I replied, giving her hand another reassuring squeeze. "But I also know that my place isn't here, in this realm. I am the daughter of Osiris, and the rightful heir to the throne of Istmere. Donika has waged a war against her own people long enough."

My mother swallowed hard, pushing her glasses back up the bridge of her nose before meeting my gaze again. "I want you to be safe. I know I can't tell you what to do anymore, that this secret has changed things between us, but I wish things could stay the same."

"A part of me does, too. But I can't let my sister kill innocents and simply turn a blind eye. I'm not alone. Tess is with me, and there is a resistance gathering in Istmere. We are not the only Shades sick of the way Donika has ruled Istmere. She has to be stopped."

"But do you have to be the one to do it?" she asked, her voice small.

I knew what she was asking, but I also knew there was no way I could come back. I didn't belong in the mortal realm...going to college and pretending none of this ever happened. There was no going back. We would have to figure out a way to explain my absence to Jake, but I would leave that to her.

"I might not be strong enough to stop her on my own...but I'm not alone. I don't see her as anything other than the woman who killed our birth mother, and there is no forgiveness for her in my eyes. Her soul is as black as the magic she has been corrupted by, and she has to be stopped."

"And how do you plan to do that?" she asked.

"I haven't quite figured that part out yet." I laughed humorlessly.

Donika was right...she has been practicing magic since before I was even born, not to mention I hadn't even touched my magic since I escaped the Stormvault. We had a hell of a fight ahead of us, and I needed to prepare. I needed to train, to grow stronger, and I *needed* that grimoire.

We had dinner with Jake, and a knot formed in the pit of my stomach knowing this was probably the last time we would be together like this...just the three of us. I would spend the night in my old room, then return to Istmere tomorrow with the grimoire. I was anxious to hear about how Tess' confrontation went with her parents, knowing that they aren't mortal like mine. It almost felt worse...knowing that they actively had magic this entire time and still kept it from her.

That they were Shades themselves.

I know they thought it was for our own safety, but all it ended up doing was letting us go into this whole situation blind. We might not have ended up right in Donika's clutches if we had known the whole story. If we had been prepared.

I took my time helping my mom with the dishes, promising to visit and write often so she knew I was ok. I cursed that cell phones didn't work in Istmere, it would be much easier to text her on occasion. So much of our modern technology interfered with casting spells, and it was a serious pain in the ass.

When I trudged up the stairs to my room for the last time, I felt the exhaustion of the day wearing on me. I couldn't wait to collapse into the safety of my own bed...but first I had to make sure the grimoire hadn't been taken by Donika's guards.

My chest felt heavy as I slowly opened the dresser drawer, expecting the worst. But there, among my underwear, sat the book of shadows.

How had Fletcher and his men not found it? And the other guards Donika had sent to ransack the house? It was practically lying in plain sight. Had the magic in the grimoire truly shielded it from the intruders, hiding it? I was relieved that it was safe and sound, and confused that even my own mother hadn't seen it here when she had gone searching.

I reached out to grab it, and as my fingers connected with the worn leather of the grimoire, an electric shock travelled up my arm. My eyes were open, but I was no longer seeing the bedroom and the dresser before me.

This had happened once before...when I had first found the grimoire in the laboratory. When I had seen The War of Siraleth, and Annelise fleeing The Stone Palace with me tightly wrapped in her arms.

The grimoire was sending me a vision.

10

I was seeing through the eyes of someone else, someone holding an intricate silver key. The hands before me weren't mine, but they were distinctly feminine as they caressed the elaborate metal designs, twisting and turning in curves resembling a den of serpents. At the center of the key's metalwork was a teardrop shaped translucent crystal, and when the stranger's hands passed over it the crystal began to glow a subtle green, light emanating from its surface.

The hands delicately placed the key atop the tattered pages of the book of shadows before me, the very same grimoire currently in my possession.

The Kotova grimoire.

The pages of the book of shadows began to sizzle, flame sparking at the edges of the parchment as the page went up in smoke and ash. When the smoke cleared the key remained, but it was no longer a physical object. They key was now drawn onto the page in the book of spells with small, cramped handwriting filling the margins. The hand reached out to close the book softly.

I snapped out of the vision as quickly as it had taken me. I was suddenly back in my room, my hand clasped around the grimoire still sitting in my dresser drawer. I stepped back, shaking my head, trying to make sense of the vision the grimoire had sent me. What significance did that key have, and how had it *become* a part of the book?

The only other time the grimoire had sent me a vision was of The War of Siraleth, of Donika killing my father Osiris, and our mother fleeing the castle after she was cast out for her magic.

What was the grimoire trying to show me?

I brought the book onto my bed and clasped it in my lap. The pages softly opened at my soft whispered incantation, the book of shadows recognizing me immediately. I flipped and flipped through the pages, but I couldn't find a page with an intricate silver key. By the time I had searched every page, my eyes were bleary with sleep, and I could barely keep them open.

I glanced at the alarm clock on the bedside table and realized it was too late to text Tess and tell her what had happened. I put the grimoire back in its not-so-hidden hiding place and climbed into bed. I knew I needed a good night's rest to make the journey back to the safe house tomorrow. I reminded myself to ask Liss for more skin spells once we met up again, I could sense that these were wearing off quickly. The black lines on my stomach and ribs were already fading.

Sleep didn't take me quickly as I had expected. I lay awake, tossing and turning for hours before my body was too exhausted to fight any longer. With my eyes wide open and trained on the ceiling above me, all I could think about was the key. Why had the grimoire sent me *that* particular vision, and what did it mean for us?

The next morning I had packed my bag quickly, kissed my mother and Jake goodbye, and raced out to the car idling at the curb. I was anxious to tell the others about the vision, and to hear what they thought. On the way to the meadow Tess and I rifled through the grimoire once more, but I hadn't imagined it, the page with the key spell was nowhere to be found.

We left the car in the same spot, parked at the edge of the dirt road leading towards the meadow. Liss led me through the portal this time, despite the sharp glare Nik gave her as she took my hand.

As we walked from Siraleth to Prins, Tess and I fell behind the rest of the group, the others realizing we needed a moment to catch up alone. I told her all about my mother, how she was mortal and how my birth mother had entrusted her to raise me. That she had planned to come back for me, but she was killed in the war. How the spell binding began to wear off, so my mortal mother brought me to Silver Oaks, as my birth mother had instructed.

I understood her reasoning for hiding this from me, thinking she was doing the right thing. Thinking she was doing right by my mother and doing exactly as she asked. Tess' parents were an entirely different story.

"Your parents fled before the war, not wanting to get caught in the middle?" I asked, walking along with Tess while I fidgeted with the strap on my pack, the grimoire safely tucked away inside. I could recognize its energy humming softly around me.

Tess nodded in response. "I was a toddler, they were raising me in Siraleth when the fighting started. They didn't want to be caught between the Nightshades and Stormshades, being only Shades themselves. They knew that things would end...badly. They still had friends left behind...friends who died in the war. They knew of Osiris, obviously, what with him being king and all. They knew your mother, but they were never close."

"At least they weren't killed in the war, caught up in the fighting," I told her.

"True, but how can you not fight for what is *right*?" she asked, shaking her head. "Instead, they turned tail and ran, simply because they didn't want to be involved. They turned a blind eye to the slaughter of thousands of Stormshades and Shades alike. If some of the Shades who thought as they did had stayed to fight, who knows, maybe Siraleth wouldn't have fallen."

"You're right. Staying out of the fray doesn't make it any better, their numbers could have turned the tides of the war, but I can understand them wanting to keep you safe. Maybe Donika wouldn't have killed my father if more Shades had stayed to fight." I shrugged.

I hadn't heard many good things about him, but there had to be *something* my mother saw in him. Something that wasn't entirely dark and corrupt.

"I am so pissed off at them for not telling me. Your mother, I understand. She was a mortal trying to make sense of it all. My parents are *Shades*. They have magic. They never wanted me to come to Istmere or to know this life. I was hoping they would join the resistance, but their minds haven't changed. They are too afraid of Donika," Tess said, shaking her head. "I am disappointed."

"They're afraid of her with good reason, I'm not sure we will be able to defeat her without a miracle, even with the numbers the resistance has been gathering. I'm anxious to get back to Prins to start training with Isaac. Having another Stormshade to train with is going to be invaluable."

Tess nodded in agreement. "And don't forget sword training, I think I'm the most excited for that."

I had to admit, I was excited about that part, too. What little training I had done with a blade had been with Nik, but it had made me feel powerful. It had felt like something I could excel at, and mother help me, I needed to learn to defend myself if I ever saw Donika again. Both with my magic, and a blade.

"Do you think you can beat me?" I teased, giving her a playful nudge.

"At least the playing field will be even unlike with our magic," she teased back with a wink.

"Did you want those skin spells or not, Kotova?" Liss called out ahead of us.

I gave Tess a grin as I sped up, catching up to Liss. I rolled my sleeve up, holding my arm out to her as we walked. She covered the bare skin of my forearm with her hands, her nails lightly marking the skin there. She closed her eyes, the whisper of a soft spell on her lips. When she removed her hands, a serpentine spell was inked freshly into the skin, my steps already feeling lighter. Without the spells Liss had provided, I wouldn't be healing nearly as fast.

Nik shot us a sideways glance, inspecting the new spell before turning back to Puck. I quickly pulled the sleeve of my shirt back down and averted my gaze.

We hadn't spoken since I had slammed the car door on him yesterday. I was still irrevocably, infuriatingly, angry at him for betraying me. He had delivered me into the hands of Donika and then disappeared for *months*. The thought of it had a tide of anger burning in my core and heat rushing to my cheeks. I shook my head, biting down on my lip to clear my thoughts.

I wondered if the grimoire would be able to tell us more about dream walking. There was so much about dream walking we didn't know, and I prayed I wouldn't be pulled into another of Donika's torture sessions again any time soon. I feared having to watch as more innocents died by her hand. Zion said he would be joining us in Prins...but when? In the dream he had still been playing the part of Donika's obedient and doting father, turning a blind eye to her immeasurable cruelty.

As we approached the pathway into Prins, a black bird passed over us in the sky, squawking as it swooped low over our heads. It was close enough that I could see its glistening black feathers, its human-like eyes set into a long, elegant head.

A raven.

But this was no ordinary raven...it was a Nightshade.

Liss stopped, turning towards the sky with an unreadable expression as the raven landed on the stone pillars ahead of us.

"Someone you know?" I asked with a raised eyebrow.

We all stopped a few feet away, the raven flapping its wings and squawking in earnest.

"Kenna," Liss nodded, her expression turning dark. "She's a messenger and a watcher. She has something to tell us. We'd better get back. Quickly."

"Did she say something?" Puck asked, stepping up next to Liss.

"That there is news," Liss nodded, but said nothing else.

The bird spread its wings and took flight without another sound, and we pressed onward in silence.

Liss and I walked together as we entered Prins, and she led us through The Shadow once more. I was anxious to get back to the safe house to find out what Kenna had brought news of.

We made it through The Shadow safely, and I was beginning to think it wasn't as bad as everyone had made it out to be. We had been through it a number of times now, and nothing had happened to us thus far. Or maybe we had simply been lucky enough to have knowledgeable guides each time, knowing which places to avoid.

Luckily there were no sightings of Tyr this time, and as we approached the safe house, even knowing it was there, I couldn't make out the entrance against the stone wall.

Liss held her hand out to the stone, and the door appeared beneath her touch. There were only a few Shades inside, and we made our way to the back of the room where Isaac was having a heated conversation with a girl who appeared to be about our age.

"Kenna, I presume?" Tess asked as everyone dropped their packs on the couch.

I held my pack tightly, not willing to let the grimoire out of my sight now that it had been returned to Istmere. I trusted the members of the resistance, but I trusted *no one* with the grimoire. Even if they couldn't open it. If the grimoire somehow made its way back to Donika, we were done for.

Isaac turned as we approached, clearly frustrated with Kenna, but happy to see us back safely.

"What happened?" Liss asked, her hand on his shoulder.

"I'll tell you what happened—" Kenna started, before she was cut off by a cutting glare from Isaac.

Kenna was beautiful, with long black hair that fell to her waist. She was petite and feminine, but something about her demeanor told me it made sense that her shifted form would be a raven.

"Not here," Isaac spoke as he shook his head, his eyes darting around the room. "It's not safe."

Tess and I glanced at each other with alarm, but followed Isaac as he led us up the narrow staircase to a room on the third floor that appeared to be an office. He closed the door behind us, moving to sit behind the desk as we all settled in.

"Isaac, what news?" Liss appeared concerned, and a lump formed in my throat before he even opened his mouth to respond.

"It's Donika. She's located a number of resistance members at an alternate safe house. She has held them captive for the past day or so. She agreed to release them if we delivered Diana to her by last night."

I swallowed down the bile that rose up the back of my throat, my stomach roiling with nausea. We were in the mortal realm last night, with no way for Isaac to even contact us to inform us of Donika's terms.

"They're gone," he confirmed with a slow nod, his eyes trained on the ticking clock that sat atop the mess of papers on his desk.

"There's nothing we could have done for them," Liss replied, lifting her chin.

Her words were cold, and they sent a shiver down my spine. Despite her callousness, I knew deep down that she was right. I couldn't turn myself over to Donika again. There's no way she would honor her word and release the prisoners or stop the fighting once I was in her custody.

She couldn't be trusted.

Trying to stage a breakout for the prisoners would have only resulted in even more losses for the resistance.

"Do you know what this means?" Isaac met her eyes across the desk and held them, a silent conversation taking place between them.

Was something going on between the two of them? I hadn't thought about it before, but the way they were acting now, it felt more intimate than merely two members of the resistance who knew each other. There was something...familiar between them. The tension was palpable.

"It can't be, we've taken every precaution..." Liss shook her head, unwilling to believe what Isaac was insinuating was true.

Nik spoke for the first time since we had entered the room, and his voice was glacially cold as he stepped forwards. "There is a traitor in our midst. The last group of people that Diana saw Donika slaughter, they were innocent civilians. If Donika found *actual resistance members*, with all the spells and safety measures we have put in place, someone has betrayed us."

Isaac nodded in agreement.

"It can't be," Liss argued, leaning forwards with her hands on the desk before her. "We have hand-picked all of these members ourselves, I refuse to believe one of them has turned on us."

"Maybe not turned on us, but never on our side to begin with," Puck offered from his place by the door. He crossed his arms over his chest. "A spy for Donika."

Isaac rubbed a hand down his face before turning to meet my gaze. "Your safety is at risk if the location of one of our safe houses has been compromised. We must move you at once and keep your location a secret. Only the council members with the highest clearance will know where you are."

"And who, exactly, is on this council?" I asked.

"It's a small contingent. Liss, Zion, Nik, Puck, Warrick, and myself. And now you and Tess, of course."

"Where will you move us?" I asked.

"We have another safe house in Dragon's Hollow. It's much smaller, and empty. Few know about it. It will be only the four of you, Liss and I will remain here as we try to determine who could have leaked information to Donika." Isaac met my gaze as he nodded to himself.

I swallowed hard. I was anxious to get out of here if there was even an *infinitesimal* possibility that Donika knew where to find us. I didn't know the members of the resistance, so I wasn't sure who we could or couldn't trust, but I trusted Liss and Isaac.

"Only the two of us"—Liss pointed between herself and Isaac—"will know where you are. Do not tell anyone where we are bringing you, do you understand?"

I nodded as I squeezed my pack tighter against my chest, the energy of the book of shadows humming softly against me. Not only did we need to ensure Donika couldn't find me, but we needed to keep the grimoire out of her reach as well.

"What were you fighting with Kenna about?" I asked.

"Kenna lost family in the raid on the safe house. A brother, and cousins. She thinks Tyr is the one who leaked our location, but he isn't aware of our locations."

"Tyr? As in...my cousin, Tyr? How would he know any of the locations of the safe houses, anyway?" I asked, confused.

Isaac gave Liss a meaningful glance before his gaze met mine again, his blue eyes hardening.

"Tyr used to be a member of the resistance, sworn to the true queen of Istmere...before he betrayed you."

11

"If I get my hands on that little weasel, I am going to wring his neck," Tess said as we traveled through the cobblestone streets behind Liss, walking to our new and secluded safe house.

"I am going to do a *hell* of a lot more than that," Nik threatened from behind me.

I turned to meet his gaze, which bordered on murderous. I desperately hoped we never ran into Tyr again, for his own sake. I had no idea Tyr had been a part of the resistance, whether his intentions were true or not, but he had given me up to Donika at the first opportunity.

I understood Kenna thinking it had to be Tyr who betrayed the safe house locations, but Isaac insisted that all the newer locations had been established *after* Tyr had led to my capture.

We traveled deeper and deeper into the heart of Prins, and I was unfamiliar with this part of the city. There were no wide streets, all the walkways were narrow and crisscrossed between the buildings as if they were street blocks. There were no Juliet balconies or vendors on these streets. They were all humble townhomes with small windows, one on top of the other.

We approached a townhome that had the bricks painted an unassuming tan color. The large wooden door had a window in it that was covered by thick iron grates. There were windows on each side of the door, and a set of stone steps leading up to it.

"This is it?" Puck asked from behind us, "I was hoping for a hidden door situation, like the last safe house."

"Sometimes hiding in plain sight is the best thing," Liss replied as she ascended the small set of steps and turned back to Puck with a glance that said she thought he was being awfully childish. "But just in case...this door is spelled, obviously."

"I'll take it," Puck conceded with a laugh as we followed Liss inside.

Isaac wasn't exaggerating when he said this safe house was smaller. The door opened directly into a small kitchen that barely had the necessary appliances to cook for ourselves. Beyond that, there was a living room with a small wooden table that sat four off to the left, a single leather couch and coffee table to the right. The back wall held a staircase with narrow, rickety steps that lead up to the bedrooms.

"She won't come searching for you here," Liss said as she crossed her arms, taking in the cottage-like townhome. "There are no neighbors. Those homes also belong to us."

"Thank you, Liss." I squeezed her shoulder gently as I passed.

Liss had done a lot for us, and without her, I might never have been able to escape the Stormvault.

"Zion should be on his way any day now. I will send word when he arrives. In the meantime, keep a low profile. Don't leave the safe house unless it is to go to the training field. We have to be safe as we gather intelligence."

"I understand." I nodded, hoping the bedrooms would be comfortable if we were going to be cooped up here together. I dreaded the idea of being stuck in such close quarters with Nik, but I would try to avoid him at all costs.

"Speaking of training, when will we get started?" I asked, anxious to touch my magic again, but nervous at the same time.

"You'll start with Isaac tomorrow, and Warrick, too."

"Who is Warrick?" Tess asked, throwing herself down on the leather couch as a cloud of dust burst forth from it.

She sputtered and coughed, waving her hand in the air.

"It's been a long time since anyone has been here," Liss laughed as Tess continued to wave her hand to dispel it. "Warrick is the sword master. He will train you with the blade. I figured you wouldn't want to train with Nik, seeing as you haven't spoken more than two words to each other."

I met Nik's gaze across the room and his expression was unreadable. Was he hoping to have continued our training we had started back in the mortal realm? I didn't trust him, and I didn't want him to think that I did. I wanted to stay as far away from him as possible, especially where blades were involved.

"Thank you," I told Liss with a tight smile.

Liss went back to the hidden safe house to speak with Isaac, leaving the four of us alone. Tess and I went upstairs to claim bedrooms, desperately hoping there were more than two rooms. I loved Tess, but I was craving some space to myself.

To my surprise, the townhome was much cleaner and cozier on the top level, with four bedrooms, each with their own washrooms. The rooms might be small, but they had canopy beds, polished furniture, and warm fireplaces.

I took the bedroom at the end of the hall, farthest from the staircase. The linens on the canopy were black and moody, with walnut dressing furniture and a window that overlooked the cobblestone streets below.

I glanced around, thinking of the best possible place to hide the grimoire, and decided on behind the dresser. I pulled it away from the wall, realizing it was much heavier than it appeared. It squeaked against the floor, and I managed to wedge the grimoire behind it before pushing it back into place. I didn't know any concealment spells, so this would have to do for now.

As I pushed it back into place and brushed my hands off on my jeans, I caught a shock of blond hair out of the corner of my eye. I jumped back, startled as Nik raised his hand to knock on the open doorway.

"I didn't mean to startle you..." he started, his other hand hidden behind his back.

"It's ok, I was just surprised, that's all. I'm a little on edge," I replied with a tight smile.

"I can only imagine." He stepped into the room, his boots heavy against the hardwood floors. "I know you might not want to train with me, or have anything to do with me at all, but I have something for you."

My brow furrowed in confusion. "What is it?"

He pulled his hand from behind his back, and in his palm was the most beautiful dagger I had ever seen...not that I had seen that many daggers.

The blade was polished silver with intricate metal designs on the handle, a beautiful golden gem set in the hilt. It was small and light, easy to wield for someone with not a lot of strength, but plenty of speed.

"Small, but deadly. Kind of like someone else I know..." Nik swallowed hard as he met my gaze, a muscle feathering in his jaw. "I had this made for you."

"When?" I asked, my voice small as I reached out for the dagger.

My skin lightly brushed against his as I clasped my hand around the hilt, sending a shock of energy up my spine.

"When you were in the Stormvault. I never had any doubt that you would get out, and that when you did, you would need this."

The dagger was incredibly lightweight and small enough to carry easily on my thigh. I turned it over in my hand, testing the weight of it in my palm.

Nik had this made...specifically for me. A lump formed in my throat and I tried my hardest to swallow it back down. I didn't want to feel any type of emotion towards the dagger, but I had to admit it felt like it cut right through the shield I was trying so hard to keep in place.

I met his gaze, and a soft smile creased his lips.

"Thank you."

"You're quite welcome." He shrugged, burying his hands in his jean pockets. Almost as if he were...nervous. "You know, every good blade needs a name."

"Does this one have a name?" I asked, running my finger carefully along the blade.

"I was thinking...Stormslayer. Like its wielder." The corner of his lip turned up as if he wanted to smirk, but he stopped himself, his eyes on his boots.

"Stormslayer. I like it." I nodded, my eyes on the blade. I could feel his gaze fall on me and I swallowed hard, heat filling my core. "And the golden gem..." I said, running my fingers delicately across it, "it looks like flames."

"It does. Just make sure to use the pointy end," he replied.

I reluctantly met his gaze, where I found an unreadable expression.

"I will," I replied with a soft smile.

My throat was thick with emotion as our eyes remained locked a moment too long. He had been thinking of me the *entire* time. He had planned my escape with Puck, Liss, and Zion, and he had this weapon forged specially for me.

Not for a *second* thinking I would be stuck down in the Stormvault forever.

Or dead.

I had accused him of not caring, of bringing me straight into Donika's clutches and forgetting all about me. Of lying to me and betraying me in the worst way imaginable, only to leave me down in the Stormvault to rot.

But I wasn't sure if that was true anymore...and I wasn't ready to admit that to myself...and face the alternative.

12

I met Isaac in a field not far from Dragon's Hollow where our new safe house was located. It was on the outskirts of the city, a narrow meadow with vibrant green grass wedged between the farthest reaches of the city and the dense forest beyond.

I had been too scared to touch my magic since leaving the Stormvault, and I hoped when I finally did, it felt as easy as it once had. I was excited to be training with another Stormshade, someone who could provide unique insight into my specific type of magic.

A part of me had been avoiding my magic because it reminded me of Nik, and those thoughts quickly dissolved into visions of him pressed against me in the tiny closet of the stone cottage in Siraleth. His leg between mine, tangled in the sheets at Eight Bells.

I wasn't ready to face any of those complicated emotions.

Despite my reservations about Nik, the dagger he had gifted me, Stormslayer, was strapped to my thigh as I walked across the field to meet Isaac.

"A beautiful day to create a storm, don't you think?" he asked with a grin.

"I'm not sure creating a storm at all is wise in Istmere, but I trust you," I replied, stopping in front of him and crossing my arms.

"I am much older and much wiser than you, young Stormshade. This glen is glamoured well enough that not a soul will be able to sense the storm magic we use here today." Isaac laughed as his eyes fell on the dagger at my thigh. "Are you planning to need that?" he asked with a raised brow.

"No, but you can never be too careful," I replied, setting my jaw. "I've already been kidnapped once...remember?"

"How could I ever forget. Our true queen...kidnapped before I even knew she had come to Istmere. Nikolai should have taken you to the resistance right away."

Little did he know, Nik had other plans. The resistance didn't know about his involvement with Donika or my kidnapping, and we decided it was best not to tell them. I hadn't entirely made up my mind to cast him out of my life forever, and I didn't know what the punishment would be for such a crime. It wasn't only me he betrayed, he broke his word to the council of the resistance, too.

I imagined the punishment was death.

"Well, I am here now, and I have lots of catching up to do," I said, relaxing my arms at my side and cracking my neck.

"Indeed, you do. What have you learned thus far?" he asked.

"Basic magic. How to move things from one place to another, how to generate an element in the palm of your hand. How to create a rainstorm and a tornado, though I haven't had much practice siphoning power from them yet."

"Very good." He nodded. "That is a good foundation. Let's begin with a simple storm spell. I'd like you to bring forth a storm cloud with rain, but don't let the droplets of water touch us."

"I can do that?"

That sounded awfully precise, and none of the magic I had done thus far had been particularly controlled. I decided not to tell him I had burned my mother's carpet the first time I had called on air and fire. And that I hadn't even reached out to my magic source since being captured by Donika.

"It's quite easy. You'll bring the storm forth as you always have, but you want to use the air to create a protective bubble around us. It uses multiple elements at once."

I nodded, raising my palms towards the sky. I had used both elements before, but never at the same time. With a deep inhale, I dove into my source, searching for that ember of magic deep within my core.

To my surprise, I found it easily, as if I had never spent any time away from it at all. My fears that Donika had spellbound me or stolen my magic were quenched as I reached into my magic, bringing it forth and out of my fingertips.

The sky above us darkened, the sun only peeking out behind the black rain cloud that quickly formed overhead. The storm cloud quickly eclipsed it, the sun winking out of sight. A soft roll of thunder sounded overhead, and I glanced at Isaac, a question in my eyes.

"Only you and I can hear the storm," he confirmed with a solemn nod.

My magic surged forth easily, and I closed my eyes to focus. I imagined the rain coming down and felt a cool drop against my cheek as I raised my face to the sky. The rain fell faster as I tried to pull up my air shield, but it was more difficult than I had first imagined. One magic working against the other. The storm came more naturally to me. The air was harder to pull into place.

"Imagine the shield around us, and we are safely within it. Nothing from the outside can touch us," Isaac encouraged.

"I'm trying."

I bit my lip as I focused harder, letting the storm go and focusing my magic on the air shield. I sensed it the moment it fell into place, the soft pellets of rain bouncing off the invisible shield with a patter. I opened my eyes, no longer feeling the rain falling against my skin. My gaze traveled to Isaac, an approving expression in his eyes.

"Very good. Now next time, maybe you secure the air shield *first*, then the storm." He laughed, shaking out his grey hair. The rain had darkened the blue shirt he was wearing.

"Sorry about that," I replied sheepishly, my own hair plastered against my scalp, the rain droplets rolling off my leather jacket, "That was more challenging than what I've done before."

"The key is to let the storm go. It has its own energy now. You don't have to hold the storm *and* the air. It can be difficult to juggle multiple elements simultaneously." He took a step closer to me, the air shields still in place. "Now for the hard part."

"That wasn't the hard part?" I asked with a huff.

"Unfortunately not. Now you have to hold the air shields in place while you reach back out to the storm to re-absorb it."

"I can't let the shields down first?" I teased with a laugh.

Isaac shook his head. "Not only would that soak us with rain even further during this demonstration, but what if it wasn't rain? What if it was *arrows* pelting against your shield? Or a sword? You'd be dead where you stand before you could even call out to the storm overhead."

"Good point," I acquiesced.

I focused my mind on keeping the air shields in place while also reaching out to the storm, which continued to rain down overhead. I could feel the magic weighing on me, as if it were a muscle I hadn't quite built up yet. It would get easier the more I used it, but I would be sore tomorrow.

I tried to reach the storm, but failed, the air shield slipping slightly as a few rain pellets fought their way through. Isaac crossed his arms over his chest as he watched me, nodding in encouragement. The air shield around us was a physical weight as I pulled more magic from my core through my fingertips towards the sky above us.

The storm responded this time, sputtering and releasing a grumble of thunder, but surging forwards again. It was raining harder this time.

I released a groan of frustration as I tried again, closing my eyes and turning my face towards the sky. I pulled even more magic through my fingertips, all while concentrating on the air shield around us.

The storm responded again, letting a bolt of lightning loose in the forest at our backs.

I startled, my eyes snapping to Isaac's.

"You have to remember, the storm isn't *yours* anymore since you let it go. You can't treat it as if it's a part of you, because it isn't. You must treat it as if it is a force all its own, *but you are stronger*. You need to find *its* source of magic now."

I nodded, rubbing my hands together, then spreading them wide again towards the sky.

I could do this.

I was a Stormshade, and a powerful one at that. I wouldn't be bested by a little rainstorm that I had created in the first place.

I pulled more magic first, but this time the intention wasn't to call the storm back, it was to capture it. I could feel my magic swirl around the storm, the clouds booming together in another clap of thunder. But this time, the storm relented. I could sense the magic source of the storm pulling through my hands and back into my core, an entirely new ember of magic to pull from.

I squinted towards the sun as it appeared once more behind the dark clouds. The clouds overhead turned from a dark, angry grey to a wispy white, then disappeared entirely.

"Very good." Isaac nodded, moving to my side.

A sheen of sweat appeared across my brow from the effort it had taken to maintain the shield and capture the storm all in the same breath. "That magic is much harder than what you have practiced so far. I am impressed."

"I had a good teacher."

The thought skittered across my mind and out of my mouth before I could take it back, and I hated myself for it. I dug my nails into the palm of my hand as I tried to banish all thoughts of Nik from my mind.

Isaac gave me a sympathetic smile as he squeezed my shoulder. "That was a big spell. I think that's enough for today. I want you to think about using your magic as a weapon *and* a shield. I know you haven't had to use it this way before, but that's the way we need to train."

"I understand," I replied, swallowing hard.

Long gone were the days of opening lockers and lifting feathers into the air for fun. I would train my magic with one goal in mind: to end Donika's reign, once and for all.

I shook my arms out, feeling as if I had finished a weight training session at the gym.

Isaac laughed. "You will be sore tomorrow, wielding magic such as this can often times be an incredibly physical activity. It takes its toll."

"Just in time for sword training with Warrick tomorrow," I replied sarcastically.

We started the walk back towards Dragon's Hollow. Isaac was determined not to let me out of his sight until I was safely back inside the safe house. He had left the glamour up so that we could sword train in the same meadow tomorrow. It was close to our side of the city, and far enough away from Akra that we didn't need to worry about our storm magic calling any unwanted attention.

Tess had mentioned training her magic with Puck, so I wasn't surprised when I found the little townhouse empty. Candles softly flickered in the windows as night descended over Prins. I used one of the candles to light a lantern as I made my way up to my room.

I used the time alone to take a long, hot soak in the claw-foot bathtub. The washroom was small, but well appointed. It had decadent smelling salts and soaps, along with soft, plush towels. I washed the day away slowly, luxuriating in the lavender scents and the hot water loosening my sore muscles. I hoped I might be able to find a jug of wine on the first floor, but I wasn't sure if the townhome would be *that* well stocked.

I could go for a pint of Dragon's Ale right about now, but doubted we would be able to show our faces at Eight Bells any time soon. Fletcher's brother, Kane, had seen us there before Donika had captured me. That might be the first place they searched for us, and I undeniably wasn't strong enough to take on Fletcher or his brother yet.

I toweled off and reached for the robe hanging on the back of the door, but thought better of it. Robes altogether now reminded me of the night I had spent with Nik. I shrugged into a too-big pair of sweatpants and a long-sleeve shirt Isaac had been nice enough to leave us. I would need to get some of my own clothes if I was going to be staying in Istmere.

I opened the door and padded down the stairs to the kitchen. I rummaged for some food that didn't require any cooking, or that jug of wine I had my heart set on. When I stood, I caught a reflection in the window before me and startled, one hand grabbing my chest, the other grabbing the edge of the counter before me.

"You scared me. I thought I was alone." My voice broke the silence, but not the tension.

"Not my intention, I apologize." Nik leaned against the kitchen peninsula, a lock of blond hair falling across his forehead.

"You're awfully quiet..." I turned towards him fully, gripping the counter behind me.

"Shadow magic, remember?" He smirked as a shadow curled around his raised hand, slinking down his arm before disappearing under the sleeve of his shirt.

I thought that seeing the shadows would bring on the same terror I had experienced when Donika had tortured me, when she had killed all those innocent people. Instead, I felt a warmth bloom in my chest that I couldn't explain.

Maybe not all shadow magic was inherently dark.

"Is there any wine in this Godforsaken place?" I asked, glancing around the kitchen and trying not to meet his gaze.

"Diana Barnes...I am *shocked*." He raised an eyebrow at me, a smile in his eyes. "Is that what you were down here rummaging for?"

"I'm not Diana Barnes. Not anymore..." I trailed off, avoiding his gaze.

"Well then, Ms. *Kotova,* let me make a deal with you. I will procure the wine you seek...if you'll eat dinner with me."

I hesitated, gripping the counter behind me tightly enough that my knuckles turned white. It was only dinner...what was the harm in that, right?

As if reading my thoughts, Nik cleared his throat before he spoke.

"It's just dinner—I'm not asking you to marry me. Have dinner with me, wine included. You can't very well drink on an empty stomach," he pointed out.

I met his gaze, and there was a challenge in his eyes.

I could do dinner. It was *just* dinner. Besides, he was right. I hadn't eaten...and Isaac's training session had left me famished.

I bit my lip. I never said no to a challenge.

"Deal."

He stood, coming around the counter to search through the cabinet under the sink. He glanced up at me, his arms resting on his knees as he knelt, and I hadn't realized how close we were until his gaze locked with mine.

"Do you know how to start a fire?" he asked, eyes locked on mine.

"Do you?" I asked, internally cursing myself for how petty I sounded.

"You know I do." His eyes smoldered, and I glanced away quickly, regretting opening my mouth in the first place.

"Of course I do," I replied, moving towards the fireplace in the living room.

"Not with magic," he called over his shoulder. I could hear bottles clinking together as he moved them around. "This place is only warded for location spells, not storm magic. If you use any storm magic outside the meadow, they might be able to track you."

"Then no, I don't know how to start a fire." I crossed my arms over my chest and pouted, despite my back facing towards him.

He laughed softly, and I could feel the sound crawling over my skin, leaving sparks in its wake. I hated that he still had that effect on me. That I knew exactly where he was, even without turning around. He placed a glass jug on the counter and came around me, kneeling before the grate to start the fire with his own magic.

"I can cook," I offered, the flames quickly licking against the wood in the fireplace.

The fire cast the room in a warm orange glow, and the heat was pleasant against my tingling skin.

"I know you can, but I want to cook for you," he replied, rising to his feet.

He was so close I could see the reflection of the flames flickering in his eyes, and despite my body telling me the exact opposite, I took a step back.

"You know how to cook?" I asked. It was my turn to raise an eyebrow.

"Don't act so shocked." He laughed as he moved back to the kitchen. He pulled out two glass goblets and filled them with a rich, dark wine. "My mom taught me a thing or two."

"Tell me about her," I blurted out, before I could think better of it.

I shouldn't want to know *anything* about him, but he was still a mystery to me. He took a deep gulp of wine and found a wooden cutting board, bringing it over to the peninsula. I sat on one of the stools as he started to chop up various vegetables, sipping on my wine as I studied him.

"What do you want to know?" he asked, slicing with expert precision, not glancing up to meet my gaze.

"Where is she?" I asked. He had said his home life had been complicated...but I wasn't sure exactly what that meant.

"Dead."

He glanced up, watching my expression from under his eyelashes.

"I'm sorry." My voice was soft, the only other sound filling the silence the flames sparking in the fireplace.

I shook my head, my eyes falling back to my wine. I shouldn't have asked. Nobody should have to deal with the loss of a parent...that was a loss I knew all too deeply. I had lost both of my birth parents, but I had never met them. They hadn't raised me. The loss of Nik's mother was entirely different.

"It was a long time ago," he replied, his voice thick with emotion. "We were close, once. I was the only child, so I always had my parents' doting affections. She and my father..." he trailed off, choosing his next words carefully. "They didn't see eye to eye on how to raise me. My father wanted to move to Akra, to put me in the queen's army. It would gain status for our family, and it would gain me visibility before Donika.

My mother never wanted that for me." He took a deep gulp of wine as he shook his head back and forth.

"What happened to her?" I asked softly, fearing the answer.

The look in Nik's eyes told me his family troubles were far more complicated than I had ever imagined.

"He will never admit it, but I think my father...*dealt* with her."

He spoke with such disdain, it was clear his relationship with his father was not a good one.

"My father has never been there for me, not once. He was a constant let down as a parent. Always pushing me to harden myself, never show my emotions, to train to be the best soldier. When I needed him the most...he was gone."

"Nik..." my voice trailed off, my grip on the stem of my wine goblet tight enough that I thought I might crack the glass.

The urge to go to him was so strong I almost pushed back my chair and came around the counter. The only thing stopping me was the image of Donika flashing before my eyes. I couldn't forget how we had gotten here, the part he had played in all of this.

"It was my father who pushed me to court Donika in the first place. I just wanted to make him proud. I wanted his acceptance, just *once*."

He met my gaze and shook his head at the sympathy he saw there.

"Like I said, all this shit with my father...it was a long time ago." He took another sip of wine before he delicately took up the knife and resumed cutting.

"That doesn't make it any less difficult to deal with," I told him.

I didn't want to feel a lick of sympathy for him, but I couldn't help it. All I wanted to feel was anger...but in this moment that had melted away, leaving something fragile and raw in its place.

"Maybe...but being upset for even *one instant* goes against everything he tried to ingrain in me. He left me to those wolves and never looked back. I don't even know where he is, and if he's alive or dead. But I've found I don't even care anymore."

He lifted his face to the ceiling, biting back the emotions that threatened to escape. I had never seen him this unfiltered, this exposed.

"It's ok to feel vulnerable. To feel emotion. You aren't just a mindless soldier," I told him.

Every voice in my head was telling me to reach across the peninsula and grab his hand, but my own hand remained curled around the wine goblet. My emotions were swirling inside of me, a tornado of battling wills. Sadness. Anger. Desperation. Vengeance. I couldn't separate them from one another, and they were so opposite I felt as if I was being ripped apart from the inside out.

"I know you won't like to hear this..." he started, meeting my gaze.

"Then don't say it," I bit out, afraid of what he might confess.

I was afraid of how it might change the way I felt about him. That it would soften me towards him. I couldn't let that happen...not again. I wouldn't punish him in this vulnerable moment, but I wouldn't open myself up to him, either.

"You brought that side out of me. I never felt more vulnerable...or emotional than when I met you. I wanted to protect you, and when I couldn't...the utter heartbreak and helplessness threatened to consume me. I've never felt like that before."

He held my gaze and I couldn't turn away, despite knowing that I should. I wasn't sure how to respond, and thankfully, he broke the silence with a humorless laugh.

"I know you don't want to hear it, but the consequences of my own actions have been *unbearable*."

He turned to the stove where he added the chopped vegetables to a pot filled with water, his back to me.

The silence was deafening.

Did I believe him? That it had all been real for him? He had said as much in the Stormvault...but after that confession I hadn't seen him for *months*. The Stormslayer dagger was proof he was, in fact, thinking of me. But I still didn't trust him. I couldn't. He had taken my heart and utterly obliterated it. That kind of broken trust couldn't be repaired so easily, if at all.

He gave the pot a stir before turning back to me, a sadness in his eyes. Maybe he knew there was no going back to the way things were before between us. That we would never be those people again, and everything that had transpired between us was...unfixable.

What we had was broken, and we couldn't put it back together.

I took a deep gulp of wine and finished the glass. Nik let out a soft laugh as he grabbed the jug to refill my goblet.

"Nothing like a little light dinner conversation."

"Tell me about it," I replied, running a hand down my face.

"At least I knew my parents," Nik said as he refilled his own glass. "I feel lucky, to have at least had that."

"I'm not sure that's any better." I laughed quietly, shaking my head. "I didn't know my parents, but at least that meant they didn't have the opportunity to disappoint me so thoroughly."

"True," Nik conceded with a grin. "We both have some pretty messed up family issues, then."

"I'll toast to that."

Nik filled wooden bowls with the warm vegetable stew, and we sat at the peninsula eating and drinking. I wasn't sure if I wanted to laugh or cry, the sentiments swirling together inside of me to create an undecipherable cyclone.

"I have to admit...this is good," I told him around a mouthful.

"I told you, I can cook," he replied, turning to me with a smirk.

"Is there anything you can't do?" I asked in challenge.

He pretended to ponder it for a moment before responding. "No, I am distinctly good at absolutely everything."

I gave him a playful shove and his foot slipped off the rung of the stool, almost causing him to fall off. "You are so conceited, *Kolya*."

If I didn't lighten the mood and change the subject, my emotions threatened to pull me under and suffocate me. I didn't know how to be here...with him. I felt exposed to him in a way that I hated, and that was the very last thing I wanted. I didn't want him to know how I felt at all. He needed to stay at arm's length...or further.

I couldn't be close to him. I couldn't let him in again.

I could feel my anger transforming into something...different. Something murkier and enigmatic. I couldn't quite determine how I was feeling, and that might have been the scariest part of all.

It was easier to stay angry with him, to let that fire fill me up and consume me.

"Hey now firecracker, I'll let you know if I ever find something I'm not good at. But so far, I haven't come up with anything. That doesn't make me conceited." He laughed hard enough that the corners of his eyes crinkled.

I realized that it was the first time I had seen him *truly* smile since everything that had happened. Despite still being angry with him, despite not trusting him, despite the emotions spiraling out of control inside of me, I couldn't help but smile back.

13

Warrick was distinctly less forgiving of an instructor than Isaac. The first few days of blade training left me unable to walk, my muscles sorer than I had ever imagined possible. I limped home and spent my nights soaking my sore and battered muscles in a hot bath before falling into bed. Liss woke me each morning, and each morning I pulled the covers tighter, dreading the inevitable.

I knew I had to train hard, to learn to wield a blade and to protect myself, but I was *tired.* I was covered in cuts and bruises in various stages of healing. Each time Liss applied a healing skin spell, I would return to the safe house with more bumps and bruises.

Tess was taking to the sword training as a fish took to water. Being naturally athletic, she was a natural. But I had to admit...my aim was better. Stormslayer was a light blade, and it felt natural in my hand. Each time I bested Warrick, pushing him back, I could see Nik smirk out of the corner of my eye.

Today Nik and Puck joined in the sparring, and we broke off in pairs. Liss was an unparalleled swordswoman, and I couldn't help but wonder how she was so skilled with a blade having been in the service of Donika as a maid, with no formal training at all. Isaac never joined these training sessions, but he did send Kenna.

Kenna was a scrappy fighter. She was slight and thin, but she was a quick thinker, and like me, she was fast. Saanvi joined us for the first time today, and I found her to be the most challenging opponent yet.

As her Nightshade form would indicate, Saanvi was cat-like in her movements. She was always one step ahead, and she certainly had nine lives. She never tired, and she was never bested. I thought she might be going easy on me, despite ending up on my back each and every time.

Warrick had brought mats out to the training field so we hopefully wouldn't injure ourselves too greatly.

Lot of good that did.

Saanvi whipped out with her leg so fast my feet came right out from underneath me, and I grunted as I hit the mat flat on my back. She was on me before I had time to roll and regain my footing, her blade poised over my heart. I brought my arm up *hard*, thankful for the leather training cuffs Liss had gifted me, and knocked her arm out of the way. I lifted my hips, rolling her over in one smooth movement.

"Yes, Diana! Use your speed, never stop moving!" Warrick called from the sidelines, clapping his hands together. Tess was whooping and hollering, cheering me on.

Warrick was much younger than I had imagined he would be, only a few years older than me. He had a strong build and was tall, not to mention incredibly handsome. His eyes were a piercing green, and I had found our first few training sessions awfully distracting.

As quickly as I had turned us over, Saanvi snuck out from underneath me and I turned, her foot coming towards my face almost faster than I could get my hands up. I took the brunt of her kick on the leather cuffs, ducking at the impact. I whirled quickly, bringing Stormslayer down in an arc, but she was equally as fast, and blocked my advance easily.

Sparring was similar to dancing, a back and forth between the opponents. It was intuitive, and even when I wasn't sparring myself, I loved to watch the other matches. There was always something to learn from the other fighters.

I ducked as Saanvi's closed fist sailed towards me, her arm swinging over my head and missing. We squared off again, pieces of my auburn hair coming loose from my tie and falling into my face. I was dripping with sweat, and while I had started off in a jacket due to the cooler spring weather, I soon found myself in only my tank top and leathers. The thigh strap for Stormslayer was tight against my leg, holding another, smaller, throwing knife.

I also had one stashed in my boot.

I lunged forwards, faking left but moving right, creeping under Saanvi's arm and hitting her on the back of her shoulder with the blunt end of Stormslayer. She fell to her knees, kicking out with her leg and hitting my legs, dropping me to the mat.

Again.

She was on me before I could think of my next move, her dagger poised to strike. I raised my closed fist and hit the mat hard, twice, tapping out.

Warrick shook his head from the sidelines, but I took his smile as an indication he was happy with my progress.

"Great match, Diana. I think you'll be able to take me in no time." Saanvi reached her hand down to help me up, a smile on her face.

I took her hand as she tossed her long black braid over her shoulder, and she pulled me upright. I took a moment to catch my breath, the wind knocked out of me.

Saanvi was my third match of the day.

"I'm not so sure about that. You are a cat, after all." I laughed, breathless.

She tilted her head in thought. "True, but you've made a lot of progress. I was certainly not this skilled after only a few weeks with a blade. It took me much longer to learn."

"She really wasn't," Puck called out from the side of the mat.

Kenna elbowed him in the stomach and he doubled over, whether with laughter or pain I couldn't quite tell.

"Whose up next?" Warrick asked, stepping forwards to the center of the mat.

I used my tank top to wipe the sweat from my forehead, Tess handing me a much-needed canteen of water.

Nik stepped forwards, a long broadsword strapped across his back.

"Anybody want to take me on?" he asked with a grin. His arrogance had me rolling my eyes at the back of his head. "How about you, Warrick?"

"I don't want to fight you, Nikolai."

Warrick crossed his arms over his chest. I had a feeling there was history between the two of them, maybe bad blood. They appeared to hate each other and avoided one another at all costs. There were always jabs or witty quips being exchanged between the two of them.

"You don't think it's time we hash it out?" Nik asked, cocking his head to the side, a gleam in his eyes.

He unsheathed the sword in one fluid movement, his stance wide.

"I'm not sure you want to be embarrassed in front of your friends," Warrick replied, his jaw tight.

"Me? Embarrassed? Never." Nik grinned at Warrick in challenge, his eyebrow raised.

I had seen Warrick spar with, and best, everyone in our group. Including Liss. But never Nik. He had laid Puck out in under a minute and Puck had complained for days that he was out of practice, and that was the only reason he had lost so easily.

Nik wasn't going to back down. "Are you afraid, Warrick? Afraid someone might be able to teach *the teacher* a thing or two?"

Warrick stepped forwards, unsheathing his own sword. We collectively backed towards the edges of the mat, waiting for the match to begin.

"Enjoy the show, ladies," Kenna murmured with a raised eyebrow and a knowing glint in her eye. She tossed her long black hair over her shoulder with a laugh.

"I'm only going to shut you up once, *Kolya*." Warrick's words dripped with scorn. "Then enough of this."

I couldn't help but wonder what had transpired between them, and why they hated each other so much. Warrick had at least a few inches of height on Nik, and while Nik was all lean muscle, Warrick was bulky. Nik had the agility in this fight, but Warrick had the brute strength.

Nik made the first move, his blade moving in a downward arc towards Warrick. He quickly parried, the steel clanking together and sending a shiver running down my spine.

Sparring with a sword was always different from sparring with a dagger. There was something so...primal about it. Nik and Warrick wielded their swords with expertise, and I was surprised to see the supposed sword master of the resistance meet his match in Nik.

As I watched Nik move, I couldn't help but admire the way he moved, his blond hair slicked back from his face, his tunic riding up to reveal the tattoos on his abdomen. I shook my head, trying to shake those thoughts loose.

Nik had betrayed me...end of story. I couldn't be thinking about his hair, his tattoos, or *anything* else. We had a civil dinner together the other night, but I had gone right back to pushing him away, keeping him at a distance.

My head moved back and forth quickly, watching Warrick and Nik move across the mat.

Nik was *fast.*

By the time Warrick could bring his sword around Nik was already onto the next move, forcing Warrick back further and further.

"Have you had enough yet?" Nik asked through gritted teeth as their swords collided again.

"In your dreams," Warrick spit out, hitting back hard enough that Nik had to take a step back, his eyes wide.

Nik was always crouched, ready to spring. He was light on his feet, and he moved with his sword as if it weighed nothing. As if it was simply an extension of himself.

He swung quickly, but Warrick managed to duck the blade, hitting Nik with the blunt end of his sword and splitting the skin on his forehead. Blood trickled down, but that didn't stop him. He spun out of Warrick's grasp and was almost able to hit him from behind, but Warrick ducked at the last minute, barely missing Nik's strike.

Nik used his tunic to wipe the blood that dripped down his face, revealing his toned abdomen for only a moment. Tess coughed not-so-quietly beside me, and I shot her a glare that had her shrinking back, but not without a smile on her face.

Warrick had first blood, but it had ignited a fire within Nik. He was moving even faster now, slicing out with such speed Warrick wasn't able to move out of the way in time. The slash to his thigh dropped him to his knees. Nik knocked the sword from Warrick's grip and pressed his sword to his throat equally as quickly, skimming the skin light enough to make Warrick wince.

"Do you yield, cousin?" Despite the effort from the fight, Nik's voice came out smooth, as if he hadn't even broken a sweat.

Cousin? Is that what this was about...more family drama? When we had spoken about his family the other night in the townhouse, he hadn't mentioned his cousin being a part of the resistance, let alone the one training me.

"Yield," Warrick spit out.

He rose to his feet, shoulders hunched. Nik was officially the one to beat, he had yet to lose a sparring match. He grinned as Puck clapped him on the back, and I could all but feel Saanvi and Kenna rolling their eyes next to us. They knew this would feed Nik's already inflated ego, and they never hesitated to remind him of it.

"Who's next to face me?" Nik asked, searching our faces.

I wasn't sure any of us would want to take him on at this point. We had been sparring all day, and we weren't at our full strength. I didn't think any of us could beat him, even on a good day.

"How about you, firecracker?" His eyes landed on me, his sword leveled in my direction.

I had yet to spar with Nik, and for good reason. I had been avoiding him ever since our dinner in the townhouse the other night, and I was doing everything in my power to keep my distance from him.

"I'm not sure I want to challenge someone who just beat the teacher," I pointed out, crossing my arms over my chest.

"And besides, I haven't been training with a sword. I'm playing to my strengths, remember?"

"I can use a dagger just as well," he replied, sheathing his sword at his back.

He moved to the center of the mat, wiping the blood from his face once more. Puck tossed him a dagger that he caught by the hilt, twisting it around in his hand skillfully.

"What are you so nervous about, firecracker? I'll go easy on you. Promise." He met my gaze with a wicked grin, and I narrowed my eyes at him.

I wanted nothing more than to wipe that smirk right off his smug face, but I had no hope against him in a sparring match. Even if he *did* go easy on me.

"I don't think so," I replied with a shake of my head.

At the same time, Tess pushed me from behind and I unintentionally stepped forwards onto the mat.

"We have a taker!" Puck announced, clapping his hands together.

I shot him a glare that silenced him immediately. Puck was—without a doubt—scared of me.

All eyes were on me as I reluctantly stepped to the center of the mat across from Nik, rolling my shoulders to loosen them.

"Do you remember what I taught you?" Nik asked with a wink.

"Mother above," Tess muttered under her breath, running a hand down her face.

I needed to put this jackass in his place.

My anger fueled me, and when Nik made the first move I was ready. Nik was fast, but so was I. He hadn't been coming to most of my training sessions with Warrick, and he didn't know my fighting style yet. It made it difficult for him to anticipate my next move.

I ducked his blade several times as he moved forwards, swinging his dagger downward and pushing me back. I rushed him, deftly slipping to my knees and turning, my dagger slicing him in the thigh as I moved past under his arcing blade.

"Well, shit," he muttered, surprised.

He cracked his neck and re-set his stance across from me. He came at me again, but I had been expecting him to make the first move. I ducked his blade and brought my own forth, almost knocking his out of his hands, but his grip was tight on the hilt.

I spun, but he anticipated it this time and kicked out with his leg, hitting me square in the hip. I winced and jumped back. I was smaller than him, and I needed to use that to my advantage. When I made my next move, I ducked and kicked, throwing him off balance as one of his feet left the ground. I pushed the advantage, knocking him off his feet. He hit the mat on his back and rolled, taking me with him. He was stronger than I was, and he had my arms pinned above my head.

A shock of heat ran through me as his hips pressed against mine, his hands around my wrists, a wicked smile on his lips.

"You know what to do!" Warrick called out from the side of the mat, grabbing my attention.

Warrick and I had gone over how to get out of this hold many times. With a grunt I bucked, my hips coming up and freeing my knee to hit him in the groin. I rolled him over as the breath left him, quickly regaining my footing.

"Maybe I shouldn't be going easy on you..." Nik coughed, breathless.

He moved forwards again, but he hadn't regained his composure. I easily knocked his arm away, my blade quickly moving to his throat. His eyebrows shot up in surprise, raising his hands as if in defeat, the dagger still in his grip.

"I have to say, I'm impressed, firecracker." He pressed closer, encroaching on my space, the blade still pressed against his throat.

"Yield," I told him through gritted teeth.

He inched closer as he raised an eyebrow at me.

"Or what?" he asked, leaning into the blade.

"Any closer and you'll get burned," I warned, my magic readily moving from my core and up my arms, towards my fingers that gripped Stormslayer.

"I've always liked to play with fire." His eyes were molten despite my blade at his throat, a sinful smirk across his lips.

"You are seriously disturbed," I replied, my jaw set.

I pressed the blade harder, ever so slightly. If anything, his gaze darkened further as a trickle of blood crept down his neck.

He held my gaze for a long, heated moment. I desperately hoped the sweat and exertion of the sparring match hid the flush of pink I knew painted my cheeks.

"Yield," he conceded, taking a reluctant step back.

I dropped my arm back to my side with a deep inhale, his eyes never leaving mine. I had thought he would happily flatten me to the mat...but he had let me win. Or had I simply caught him by surprise? I could practically feel Warrick's disapproval from the sidelines.

"Intoxicating," Nik murmured as he stepped back, loud enough for only me to hear.

My eyes blazed, and I hated myself for the reaction my body still had towards him. That his words could still raise the hair on my arms and set my core on fire. I narrowed my eyes and his gaze only intensified, a spark of electricity taught between us.

Tess cleared her throat, loudly, and broke whatever spell I had fallen into. I stepped away, rejoining her at the side of the mat and guzzling back the remainder of the canteen.

I needed a hot shower.

Or maybe a cold one?

I pinched my fingers on the bridge of my nose and internally cursed myself. How could I let myself feel *anything* but anger towards him?

The sun was beginning to set, leaving the meadow swathed in pink, dusk sunlight. I couldn't wait to wash this day off and crawl into bed and stay there. Preferably for the next several days.

"What was that?" Kenna asked, pointing towards the forest.

"What was what?" Saanvi asked, turning.

"That black figure..." Kenna trailed off as we all turned towards the tree line.

Without much natural light to see by it was difficult to make out the shape of the figure, but it was certainly nothing

I had ever seen before. The *thing* that emerged from the trees was a creature from the deepest depths of hell, or my darkest nightmares.

It had the legs of a spider, long and spindly, the creature standing at least ten feet tall or more. Its body was round, with a head that was distinctly human-like, but it was completely eyeless. Its teeth were razor sharp with long, protruding fangs. It had a barbed tail that swished about in agitation.

Or was there more than one tail? The creature moved in the dim light and my eyes had difficulty tracing its movements against the backdrop of trees.

"What...the hell...is that?" My voice came out small as I backed away, Stormslayer tight in my grip. "Are there *monsters* in Istmere?"

"No." Nik replied, his jaw tight. "At least...there weren't."

The creature advanced, moving rather quickly despite its immense size. It was flanked by two more, and as the sun set behind us the horrible creatures let loose a bone chilling shriek.

What the hell were those things?

"Get behind me," Nik instructed, pushing me back and shielding me with his body.

The creatures advanced and Warrick moved to meet them, slashing forwards with his sword. He was able to slice off one of the creature's many legs and it howled in pain, easily reaching out with another of its legs and knocking him to the side effortlessly.

Nik moved to advance on the one before us, jumping up and trying to slice his sword and catch the creature in the head.

It reared back with a horrible sound, and Nik slashed out, lodging his sword directly in its forehead. He pulled it loose with great effort and hacked forwards again, slicing its head clean in half. It fell in a heap at his feet, and equally as fast it disintegrated into a puff of black smoke, leaving nothing but black sludge in its wake.

Was that black liquid...its blood?

"What the..." Tess spoke from beside me as we continued to back away.

I wasn't ready to face any real threat, I hadn't trained enough. What were these things, and where had they come from?

As Saanvi jumped onto the back of another creature and drove her sword down through the top of its head, I had a sinking feeling these creatures were sent by Donika.

"Diana, watch out!" Warrick's voice rang through me as a spider-like leg lashed out and knocked me off my feet as if I weighed nothing at all.

I hit my head against the ground as I landed in a heap, Stormslayer skittering from my grip. I tried to crawl through the grass to reach it, but the creature placed a hairy, spindly leg on my back to stop me. I could hear the wet, grinding noises it was making as it lowered its head towards mine. I tried with all my strength to push out from underneath it, but I couldn't budge. Nik was still too far away, and I wasn't sure where Warrick or Puck were.

My magic surged up without even calling on it, as if to remind me it was right there, waiting. As I dipped into the core of my energy, a whirling ball of fire in my palm, a wet, gushing sound filled my ears. Someone was on top of the creature and had beheaded it, its head rolling to the ground beside me in a sickly, wet thud. Its eyeless face met the dirt and came to rest mere feet from where I lay.

The creatures body slid to the ground and disappeared in a cloud of smoke. The figure deftly jumped to the ground and rolled, never losing grip of their sword.

I raised my eyes to theirs, my brow furrowing in confusion.

What was he doing here?

He had saved my life. He could easily have let that monster consume me...but he hadn't.

And I wanted to know why.

"What are you doing here, Tyr?"

14

"You'd better start talking, or it will be *your* head that is sliced clean off next," Nik seethed, his sword pointed at the back of Tyr's neck.

Tyr lifted his arms and turned slowly, meeting Nik's furious gaze.

"I just saved her life." He gestured towards me where I still lay in a heap on the ground, covered in the black, thick liquid I believed to be the blood of those creatures.

"And you almost lost it once before. Talk. Now."

Nik's tone brooked no argument. Tyr glanced between the two of us before deciding he had a better chance of reasoning with me. Nik never lowered his sword.

"I came to warn you, but it appears I almost didn't make it in time. Donika sent these creatures after you. They're the product of her blood magic, they are dark, magical beings. And they aren't the only ones, she is working on more," Tyr said.

“Why would you come to warn me?” I asked, my brow furrowing in confusion.

I got to me feet and dusted off my pants, now ruined with blood and grime. I bent to retrieve Stormslayer, securing it back to my thigh.

“We got off on the wrong foot…” Tyr started.

“That’s the understatement of the century,” Puck replied as he joined us, grabbing Tyr around the back of the neck and motioning for Nik to lower his sword.

Tyr was far outnumbered.

“What I mean to say is, I am *not* an ally of Donika. I never was, and I never will be. I didn’t go to her willingly with the information that you were in Istmere,” Tyr explained.

“That doesn’t explain how she got the information, then, does it?” Nik asked, cocking his head to the side.

“She tortured it out of me.”

Tyr met Nik’s gaze with a cold glare of his own.

“And you sold out your cousin to die at the hands of that psychopath, it was that easy?” Nik replied, taking a step closer.

Puck shot him a warning glare, his grip still firm on Tyr.

“No, it wasn’t that easy. I didn’t want to tell her. She threatened my mother, she threatened my family. I never wanted to betray Diana. I have felt *awful* about what I have done.”

“I’m sure you have,” Puck replied, his voice dripping with sarcasm.

“I am telling the truth. I heard things, when I was at the castle. Things about the creatures she is creating. The moment I was free I came straight to find you, which proved quite difficult."

Tyr wiped the sweat from his forehead and turned to me with a pleading gaze. "I never meant to hurt you, Diana, I support your claim to the throne. I came here to warn you as soon as I could."

"Bullshit," Nik spat, taking another step closer, his grip on the hilt of his sword so tight his knuckles were white.

"He saved my life. We at least have to bring this decision back to Isaac and Liss," I offered, my palm out as if to stop him. "The council has a say in this."

"And I am a member of said council," Nik pointed out, his eyes narrowing.

I bristled. His reminder that he had played both the doting boyfriend to Donika while gaining the trust of the council and feeding that information back all the while made my skin crawl.

"I am aware of that, but you aren't the only member. We need to discuss this with the others, and nothing will be done to him before we do so. Do I make myself clear?"

My voice was confident, and it surprised me a little.

I sounded like a queen.

Nik met my gaze and nodded softly.

"Thank you," I replied. "We can't exactly bring him straight to one of our safe houses, so what do we do with him?"

"I volunteer to stay here and watch the little lad," Puck smiled, tightening his grip on Tyr.

"I will as well," Warrick offered.

"I can spell him, he won't be able to leave," Saanvi offered, speaking for the first time.

I had almost forgotten she and Kenna were still here.

"Good, let's get it done." I turned, joining Tess and walking back to the hidden safe house we had first stayed in when we escaped Donika.

Nik was close on our heels, Kenna having stayed back to walk with Saanvi after the spell was complete. I was confident that even if Tyr managed to get out of the spelled circle...he was no match for Puck and Warrick.

I had to ask Nik for directions back to the safe house many times, but we eventually found it. The spelled door opened beneath my touch and Isaac and Liss were already downstairs, as if they had been waiting for us.

"What the hell happened?" Liss asked, rushing towards us when she took in our appearances, covered in blood and dirt.

"It's a long story, can we talk somewhere private?" I asked, casting my gaze around and noticing several other Shades strewn about the safe house.

"My office," Isaac offered, nodding towards the back staircase.

Once safely behind the closed door of Isaac's office Tess collapsed into the chair across from Isaac's desk with a huff.

"Long day?" Isaac asked, raising an eyebrow.

"You've got no idea," she replied, shaking her head.

"Fill me in, what is going on?" he asked, sitting in the chair at his desk. "Why did you come to the safe house without contacting us first?"

"It was an emergency," I explained. "We were training with Warrick, and we were attacked."

"Attacked?" he asked, shooting to his feet, gripping the desk with both hands. "By whom?"

"Not a who, but a what. Creatures. Donika has used her blood magic to create monsters to come after us. I guess her Nightshade army wasn't getting the job done."

"Are you all ok?" he asked, checking each of us over. His gaze roaming over each of our faces.

"Yes, but there's one tiny little problem."

"And what might that be?" Liss asked, her arms crossed over her chest.

"Tyr was the one to kill the last of the three creatures. He says he came to warn us, that he never meant to have me captured. He didn't go to Donika, he was captured and tortured for information," I replied.

"But how would Donika have known he had any information *to give*?" Liss asked, her brow furrowing.

"Exactly," Nik nodded.

I shot him a warning glance, and he had the decency to appear sheepish.

"Spies?" I offered, "she has them everywhere. There's no way she wasn't tracking him, especially if she suspected he was a part of the resistance. Not to mention he was 'tasked' with retrieving the grimoire. He is a Kotova after all, it could have chosen him at any point. She would have wanted to have eyes on him."

"That's a good point," Isaac said, sitting back in the thick leather chair and running his hand along the scruff on his cheek.

"But *he* is one of her spies," Nik insisted, his voice gruff.

"I'm not sure," I replied, shaking my head.

"Don't let the fact that he is family cloud your judgement," Nik said, his eyes softening.

"I'm not," I spat, my gaze turning cold. "I believe him. I know what it is to be tortured by Donika. Tyr was desperate."

"What did Puck think of this? He has a place on this council as well as Saanvi," Isaac replied.

"Saanvi should be here shortly, and she can tell you her thoughts herself. I'm sure Puck would side with Nik." I cast him a sidelong glance.

"And what, exactly, do you think?" Isaac asked, turning to face Nik.

"I think the little weasel is a spy, trying to get back into our good graces."

"Why would he do that? He could have let that creature kill me, then he wouldn't need to be back in *anyone's* good graces. I would be dead. If he was under Donika's control, I wouldn't be sitting here right now," I seethed. "I saw him in The Shadow the other day. I think he has been searching for us."

"She has a point," Isaac replied, giving Nik a knowing glance.

Nik refused to budge. What a stubborn, frustrating, pig-headed...

The door swung open, saving me from finishing that thought, and Saanvi slipped in quietly.

"Your thoughts on the issue of Tyr?" Isaac asked her as we all turned towards her.

"I don't believe he meant to harm Diana. Donika threatened his family, he only gave up the information under duress. He is only a kid, after all," she replied, sympathy in her eyes.

"My thoughts exactly. He can't be more than fifteen years old. He is far from an evil mastermind," I agreed with a nod.

"I have to agree," Isaac responded. "Tess?"

"I'm with Diana," she replied, grabbing my hand and giving it a squeeze. "Always."

"Liss?"

"I don't trust that rat bastard as far as I can throw him. Not when it comes to Diana," she replied resolutely.

"It's down to Puck and Warrick, then. Where are they?" Isaac asked, standing from the desk and coming around to the door.

"Back on the training field, I spelled them to stay put with Tyr. Didn't want him to know the location of this safe house and have to move...again," Saanvi replied.

"Thank you." Isaac gave her shoulder a soft squeeze as he moved to the door, and we followed.

"And if Puck and Warrick agree with me?" Nik asked, "what will you do then?"

"You know what we do to traitors," Isaac replied, his voice somber.

They would kill him? Based on a vote?

I understood he betrayed the resistance when he gave up the information that got me captured, but he was *just a kid*. His family had been threatened. He saved my life when he easily could have let that hell creature consume me.

We walked to the training field quickly and in silence under the cover of night, uneasy to be out after dark, outside the safe walls of the spelled townhome. Luckily, we were all well-armed.

Puck, Warrick, and Tyr were right where we left them. Puck was sitting in the grass and appeared to be searching for a four-leaf clover. Warrick stood watch over Tyr, who was still trapped within Saanvi's spelled circle.

"We have all voted, gentlemen. It comes down to you," Isaac said, nodding his head towards Puck and Warrick.

"Voted?" Tyr asked.

He sounded so young, his eyes wide as he searched our faces.

"You know our rules, Tyr." Isaac's tone was cutting.

Tyr set his jaw under Isaac's gaze, but his hands were shaking.

"I'm with Nik," Puck replied. "Too much of a coincidence that he found us, if you ask me. He betrayed us once before, he will do it again."

"Surprise, surprise," I murmured under my breath.

"If Warrick agrees Tyr is a traitor, it will be a tie," Tess muttered quietly beside me.

I could only hope that Warrick wouldn't sentence a child to death. That made us no better than Donika herself.

It felt as if we all collectively held our breath as we waited for Warrick to speak. Would they let him back into the resistance if the council voted that he wasn't guilty?

The tension in the air was almost tangible as Warrick met my eyes. I didn't believe Tyr meant for any of this to happen, and I desperately hoped Warrick felt the same.

"I don't believe he meant to betray us," Warrick finally spoke.

I wanted to rush forwards and hug him, but feared that might set Nik straight over the edge and past the point of no return. Nik's jaw was set, his eyes hard.

He wanted nothing more than to kill Tyr for his betrayal of me, intentional or not.

"Tyr Kotova." Isaac's voice was deep as it reverberated across the training field. "You have been found *not guilty* of the crime of betraying our true queen."

15

The events of the day had worn me to within an inch of my sanity. I could barely process the fact that Tyr was back, and that he hadn't meant to betray me. I certainly couldn't come to terms with the creatures from hell Donika had created with her dark magic. Araneoch, Tyr had called them. I made a mental reminder to check the Kotova grimoire for any such spells once I got some rest.

The long soak in the claw-foot tub still couldn't scrub the images of the creatures from my mind, and when I fell into bed, I was desperate for a dreamless sleep. The only thing I could see behind my closed eyelids were those hairy, spindly legs. That eyeless head and those razor-sharp fangs.

I curled onto my side, my wet hair cascading down the pillow, but it wasn't a dreamless sleep that I found waiting for me. I was pulled into a dream entirely against my will...the sensation becoming all too familiar.

I was dream walking.

Donika descended the steps of the dais slowly, her heels clicking against the marble, her eyes darkening.

"If I may, My Queen, it appears the experiments have been failing on some and a success on others. I have noticed that since Zion left you have pushed to run the tests before the subjects are ready..."

"What is your point, Corian?" Donika sneered, approaching a figure that lay in a pile of limbs on the cold tile.

She used her heel to turn the figures face upwards, and I gasped at what I saw there. It was a human, or at least, it used to be. It had black, lifeless eyes like Donika, but the blackness spread across the figure's entire face as if it were a spiderweb of veins. The veins on their hands had also turned black beneath their translucent skin. The figures mouth was slack, the hint of fangs showing in their dark mouth. What was *this thing?*

It resembled the Araneoch we encountered on the training field yesterday, but it also...didn't. This had once been a person. Human. This wasn't some pieced together monstrosity.

"If we could simply ask Zion to come back, if we could find him—" Corian started, but his words trailed off as he met Donika's gaze.

"Zion is not coming back," Donika spat, giving the figure before her a shove before advancing on Corian. "Bring in the next one."

"At once, your majesty." Corian nodded towards a guard at the double doors leading to the throne room, and another figure was led in. This figure was slumped between two guards, her head hanging limply, her blonde hair covering her face.

"This is the one who has lived?" Donika asked, crossing her arms over the bodice of her diamond-adorned gown.

"Yes, your majesty. This one thrives."

It didn't appear as if she was thriving to me. As soon as the guards released her, she fell into a heap, her knees hitting the tile with jarring impact. Donika cocked her head to the side as she examined the girl. Her shadows reached out and curled around the girl's chin, turning her face towards her.

The girl's eyes snapped up to Donika's, and she released a fierce hiss, more animal than human. Her eyes were the same as the dead figure beside her, entirely black and webbed with black veins. As if the very magic that had corrupted her was pumping through her blood. Her nails were sharpened to points.

No...not nails. Claws.

A slow smile crept across Donika's lips as she glanced at the girl with satisfaction. "Very good, Corian. How many others are there?"

"Thus far we have lost four, but we have almost ten who have not succumbed to the magic yet. Only time will tell if they survive."

Donika nodded thoughtfully. "And their magic?"

"Stronger than ever, My Queen. All of their innate abilities have been amplified tenfold. If we can continue the experiments, you will have your army."

Army.

She was building an army of...what exactly were *those things? Humans corrupted with dark magic past the point of all return?*

I wish this were a nightmare.

I wish I didn't know, deep in my bones, that what I was seeing was real.

How would we stand a chance against an army of corrupted witches, pumped full of black magic?

Donika wasn't only murdering innocents anymore, she was experimenting on them. Altering them.

Changing them at their very core and corrupting their magic. Where would it ever stop? There was nothing Donika wouldn't do to win this war, and to see me dead.

"Very good, Corian." Donika turned on her heel and moved towards the hall, her wolves at her side. "You'll see to it this is kept a secret?" she asked, glancing over her shoulder.

"Of course, your majesty. But what of Zion?" Corian replied.

"It's too late to do anything about him now. I was hoping any knowledge he had would die with him. I've sent Nightshade soldiers after him, but Zion won't be found if he doesn't want to be. He has betrayed us all, *and I will not speak of him again. Am I understood?"*

"Yes, your majesty." Corian bowed deeply, averting his gaze.

"He has chosen his side in this war, and he has sided with traitors. He will pay with his life for what he has done, as will the Stormshade bitch."

"Your sister?" Corian asked, not meeting her gaze.

"Who else would I be talking about?" she asked, as if Corian was more dimwitted than she originally thought. "Unless you have found more for me?" She raised an eyebrow at him.

"Not since the last batch we took. We only found the one, your majesty."

"And they all paid for the sins of that one, didn't they?" Donika's smile was cruel as she turned again, disappearing through the doorway.

I wanted to scream. *Playing with swords and training with Isaac wasn't going to win me this war. I was completely and utterly hopeless. I shook my head back and forth, willing myself awake, but the dream wasn't done with me yet.*

Corian moved forwards and motioned to the guards to remove the girl. She became limp once held in their grasp. Where were they taking them? I tried to follow, to pass through the doors with the guard, but it was as if an invisible barrier kept me here in the throne room. I couldn't pass.

Corian knelt at the side of the dead figure and laid a hand across his face. A surge of magic traveled forth, a blinding flash had me shielding my eyes, and when I finally opened them the figure was moving.

No...it wasn't him that was moving...it was something under *his skin. It appeared as if there were a million little creatures moving under the surface, and they all crawled upwards, towards his head. The figure moved with a shock, blinking and turning towards Corian with a smile.*

Cold dread settled in my gut, and if I was awake, I knew I would be retching. The figure sat up, his movements jerky and uncoordinated.

Corian had reanimated him.

They weren't simply creating these dark creatures, they were re-animating the dead.

"Don't think I don't see you there..." Corian practically whispered.

He stood, his eyes landing on me. But he couldn't see me, could he? His lips curved into a sinister smile and I let out a guttural scream, pulled from the very depth of my soul when I saw that the eyes looking back at me were now entirely black.

"Diana, Diana!" Nik's voice was frantic, his hands on my shoulders, shaking me awake. "Diana! You need to wake up!"

I blinked back the tears that welled in my eyes, the familiar sight of my bedroom in the Prins Townhouse coming into focus. I couldn't catch my breath, no matter how hard I tried to fill my lungs with air.

"I've got you, I've got you. Just breathe." Nik's voice turned soothing as he saw my eyes snap open, the tears rolling softly down my cheeks.

He held me to him, rubbing a hand in soothing circles against my back. I blinked, the tears staining his shirt as I grabbed it in my fist.

"What are you doing here?" I asked, my voice sounded rough and broken.

I felt absolutely and completely hopeless.

"You were screaming," he replied, his eyes soft.

Again.

Nik had woken me screaming...again.

When would the nightmares end? Except these weren't nightmares at all, they were reality.

"I...I..." I tried to speak, but the words wouldn't come out. I was paralyzed by my own fear. Paralyzed by what I had seen in the dream. By what Donika was capable of.

"It's ok. Just breathe. You don't need to speak yet. Just breathe."

Nik held me tighter, his arm wrapping around my shoulder as the tears fell in earnest now. I sobbed into his chest, the visions of black eyes haunting me from behind my closed eyelids.

The only clear thought that could make it through the haze was that I needed to study the Kotova grimoire, and I needed to do it now. I needed to find a spell to even the scales, no matter what it took. Donika was creating an army of corrupted Shades, and if she succeeded, we had no hope of winning this war.

Of surviving.

"Zion is coming back," I stuttered, pressing back enough to look into Nik's eyes.

Mother above, I *hated* him, but I couldn't help but think...he was always here when I needed him the most.

He searched my eyes in the dark.

"What do you mean?" he asked.

"I saw Donika," I choked out. "She said Zion had left. That he had betrayed her. She sent soldiers after him...but wasn't hopeful she would find him."

Nik nodded. "Good, we need his help. It's about time he stopped playing spy and joined the right side of this war."

"That's not all." My voice sounded strangled as I wiped the tears from my cheeks. I needed to tell him what I saw.

"Donika is creating...monsters," I started, biting my lip.

"More monsters similar to the Araneoch?" he asked, his hand falling from my shoulder to my thigh where he gave me a reassuring squeeze. My eyes fell to that hand, and I swallowed hard, shaking my head.

"No, not like the Araneoch. People. She is using her black magic on people, infecting them. They are horrible, Nik. Their eyes are as black as hers, but that's not all. Their veins...they are black, too. Their hands have turned into claws and their teeth into fangs. Their magic is amplified, more powerful than ever. She is creating an army."

Nik reached out with his other hand, turning my chin up towards him so I would meet his eyes. When I blinked, another tear spilled forth as I stifled back a sob. I wanted to be strong, but I felt as if I was falling apart. I had tried so hard to push all of these emotions down after escaping the Stormvault, but they were all bubbling to the surface again.

"We will face whatever it is she has done, and we will win."

"You can't know that," I replied, shaking my head, his grip on my chin never wavering.

"Diana...whatever happens, I will be by your side. First thing in the morning we will take this knowledge to the council as we wait for Zion's return. He might have more information."

I nodded, wanting nothing more than to forget the dream entirely and fall endlessly into his deep blue eyes. How were they still *so damn* blue, even in the darkness of the room? I took a deep breath, trying to center myself.

"We will *fight,* Diana. I will be right there with you."

A moment of silence fell between us as I gathered myself, breathing deeply. Nik's eyes never left mine.

"Thank you," I whispered, still breathless.

Nik nodded, moving to stand.

"Wait—" I grabbed the hem of his shirt as he turned to leave, one leg still on the bed. He turned back to me, a question in his eyes.

"I can't...I can't sleep here alone."

Nik said nothing, his expression entirely unreadable in the darkness of my bedroom. *Mother above*, I would give anything to know what he was thinking right now. What was *I* thinking? Did he think me pathetic that I pushed him away, time and time again, only to reel him back in by asking him something like this?

"You want me to stay the night?" he asked, his voice soft.

His response surprised me. No teasing...no crude jokes...only a fragile hope in his voice.

"It's not like that—" I started, shaking my head. "I just can't be alone right now."

Not after the nightmare I had. The fact that it was real, that I would have to face this in the morning, made it all ten times worse.

"Do you want me to get Tess?" he asked, his eyes searching mine.

I shook my head, my gaze never wavering from his. "No."

His throat bobbed as he swallowed hard. He nodded once, moving the blanket aside to crawl into the bed next to me.

I only wanted his steady presence beside me. I needed his warmth, the soft sound of his breathing. I feared the silence of the night if he left. It was only a few hours. What could a few hours hurt? I could go back to hating him in the morning.

As much as I told myself that, I could feel the outer shell of my anger beginning to crack. I was softening towards him, and I didn't want to admit it. Not to myself, or anyone else. He had betrayed me, and for that I could never forgive him. But there was a piece of me, and I wasn't sure how small that piece might be, that felt as if I was falling all over again.

I turned my back towards him, pulling the covers up to my chin and rubbing my feet together under the blanket. It was something I did when I was anxious, something that had always soothed me. He didn't reach out to touch me, and he didn't say a word.

We fell asleep like that...lying next to each other, but still worlds apart.

16

The next morning, I woke to an arm wound tightly around my waist, my back pressed against a hard chest. I moved slightly as Nik's chest expanded, his breathing deep and even.

He was still asleep.

How had we ended up wrapped in each other's arms in the middle of the night? We had fallen asleep on entirely opposite sides of the bed.

The fact that I wasn't entirely displeased felt like a knife in my chest, as if I was betraying myself by letting him get this close. I desperately needed him last night, but in the light of the morning, I was seeing things more clearly. I had been slipping up lately, letting him get close again. Despite my feelings on the matter, I couldn't let that happen again. I still couldn't trust him...not entirely.

Tess *did* always call me a grudge holder.

As I made the decision to sneak out of bed, the door banged open.

"You better be decent, you little witch..." Tess trailed off as she took in the scene before her.

Nik and I were in bed together...his arm wrapped around me. Thank *God* we were both clothed, otherwise I would have some serious explaining to do.

We both jumped with a start, my eyes going wide. Nik had been woken from a sound sleep by the sound of Tess barging in.

"Mother above, I didn't mean to interrupt." Tess smirked, raising her eyebrow at me.

"You aren't interrupting anything," I replied, extricating myself from Nik's arm and sliding off the bed.

I wrapped myself in the sweater hanging from the armoire and slipped my feet into my cozy slippers. Nik rubbed the sleep from his eyes, letting out a groan.

"Good morning to you too, Tess. Always good to see you." He leveled her with a deadpan stare.

She truly did have incredible timing, another few minutes, and I would have already been downstairs drinking my coffee.

The awkwardness of the situation was not lost on me, but the memories of last night came flooding back, reminding me I needed to tell Tess and the rest of the council what I saw in my dream.

"We need to talk," I told Tess.

She hadn't left, simply crossed her arms over her chest and stared Nik down with a cold glare.

"I was coming in here to talk to you. I think we need a girls' day in town. Shopping and all that. You down?" she asked, turning towards me as her expression softened.

"I had another dream," I explained, pushing the curls back from my face. "I have to talk to the council."

"Can't that wait?" Tess whined impatiently. "We haven't had time to ourselves in ages, and I, for one, need a break from all this gloom and doom."

I started to shake my head, but Nik spoke from his place in the bed. "I think that's a great idea, actually. If Zion is on his way, it will be easier to loop everyone in together. You need a break, Diana."

Tess shot him a glare that said he shouldn't be telling me what I do or don't need, before turning back towards me. "See? Even he agrees."

"I don't know..." I started.

I wasn't sure I was up for anything as lighthearted as shopping when the knowledge of Donika creating a black magic army complete with disfigured monsters was looming over me.

"You have to wear a glamour. I have some in my room." Nik slid out of the bed, stretching his arms over his head.

I averted my gaze, cursing myself at how easily both my thoughts and my eyes traveled to the tanned toned strip of bare skin revealed above his pants.

"I don't need you to agree. I am kidnapping you either way," Tess told me, wrapping an arm around my shoulder.

"A glamour?" I asked, skeptical.

Nik nodded, joining us by the door. "And Kenna and Saanvi as bodyguards. At a safe distance...of course. Girls' day and all that." Nik winked, turning to pad down the hallway to his room, presumably to grab the glamours.

Back to his old self, I see.

"We need to debrief, especially seeing as I just caught you in bed with loverboy," Tess whispered, looping her arm through mine.

"It's not what you think." I sighed, running a hand through my mess of curls.

"That's the point. I don't know what's going on with you. All of your spare time is taken up by Isaac or Warrick. What about Tess time?" She gave me her best fake pout.

I shook my head, laughing softly. "Fine, but only for today. Tomorrow, it's back to magic training. And we need to dig into the Kotova grimoire."

"Agreed." Tess flashed me a toothy smile as Nik appeared outside the door to his room down the hall.

"Catch," he called, tossing two glass vials one after the other. Surprising myself, I caught them both.

"You're lucky I've been training, or these absolutely would have been wasted all over the floor," I told him.

"I have every confidence in your training, firecracker. Have fun today. We can talk to the council later tonight."

I nodded. I did need a day to unwind, even if I felt like I needed to train harder—now more than ever. I needed to wield stronger spells with my storm magic, and I needed to find a spell in the Kotova grimoire that could save us all.

I couldn't help but think of the vision the grimoire had sent me, and how the spell with the key had been missing when I had gone searching for it. Could that spell be exactly what we needed to defeat Donika? Is that why the grimoire had sent me that particular vision?

I dressed quickly, Tess waiting impatiently on the edge of my bed. We found Saanvi and Kenna waiting downstairs for us, having already been called over to the townhouse by Nik. They agreed to follow us at a safe distance, in case anything should happen.

"I guess it's time to take this glamour," I said, investigating the contents of the tiny vial with suspicion. "You go first."

"Why me?" Tess splayed her hand over her chest, feigning offense.

"Because this was your idea," I reminded her.

"Yeah, yeah." She rolled her eyes, un-corking the glass vial and holding it out. "Cheers."

She clinked her vial against mine and downed the bright red liquid in one gulp.

"Well?" I asked.

"It's surprisingly...sweet," she replied as her features began to change.

At first it was subtle, but as I blinked and refocused, I couldn't recognize her any longer. Her hair, which was once a rich chocolate color, turned black, her eyes turned a muted shade of brown. Her warm complexion turned porcelain, and her features almost...blurred. As if you couldn't focus on any one feature too closely.

"Well...that worked," I replied hopefully, inclining my head. "I definitely cannot tell that it's you."

I un-corked my own vial and downed the liquid, surprised at the sweet, tart flavor. To be honest, I had expected it to taste terrible. I didn't feel anything, but by the widening of Tess' eyes I could tell the glamour had already taken effect.

"Well?" I asked, doing an exaggerated spin for Tess.

"Unrecognizable," Tess replied resolutely with a nod of her head.

I pulled a lock of hair forwards and was surprised to see the shock of auburn faded to an ashy blonde, the curls falling in straight strands.

"And nobody will recognize Kenna or Saanvi?" I asked, grabbing my bag and moving towards the door.

I unconsciously ran my fingers along my thighs to ensure Stormslayer was safely sheathed there along with the throwing knives Warrick had gifted me.

"Nobody knows who *we* are," Saanvi replied with a raised eyebrow.

"Good point."

Kenna and Saanvi kept a safe distance away from us as we made our way through the cobblestone streets of Dragon's Hollow and past Alastir's charm shop towards the shopping district. I told Tess about the dream I'd had and how we desperately needed to prepare ourselves. I had no idea what those creatures were capable of, and we needed to be ready.

Tess and I ducked into a shop that sold clothes similar to what you would find in the mortal realm.

"This is absolutely your color." Tess laughed as she pulled a leopard print blouse out from the rack of clothes.

"Ha, Ha. Very funny." I smiled, giving her a gentle nudge back.

It had been so long since we had time together, only the two of us. In this moment I felt lighter. As if maybe the fate of the realm of Istmere didn't rest on mine and my friend's shoulders. As if Donika wasn't searching for me and creating armies of mutilated monsters and deranged witches to fight us.

It was just me and Tess.

"Are we going to talk about this morning?" Tess asked, watching my expression out of the corner of her eye.

"What about this morning?" I asked, feigning confusion.

I thumbed through the rack of clothes, not meeting her gaze. Tess could always see right through me.

"Oh, I don't know, maybe how I found Nik in your bed?" she asked, her tone light as she glanced at me from under her eyelashes.

I shot her a deadpan glare. "We were clothed."

"Yes, clothed. But he was still in your bed," she pointed out.

"And?"

"And? Diana...the last time we talked boys, you wanted to stab him in the eye. How did we get from stabbing to cuddling?" She sighed.

"We were *not* cuddling," I replied.

"That's not what it looked like to me. His deliciously tattooed arm was wrapped around your waist, if I remember correctly."

I shook my head at her. “We must have tangled together during the night. He was only keeping me company after the nightmare. I didn’t want to be alone.” I bit my lip, meeting her searching gaze.

“Sure. I’m sure that’s all it was...” she trailed off.

“There’s nothing going on,” I replied, grabbing a black t-shirt that appeared to be my size.

“Not yet, there isn’t,” Tess replied.

“What is that supposed to mean?” I asked, raising my brow at her.

“It means that I could see this coming a mile away. He has been weaseling his way back in, and you are letting him, whether you want to admit it or not. There’s no judgement from me. I know the connection you two have. I only want you to be happy.” She gave me a half-smile as she took the black shirt from my hand and placed it back on the rack. “No more black clothes, you have enough.”

I rolled my eyes at her. “And what about you and Puck? You were awfully quick to forgive him, if I remember correctly.”

“That’s different.” She shook her head. “Besides, we aren’t talking about *me*. We are talking about you.”

“I haven’t forgiven him if that’s what you’re getting at.”

I threw the straight blonde hair over my shoulder as it fell into my eyes. I could never get used to the appearance of this hair and was glad the glamour was only temporary. We would have to get back to the townhouse before it wore off.

“Does that mean you have zero feelings for him?” she asked.

"I don't know. I really don't. I don't forgive him, but he has been there for me when I've needed him. He had Stormslayer crafted for me when we were locked in the Stormvault, and he just..." I trailed off.

"Just been a wee bit overprotective, don't you think? You know he picked that fight with Warrick to show off for you, don't you?"

"He has nothing to worry about with Warrick," I replied.

"No?" Tess' eyebrows shot up her forehead as she gave me a pointed look. "Things appeared awfully hot and heavy during your training session the other day."

"We were only *training*," I told her.

"Whatever you need to tell yourself."

She nudged me in the side with a wink as she handed me a slinky silver number. Where on earth would I have a chance to wear that between training my storm magic, learning to wield a dagger, and defeating Donika? I pointedly shoved the top back onto the rack.

"Things are too complicated right now. The last thing I need is boy problems. I need to focus on controlling my storms and studying the grimoire. If Donika were to find us, if she were to set that army of black magic infested creatures on us...we need to be ready."

"Amen to that," Tess replied.

"But...what *is* going on with you and Puck?" I asked.

"Things are...complicated," she replied with a laugh.

Complicated appeared to be the theme of the day.

"But you've been spending the night in his room?" I asked.

"How do you know that?" she asked, scandalized.

"Tess, my love, you are many things, but discreet is not one of them," I told her with a shake of my head.

"If you are asking if we are back together...I guess the answer is yes."

"Good." I smirked. "I've always liked Puck."

"So you'll forgive Puck but not Nik?" she asked, leveling me with an expression I knew all too well.

"That's different," I replied. "Puck didn't quite *deliver* us into the hands of Donika like Nik did."

"But Nik *didn't,*" she reminded me. "He told you to run. He never wanted you to be captured. And you said it yourself. He never thought for a moment there would be a reality where he didn't figure out a way to get you out. He played his part to stay under the radar, all while plotting our jailbreak and crafting your custom little blade." Her eyes moved to Stormslayer, strapped at my thigh.

I opened my mouth to respond...but nothing came out.

I wasn't even sure what to say. In a way, Tess was right. But in my stubborn heart, I still wasn't ready to believe him yet. I didn't want to open myself up to being hurt by him...again. I didn't think I could handle that heartbreak a second time. I had been so *angry* at him, and that anger had turned to hatred in my time locked in the Stormvault. But since our time in Prins, I have felt a crack in my armor, and that anger and hatred have slowly started to dissipate.

I wasn't ready to come to terms with it yet. Things were still volatile, and with Donika's ongoing threats looming over our heads, my emotions were all over the place.

I needed to focus on the resistance and on training. I didn't have time to be thinking about Nik and how I did or didn't feel about him. I shook my head as if to clear my thoughts and turned back towards Tess.

"I'm not ready to move on yet," I told her resolutely.

"I understand," she replied with a nod. "You always were a tough nut to crack."

I shook my head at her and laughed. Leave it to Tess to make me laugh even when I felt as if I was drowning in my own emotions. Nik had been right about one thing...I needed this. Flipping through racks of clothing and having girl talk with Tess was its own kind of healing, and thoughts of dark magic were pushed to the back of my mind...for now at least.

By the time we had filled our arms with shopping bags, the glamour was starting to wear off, and we made our way back to the hidden safe house to meet with Liss and Isaac.

When we entered the safe house, it was completely empty, the lamps on the first floor having burned out. A trickle of fear slid down my spine at the sight of the empty bar stools, the darkness covering every inch of the first floor.

We made our way to Isaac's office, and Kenna and Saanvi went first, opening the door with their daggers in hand. Inside the tiny office were Isaac, Liss, Warrick, Nik, and Puck, along with a figure sitting across from Isaac with shorn black hair that appeared awfully familiar from the back.

As he turned towards us, I met his hazel eyes, and relief washed over him as he stood. He closed me into an embrace, his arms so tight around me I couldn't take a full breath.

"Diana, you are safe. *Thank the mother you are safe.*"

"Why wouldn't I be?" I asked, extricating myself from his grasp, confusion creasing my brow.

"Donika didn't only send Nightshade soldiers after me when I left The Stone City. She sent her Noctani. They have unparalleled speed and power, if they had found you..." his words trailed off as he hung his head.

"Noctani?" I asked, meeting Liss' gaze, then Isaac's.

It was Isaac who answered me. "Her idea of the perfect Shade. She is creating an army of demon witches corrupted by black magic and blood magic."

"Like what I saw when I was dream walking?" I asked, my eyes flickering towards Nik, who stood in the corner, his arms crossed over his chest.

He nodded. "Yes, I have filled them in."

Good. The less I had to relive that nightmare, the better. My eyes softened as he met my gaze and gave me a half-smile, the corner of his mouth turning up.

"Why am I seeing Donika?" I asked, turning back towards Isaac and Zion. "I have dream walked before, but I never have control of where I am or what I dream. The last two times I dream walked, I have been pulled into her throne room."

"I think you were linked, somehow," Zion replied.

"Linked?" My voice came out somewhere between a squeal and a croak.

Zion nodded. "During your time at The Stone Palace, your magic recognized her magic. You are sisters, after all. I'm not sure if it goes deeper than that, if she performed a spell or not."

"That's great," I huffed. "Exactly what we need. We are trying to plan her demise, but I might be linked to her? If she dies, will I?"

"We aren't sure," Liss replied from the corner where she stood next to Nik. "But I believe the answer we are searching for will be in the Kotova grimoire."

I nodded. One more thing I needed to find out from that grimoire. Maybe I would get lucky, and the grimoire would send me visions of exactly what I needed...but the chances of that happening were slim. The grimoire had a mind of its own, and thus far it had only shown me exactly what it wanted me to see. Which still didn't explain the spell with the key...

"We will study it. We will find out if they are truly linked or if it is merely...a familial connection," Tess offered.

"Good," Isaac replied, pushing out from the desk and standing. "For now, Zion needs his rest. He has had a long journey from The Stone City."

"And you're sure you weren't followed?" Nik asked, his eyes narrowing on Zion.

Zion might have helped us escape Donika's prison, but if I had to hazard a guess, Nik didn't trust him as far as he could throw him.

"I wasn't followed," Zion replied, meeting Nik's gaze with a challenge in his eyes.

Nik returned his gaze with his chin turned up, his jaw set.

"Diana, I will see you tomorrow for our next session," Isaac said, inclining his head towards me.

I nodded, following Tess and Nik out the door. I had so much on my mind between the Araneoch and the Noctani. What else was Donika conjuring up? We would need to attack her offensively once we were ready—once we had the numbers. Isaac estimated we were nearing close to four thousand members in the resistance, but I wasn't sure if it would be enough. Maybe if we were only fighting her Nightshade soldiers...but her monstrous creations?

I needed to split my time between studying the grimoire and training with Isaac and Warrick. We needed to figure out why the spell with the key was missing, what spell was in the grimoire that Donika was after, and if Donika and I were magically linked. There would be no more time for shopping trips into town with Tess.

Donika was killing and experimenting on more innocents by the day, and we needed to put a stop to it. We needed to win this war, and that meant it was time to start acting like a queen.

17

I was tired when I met Isaac on the training field the next day, having not slept well that night. I hadn't dream walked again, but I *did* have nightmares. I spent half of the night tossing and turning, throwing the bedsheets off when they were covered with sweat. My mind was racing with a million thoughts, unable to settle into a comfortable sleep.

I had come a long way with training my storm magic, but I hadn't created any big storms yet. Isaac asked me to create an intense thunderstorm with lightning and rain, and to not only let it go, but reign it back in once I had.

That was always the hardest part for me.

He assured me the storm would be held within the barriers of the wards he set up around the training field, but I was beginning to feel as if our practice space wasn't nearly big enough.

Isaac watched as I pulled the magic out of my core and through my fingertips, the sky darkening overhead. No one had come to the training session today, and I was thankful to not have an audience. I always felt more pressure on those days, as if I didn't have enough on my shoulders at the moment.

"Very good. Now create each element of the storm," Isaac said, folding his arms across his chest as he watched.

Creating a storm of this magnitude would take quite a bit of magic, and I hoped I had the strength for it. The magic left my fingertips as the rain began to pour down, soaking through our clothing. There would be no protective air shield today. Thunder boomed overhead, a crack of lightning striking through the sky at the other end of the field.

I closed my eyes in concentration as I thickened the clouds with my magic, the rain turning into a torrent against my skin. The thunder sounded close, much closer than I had ever dared before. Lightning struck again, splitting a tree straight down the middle with a loud clap.

My eyes popped open, searching for Isaac. The driving rain didn't allow for much visibility, but I could make out the shape of him a few feet away.

"You've driven enough power into the storm. Now let it go," Isaac instructed.

Despite a little voice in my head telling me not to, I did as Isaac said, and I let go. The storm quickly intensified outside of the grip of my magic, the black clouds swirling angrily overhead. The rain pelted down so hard it bounced off the training mats. Thunder clapped loudly enough overhead that I could barely hear Isaac's next instruction.

"Now rein it in."

I easily found the center of the storm's magic, having practiced this part quite a few times before. I took that center and imagined pulling it into myself, that the magic of the storm would now become *my* magic.

The magic began draining into my fingertips, but with a start it sputtered out, a zap at my fingertips causing me to draw back. I glanced at Isaac with alarm, but he remained impassive, his arms still crossed. I tried again, reaching out to the storm, but this time it actively pushed *back*.

It couldn't do that, could it? It did have its own magic, but...mine was stronger. I imagined consuming that power, taking it into my core and melding it with the magic I already had. The storm reared back, lightning striking so close to my feet the ground sizzled. I could smell the faint burning of my rubber-soled shoes. The clouds darkened further, the loud cracks of thunder and lightning breaking my focus.

"Diana, you need to pull it in. *Now*!" Isaac bellowed over the violent stream of rain that fell between us.

"I'm trying!" I cried, marking the center of the storm's energy once more.

The storm pushed back *harder* this time, and I fell to my knees, the energy leaving me in a rush.

The storm...it had...no. No. It wasn't possible. Isaac would have warned me. Unless...did Isaac not know?

The storm had *stolen* my energy. Stolen my magic.

Isaac raised his hands to the sky and tried to contain the storm I had created, but his face soon crumpled from the strain. I lifted my palms to the sky, my hands feeling as if they were on fire from the amount of energy pulsing within them.

I had to get control of this storm, or it would kill us both.

I pushed to my feet, my palms still facing the sky as I tried to pull the energy back. I needed to be stronger than this storm; I had no other choice. I had no control of this storm—it had taken on a mind of its own. Had I fed too much of my magic into it? Was this the risk?

The storm struck out once more, and this time it hit its mark. I fell to the ground with a cry, clutching my shoulder with my hand. It felt as if a hole of pure energy had burned through my skin, all the way to the bone.

"Diana!" Isaac called out, rushing to my side.

I shook my head at him, speaking through gritted teeth. "We need to get control of this storm."

There was no way we could heal my shoulder in this melee, the rain still violently pouring down around us, the thunder still booming directly overhead. Lightning struck all around us on the training field.

"My hand. Take my hand, Diana."

I did as he asked, blood pouring down my arm the moment I removed my own hand from the wound. I joined my hand with his, and with every ounce of energy left in my body, I pulled on the storm.

I pulled and pulled and pulled until I couldn't bring any more magic in. Until I was full to the brim with the restless energy, my fingertips numb. My vision flickered, darkness descending despite the clouds beginning to dissipate. I was blacking out—from the pain or the magic I wasn't sure.

The last thing I saw before descending into total darkness was the expression of alarm on Isaac's face.

It was a look I wouldn't soon forget.

18

"Did you know?" Nik seethed.

My eyes were closed, my body hurt *everywhere*. Where was I?

"Did. You. Know." Nik spoke each word through clenched teeth.

"Do you think I would have asked her to do that if I had known?" Isaac's voice sounded terrified. "It's not as if there are a lot of Stormshades left to turn to. This magic isn't an exact science, and everyone who knew how to wield it is *dead*."

I tried to open my eyes, to speak, but my limbs were too heavy. I was fighting sleep. Had they given me some type of sedative tonic?

"You're telling me you have *never*, in all your years of using storm magic, had a storm turn on you?" Nik's tone was glacially cold.

"Never, but I am not *nearly* as strong as she is. I could never have created a storm of that magnitude in the first place." I could hear Isaac run his hand along the scruff on his face, letting out a strangled cry. "I'm sorry."

"Where is your book of shadows?" Nik asked.

"I never found it," Isaac answered quietly.

"You're telling me the only thing we have to rely on is the Kotova grimoire and *you*. There are no other resources for storm magic?" Nik spat.

"Not that I am aware of."

"God dammit, Isaac. I never would have brought her here if I had known this could happen."

"It's not as if you had a choice. She is the rightful queen, Nikolai."

"She won't be if she ends up *dead* from one of her own Goddamn storms!" Nik replied angrily.

I peeled my eyes open just enough to see Nik running a hand through his mess of blond hair, his eyes red and bloodshot.

"I knew storms could have a mind of their own, but I didn't know storms could turn. There hasn't been a Stormshade as powerful as Diana since The War of Sir-aleth. There is only so much magic one person can wield," Isaac said, sitting on the bed next to mine, his hands on his knees.

I was in an infirmary of some sort, and they hadn't yet realized I was awake. I was lying on a white bed in a room filled with them, the fluorescent lights overhead causing my head to throb.

"And that's it, then? She has too much magic for one person to wield? What the hell is she supposed to do with that? She can't risk her life every time she generates a storm." Nik shook his head furiously.

"I know. If we can't figure out a way to tame her magic, we won't be able to use it against Donika," Isaac answered.

"Are you serious? *Fuck* using her magic against Donika, her *life* is in the balance, Isaac! That's the only thing I care about. If I have to bring her back to the mortal realm and spell bind her to keep her safe and out of Donika's reach, that's what I'll do. Make no mistake, my concern is for Diana and Diana alone. This war can go to hell for all I care."

"You don't mean that." Isaac met Nik's seething gaze.

"I mean *every word*. My only concern is for Diana and her well-being. If she is at risk wielding her magic, then she won't wield it. It's as simple as that."

"Nikolai, you and I both know it isn't that simple."

"Don't you dare play the concerned father role with me, Isaac! I have known you for a long time, and I know that you would sacrifice *anything* for Istmere to be safe for Stormshades again. Diana included. I am not willing to make the same sacrifice."

"That isn't true. But it doesn't matter, it will not come to that." Isaac's voice sounded tired.

How long had they been arguing?

"You can't promise that, after today. After what happened." Nik ran a hand down his face.

"We will find a way to control her magic. The solution has to be in the Kotova grimoire. We must not be searching hard enough." Isaac's gaze met his feet, his eyes moving back and forth rapidly, deep in thought.

"I...I can control it," I spoke, my voice sounding like sandpaper.

"Diana," Nik breathed, kneeling at the side of my bed.

His hand cupped my cheek, the heat from his skin instantly warming me. My eyes found his, and I felt that warmth pool low in my stomach.

"Are you ok?" he asked, his eyes searching mine.

"I will be."

I smiled, but even moving the muscles in my face hurt. Whatever tonic they had given me was beginning to wear off, and a searing pain in my shoulder was returning. I turned my head to the side to see the flesh there completely singed, mottled beyond recognition. The burn was severe, reaching from my shoulder down part of my arm.

"Don't look," Nik shook his head. "Liss is on her way. She is the most powerful healer we have, not to mention the best at skin spells."

I wasn't even sure my skin would tolerate a skin spell at this point. Every nerve ending felt as if it had been set on fire. I never knew what it felt like to be singed by your own magic, and I never wanted to feel it again. I didn't imagine Liss would be able to heal it entirely. I would have a hideous scar.

"Where am I?" I asked.

I knew I was in an infirmary...but where?

"Another safe house. We had to leave the last one behind. Your storm broke through the wards on the training field—we had to find a new place to hole up. The townhouse is still safe, but the other safe house is too close. It was compromised. Donika's army will be thoroughly searching the area for us," Nik replied, running his thumb across my cheek in a soothing motion.

I closed my eyes, the events from earlier today coming back to me. I had created a storm I couldn't control...and it had turned on me.

It had *hurt* me.

Stolen my magic.

I shook my head as tears stung the back of my eyes. All I did was cry lately. It was one step forwards and two steps back. I couldn't catch a break. My entire body felt as if it had been burned from the inside out by my own magic.

"I have to try again," I told Nik, blinking away the tears and meeting his eyes again.

"That is out of the question." A muscle feathered in his jaw as his teeth snapped together, his eyes darkening. "I will not put you at risk again."

"But I need to learn to tame this magic," I insisted.

"We will find another way. Isaac thinks the answer might be in the Kotova grimoire." His eyes traveled to my shoulder quickly before meeting my gaze again.

"I think we should pause any of our training sessions until we have combed through the grimoire. Even with our storm magic combined, we could barely contain that storm," Isaac said from his spot on the bed next to mine.

"I want to try again," I insisted.

After everything I had been through, I wasn't about to let this magic get the better of me. My mother was a powerful

Stormshade, and so was I. I would not give up after one storm gone wrong.

"Where is she?" Liss' panicked voice sounded from the doorway.

"Over here," Nik called over his shoulder before turning back to me. "We will talk more about this later."

He stood, my cheek instantly cold where his hand had been. I already missed the sensation of his skin against mine, his steady presence at my side.

Liss took his place, kneeling by my bedside and taking out a medical bag. Instead of being full of bandages and ointments as a typical kit would be, this was filled with herbs and spices. She rested her hands against my good arm, reciting a spell under her breath.

When she removed her hands, my skin was marked with the dark ink of a skin spell, the color already fading from a stark black to a charcoal as it went to work healing my shoulder.

"Can one of you put a kettle on for me? I'll need it for the tea," Liss spoke, not bothering to glance their way.

Liss was stoic, but the way her hand shook as she ground the herbs with the pestle told me she was shaken.

They all were.

Nik glanced at Isaac when he didn't move. "I will not leave her side."

Isaac groaned, reluctantly getting up to find wherever the kitchen was in this new safe house.

The skin spell took the immediate sting out of the wound, but the deep, throbbing pain remained. Liss created a paste with the herbs and packed them against the wound, a hiss escaping through my lips. She slathered the poultice on liberally before sitting me up, wrapping the wound with gauze to keep the poultice in place.

I wasn't sure how long I had slept before, but exhaustion was taking over now. My body needed rest, as did my mind. The amount of magic I had to wield to contain the storm again left me weary.

"She will need to rest," Liss called over her shoulder, speaking to Nik.

"I'm not leaving. I will let her rest, but I will be by the door."

He reluctantly pushed off the wall across from me, making his way towards the door as it opened. Isaac shuffled back in with a mug full of hot, steaming water. Liss stirred in a different mixture of herbs and handed me the mug of dark liquid.

"You need to drink *all* of this, despite it tasting like dirt," she instructed, closing up her healing bag.

The first sip almost landed me flat on my back. I think dirt would actually taste *better*, this tasted like...licorice gone bad. I did as she said, draining the mug of hot tea as she propped me up with more pillows.

There must have been another sedative in the tea to help me sleep, because it wasn't long before I found myself dozing off again.

It was the first time I had met a dreamless, restful sleep in a long, long time.

19

I had spent days healing my shoulder wound in the safety of the townhouse in Dragon's Hollow, Tess never leaving my side. Zion had come to visit, and I was finally well enough to move around on my own and to touch my magic again. Isaac had insisted we move to the new safe house permanently, but Nik had fought him tooth and nail, not wanting me to be around the other Shades.

We didn't want anyone else to know my storm had turned on me. The resistance was relying on my storm magic to turn the tides of this war, and if I couldn't control it, we had no hope of defeating Donika. Fletcher had been spotted near the training field as Isaac suspected. My blast of storm magic had sent out a magical signature so strong it broke the wards and had Donika's Nightshade soldiers coming for us.

"What do you know about the Noctani?" I asked Zion, sitting up in bed and taking a sip from the mug Tess handed me.

More healing remedies from Liss. "It's only a matter of time before she sends them after us, too."

"I have to admit I don't know as much as I would like, I had to leave before I was able to gain too much information. Her mad scientist was onto me, whispering in her ear. Donika had already turned her trust away from me."

Her mad scientist...that must have been Corian, the man I saw when I was dream walking. The man who *also* saw me. Had he told Donika what he saw?

"What *exactly* are they?" Tess asked, gathering her knees up against her chest as she sat next to me on the bed.

Nik and Puck were out scouting a new training area for when I was well enough to work with Warrick again. Isaac had meant it when he said we wouldn't be training my storm magic again, not until we had some answers.

"They are human. Donika has corrupted them with her dark magic, creating a monster similar to the Araneoch. Those aren't the only creatures she has been busy creating."

"But they have fangs, and claws," I pointed out. "Even if they were once human, they aren't anymore."

"You're telling me that Donika has created *vampires*?" Tess asked, shaking her head back and forth. "Great, that's *exactly* what we need."

"Not vampires, not exactly," Zion answered, running a hand against the scruff on his cheek.

He and Liss had been almost inseparable since his return, and it had me thinking they were much closer back at The Stone Palace than I originally thought.

"If they're not vampires then why would they need fangs?" Tess asked.

"They feed, but it isn't blood they feed on. Not alone, at least. It's magic. The Noctani were designed to suck the blood out of you, thus siphoning your magic as well," he replied, his eyes downcast. "We cannot let them get near Diana, under any circumstances."

The thought of a Noctani sinking their teeth into me and sucking the magic out of me had my stomach doing a flip, the herbs sitting in my stomach like a weight.

"Wait a second—" I started, placing the mug on the nightstand and moving to my feet. "Did you say siphon?"

Zion nodded, watching me cross the room with a furrowed brow.

"When we were searching through the grimoire to find out if Donika and I were magically linked, I came across a siphoning spell."

I pulled the dresser away from the wall and slipped the leather-bound grimoire free, placing it on the floor before me as I knelt and flipped through it.

I was relieved when Liss found the spell in the Kotova grimoire to confirm we weren't magically linked. The reason she haunted my dreams was no more than familial connection. All it had taken was a few drops of my blood and the spell to determine I wasn't magically linked to anyone...thankfully. But in our search of the grimoire we hadn't found the spell Donika would be so desperate to get her hands on. The spell Tyr was willing to risk everything to transcribe for her.

"Here." I pointed to the page before me, skimming the words. "This must be the spell Donika was desperate to get her hands on! The reason she wanted the grimoire in the first place. She wants to siphon magic."

"But she never got the grimoire, how could she have the siphoning spell?" Tess asked, peering at the spell over my shoulder.

"She must have found a work around with her blood magic. The dark creatures she created must serve her purpose. She couldn't get her hands on this siphoning spell, so instead she created the Noctani," Zion explained. "Clever girl."

I shot him a glare that had him shrinking back in his chair.

"This spell is dark magic," I said, reading the words over and over again. "This type of magic allows you to steal a witch's power, leaving them mortal. Did Tyr transcribe enough of the spell that Donika was able to replicate it?" My eyes met Zion's, panicked.

Donika might not have needed this spell after all, she had found a way to siphon magic, although indirectly.

"But whose magic does she want to siphon? Isn't she supposed to be the most powerful witch in the entire realm?" Tess asked.

I turned to her, the answer already in her eyes despite having asked the question. It was *my* magic she wanted. If Donika could siphon my storm magic and leave me mortal, there would be no stopping her.

The realization dawned on Zion at the same time, and he abruptly stood.

"We have to bring this back to the council. Your safety is more paramount than ever. We cannot let Donika's Noctani *anywhere* near you."

"We need to figure out a way to stop them." I bit my lip, thinking about the other spells in the grimoire.

What other spell could help us to take down the Noctani before Donika set them loose in this war?

"When Nik and Puck return, update them on our new theory. I am going to debrief Liss and Isaac. This could change things. We may need to move you to the mortal realm, where Donika can't reach you," Zion said as he moved towards the door.

"I will not run." My words were sharp, and Zion turned to meet my gaze.

I wasn't sure what he found there, but he reluctantly nodded before letting himself out.

"Let me see," Tess said, leaning across me to get a better look at the siphoning spell. The grimoire snapped shut, a cloud of dust wafting into her hair. "I will never get used to that."

I laughed, murmuring the opened spell and letting Tess see it from over my shoulder again. I wondered if the grimoire would recognize Donika, and if it would react similarly, despite her Kotova blood. Could it also sense the darkness roiling within her?

We needed to confront Tyr about how much of this spell he was able to transcribe for her. I had come to think of the townhouse as a home away from home, and I hoped we wouldn't have to move again. Fletcher and his men hadn't found us yet, which meant the wards were doing their job. Since I broke the wards around the training field, I hadn't been outside other than moving from one safe house to another.

"How will we beat her Noctani if they are going to suck the magic right out of us?" Tess mused, moving to rest her back against the footboard of the bed.

"We don't let them get their fangs into us," I replied with a half-smile. "I don't know if they have true magic of their own anymore. They have been so corrupted by the darkness of Donika's magic. She said their abilities were amplified tenfold, but maybe that's only their strength and speed. I find it hard to believe they still possess magic. I think they are simply a vessel now. With the training we have been doing with Warrick, I think we stand a chance. I only need to get a handle on my own magic."

"You heard what Isaac said," Tess reminded me. "We have combed through this grimoire day and night, and we haven't found a spell to help you control your magic yet. What if..." she trailed off, not meeting my gaze.

"What?" I asked, grabbing the grimoire and joining her at the foot of the bed.

"What if there isn't a solution? What if your magic is too much to handle, and you can't do more than parlor tricks?" she asked.

"We will have to cross that bridge when we come to it," I replied.

"Honey, I think we have come to it. You have to admit, there is a possibility you won't be able to use your magic against her."

"I'm not ready to believe that yet," I told her, shaking my head. "I will exhaust every resource before I give up. I can't simply give up after one bad storm."

Tess' eyes moved to the scar on my shoulder, the red burn streaking partly down my arm towards my fingers.

"It wasn't merely a bad storm." Her voice was solemn.

Liss had applied skin spell after skin spell, but the wound was still puckered and angry. I applied the salves she had given me, but I knew that the permanent reminder of that storm would remain with me forever.

I swallowed hard. "I know."

"I only want you to be careful. I can't lose you." Tess gave my arm a squeeze.

"You won't," I reassured her.

I wasn't sure if that was a promise I would be able to deliver on, but I was going to try my hardest not to let her down. To let any of them down.

If there was a way to defeat Donika and her Noctani while learning to control my magic, I was going to find it.

And soon.

Time was ticking down and as always, it was not on our side.

20

Another week passed, and I was feeling much better. Liss' healing had done the trick, and though I still had a scar on my shoulder, all residual pain was gone. I had full mobility in my arm again, and since Warrick had gone on a scouting mission with Puck, I was meeting Nik to train with my dagger.

Isaac had cleared out one of the rooms at the new safe house to lay down training mats, the far wall covered in weapons of all types. The windows were barricaded shut, allowing no natural light to pass through, despite the room being located on the third floor. Even if our wards did fail, nobody would be able to see us in here.

This safe house was much larger than the last, and also more hidden in plain sight. It was only a few blocks away from Eight Bells, and every time I walked here with Tess she begged to stop and grab a short stack at The Giddy Griddle. I could practically smell the savory flapjacks from the doorway as I pressed my hand to it, reciting the spell under my breath.

"*Ego sum resistentia. Instrumentum sum in hoc bello.*"

The door swung open beneath my touch, and I cast a glance left and right to make sure no one had followed before passing through. Stormslayer was strapped to my thigh, and I had worn my training leathers today. I knew Nik wouldn't go easy on me, despite only recently recovering from my injury.

I scaled the stairs to the third floor and found that I had arrived first. I dragged one of the punching bags out to the center of the floor, the chains holding it to the ceiling jingling as it slid across the tracks. I might as well get warmed up while I waited for Nik.

Tess was spending the day with Puck, and it had been the first time I had made the walk from the townhouse to the safe house by myself.

Things had died down in the last week. There had been no more sightings of Fletcher or Donika's other Nightshade guards, and for that I was thankful. I tiny voice inside my head said it was too good to be true. That there was no way they had stopped searching for us, and that this was the calm before the storm.

I took all my anxiety and uncertainty out on the bag, pounding it with my fists until my knuckles came away streaked with blood. I would have to ask Nik if he could wrap them for me before we returned to the townhouse.

Without being able to work with my magic, my current priority was becoming the strongest I possibly could, physically. I had been running with Liss and Saanvi every morning, and

I had been lifting weights with Isaac and Warrick. Nik and I had been training with the sword and dagger, and I was beginning to feel confident in my fighting abilities.

I added a kick to the combination, the bag spinning away from me on the tracks as it gave way behind the force of my boot.

"Now what did that bag ever do to you?" Nik asked, shouldering the door open with a first aid box in his hands.

"How did you know I would need the wraps again?" I asked, my eyebrow raised. "Am I that predictable?"

"You are decidedly *un*predictable," Nik said, meeting my gaze as he set the box down on the bench by the doorway. "But I know why you train as hard as you do."

If there was anyone who could understand my need to prove myself, it was Nik. He had spent his entire life trying to prove himself to his father, to earn his favor. In the end it had never been enough. Isaac had become a father figure to Nik, despite Nik's actual father still being out there...somewhere.

"I wouldn't have to if I could use my storm magic," I told him, inclining my head in a knowing way.

"I don't make the rules," Nik replied, palms up. "If you want to go toe to toe with Isaac, be my guest. But I must warn you...you won't win."

"My magic is stronger than his," I reminded him, pushing the punching bag back against the wall.

"But he has resolve of steel, trust me. Once he has made up his mind, there is no changing it," Nik replied. He sheathed a dagger onto his thigh and strapped a few throwing knives to the sheaths at his ankles.

I turned back to Nik, waiting for him to join me on the mat. I hadn't told Tess what I had overheard Nik and Isaac talking about in the infirmary...maybe because I wasn't ready to even think about it myself.

Nik hadn't known I was awake, and yet, he fought for me. He had told Isaac I was his only concern, and that thought sent a shiver down my spine. I had been keeping him at arm's length, and that resolve was beginning to whither bit by bit. How could it not when he was one of the few people that cared more for me than they did for seeing an end to this war?

He was chipping away at my armor...and I was letting him. He had gotten under my skin...again. A part of me desperately wanted to forgive him, to give in to the feelings that had crept up on me. But a bigger part of me still stung with his betrayal.

I knew that he was not on Donika's side. That everything he had said about his relationship with her had been true, but the fact that there had been a relationship at all still bothered me.

Things had changed for Nik somewhere between when he had met me in Silver Oaks, and when I had been captured at The Stone City. But I wasn't ready to let him back in yet. To risk breaking my heart again. The worry in his eyes when he had seen me in that infirmary bed had undoubtedly softened me towards him, but I needed to keep my shields up around him.

As I told Tess, there was a war at hand, and the last thing I needed was to deal with boy problems. Tess' boy problems had disappeared entirely, and I was sure she and Puck were destroying the townhouse in our absence today. I would stay here and train as long as I could to give them their privacy.

"You ready, Firecracker?" Nik joined me at the center of the mat, looking every bit the avenging angel. His blond hair was a stark contrast to his black training leathers, and when he smiled I could see the dimple on his cheek pop.

"I was born ready," I replied, unsheathing Stormslayer.

"I'm not sure I'd say that..." he replied with a mischievous grin, moving into his fighting stance, feet apart.

"Now, Kolya, that's not very nice." I began to circle him, my feet light on the mat.

"I never claimed to be nice," he responded, a wicked glint in his crystal blue eyes.

His shadows whirled out from behind him, fanning out to come at me from both sides.

"That's cheating!" I moved towards him, bringing Stormslayer down in an arc towards him. "We agreed no magic."

"Did we?" he asked innocently, deftly moving out of the way. "I thought that was only *you* who couldn't use magic," he teased.

I ducked under his arm and hit him hard in the back with my elbow, sending him to his knees on the mat. He whirled, his foot coming towards me too fast for me to get out of the way as he swept my feet out from underneath me. I caught myself on one knee, rolling into a somersault to escape his dagger as it swept towards me. I sliced out with Stormslayer as I passed him, leaving a cut in the side of his leathers.

"One point for you, firecracker." He nodded, a smile on his lips as if he was proud I had drawn first blood.

He moved towards me first this time and I parried, my dagger smashing against his forcefully. I thrust my other fist up and hit his chin, his head snapping back, surprise in his eyes. He deflected my next blow with his forearm, pushing forwards to try to disarm me.

I sliced through the air to keep him back, dodging his next strike with ease. I could wield Stormslayer confidently now, all of those training sessions with Warrick had certainly paid off. Warrick kept things clean and straight forwards, but I learned the risky tricks and the real skill from my sessions with Nik. He wielded his weapon as if it were an extension of himself, as if he and the dagger were one.

He came towards me again, but I used my smaller stature and my speed to duck under his arm again, but this time he was expecting it. He caught my thigh as I passed and he tackled me to the ground, abandoning his own dagger to grapple with mine. He was the stronger of the two of us. With his knee still firmly planted on the mat and me flat on my back, it wasn't long before he was able to wrestle Stormslayer away from me and pry it from my grip.

He threw my weapon to the mat, bending over me to grab me by the wrists.

"Do you yield?" he panted, his breath warm against my cheeks.

"No." I struggled against his hold, trying my hardest to get my legs back up underneath me to shove him off. His knee was still firmly fixed to the mat between my legs. He pinned my wrists above my head and leaned over, a drop of his sweat beading down to fall against my throat.

"Well, isn't this familiar," he teased, his eyes darkening.

My arms were pinned above me on the mat, his hands around my wrists. His knee was pressed between my legs, and a blush so deep I was sure I would die from embarrassment flushed my cheeks.

"I don't know what you're talking about."

I tried again to push him off, but he held me firmly beneath him. My core felt molten, and I struggled against him, trying not to let thoughts of that night at Eight Bells consume me.

His lips were only a breath away from my ear, the scent of coffee and cinnamon rolling off him.

"Do. You. Yield?" His voice was a soft caress in my ear, and it almost broke any and all fight I had left in me.

Almost.

I met his eyes with a wicked grin of my own. His face was so close to me, it would only take one small movement to close the distance between us. I remembered the feeling of his lips brushing against mine. The taste of him. The feel of his bare chest beneath my hands.

I bucked my hips hard enough that his knee slipped on the mat, and I pushed with all my strength, flipping us over. I knocked his arms away, using my hips to press him into the mat. I grabbed his wrists and pinned them above his head, mimicking his movements. A smirk crossed his lips as he fell against the mat, not fighting against my hold.

"Do you yield?" I asked, pressing him harder into the mat with my hips. His smile deepened. He was enjoying this far too much.

"Yes, Diana. I yield." He lifted his head off the mat and our mouths were only inches apart, my grip still tight on his wrists.

He had yielded, so why was it that I couldn't bring myself to let him go? To roll off him?

I could detect every place where our bodies were connected. My hips against his, my legs resting on the outside of his thighs. My ankles hooked behind his knees. My hands on his wrists.

My eyes traveled down to his mouth, and I couldn't help the traitorous thoughts that filled my head.

I wanted his mouth on mine.

I wanted his lips to taste me, to trail along my skin. I wanted to feel his hands on me, exploring beneath my training leathers.

Between my thighs.

Nik must have guessed where my thoughts had led me, his gaze turning molten. "Diana?"

The sound of my name in his mouth threatened to break me, to shatter every ounce of resolve I had left in my body and turn me to dust. One movement from him and I would come undone.

Just once, I wanted to forget about *everything* and give in. To forget about Donika and her army. To forget about my storm magic turning against me and the resistance depending on me. I wanted to forget about everything pressing down on me and simply exist in this moment.

And in this moment, I wanted Nik.

His voice broke through my thoughts, my eyes meeting his. "I will not touch you unless you ask."

I had been so adamant with him that I regretted *everything*, but here I was...*wanting*. I *wanted* him to touch me, to strip my leathers off and explore my skin. I wanted *more, more, more*.

I had told him he would never touch me again, but that had always been a lie, hadn't it? He had been the only one who could ever make me feel this way, and right now, I wanted to feel strong and powerful. Beautiful.

"Touch me, Nikolai."

I didn't have to tell him twice. I uttered those three words, and his mouth was crashing against mine, his hands slipping free from my grip to grab hold of my hips. He pulled me down onto him, and I could feel the length of him against my thigh. A soft gasp escaped my lips as he nipped at my neck. He hadn't even touched me, and yet he was already hard against me.

"Say it again."

A gentle sigh escaped me as his lips moved to my ear, then back to my throat. "*Touch me, Nikolai.*"

He flipped us over so fast I could barely comprehend it, his hips pressing me down into the mat, his hands working the laces of my leather training vest as his lips found mine again.

"*Diana.*" He whispered my name as if it were a prayer, over and over against my skin. My mouth.

My vest came loose, and I pulled at the white shirt beneath, tugging it over my head and settling back beneath him. The bare skin of my back stuck to the mat as I pulled his shirt over his head, leaving him bare from the waist up.

The sensation of his warm skin against mine threatened to send me over the edge. His lips found mine once more, and I ran my hands along his back, up his shoulders, digging my nails into the skin and dragging them back down.

A hiss of pleasure escaped his lips as he pulled me closer, his hands on my hips, beneath my waist. I wanted to erase any distance between us, to feel him against my hips...my thighs...

"I want this." My voice came out barely above a whisper as I dug my nails beneath the waistband of his pants. I pushed them down, using the friction of my legs to push them even further to pool around his ankles.

Nik let out a soft laugh. "I think about this every day. About you. How fucking *gorgeous* you look beneath me. How you sound when you say my name."

One of his hands remained firmly behind my waist, pulling me against him, as the other traveled down over my pants and between my thighs.

A cry escaped me as he pressed against my core over my pants, the sensation so much but not nearly enough. He worked the spot between his two fingers and pressed harder, another cry escaping my lips as I pressed harder into him, chasing the sensation.

"You like that, firecracker?"

I bit my lip, my head thrown back against the mat, my auburn hair surrounding me, spilling outward in a halo.

"Yes," I breathed.

His mouth found my throat again, kissing a trail over my collarbone, my bra, down my sternum, as he worked me with his fingers. This was pure *ecstasy*. I ran my fingers through his mess of blond hair as he glanced up at me through his eyelashes, his mouth still on my skin.

The sight of him like that...

We both startled as the door to the training room burst open, Nik falling to the side of me to cover me from view. Isaac stormed in, not noticing he had interrupted something at first.

"I-" he stuttered, casting his gaze down to his feet, his jaw tight. "Sorry to interrupt. The two of you need to get dressed, now. Warrick and Puck have returned. There has been a sighting of Donika in Prins."

21

Tyr was dragged into Isaac's new office in chains. His cheeks were red, his eyes covered with a thick black piece of cloth. Nik and I had dressed as quickly as we could and joined the rest of the council, my hair mussed, and my face flushed. Tess shot me a glance, letting me know I wasn't the only one who had been interrupted by this revelation.

"*Exactly* how much of the spell did you successfully transcribe for her?" Warrick asked, his voice hard.

He knelt before Tyr so that his face was level with his before ripping the cloth from his eyes. Tyr startled, flinching backwards as his vision adjusted to the room around him.

This office was much bigger than the last one Isaac had claimed in the other safe house, and it was lined with windows, the shades now drawn shut against the oncoming night.

A chill ran down my spine all the way to my toes.

Had Donika found us?

Isaac had said there had been a sighting of Donika in Prins, and to my knowledge she *never* left The Stone Palace. Ever.

"Cousin, I am much better at playing the bad guy, if you would just—" Nik started, his arms crossed.

His words were cut short by the glare of pure loathing Warrick shot his direction. Things had been even more tense than usual between the two of them over the past few weeks.

"I didn't... I didn't get that far in the transcription. Not nearly far enough that she could wield an actual *spell* out of the damn thing!" Tyr's voice shook with his words, his eyes darting back and forth.

He had been found innocent by the council, but Isaac had still thrown him into the prisons of the resistance the second Donika had been spotted far too close to where we had been hiding. Tyr wouldn't admit it, but Isaac suspected he had given away our location.

"Then how do you explain the Noctani?" Warrick asked, gripping Tyr by the back of the neck hard enough to make him gasp.

"I don't know!" Tyr spit out, struggling to get away, his hands still bound. "I swear to you! I never even knew the location of the new safe house—I *couldn't* have given away your position. I only transcribed *some* of the siphoning spell, not enough for her to have created those monsters. I swear it!"

"Do you believe him?" Warrick asked as he turned towards Isaac, his grip still tight on the back of Tyr's neck.

A muscle ticked in Nik's jaw as he met my eyes. I could tell he wanted to be the one interrogating Tyr, and if that were the case, we would be having a very different 'discussion.'

"I'm not sure what to believe anymore," Isaac replied, running a hand down his face.

He appeared tired, as if he hadn't had a good night's sleep since that day I lost control of my own storm. Liss had been taking care of him, but the lines of exhaustion were clear on his face.

"Most of what Donika did with her Noctani was done after Tyr escaped Akra. I don't believe he had anything to do with it, for what it's worth," Zion said from the far corner of the office, his arms crossed over his chest. His eyes were narrowed on Tyr and Warrick in the center of the room.

"There's nothing we can do about that now," Liss pointed out, joining Zion and resting her hand on his shoulder. "She has already created the monsters who siphon. Our only path forward is to figure out how to stop them. The problem now...is how Donika was spotted this close."

"My point exactly." Warrick clenched his jaw shut.

He let go of Tyr with such force Tyr rolled backwards, unable to catch himself. "Who do you think told her where we were?"

"I couldn't have—" Tyr's words were cut short with a gurgle, and blood spilled forth from his lips. Startled, I jumped forwards, my arm on Warrick's.

"*Stop it!*" I hissed.

His gaze never strayed from Tyr, whose gurgling continued, causing blood to spray across his shirt and the hardwood floor beneath us.

"*Warrick*," I warned.

"There is no way he could have given our location away if he didn't know it in the first place, mate," Puck said, moving forwards as if he would stop Warrick himself if he needed to.

Warrick still didn't move. My eyes narrowed on him, and I reached into the core of my magic, ready to call on it if needed. My magic surged forth readily, *desperately*. It wanted to be unleashed equally as much as I wanted to unleash it.

"Don't make me warn you again." My voice was deadly calm.

When Warrick still didn't glance away and Tyr's gurgles became panicked gasps, I raised my hand towards Warrick, letting a surge of amethyst magic burst forth.

Warrick was standing in front of me one moment, and in the next he was across the room being thrown into the bookshelf. The bookcase rocked back against the wall, books and supplies falling forth as Warrick slumped to the ground with a grunt.

"Warrick, you are out of line." I moved forwards, my hand still extended towards him.

I relaxed when he didn't move, only stared up at me in shock, his jaw slack.

"Might be the last time you don't listen to her." Puck laughed under his breath as he shot Nik a proud glance from across the room.

"That will be the last time you use your magic on him like that. Do you understand me?" I asked, my expression cold.

"Diana..." Warrick shook his head, stunned.

"I said...do you understand me?" I repeated.

Nik silently moved to my side and without a touch or a word, I could sense his strong presence at my back.

"Your queen asked you a question. I believe it's in your best interest to answer her. Now." Nik's voice was stern, his shoulders taut.

He was prepared to act on my behalf if needed, but I had thrown Warrick across the room by simply raising my hand. I might not be able to wield my storms right now, but I was still a damn powerful witch, and I would not be walked all over.

I could fight my own battles.

Tyr had slumped over, unconscious, a pool of blood surrounding him. Liss moved forwards silently, pressing a hand to his forehead and reciting the words of a healing spell she knew like the back of her hand. His eyelids fluttered, but they did not open.

Isaac moved around the desk, his eyes on me, his expression reverent. When I first met Isaac a few weeks ago, I had been the scared, fragile Stormshade who had just escaped the Stormvault.

But I was a queen, and now I was starting to act like it.

"I understand," Warrick replied, his voice hoarse.

"If you try to kill a prisoner without the vote of this council again, you will no longer be a part of it." Isaac's voice was barely above a whisper. "Liss, if you would please tend to him. We need to discuss the matter of how to proceed with accommodations."

Liss and the guards who brought Tyr in exited quietly, the only thing left of them was the pool of blood before us.

"Is the location of this safe house not compromised now as well?" Nik asked, turning towards Isaac.

"I believe only the last location has been compromised. Donika was spotted on those streets, a long-haired male Shade at her side," Isaac replied.

Could the long-haired Shade have been Corian, the one I had seen experimenting on the Noctani with her?

"And the townhouse?" Puck asked with a raised brow.

It didn't escape my notice that Tess' hand was firmly planted inside his, their fingers interlaced. A sly smile played on my lips that I fought to hold back. Now was certainly not the time, but I couldn't help but be happy for her, despite the seriousness of the situation.

"I believe Dragon's Hollow is the safest place for all of you at the moment. I ask that you go there tonight, and you don't leave again until I have sent for you." Isaac stopped to search each of our faces. "If Donika is in Prins, it isn't safe. We don't have the numbers to fight yet. We aren't ready to make any offensive move against her. Defending against an attack will only whittle our numbers further. We have no stronghold. No castle to defend. We are spread out, in hiding across the city. An attack would be detrimental to our cause, not to mention her goal is likely to capture Diana again."

"Have the Noctani been spotted?" I asked.

Puck's gaze fell on me. "No, it was only the two of them. Not even soldiers from their forces, they appeared to be alone."

"Why would she come scouting without a force behind her?" Nik mused. "That doesn't make any sense. Something isn't right."

"I have to agree," Isaac sighed, moving towards the bookcase to pick up the fallen books and place them back onto the shelf. "She would have come with a force if she knew our exact location and planned to take Diana. Or even to diminish our numbers. Something else is afoot here, and until we know her motives, we need to be *very* careful."

"Did you see her yourself?" Nik asked, his gaze meeting Puck's.

Puck gave a gentle shake of his head. "No, only reports of her sighting."

Nik gave a thoughtful nod, his expression unreadable.

"How long are we supposed to stay holed up in the townhouse for?" Tess asked, her brows knitted together.

I wasn't the biggest fan of the idea of hiding out indefinitely either, but Isaac was right. We needed to stay safe, and we couldn't risk recapture. Simply returning to the townhouse tonight would be nerve-wracking enough, knowing Donika was here in Prins somewhere.

"Until the threat passes." Isaac sounded tired as he moved towards the door.

"And if it doesn't?" Puck asked, cocking his head to the side.

"Then you don't leave," Isaac replied simply. "I mean it, Petyr. You four are to stay in the townhouse until further notice. We have another scouting mission leaving in the morning, and until there is more news, we are all to stay put."

"And you don't think Tyr had anything to do with the information leak?" Zion asked from the corner of the room.

He had stayed silent throughout the whole exchange with Tyr and Warrick, but now he pushed off the wall and moved towards us.

"I agree with you, Zion. I don't think Tyr was involved. He has been under our thumb since he came back, and we never revealed that location to him. We knew it was compromised, hence why we moved here, but I never thought Donika herself would be spotted there."

"Me neither," Zion agreed with a shake of his head. "Do you need an escort back to the townhouse?"

"I'm not sure if you missed the part where Diana threw a grown man into the wall earlier, but I think we will be fine," Puck replied, the corner of his mouth lifting into a smirk.

Tess giggled and pushed off the desk, moving towards the door with Puck in tow.

"You will let us know when you have more information?" I asked as Puck and Tess filed out behind Zion with Nik on their heels.

"Of course, Diana." Isaac gave my shoulder a reassuring squeeze. "There's one more thing..." His eyes flashed to the door before moving back to rest on me, and heat immediately rushed to my cheeks.

I thought we might be able to avoid this conversation entirely, given the tenor of the earlier topic of discussion.

"Isaac you don't—" I started, but he cut me off with the raise of his hand.

"All I was going to say is...I am happy to see you happy."

"Nothing is going on," I insisted, realizing what it might have looked like to an outsider.

I couldn't explain it to Isaac, but it had been a moment of weakness and *wanting*. There was nothing else going on between me and Nik because I still didn't trust him. I didn't know *if* or *when* that would ever change...it was complicated.

"Whatever the case...Nikolai is a good man, and I have known him a long, long time." Isaac's expression was soft, his eyes knowing.

"Thank you, Isaac. But in truth, it was nothing."

"I understand," he replied with a wink.

Isaac had been a father figure to Nik, and this conversation felt awfully fatherly as well. Isaac was a good man, and I found myself secretly hoping something *was* going on between him and Liss.

But things had changed since Zion came back, leading me to think there was a love triangle going on between the three of them.

I gave him a playful shove before moving towards the door to join the others. "Thank you, Isaac."

"Anything for you, My Queen."

Puck, Tess, and Nik were waiting for me outside the compound and, despite my protests of not wanting to be stuck looking like a stranger for the next few hours, we all drank glamours for the walk back.

The night had descended upon Prins and the streets were dark and filled with people and creatures alike lurking through the shadows. I didn't expect to run into any Araneoch in the city center, but as we walked towards Dragon's Hollow, we needed to be vigilant that Donika was near.

Puck and Tess walked hand in hand ahead of us, leaving Nik and I several yards behind. I was worried that he might bring up what had happened earlier, and I wasn't sure if I wanted to talk about it. I had been caught up in the heat of the moment, his hands had been on me, and the position...it had brought back a few memories.

That's all.

He glanced at me out of the corner of his eye before clearing his throat. "That was pretty impressive back there, with Warrick."

I took a deep breath, relieved he hadn't decided to bring it up. Maybe he was feeling the same way I had, and he had only been caught up in the moment. There was no reason to believe it was anything more than that on his part, either. Maybe he didn't even feel that way about me anymore. I shook my head to clear my thoughts and gave him a lopsided grin.

"Well, I did have a good magic teacher."

"A *great* magic teacher," he corrected with a grin. "I knew it would be as easy as breathing for you if you practiced. I know you are upset about not being able to use your storm magic, but I promise that doesn't make you weak. Look at what you did back there...you are stronger than you know, even without having to tap into that side of your magic."

"And when I pull on too much power and gas out?" I asked, raising my brow at him.

We turned towards Dragon's Hollow and the streets grew darker and emptier. The lights weren't turned on outside the shops on this side of town, the people already having turned in for the night. The only sound was our hushed voices and the soft clip of our boots against the cobblestone street.

"That hasn't happened yet, so let's not think about it."

"That's a great way to think about it. We will cross that bridge when we come to it...so let's never come to it. Simply don't pass out."

"Exactly." He grinned, playfully nudging me in the side. "Just don't pass out."

"I'll try my best," I replied.

"Did you know those two were back together?" he asked, nodding towards Puck and Tess ahead of us.

I swallowed hard. "Yes. I assume you didn't?"

He shook his head. "Puck and I...we haven't exactly talked...about any of that."

A blush heated my cheeks and I was thankful for the dark cover of night. There was no way Nik would be able to see the flush under the dim light of the moon.

I wondered if he would tell Puck about today, or if they hadn't spoken about it because it didn't mean anything to him anymore. Maybe his protectiveness in the infirmary was simply protection of the heir to the throne, to the true queen.

Maybe there was nothing romantic about it.

I laughed, but the sound was hollow in my own ears. I hoped it was convincing enough as my mind ran away with my thoughts. As we reached the door to the townhouse, Puck and Tess stopped for a quick kiss in front of the stone steps.

A sudden chill ran down my spine, unsettling me. I glanced behind me, but the street was dark and empty. Why did it feel as if someone had been watching us?

I broke away, the sound of Nik's voice calling after me as I turned around the side of the building. Something was drawing me in that direction, and I couldn't explain what.

I felt a tug, like a physical pull that I couldn't push back against even if I tried. I felt eyes on me, and when I turned the corner of the townhouse, the sight before me sent a shiver through me that threatened to freeze me in place, despite the warm spring air.

Before me were two mounted horses. The first rider rode a horse of milky white, his shoulder-length hair familiar though I had only set eyes on him once before, when I was dream walking. My eyes passed over him, already knowing who I would see next.

The second horse was all black, its mane long enough that it almost trailed along the ground. The rider carried a long, black staff with an amber gem set in the bezel. It had black textured serpents crawling up the side of the staff towards the gem, where they appeared to open their mouths towards it, their fangs extended. My eyes traveled upwards further, to black tourmaline eyes and white and blue hair that was striking against the black of night.

My breath left me as if it had physically been squeezed out of my lungs. I could hear Nik calling my name, but when I turned back, he was gone.

I couldn't see him anywhere.

"*Diana! Diana!*" His voice was strangled as he said my name, over and over again.

There was nothing behind me but the quiet of Dragon's Hollow, shrouded in a dense black fog.

I turned back towards Corian and Donika, my hands shaking.

The glamour must have worn off...but it hadn't been that long...how was that possible?

Corian's mouth curved into a sinister smile as he glared down at me, his hand moving towards the sword at his hip. Donika moved the staff towards me, and the amber gem lit up brightly enough that I had to shield my eyes with the back of my hand. When the light cleared, my eyes met hers, a pit in my stomach, my feet rooted in place.

Her lips were coated in bright red lacquer, the corner of her mouth lifting as she peered down at me.

"I've found you, little Stormshade."

22

The blood in my veins ran cold as my eyes locked on Donika's, a sinister smile curving across her lips. Corian snickered at her side, but my eyes held Donika's gaze.

She had found me.

How had she found me?

I opened my mouth to scream, to call for Nik, Puck, or Tess, but nothing came out. The sound of Nik's voice screaming my name sounded further and further away until I couldn't hear it at all anymore. Wherever they were, they couldn't see or hear me.

It must be some type of spell Donika concocted to single me out. A small wave of relief washed over me at the thought of them being safe, that it was only *me* she would take prisoner this time. That Tess was safe.

I wet my lips against the cold chill that suddenly hung in the air. Only moments ago it had been a balmy, warm spring night. I set my shoulders and glared at Donika from under my eyelashes.

She would not see me afraid.

My fingers twitched to the Stormslayer dagger strapped to my thigh, but I made no move for it. I was outnumbered with Corian here, and I wasn't sure I was ready to face Donika in a duel.

"What's wrong, little Stormshade?" She laughed, throwing her head back. "Cat got your tongue?"

"How did you find me?" My lips thinned as I watched something swirl in the amber crystal of her staff.

Magic.

It was holding some type of magic, I realized. But what?

She had no way of knowing I couldn't use my storm magic, that it had turned on me. In her eyes, I was still a threat, and I would act like it.

"You came here all alone?" I asked, my brow raised. "Not so wise for the *queen* of this realm."

I pulled on enough magic for thunder to crack loudly overhead. If I hadn't been watching her, I might have missed the way her brow flinched, just a little.

"I see no reason to be afraid for *my* safety. You are alone, and only a *little* Stormshade, after all."

"There is nothing *little* about my magic, Donika. It has been weeks since you have seen me last."

I clenched by jaw so tight I could feel the pain radiate into my temples. I pushed a lock of auburn hair over my shoulder with ease.

I would not let her see me shaken.

"How easily you forget your time in the Stormvault. Maybe you need a reminder."

She flicked her staff and Corian moved to dismount, his white horse whinnying a hot exhale into the cold night air.

"Do not come any closer," I warned, my arm outstretched between us.

A smile lifted the corner of Corian's mouth, but he stayed by his horse as a streak of lightning crossed the sky, striking the ground a few yards away. If I wasn't careful, I would lose a hold of this magic. I needed to use *only* enough to let them see I could wield it.

Only enough to let me escape.

But where would I go? I couldn't lead them to the townhouse where Nik, Puck, and Tess were. I would never make it back to the safe house before they captured me. I swallowed hard, racking my brain for a way out of this.

"I saw you." Corian's words were soft as he took a step forwards, then another.

"I said don't come any closer."

I tried to put as much steel into my voice as I could, but I couldn't risk channeling any more storm magic.

"I saw you, spying on us." His lip lifted into a sneer.

"What are you talking about?" I asked, shaking my head back and forth, my hand still outstretched between us.

"*Dream walker*," he spat, as if the word were a curse.

Donika's expression did not change. She simply moved the reins of her horse to her other hand, her grip on the staff tightening.

"If you saw me, that means you, yourself, are a dream walker. Do you deny this?"

"I do not deny it. The mother thought fit to curse me. I am a dream walker, but I am also the right hand of the queen now that Zion has betrayed our cause. *How much did you see, little Stormshade*?" His mouth twisted into a grimace as he spoke.

How could he hate dream walkers this much when he was one himself?

I only shook my head in response. I had seen Donika's Noctani, but Zion had confirmed as much. They were no longer a secret to protect. Neither were the Araneoch, who she had sent to attack us on the training field. We might not have made it out of that alive if it hadn't been for Tyr coming to warn us and kill one of them himself.

"No matter, I will know what you saw soon enough."

How could that be possible? Was there something...*more* to his dream walking abilities?

"I think you'd better leave." My voice was cutting despite the shake I could feel in my outstretched hand.

"I think not, Diana. You will come with us, back to The Stone Palace, by choice or by force. But you *will* return with us," Donika replied.

She appeared utterly bored by the entire exchange, and my heart hammered away in my chest. Was there something I could do to break the spell that hid me from my friends? Did it have to do with the magic in Donika's staff?

I dipped into the magic in my core, channeling it out of my arms and through my fingertips to taste the magic in the amber crystal.

My magic immediately reared back, recoiling. It recognized this magic as something *dark*. Something awful. I pushed once more, urging my magic to reach out, but whatever spell was held inside the amber crystal, it wasn't the spell that had hidden me here.

That meant this was Corian's doing. I lifted my palm towards him, and without giving him time to react, I let loose a burst of amethyst magic as I had with Warrick earlier. Just as Warrick had, Corian whirled back. His horse whinnied, its eyes wild. It stomped its hooves against the ground, preparing to run off.

As Corian flew back, I could see a black surge around him, as if it were a ripple in time.

What was that?

As he tried to get up, I unleashed another blast of magic, knocking him to his knees. Again, I saw that darkness ripple around his figure.

My voice came out barely above a whisper. "This is a dream."

My eyes lit up with the recognition of what that ripple truly was.

It was my magic fighting his. He had created this space for us, and us alone. That meant I could break free of it.

"You *witch*," he spat, trying to regain his footing one last time.

Donika's gaze darted between us, as if she finally realized that I knew. She urged her horse forwards, her staff outstretched towards me. Before her staff could strike me, I created a bubble of protection around myself, as Isaac had taught me.

A magical shield.

The magic rippled with purple light around me, and I could once again hear the faint sound of Nik's voice screaming my name. I pushed more and more magic into the veil of protection, and the thick, black fog began to dissipate. The image of Donika and Corian undulated before me as she beat against my magic shield with her staff.

"Diana! Diana, can you hear me? I need you to hear me, Diana!"

Before she could break through my hold and shatter my magic, I took a deep breath and pushed one last surge of storm magic into the protection veil.

I was exhausted, and I slipped to my knees as the image of Donika and Corian faded entirely. I blinked furiously to refocus my vision.

Before me was Nik, roughly gripping my shoulders and shaking me, his voice loud in my ear. He called my name, over and over. The dense fog was gone, replaced by the streets of Prins as they had been only a few moments ago. The balmy spring night was back, and I could see Tess and Puck out of the corner of my eye.

Donika and Corian were gone.

It had been a dream. But...*how*? I hadn't been sleeping...I had been awake. Did Corian have the ability to pull me into a dream while I was still waking? If so, he was far more powerful than I had originally given him credit for.

"Nik." My voice came out as a whisper, and I gripped his leather jacket in my fingers tightly.

"*Diana*. Mother above, *you can hear me*." He pulled me tight, so tight I couldn't breathe, but I buried my face in his shoulder, regardless.

I gripped his jacket, pulling him closer until there was no space left between us. The feeling of his arms around me grounded me back to this reality. I recognized a tickling sensation in the back of my mind, as if someone was trying to break through my consciousness. I had no idea dream walking could be linked to the magic of the mind, but I now recognized the sensation of Corian trying to pull me back into the dream. I squeezed my eyes closed and shut him out entirely.

"Are you ok?" Tess' voice was panicked as she kneeled before us, her hand on my back. "We were all walking and you just...stopped. You were blinking, but not responding. As if you couldn't hear us."

Nik released me only enough for me to respond to Tess, his grip still tight around my shoulders.

"I was pulled into a dream by Corian."

"Who the hell is Corian?" Nik asked, his voice ragged.

"I saw him in the dream, the one where I saw the Noctani. He had seen me there...he is a dream walker, too. He pulled me into a dream against my will...and he and Donika were both there."

"Donika was there?" Tess glanced at Nik, but he didn't take his eyes off me.

I nodded. "She had a giant black staff covered in serpents, and some type of dark magic spell trapped in an amber crystal set in the bezel. I don't know what the spell was. She said she had found me, and that by choice or by force I was going back to Akra with her."

"Well, that sounds like quite the dilemma. I never was one for multiple choice." Puck crossed his arms over his chest as he watched us.

Nik pulled me to my feet and Tess caught me, holding me upright.

"Do you think she actually knows where we are? Or did she only mean that she had found me in the dream?" I asked.

Nik shook his head. "None of us know that much about dream walking. Despite now knowing of *three* dream walkers, it isn't that common."

"We can't stay here tonight," Tess protested, gesturing towards the townhouse before us.

"Where else would we go?" I asked. "It's almost midnight, and the last thing I want to do is lead anyone back to the safe house. It's not as if we have another place on hand. Isaac told us to stay put."

"Actually—" Puck started, but his words were cut off by a sharp glare from Nik. "What? Tess is right, we can't stay here. He's our last option. I wouldn't suggest it if it weren't a last resort."

"I don't trust him with this," Nik replied, inclining his head in my direction.

"What other choice do we have? He is an old witch, and incredibly strong. If Donika or Corian found us there, he's our best bet at keeping everyone safe." Puck tensed as he spoke.

Who were they talking about?

"Do you forget that he was right hand to The Dark King, Osiris?" Nik asked, his eyes narrowing.

"My father?" My voice sounded small between them as Nik's gaze cut to mine.

"Yes, your father. He might have been slaughtered by Donika, but he was no saint himself. He, too, had a vendetta against Stormshades." Nik ran a hand through his hair as he paled.

"If you can think of a better option, Kolya, I'm all ears."

"Does anyone want to fill us in?" Tess asked, crossing her arms over her chest and facing Puck. "What are you two talking about?"

"Alastir." Puck's tone was clipped as his gaze traveled from Nik to Tess.

"The owner of the charm shop?" I asked, my head throbbing.

"Yes. There is a reason we didn't let you meet him that day. I don't think I trust him with the knowledge that you are a Stormshade, and that we are running from Donika."

"But he *hates* Donika," Puck pointed out. "We have been trying to get him to join the forces of the resistance for *years*. Maybe this is our chance."

"And if he turns her in?" Nik asked, his jaw set. "Leads Donika straight to us?"

"She is his *daughter*, Nik. I think it's a chance we have to take. Unless you want to go to bed up there and wake up in the Stormvault." Puck gestured towards the townhouse behind us. "Or lead Donika and Corian directly to our numbers in the safe house, thus extinguishing any chance we have of winning this war."

"You know I don't want either of those things," Nik ground out.

"Well, if you know of another place for us to stay tonight, I'm all ears. I, for one, do not plan to find out if Donika knows our *actual* location or only our *dream* location. Alastir is a risk worth taking, if you ask me."

"He has a point about Osiris. If he was so loyal to him, there's no way he would lay a hand on his only daughter," I replied, giving Nik a reassuring half-smile.

Or at least, I didn't think so.

Nik glanced between all of us, weighing our options before he finally spoke. "Just for tonight."

"Obviously," Puck huffed as he turned on his heel and started down the cobblestone street in the other direction. "The old man probably has at least one hundred cats. And you know how I feel about cats."

"Hey, I love cats," I replied, following behind with a frown.

"It's nothing personal, love. They scare me, that's all."

"Are you scared of Saanvi, then?" My brow raised at Puck in the darkness.

"Quite," he admitted with a lopsided grin.

That had us laughing, at least. We headed down the main street towards Alastir's charm shop, and luckily the gas lanterns were lit in this part of Dragon's Hollow. The streets narrowed as we rose over the crest of the hill leading towards the shop, and we all stopped out front. The door was shuttered for the night, a 'closed' sign prominently hanging in the window. From what I could tell, there were no lights on inside.

Nik raised his hand to knock, but the door swung open before his fist connected with the wood of the door.

"Alastir," Nik's voice was relieved, as if he half expected him not to be here. Or to answer.

"Kolya. I should have expected it would be the two of you troublemakers waking me in the middle of the night." His eyes traveled over our group and stopped when they landed on me.

Alastir was older, likely in his late seventies, with a scruff of grey hair on his face and a permanent slouch. He held a cane in his hand that didn't do a very good job of keeping him upright. This was the *powerful* witch they were speaking of? He appeared awfully...frail.

His brows lowered as if he could guess my thoughts, and his gaze snapped back to Nik. "You dare bring her here?"

I swallowed hard, stuffing my hands into my pockets. Maybe it wasn't such a good idea to come here after all.

"We have nowhere else to go," Nik explained quietly. "You know who she is?"

"Of course I know who she is. I am no fool. Now, inside with the lot of you, quickly." Alastir glanced back and forth down the street before stepping aside and letting us pass through the open doorway.

His shop was exactly as I had pictured it, littered with potions and charms placed on rickety wooden shelves. The back wall was filled with bookshelves that almost swallowed the little door set into it that likely led up to the living quarters above the shop. The floor was carpeted with a dark blue tapestry, and the wooden floors beneath creaked as Alastir led us towards the back of the shop.

"Upstairs, quickly."

He ushered us up the narrow staircase, one after the other, before shutting the door and sealing it with a spell. The door glowed an indigo hue before we heard a pop, and Alastir followed us upwards.

His living quarters were quaint but comfortable. There was a small kitchen and a wooden stove that roared with a crackling fire. There were two comfortable-looking couches, and two bedrooms off the main room. To my dismay, there wasn't a cat in sight.

Alastir lifted a hand and the shades on all the windows rolled closed with a snap. He moved to the small kitchen and poured himself a mug of steaming hot coffee from the pot on the stove.

Had he been...expecting us? He rubbed the sleep from his eyes and turned towards us, his cane in one hand, the mug in the other. "I have spelled these walls so nothing can be heard from outside them."

Alastir moved to the living room and fell into a chair by the fireplace. "Now...would one of you like to explain why you brought the heir to the throne, the daughter of my dear friend Osiris, to my house in the middle of the night?"

23

We joined Alastir and curled up on the sofas surrounding the fireplace. I brought my knees up to my chest, resting my chin on them.

"Well? Would one of you care to explain?" Alastir watched us quietly from his chair, taking a sip of his midnight coffee.

"We can't just pay you a visit, old man?" Puck grinned, throwing his arm over the back of the sofa behind Tess.

Alastir's mouth thinned as his gaze fell on Nikolai.

"Explain. I know more than you think, so don't try to hide anything from me."

"Did you see us coming?" Nik asked, rubbing his hands together in front of the flames.

Alastir held his gaze before subtly nodding once. How was that possible? How could he have seen us coming?

"I am a seer, girl," Alastir replied as if reading my thoughts, his eyes darting towards me. "And no, I cannot read your thoughts."

"I have a name," I bit out.

"Ah, yes. Diana. The youngest Stormshade of the Kotova bloodline." Alastir gave me a wry smile before turning back to Nik.

"We didn't have any other choice. Donika is coming after us, and she might know of our location. She has a powerful dream walker at her side, Corian. He pulled Diana into a dream against her will and tried to hold her there. They claimed to know our location. They want to capture her again, throw her in the Stormvault. She has created these demons with her darkness that siphon magic. I don't know if she plans to siphon Diana's magic and turn her mortal, or steal it for herself, but either way...I won't let Donika get her hands on her."

Nik swallowed hard, running a hand through his mess of blond hair. He leaned back against the couch, exhausted. It had been a long day for all of us.

"And you knew this is the one place she wouldn't be able to find her," Alastir replied simply.

"Yes," Nik admitted. "We will leave tomorrow, but we didn't want to lead her back to the resistance."

"I understand. You came to the right place." Alastir nodded.

"You knew who she was this whole time?" Nik asked.

"Yes. I have known who she is since the moment she was born. Osiris was a dear friend of mine. I have watched over her these past years, ensuring her safety, for his sake. I sensed her outside the charm shop that day you came in, and I saw you coming here, tonight."

"What else have you seen?" Nik asked.

"Nothing that will help *you.*" Alastir held Nik's gaze a moment longer before turning towards me, his gaze haunting. "Have you lost control of your magic yet?"

I reared back as if slapped.

Had he seen that, too?

"You are not the only Stormshade to be granted *too much* power. Too much to wield. Too much to control."

"I'm not?" I asked, my voice strangled.

If there were others that had been in this same predicament, did that mean there was an answer to this? A way for me to learn to control this magic?

Alastir shook his head. "You certainly are not the first. The Kotova bloodline has always been particularly plagued with this affliction. This level of power. It isn't a blessing, as I'm sure you've seen. More of a curse."

I swallowed hard, my mind reeling. "What do I do?"

"You already have part of the answers you seek," he replied cryptically.

"What does that mean?" My chest rose and fell with rapid breaths, my mind spinning with the possibilities.

"It means...your grimoire has already shown you the answer."

"The key?" I asked, my gaze darting towards Tess.

She is the only one I had told about that dream, the one with the key spell. The one where the page must have been ripped out of the grimoire...because no matter how long I searched and searched I could not find that spell in the book of shadows.

"What key?" Nik asked.

My gaze fell on him. "I had a vision. My grimoire showed me...as if I was watching from someone else's point of view. Someone else's hands before me. The vision was short, and I had absolutely *no* idea what it meant."

"The key is a spell from the Kotova book of shadows. It is the only way a Stormshade can control her powers. Without that spell, without the key, there is no other way," Alastir replied.

No other way?

What about those Stormshades who never had the good fortune of knowing the spell existed? What happened to them?

"But I searched the grimoire over and over again, that spell wasn't in there," I insisted.

Alastir nodded, taking another sip of his coffee. "It has been ripped out. You will have to travel to The Shadow to find the answers you seek."

"The Shadow?" Nik's reply echoed my own thoughts.

"Why would the spell be in The Shadow? Is that where the person is who ripped it out? Why would they *do* that?" I asked, the questions spilling out of my mouth.

Alastir held my gaze with a knowing expression in his eyes. "Not everyone *wants* a powerful Stormshade to have the ability to control their magic. Not every Stormshade requires the key, and those that do are *exceptionally* powerful."

"How did you know I would need it?"

A smile tugged at the corner of his mouth as he replied, "I saw it."

"If you saw it, why didn't you tell us?" Nik asked, his voice ragged as he ran a hand down his face, exhaustion threatening to take over.

"Because that would have interrupted the sequence of events. If I had intervened and told you earlier, we never would have been here, now, having this conversation." Alastir inclined his head in Nik's direction. "You know I cannot interfere in what I see. My gift is from the mother above, and she can take it away just as easily as it has been given."

"So, who do we need to go searching for in The Shadow? We can't exactly go waltzing in asking questions. Diana's location must be kept secret, and The Shadow is full of questionable Shades. Have you seen that much, at least?" Nik asked, exasperated.

"The man you are searching for is named Phineas Wolfe. He is a Nightshade, as you are. He is a wolf, as you are. And he has the answers you seek."

"What does that mean?" I asked, more than mildly irritated. I ran a hand through my auburn curls, wanting to rip them out. "Does he have the spell, or not?"

"I have given you all the information the mother will allow," Alastir replied simply. "You can stay here for the night, and journey to The Shadow in the morning. After that, you'll need to find new lodging. I am too old to be pulled into this war. I have seen enough war for my lifetime, and many more."

I wanted to curse the mother above for what little information we were given. I wondered if we might be able to get Liss or Saanvi to escort us tomorrow as they had in the past. We didn't know our way in and out of The Shadow, and it was too unpredictable of a place to get lost in. We had no idea what this Phineas looked like, or where we might find him. He might not be willing to give up the spell so easily, and we would need to be ready for a fight.

I wanted to know how he got his hands on it in the first place. The spell was part of the Kotova grimoire, and only Kotova blood could open it. How had he had the opportunity to steal it?

"We will leave first thing in the morning," Nik agreed.

Alastir nodded to one of the rooms off the small living space, getting up slowly from his chair. "There is a spare bedroom there, the rest can sleep out here. Rest easy tonight, Donika cannot find you here. You'll give my best to Isaac?"

Nik met Alastir's expression with one of shock. "How do you know Isaac?"

Alastir only smiled knowingly before dumping the remainder of his coffee in the sink and disappearing into the other bedroom.

Tess and I had taken the spare room, curling up under the coverlet together and falling asleep quickly. We could hear Nik and Puck whispering out in the living space into the early hours of the morning before sleep eventually took them, too.

Puck woke with the sun and gently shook us awake, careful not to wake Alastir in the adjoining room. I wasn't sure how much help he had been with how vague his answers were, but I was thankful we at least had one answer: The spell we needed to control my magic was the key, and it was in The Shadow.

I rubbed sleep from my eyes as I bundled myself into my black cloak, tying it at the neck and draping it across my shoulders. The others did the same, hoping to stay somewhat inconspicuous as we traveled through The Shadow.

Nik didn't want to travel back to the safe house to get Saanvi or Liss to escort us, and I understood why. Donika might not know our exact location anymore, but she knew we were in Prins, and she knew we were in this part of the city. It was too much of a risk to lead her straight back to the members of our cause. We would need to find our way in and out of The Shadow on our own.

We took to the streets with our hoods up and fell into step with the foot traffic down the hill, towards the main part of the city. Alastir's wasn't too far from The Shadow, and it wasn't long before we were facing the staircase that would take us down into the darkness.

The sky overhead was gloomy, as if a rainstorm threatened to cascade down on us at any moment. The clouds swirled together angrily, and I hoped we wouldn't get caught in a driving rain—in a place we weren't familiar with.

We paused before the steep stone staircase, steeling ourselves before we ventured down. Tess gave me a reassuring smile and followed behind me as I made my ascent. Puck had proposed we start at a pub, it was as good a place as any to try to find someone. We had passed a few pubs on our travels through The Shadow before, so at least we had a starting point.

We traveled through the long, stone tunnel to the streets located beyond. The road was inlaid with cobblestone as it was in the rest of Prins, but here, it hadn't seen the sunlight in decades. The stones were a muddied, filthy brown, and you couldn't avoid sloshing your boots in a dirty puddle as we made our way around the first corner.

There were no people busily walking the streets here. No stores open, no shop owners hawking their wares to passerby.

It was utterly quiet.

A crow circled overhead, calling out, and I peered through the sheets draped between buildings to see. I had a sneaking suspicion it was Kenna, but couldn't be sure. A woman with a cane and a suspicious looking green bottle of liquid tried to stop us, but we ignored her and pressed on.

We popped into the first pub we saw, and despite having our hoods drawn up, all eyes immediately turned our direction. We stuck out here, and that would only make finding Phineas even more difficult.

Nik and Puck sidled up to the bar, and I had a feeling whatever they served here *wasn't* Dragon's Ale. The bartender had a cap pulled low over his eyes, and he watched us as he polished an amber bottle with a dirty rag.

"Aye, you lot aren't from around here, are ye?" he asked, placing the bottle back on the bar top and slinging the rag over his shoulder. "What can I get ye? Two hundred pounds could buy you a good time..." he trailed off as Puck shot him a glare.

"We aren't patrons of your...establishment." Nik cleared his throat. I glanced around, and for the first time I realized exactly what kind of *establishment* this was. It surely wasn't Dragon's Ale they sold here. "We are searching for someone."

"Aye, everyone is searching for someone, ain't they?" The bartender peered at Nik under hooded eyes. "Can't help ye."

"You don't know who we are looking for," Nik protested as the bartender turned his back towards us.

"Nobody in The Shadow is lookin' for anybody good, of that I'm certain. Run along," the bartender replied, shooing us away from the bar top to make room for other, paying, patrons.

"Well, that was a bust," Tess sighed as we moved towards the door.

"We'll have to try another place," Puck agreed.

As we passed through the door Nik stopped and engaged with a man standing there, an ale in one hand and the other firmly planted inside his jacket. "Do you know a Phineas Wolfe?"

"Boy, are you stupid?" The man screwed his face up at Nik. "Bugger off."

"It was worth a try." Nik shrugged.

"Now the question is, did he think you were stupid because you asked about Phineas, or for more obvious reasons," Puck asked with a laugh as we made our way back out onto the street.

"Not helpful, Puck." Nik sighed, turning his face skyward.

"Where do we try next? Where would a sinister spell-stealer be hiding out?" I asked, peering up and down the deserted street.

"What about that pub you thought you had seen Tyr going into?" Tess asked. "Surely if they let a fifteen-year-old in, it can't be as seedy as this one. Maybe we would have better luck there."

She turned and grimaced at the front door of the pub we stood outside of, a shiver running down her spine.

"True," Puck agreed. "And if Tyr was welcome there...those folks might be running in circles that have them associated with the Kotova bloodline."

Tyr wouldn't have stolen the spell...would he? Tyr was a Kotova, but he wasn't a Stormshade. He would have no need of the spell for himself.

We carefully crossed The Shadow, following the way Liss had led us last time we had been here. We were careful to keep our heads down and eyes up, alert to any possible threats. The Shadow appeared more deserted than usual today, which was certainly saying something.

Quite a few of the seedier shops had closed since our last pass through, their windows and doors boarded up. The second pub was near the base of the staircase that led back up out of The Shadow on the other side, and it was nestled at the end of a long stone corridor.

We rounded the corner and were surprised to find this pub much livelier than the last. There were girls dancing on the bar top, ale sloshing from their mugs, and men pounding their fists against the bar as they cheered. The music was coming from a live folk band nestled into the back corner of the pub, where there appeared to be some type of poker game taking place.

There were both young and old patrons, and the clientele didn't appear nearly as questionable as the last place. Nik and Puck pushed their way through the crowd to the bar where they perched on a couple of stools. Tess and I followed, keeping an eye out for any of Fletcher's men who might frequent a place such as this.

"Hey!" Puck called out, raising a hand to get the attention of the bartender.

A younger man with a mustache approached, leaning across the bar. "What can I do you for?"

"We are looking for someone. Do you know a Phineas Wolfe?" Puck asked.

The bartender raised his brow and glanced down the bar to see if anyone was close enough to hear.

"You're not likely to find Mr. Wolfe in a place like this. Your best bet is Madam Dougherty's over on West. Do me a favor? Don't tell him I sent you."

Puck nodded, and the bartender disappeared behind the bar to tend to the next patron. We had passed West street on our way here, we would only need to backtrack a bit. Was Madam Dougherty's a brothel? What kind of business was this Mr. Wolfe into, anyway?

We shuffled back out of the bar, avoiding the sloshing drinks of the drunk patrons as we made our way back onto the street. I had to admit, that bar looked like a good time, and I was a little sad to be leaving so soon. I knew we needed to focus on retrieving the key spell, but I had a craving for a *large* mug of ale right about now.

West street was a few blocks away and only took us a few minutes to walk to. I was surprised we hadn't gotten lost yet, but didn't want to mention that out loud and jinx it.

We found a stone building stained with moss that had a small, wooden sign hanging out front declaring this to be Madam Dougherty's. There was no indication of what type of establishment it was, and there were no windows to peer into.

Nik pulled on the heavy wooden door, and we entered into darkness. The door led to a staircase which we descended, finding an attendant at a wooden stand asleep across his books at the bottom.

Nik cleared his throat, but the attendant didn't budge. Puck gave him a slight nudge, and he woke with a start, whipping his head up. He took our group in with a scrutinizing gaze before turning to Nik, deciding he must be the leader.

He cleared his throat. "Appointment?"

"We don't have an appointment," Nik started, shifting uncomfortably. Maybe we *had* walked into a brothel after all. "We are looking for someone. Phineas Wolfe."

The attendant nodded before disappearing behind the black curtain behind him. A moment later he returned.

"Follow me."

Had we found him already? Could it be that easy?

The simple part would likely be finding him...getting him to give up the spell on the other hand was something else entirely.

We followed the man behind the curtain to a small room with a folded table at the center. A woman sat atop a tall chair, a scrying glass before her, an empty seat across from her. So, not a brothel after all. I breathed a sigh of relief.

It appeared Madam Dougherty was a fortune teller of some sort, and I doubted any fortune she might tell would be a positive one based off on her moody expression.

"Madam, we are looking for Phineas Wolfe. Do you know where we might find him?" Nik asked, leaning over the chair across from her to bring himself down to her level.

She glanced up at him and her mouth thinned. "You just missed him."

Tess and I visibly deflated. How many places were we going to have to search in order to find this man?

Nik sighed, clearly frustrated. "Do you know where we might find him?"

The woman shook her head. "I don't keep tabs on Phineas Wolfe, and if you had any brains in that beautiful blond head of yours...you wouldn't either. But I can offer you a bit of information...something that could change the path before you, should you be open to it."

"Hard pass," Nik replied, standing straight. "I've had enough 'seeing' for one day, but thank you for the offer."

We shuffled out onto the street, unsure where to go next. It had to be about midday based on what little of the sun we could see from down here. That meant we had already spent a few hours searching for Phineas with no success.

Each person sent us to the next location without any other information, like a treasure hunt. Except...the treasure was a spell I *desperately* needed and was anxious to get my hands on.

"Where do we go now?" Tess asked, hugging her arms around herself.

A cold chill ran through the air, but the angry storm clouds above hadn't broken yet. I was thankful the rain had held off thus far. I felt the same chill run down my own spine and hugged my cloak tighter around me.

"We could always try another pub?" Puck offered.

"Did you see any other pubs? I'm hesitant to stray from the main streets without a guide," Nik replied, his expression tight.

Behind Nik and Puck, I saw a flash of black at the mouth of the next alley. It was gone as quickly as I had seen it. Just like with Tyr.

"Did you see that?" I asked, pointing.

"I didn't see anything," Tess replied, turning towards the alley.

"That!" I pointed as the black figure passed the opening of the alley again, so quickly you could blink and miss it.

"Stay here," Nik instructed, his hand on the sword at his hip.

My own hand subconsciously moved to my thigh sheath to find Stormslayer safely secured there with my throwing knives. Nik and Puck moved towards the alley soundlessly, and Tess and I quietly followed behind.

"Did I not say to stay there?" Nik hissed as he turned to glare at us, his gaze hard.

"I'll do as I please," I replied frostily.

Nik snickered under his breath, inching forwards. "I would expect nothing less, firecracker."

A dark figure shot out, knocking Puck to the ground. His Katana went skittering across the cobblestones and out of reach, the black figure pinning him to the filthy street. Nik took one look at the wolf snapping its jaws in Puck's face and turned form himself.

One moment he was standing before us in his cloak, his sword in hand. The next he was a wolf, his great black haunches poised to lunge, his mouth peeled back in a snarl. With his hackles raised he lunged for the throat of the wolf that had pinned Puck to the ground.

He was able to throw the wolf off using surprise to his advantage, but this other wolf was bigger than Nik was. It had warm brown eyes, and its coat was streaked with grey and white fur. I didn't recognize it, and was sure I had never encountered this wolf before.

"Stay back!" Puck called to us as he scrambled for his Katana, ready to back Nik up if he needed it.

My hand moved to Stormslayer and remained steady on the hilt, ready to wield it if needed.

Nik dodged the bigger wolf, using his smaller stature and speed to his advantage. He was able to catch the other wolf by the back leg, using his sharp teeth and strong jaw to drag it backwards.

The grey and white wolf let out a yelp, turning over to show Nik its stomach. Nik didn't move, his lips curled back over his muzzle in a snarl as his eyes held those of the grey and white wolf.

Puck pointed his sword at the chest of the enemy wolf as it lay sprawled against the cobblestones, his expression stern. "Who are you?"

The other wolf glanced back towards us, then his eyes fell on Puck once more. In the blink of an eye the wolf turned into a man, one I had never seen before.

He had salt and pepper hair and a strong jaw. He was handsome for an older man, and he raised his hands in surrender, palms up. His smile was that of a fox caught in a trap, and something about him unsettled me to my very core.

"I'll ask again...who are you?" Puck didn't move, the Katana still pointed at the man's heart.

Nik remained in his wolf form, his chest rising and falling rapidly from exertion.

"The name's Phineas Wolfe," the man replied with a mischievous smirk, "I heard you're looking for me?"

24

We had done it…we had found Phineas Wolfe, and it had only taken us a few hours of searching through The Shadow. He watched Puck with a playful grin, propping himself up on his elbows against the cobblestone street. It appeared no one had heard the brief scuffle, and for that I was thankful.

The crow that had been watching us from above cawed out overhead, and I peered through the fabric to see it circling above. That most certainly had to be Kenna, sent by the council to watch over us. It had been tracking our every move since we entered The Shadow despite it being difficult to see our movements from above, with most of the view blocked off from that vantage point.

"What can I help you with?" Phineas asked, his grin still plastered across his face despite Nik snarling before him and snapping his jaw, Puck's Katana still pointed at his chest.

He was at a major disadvantage here, but you could never tell from his countenance.

"We need your help with something," Puck replied, his jaw set.

"I don't help people for free."

"You stole something that belongs to us," Puck rephrased, his eyes darting towards me for a fraction of a second.

"You're going to have to be far more specific, I've stolen a great many things in my lifetime," Phineas replied with a wink.

I stepped forwards and joined Puck, my fists clenched. "You stole a spell from my grimoire, and I want it back."

"You *want* it back, or you *need* it back?" He laughed, and the sound bounced off the walls of the alley, echoing as it went.

"That's not of your concern. You have the spell, and it belongs to me." I crossed my arms over my chest.

"Again, you'll need to be more specific. You see, one steals many spells when they are in the business of...stealing spells."

"You steal spells...as a job?" My eyes flashed with anger as I peered down at him.

I wanted to wipe that grin right off his face.

"What do you think we do in The Shadow to make ends meet? We make do with the skills we have, and I happen to be *very* skilled at stealing spells." He shrugged, the movement making Puck's Katana snag on the fabric of his tunic.

I shook my head, anger bubbling beneath the surface. "The key...we are searching for the key. It's a spell from the Kotova grimoire."

"The Kotova grimoire?" The man laughed, raising an eyebrow at me. "Now that would have fetched a *hefty* price. You know our sovereign queen belongs to the name Kotova, though she won't claim it for herself. Any spell from that grimoire would be equivalent to a lifetime's worth of gold."

"Do you have it?" I asked, my fingers twitching against the knife sheath at my thigh.

"Let's discuss a price—" Phineas started, but was cut off as I whipped Stormslayer from its sheath and bent over, pressing the blade to his throat.

I could hear Nik's human chuckle sounding behind me, he must have changed back into his human form. He *would* find me pressing a knife to someone's neck humorous.

So twisted.

"Let's not. How about you give me the spell, and you get to leave with your life. Sounds like a good deal to me." My voice was cold as I pressed the dagger hard enough for a trickle of blood to trail down his neck to pool in his clavicle.

"You're her, aren't you?" he asked, laughing. The movement made the blood come faster, and I was almost certain this man was completely out of his mind. "You're the Stormshade witch they're all talking about. *Sister* to the queen. The rightful heir, and all that nonsense."

"Shut up," I ground out, pressing a knee into his chest.

This was all too amusing to him. I wanted to scream in frustration.

"I would listen to her if I were you," Puck said, sheathing his Katana. "She's got a temper, that one."

"Even if I had the spell, which I don't, I couldn't give it to you," Phineas replied.

I released some of the pressure on the blade.

"And why not?" I asked through my teeth, my patience wearing thin.

"It was the queen herself who contracted me to steal it. That would be *treason*."

"So you did have it...and you gave it to Donika?" Hopelessness swelled inside of me.

If Donika had the spell for the key, she had surely destroyed it. If Donika had the spell...there was no hope in gaining control of all of this power. I would be reduced to parlor tricks for the rest of my life, and that type of magic would not help us win this war. I needed to equal Donika's power, and that meant I needed to draw on a tremendous storm.

"That's not what I said," Phineas replied, his smile sinister.

I inclined my head towards him, my eyes narrowing. "What do you mean?"

"I mean, the queen contracted me to steal it. Over a decade ago. I did steal it...but I never said I gave it to her."

"Then where is it if you never gave it to her, but you also don't have it?" I asked, my frustration brewing.

I had to ask the *exact* right question with this man, and his smug demeanor was wearing on me.

"It simply disappeared. That Kotova grimoire has a mind of its own, if you hadn't noticed. It was with me one moment, then it was gone the next. It was in my jacket pocket right here." He patted the vest he wore showing the pocket was empty. "It was here, then it wasn't. Simple as that."

"That's just great," Tess moaned from behind me, throwing her arms up.

I pushed off Phineas with a frustrated grunt and he sat up, rubbing away the trickle of blood on his neck.

"Wish I could be of more help. Truly, I do," his voice held a mocking edge, and I had half a mind to press the blade back to that same spot again but finish the job this time.

The book of shadows did, indeed, have a mind of its own. How could the spell have simply...disappeared? Someone else must have stolen it. If it was truly gone, why would the grimoire have shown me the vision of *that* particular spell? Something wasn't adding up, but I wasn't sure what, exactly, we were missing.

"Are there any other spells she contracted you to steal?" Nik asked, his arms crossed, brow raised.

"I don't kiss and tell," Phineas replied tightly.

"I'm not as nice and forgiving as our true queen, here. I *will* hurt you." Nik's gaze was dark as he searched Phineas'.

"I'm not sure she's nice *or* forgiving. But I *am* sure it's not in my best interest to answer that question," Phineas replied with a tight smile.

Before I could even register what Phineas had said, Nik's arm whipped back, slinging forwards to hit Phineas square in the jaw with a closed fist. Phineas fell back with a grunt, his hand cradling his jaw where Nik had punched him. He spit blood, and what I believed to be a tooth, before fixing Nik with a cold glare.

"That was highly unnecessary," Phineas spat, his expression cross.

"I think it was quite necessary. Not only did you speak ill of your true queen, but you're jerking us around. I'm done playing games. What other spells did the queen hire you to steal?"

"Does it matter? The Kotova grimoire hasn't been seen in over a decade, nobody knows where it is," Phineas replied.

Little did he know it was currently in my possession and had been for quite some time. I hadn't noticed any other spells missing or pages ripped out, so I thought it was unlikely he had succeeded in stealing anything else. He would had to have manipulated a Kotova witch to have gained access to the spell in the first place, and deceiving one a second time would be near impossible.

"It matters," Nik bit out. "Tell me what other spells she wanted you to steal, and I'll spare the other side of your face."

Phineas ran a hand through his greying hair and his eyes fell on his feet with a huff. "Only one. But as I said, I told her it was impossible. She asked me to steal a siphoning spell. But the grimoire is missing, and no one knows its location."

She had wanted both Tyr and Phineas to steal that spell for her, but she had made do, even without it. She had still managed to create her magic siphoning Noctani.

"If I find out that you are lying to us, that the key spell is in your possession, I will not be so kind the next time we meet." Nik's voice was hard as he stepped forwards and glared down at Phineas.

"I don't think you were particularly kind to begin with," Phineas grumbled, rubbing his jaw.

Phineas Wolfe had been a dead end, so why had Alastir sent us after him?

He *had* stolen the spell, but somehow lost it. Or the spell left on its own…if that's even possible. If that was the case, why couldn't the grimoire simply show me its new location?

The visions sent to me from the book of shadows were selective, I could never decipher initially what it meant. What the book was trying to show me. We were still missing a piece of the puzzle, and I prayed that the spell hadn't ended up in Donika's hands in the end.

"One last thing—" Phineas started, cut short by Nik's violent glare. "You'll want to know this, friend."

"What is it?" Nik asked through gritted teeth. A muscle feathered in his jaw, and I could see that he was losing his patience, too.

I didn't want to draw any more attention to us, and I certainly didn't want to leave a reputation behind of causing trouble in The Shadow. As it was, people knew we were here now. Phineas knew who we were. Word would get around that Diana Kotova, heir to the throne, had been in The Shadow. We didn't need trouble, and we didn't need people searching for us. Especially those loyal to Donika, or those in her army.

"There's one *little* piece of information I've left out…" Phineas grinned, moving to stand and dust the dirt off his leather riding pants.

"And what might that be, *friend*?" Puck's voice dripped with sarcasm as he moved to stand beside Tess.

A figure appeared at the mouth of the alley, and they didn't appear very happy. We needed to get out of here...now.

"You wouldn't be able to perform the spell anyway, even if you had it in your possession."

"And why is that?" Puck asked, scorn thick in his voice as he pushed Tess towards the other end of the alley. Towards a crossroad that would lead us up and out of The Shadow.

Another figure joined the first, and Phineas' grin deepened.

"It's a *binding spell.* In order to bind it, you need *two* generations. A bloodline. Afraid you're fresh out of luck where that is concerned," Phineas replied with a shrug.

I wanted to cross the space between us and strangle him with my bare hands. Even if we found the spell, it would be useless to me because Donika had killed my mother. The only other witch in my direct bloodline that was still alive was Donika.

I bit back the tears that stung the back of my eyes, and Nik moved to block my view from Phineas.

"Run along," Phineas cooed, moving closer now that he was flanked by a few of his men, his confidence renewed. "I hope we meet again soon."

"Let's go, Diana," Nik's voice was soft in my ear as he placed a hand against the small of my back to guide me.

We moved towards the mouth of the alley where Puck and Tess waited, and Phineas and his men followed suit.

"Faster," he urged in my ear as he pushed me to walk before him.

He turned his back towards us as we retreated. As if he would fight all three men by himself. But after one long glance at Phineas, Nik took off after us.

We rushed through the streets at a clipped pace, following Puck's lead as he appeared to know where we were going. I recognized the long, dark, tunnel and the spelled door on the other side of it. We raced up the steps and out of The Shadow, and it wasn't until we were safely a block away from the staircase that I allowed myself a relieved sigh.

I bent over, my hands on my knees as I caught my breath. Nik had made sure we weren't followed, but there was no way we could enter The Shadow again any time soon. Phineas and his men would spread the word, and it would be one of the first places Donika and her men would search for us.

"Well...that was a bust," Tess' voice was ragged from running. "I'm sorry, Diana."

I shook my head to clear my thoughts, turning my face towards the sky that still threatened rain. "We will have to find another way. Another spell. It can't be the only way. It can't."

Tess nodded in agreement.

I couldn't give up so easily. There had to be another way, and we would find it. Maybe my grimoire would sense our change in direction and show me a new vision, guide us on a new path.

I let out a heavy exhale, and with it, my disappointment. As Alastir had said, I was hardly the first Stormshade to be granted an unnatural amount of power. There were those that came before me that struggled to control their magic, and I was no different. If there were answers to be found...I would find them.

I moved to unclasp my cloak around my neck, suddenly hot, when I felt something rustle in my jacket pocket. I patted it lightly, and it made the sound of crumpling paper.

Tess raised a brow in my direction, a smile on her face. "What is *that*?"

"I'm not sure," I replied, reaching into my jacket and taking out a folded piece of paper.

It was brown parchment, aged by weather and time. I unfolded it carefully, a gasp escaping me.

"You have *got* to be kidding me." Tess laughed, the realest laugh I had heard in a long time.

"What?" Nik asked, moving to see what it was that I had in my grasp.

On the paper before me was the key, a little worse for wear, but it was right here. "What the hell?"

"That was in your jacket pocket?" Puck asked.

I nodded. "It obviously hadn't been there the whole time..."

How had it just...appeared there?

"Phineas had said the spell simply disappeared. Maybe it hid itself, sensing his intentions or that he wasn't a Kotova. If it was still on his person, because he didn't know it, it might have sensed you, too. The grimoire chose you after all, and that is a part of the grimoire," Nik pointed out.

"You think it was invisible until another Kotova came along to claim it?" I asked.

"It's not the most outlandish thing to consider." Puck shrugged. "The Kotova grimoire does have a mind of its own, right? As your magic does. There is a lot we don't know about your bloodline or your magic. I think the spell chose you, the same way the grimoire did."

"I think the most outlandish thing about this whole situation is that Phineas wore the same vest for over a decade..." Tess replied with a grimace.

I couldn't help but laugh. A swell of relief filled my chest—until I remembered the last thing Phineas had said.

"The spell may have hidden itself away in my jacket, but that doesn't change the fact that we need *a bloodline* to bind my storm magic. A bloodline we don't have."

"Maybe there's a loophole?" Tess offered.

"Maybe," I replied, biting my lip.

I studied the words on the page and quickly realized a translation would be in order for this spell. The key needed to be physically removed from the paper, as I had seen in the vision the grimoire had sent me.

I folded the paper carefully and tucked it back into my pocket, shaking my head. The grimoire certainly was *magical.* To think that Phineas had the spell in his possession for the last decade and didn't know it brought another smile to my lips. Maybe Tess was right, maybe there was a loophole.

"I'll have to return this to its rightful place later, we need to update Isaac and the council on what's happened."

"Agreed." Nik nodded, motioning towards the road that would take us to the safe house.

I prayed no one had followed us up and out of The Shadow, and that we weren't tracked as we made our way to the safe house. I hadn't seen Kenna since our spat with Phineas, and a string of unease unfurled in my gut. I had half expected her to meet us once we had come back up the stone steps, but she was nowhere to be seen.

We took a roundabout way to get there—to be sure we weren't being followed. It took twice as long as it normally would, but there was a sense of relief that had settled between us that we had at least *found* the spell Alastir sent us to search for. Alastir hadn't steered us wrong. That was the first step, the rest we could figure out later.

The closer we got to the safe house, the more a sensation of uneasiness settled in my chest. The sky overhead still hadn't cleared, but it also hadn't stormed yet. It had been teetering on a precipice all day, not moving one way or the other.

I thought I might have heard a scream in the distance, but searched the faces of the others and shrugged it off when it appeared they hadn't heard anything themselves.

As we drew closer, I felt a swell of magic. As we turned the corner to see the safe house a few blocks away, my blood ran cold.

Witches filled the streets, magic swirling angrily in the air. The sound of screams and clashing metal and iron filled my ears, sending a chill down to my bones.

I exchanged an alarmed glance with Tess, but Nik and Puck were already off running. We were close on their heels, pumping my fists harder and harder as I pushed myself to keep up.

The first thing I saw was Isaac, blood smeared across his face, his sword clashing fiercely with a Nightshade guard from Donika's army, her seal proudly displayed on his breast plate.

The rest of the resistance was out here, too.

Fighting.

They were fighting for their lives.

Dusk had ascended over Prins and smoke filled the streets, making it hard to see who was fighting who. The only relief I allowed myself was that I didn't see any Noctani among the chaotic fray.

I pulled Stormslayer free and dove after Nik into the melee, my dagger tight in my grip. He shot me a glance that told me he knew there was no way to keep me out of the fighting, and that I *better* keep myself safe.

I nodded at him before he disappeared into the smog after Puck. I scanned the entrance to the safe house which had now turned into a raging battlefield, blood and bodies strewn about. Bile rose in my throat, but I quickly swallowed it down.

There was no time for second guessing. No time to be afraid.

This was everything I had trained for, and whether I was ready or not, the time to fight had come.

I stopped dead in my tracks when my gaze snagged on a familiar face. It wasn't the one I had been expecting, but it sent a shiver down my spine all the same. His lips stretched into a menacing grin as he caught my eye, moving towards me with his sword raised.

Fletcher had found us, and he had brought an army.

25

The sky was on fire.

The sun had set, escaping below the horizon and cloaking Prins in darkness, lit only by the flames of the buildings as they burned relentlessly. I gripped Stormslayer tightly in my fist as Fletcher advanced, a smirk across his lips. I whirled, searching the smoke and flames for any sign of Nik or Puck, but they had already jumped into the battle.

My breath caught in my throat as I stood my ground. I blinked away the tears from the smoke and dipped into my well of magic to be sure it was ready. There was no time to think about whether my magic would escape my control again or not.

This was life or death, and I would not die here today.

"Funny seeing you here," Fletcher called out over the sound of clashing blades and gurgling screams.

"How did you find us?" My voice was almost swallowed by the sounds of the fighting, but it didn't waver.

"Our dear friend Corian. You all but gave yourself away in that dream, Diana. You never did understand we are smarter than you, always one step ahead. If you surrender now...I'll take you and your friends back to The Stone Palace and leave the rest of your *resistance* alone." Fletcher laughed, as if our resistance was a force so meek he could crush it beneath his boot.

"And what will you do with us?" I asked, raising Stormslayer between us to keep him at a safe distance.

Fletcher's eyes moved to the blade, then met my gaze again with a smile.

"You don't think you could take me on, do you?" He laughed, taking another step forwards. "If you surrender, only *you* will face Donika's wrath."

"I don't believe you." I swallowed hard, holding his gaze. My grip on the dagger was tight despite the sweat greasing my palms.

"It doesn't matter either way. Either you die here, along with everyone else, or you die in the Stormvault. Your choice."

"Not much of a choice at all, is it?" I asked, dipping into my magic and allowing it to flow through my fingers. "I am a Stormshade of the Kotova bloodline, *and you cannot break me.*"

I made the first move, bringing my dagger down in an arc towards Fletcher's face. His expression lit with surprise, but he managed to duck and avoid my advance. He hadn't been expecting me to make the first move.

Adrenaline pumped through my veins as I remembered everything Warrick and Nik had taught me. Stay low. Use my speed and my size to my advantage. Don't let him back me into a corner.

Fletcher brought his blade around and I blocked his forearm with mine, my teeth clashing at the force with which we collided. The elbow of his other arm shot out and hit the side of my head *hard* and my vision swam. Before I took a step back, I brought Stormslayer up and caught his jacket with the blade, tearing it open.

Fletcher's eyebrows lifted in surprise as he sliced at me again. This time I whirled, kicking at the back of his knees with my leg to sweep his feet out from under him.

Was I going to have to kill him?

Was I capable of that?

Fletcher's eyes were cold as he hit the ground on his back, the wind knocking from his lungs. He rolled quickly, finding his footing effortlessly. He was clearly a seasoned soldier. We circled each other as the battle raged on around us, my eyes flicking to the higher ground to see if Donika watched.

Was she here, or had she simply sent her army to slaughter us all?

Fletcher advanced quickly, his blade slicing my thigh before I had a chance to block, and a scream tore from my throat. The blade cut deep, blood dripping onto the cold ground. I held my hand to my thigh, the blood oozing around it and through my fingertips.

A smirk filled with malice graced Fletcher's lips as we circled once more.

I needed to heal myself. *I needed to find Liss.*

I would have to end this...I had no other choice. The only way I could keep from killing him was to go with him willingly...and that was not an option.

I had survived Donika's torture in the Stormvault.

I had survived the loss of both my mother and my father.

I had survived Nik's betrayal.

I would survive this, too.

I set my chin, resolute. I didn't want to be responsible for killing *anyone* in this war, but there was no way I would make it out without getting my hands bloody. Fletcher would either kill me or bring me back to Donika.

It was kill or be killed...and I was a survivor. A fighter.

I was the rightful heir to the throne of Istmere, and I would not fall in battle today.

I spun, my auburn hair cascading around me as I kicked Fletcher in the side, my blade slicing through his chest as he staggered back. I grunted as I kept coming without mercy. I was lucky he hadn't chosen to wear armor today, whether it be arrogance or stupidity, I was thankful. I came at him again.

I kicked out once more, pushing him back. Stormslayer sang through the air and sliced his arm, Fletcher pulling back with a hiss. I pushed him back again.

Again.

Again.

A wild expression clouded Fletcher's features as he fell, his dagger sliding away from him into the rubble of what had once been the safe house. His eyes were wide as I held

Stormslayer over my head with both hands, poised to bring it down.

One moment my vision was filled with smoke and ash, Fletcher's body kneeling in the rubble before me. In the next, a vision passed before my eyes.

Donika standing before my mother, her sword poised over her body. Her eyes were dark, bottomless. She smirked, bringing the sword down with all her strength.

"Diana!"

Nik's voice cut across the battle and my eyes came back into focus, searching for him. My grip on the dagger relaxed ever so slightly. Nik was racing towards me, soot and dirt smeared across his face, his blue eyes wild and terrified. He cut down a Nightshade soldier in his path with nothing but a thrust of his sword as he pushed through the crowd of bodies.

In the moment I had glanced away, the moment the vision had flashed before my eyes, Fletcher had found his feet again.

And his sword hand was empty.

He looked at me with...was that pity? His eyes almost... sad. No, that wasn't right. My brow creased in confusion. I didn't understand.

Not until I felt the searing pain in my chest where his dagger was buried.

My mouth fell open as my arms dropped to my sides, Stormslayer clanging against the ground as it fell from my grip. Fletcher's dagger was buried in my left shoulder, so close to my heart. My eyes snapped up to his, and I shrunk back at his expression, his teeth bared in an angry snarl. Hot blood pooled against the material of my tunic. I reached up and grabbed the dagger with both hands, sliding it free as I ground my teeth against the pain.

The dagger tumbled to the ground as I fell to my knees, a cloud of soot whirling through the air around me.

"Diana!"

Nik's voice was in my ears again, but my vision swam before me.

I couldn't find him.

I couldn't see anything.

I blinked back the tears that clouded my vision and Fletcher peered down at me as my hand went to my chest to stop the bleeding.

I could hear another voice, calling out my name, but I couldn't place it. I heard it over and over as it came closer, and Fletcher bent to pick up a sword among the rubble.

Where was Tess? Puck?

I wanted to close my eyes, the pull so strong that I fell forwards, barely catching myself with my other hand. I pressed against my chest firmly, but the blood wouldn't stop...it just kept coming. It dripped onto the stone beneath me, and I startled as it began to pool there.

I was dying.

I reached into the core of my magic, needing it desperately in this moment, and felt it whisper back softly.

It was weak.

The sound of clashing swords rang loudly in my ears as a body appeared before me, parrying Fletcher's attack. I opened my mouth to cough, and blood splattered the cobblestones before me.

I needed to heal.

I needed my magic, and I needed it *now.*

"Diana! Fuck, Diana. No, no, no..." Nik had found me, his hands shaking as he pulled me against him.

The orange flames danced in the reflection of Nik's eyes as he knelt before me. He pressed his palm to my chest wound much harder than I had the strength for. His lips moved in a spell, but I could barely hear the words.

"Listen to me, Diana. Stay with me. I need you to stay with me. Baby, *please.*"

His face was blurry, but I could see the utter terror in his piercing blue gaze. The hard set of his mouth. His brow creased with effort as he spoke the spell again and again, swearing under his breath.

If Nik was here with me...who was fighting Fletcher?

As my eyes focused on the fight over Nik's shoulder, a guttural scream tore forth as Fletcher's sword hit home. It sliced through the stomach of the witch before him, all the way to the hilt.

The sword looked odd protruding from his back as the witch fell to his knees, red staining his mouth as he gurgled blood. He sank to the rubble in a lifeless heap, his face turning towards me as he fell. There was sorrow in his eyes right before they glassed over.

He took one final breath, then his body was still.

Tyr.

Tyr had fought Fletcher to protect me, to protect all of us, and he had paid the ultimate price.

Tyr was dead.

26

The sight of Tyr's lifeless body lying among the rubble would live with me until my last days.

Tyr was my cousin.

He was only a *boy*.

He had his whole life ahead of him, only for it to be snuffed out. All because of me.

Tyr was dead, and it was my fault.

Rage brewed in my gut so deep it pulled my magic free of its own volition, thunder cracking loudly overhead. Fletcher's eyes turned to the sky in alarm before falling back to Tyr's limp form. He braced his foot against Tyr's chest as he slid the sword free.

Flames swam before my eyes as my magic swelled inside of me, and all I could see was *red*. The wound in my chest was nothing but an afterthought as I pushed to my knees, Nik's voice calling out for me. I could hear his voice, but not the words he spoke.

The sound of my own blood pumping through my veins was rushing through my ears as I pulled on my magic again, a burning sensation reaching my fingertips as lightning shot out of the sky.

The screams of the surrounding witches were drowned out by the spitting rain that violently tore from the sky, torrents of it cascading down on the battle. My hair stuck to my forehead, the back of my neck, as I pushed to my feet. Rivulets of water ran down my face, washing away the dried blood and dirt.

"Diana..." Nik warned, his grip tight on my arm as I raised my palms towards Fletcher.

My chest rose and fell rhythmically as I drew on my magic. I drew, and drew, and drew until it filled me up to the brim. I almost buckled under the pressure of the storm, the intensity of it, as it swirled overhead. But I held my footing.

Fletcher shuddered as the sword dropped from his grip.

"Diana, you are drawing on too much magic." Nik's voice was a whisper in my ears, one I could easily ignore.

I reached out to the angry clouds overhead and grabbed its magic. An earth-shaking thunder enveloped everything, leaving a ringing in my ears. A smile graced my lips as my eyes fell on Fletcher. I cocked my head to the side, another crash of thunder sounding overhead.

The wind was picking up, whipping my wet hair back and forth, cloaking the battlefield in a haze of driving rain. I reached out to the storm again and grabbed whatever power it had left. I waited until it filled me to the point of *physical pain* before I unleashed it.

Lightning struck out haphazardly around us, the ground sizzling and flaming where it had struck. Fletcher's expression was wild as he backed away.

"Your eyes..." he uttered, scrambling backwards over the rubble.

My eyes?

I found the lightning in the cloud again...and this time I would not miss. Fletcher had killed Tyr, likely the only blood family I had left. The council had accused him of betraying the resistance, and they had thrown him into the dungeon for crimes they couldn't prove he committed.

In the end, he *had* been on our side. He *gave his life* to save mine.

At some point, the blood had stopped pooling on my tunic, and the pain had drained away to leave nothing but raw, unfettered vengeance and rage.

I watched as I released the lightning and it struck out again, violently stinging the ground around us. Several Nightshade soldiers fell to the ground, including Fletcher.

His body was motionless against the cobblestones, his eyes wide. I stepped forwards slowly, one foot after the other, the sound of Nik's voice fading in my ears.

"Tess! Tess, I need you!" I could hear Nik yell out behind me. "I can't bring her back. She can't hear me!"

I stalked forwards, kneeling next to Fletcher's limp body as thunder crackled loudly overhead once more. Fletcher's eyes were trained on the sky, unblinking. His chest was sliced open, the cut blue around the edges and seeping with bright red blood.

It was as if my lightning had *cut him down the middle.* My eyes traveled to the others around him, and I realized I had taken down at least a dozen other Nightshade soldiers with my lightning strike, but the battle raged on.

But not for long.

I stood again, pulling on more of the magic the storm had left, letting it well up inside of me once more. I threw my head back, turning my face to the storm above with a smile on my lips.

"Diana! Listen to me, Diana!" It was Tess' voice in my ears this time, and a voice deep down told me to look at her.

My face turned, my eyes meeting hers.

"Your eyes..." She backed up a step, her hand flying to her throat. "They're...glowing, swirling with storm magic. Diana, come back to us."

"Why?" I asked, my voice sounding foreign in my own ears. Darker. Colder.

It was Isaac's voice that rang out this time. "Diana, you need to focus on letting the storm *go.* It has no more energy for you to take."

I turned to him, my brow creasing in confusion. "Why would I do that? I killed over a dozen enemies in one fell swoop. I could end this battle right here and now."

"But at what price?" Isaac asked, his voice raised over the storm that surged around us. I must have said those words out loud, I realized. "Diana, *there is a price to this kind of magic.*"

The storm thundered around us, out of control. Lightning struck against the rubble, rocks flying into the air and hitting those unfortunate enough to be standing within striking distance. The rain was falling so hard it stung against my skin, pools of rain and blood forming around the battlefield.

My eyes searched once again for Donika, but she wasn't here.

She had sent her minions to capture me, not wanting to face me herself. Was Corian here? Who else had she sent after me?

I would take them all down. Every last one.

"Diana, please let the storm go," Tess pleaded.

She took a tentative step forwards, then another. Lightning struck between us, and she jumped back. My eyes moved from her frightened expression to that of Nik, who stood over her shoulder. His jaw was set, his eyes pleading.

"I can't," I choked out, my feet rooted in place.

The storm raged around me, and the same as last time, I had lost control. I had *wanted* to kill those witches, and the thought made my stomach twist. What was happening to me? Was *this* the price of this kind of magic?

Bloodlust?

I wanted to fall to my knees and wretch at the thought of those I had murdered, but the storm and its magic held me rooted in place. It hadn't been only Nightshade guards that had fallen when my lightning struck—it had been resistance members, too. Lightning struck again, dangerously close to where I stood. I didn't own this storm...not anymore.

Nobody did.

It would strike *me* down as easily as it had my enemies.

"Please, Diana." Tess' voice rang through my ears again.

I closed my eyes, focusing on separating my mind from that of the storm. I grit my teeth against the pain. It felt as if I was *pulling a part of myself out* as I tried to separate the two.

But the storm and I were one. Despite not owning this storm any longer, despite it being out of my control, it felt as if it intrinsically belonged to me, and I belonged to it.

If the storm died, *I would die.*

I fell to my knees again, the rocks biting into my skin as I ground my teeth together.

The storm didn't want to let me go.

I tried and tried to pull the energy in, but it bucked against me, striking out wildly. Isaac joined me, kneeling before me and tentatively reaching out to grab my hand.

"You *can,* Diana. You are the strongest Stormshade I have ever known."

My eyes met his, and a tear fell down my cheek, mixing with the rain sticking to my skin. I could sense Isaac's magic here, now. It pulled with mine, breaking the storm in two. My other hand buried into the dirt as I curled my fingers, trying not to think about the pain as we cleaved the storm in half with our magic.

I knew the moment Isaac was able to break off a piece of the storm and absorb it, as if a physical weight lifted off my shoulders. With the storm severed, I was able to wrangle its energy, absorbing it back into myself.

The last drop of rain fell against my cheek as the storm dissipated, the thunder rumbling off into the distance. The sky was still black with fog and smoke from the flames, but the storm was gone.

Bone deep exhaustion consumed me and I fell forwards, Isaac catching me in his arms. I had never drawn on that much magic, not even when the storm had turned on me in the training field.

My well of magic felt...empty.

I felt empty.

I reached into my core to touch my magic, but there was *nothing*.

A sob escaped my throat as Tess found me, her arms encompassing me.

"Isaac, behind you!" Nik called out.

Isaac turned in time to parry an attack from a Nightshade soldier who had seen our opportunity of weakness and decided to strike.

The battle raged on around us, far from being over, despite Fletcher and many of his men lying dead a few feet from us. I held tightly onto Tess, my nails digging into her shoulder.

"I've got you, Diana. I've got you." Her hand found the back of my head as she pulled me closer. "I've got you."

Nik knelt before us, sliding Stormslayer back into my grip.

"I can't," I sobbed, meeting his eyes through the well of tears. I didn't want to feel the hilt of the blade in my grip again. Didn't deserve to.

"I'm afraid we don't have a choice."

His expression was grim. How many had we lost in this battle? Enough to set us back...years? How many of those lives was I responsible for with that erratic lightning strike?

We would never be able to storm The Stone Palace now...not with our numbers practically halved.

"Can you fight?" Tess asked, her soft eyes meeting mine but her expression firm.

I wanted to tell her that's all I have been doing. *Fighting*.

From the moment I found out I was a Stormshade, I had been fighting. I was utterly exhausted, my muscles sore, my resolve weary, my emotions fragile.

I glanced down at my chest and realized the wound had healed itself. Had it been my magic? Had pulling on *that* amount of storm magic healed me?

"Yes, I can fight," I replied, setting my jaw.

I swallowed back all the emotions threatening to drown me.

I couldn't let these witches give their lives for me, as Tyr had, without fighting beside them. Fletcher was gone, but his numbers were still fierce. They battled on, and the sight of the dead bodies strewn across the cobblestone street had me swallowing back bile.

Tess helped me to my feet and gave my shoulder a gentle squeeze to steady me.

Stormslayer was tight in my grip once more, the weight of the dagger bringing me little comfort as the sounds of clashing metal and screams filled my ears.

27

My magic was utterly depleted, and I couldn't even pull on it to push myself faster on the battlefield. When I dipped into the well of magic in my core, I felt *nothing*.

Blood and dirt smeared my face despite the driving rain my storm had brought on. My hair was wet and tangled, plastered to my face as I followed Tess, Nik, and Isaac back into the battle. Puck was somewhere among the fray, as were Liss, Warrick, Zion, Saanvi, and Kenna.

The battle was a mixture of Nightshade's shifted into their animal form and those that preferred the sword and dagger. Everywhere I searched there was a new sight, whether it was a jaguar, wolf, bear, or tiger. Nik remained in his human form as he fought back-to-back with me, a second wind hitting me as I gripped Stormslayer in my fist.

These people were risking their lives for *me* and for the promise of a better future for Istmere, and they would not defeat us so easily. I was thankful that Donika had chosen not to join this battle, and her Noctani and Araneoch were nowhere to be seen, either. Corian was noticeably absent as well.

I didn't recognize any of the other soldiers as I cut them down, my mind numb with the chaos of battle. I felt like a robot as I went through the motions, pure adrenaline driving me.

We needed to survive this.

All of us.

We had been fighting for hours, but darkness still blanketed Prins, the sunrise nowhere in sight.

I wiped sweat from my brow with the back of my hand as we fought on, my eyes always searching to make sure Nik and Tess were safe. Isaac and Puck had drifted off into the melee of the battle, and I had lost sight of them quite some time ago. I prayed that they were safe, and that we would all make it out of this alive.

My thoughts kept traveling back to the witches I had killed, back to Tyr. But I shook my head to try to clear my thoughts and focus.

I would have time later to grieve.

To process.

Right now, I simply needed to *move.*

"Behind you!" Tess called as the Nightshade before her fell to his knees beneath her blade.

I whirled around and ducked as a soldier's sword swung over my head. One moment later, and it would have separated my head from the rest of my body. I ducked under the soldier's arm, jabbing him in the back with my dagger. His sword fell to the ground as he turned, his hand reaching out fast enough that I couldn't stop it before it closed around my throat.

I sliced through his forearm with Stormslayer, and he withdrew with a hiss, stepping backwards right into Nik's sword. He fell to his knees as Nik slid his sword free and the soldier fell among the rubble.

"Teamwork makes the dream work," Tess called out, and I couldn't help but shake my head and indulge her a little. Leave it to Tess to find a lick of humor in a situation such as this.

It was short-lived as another soldier stormed forwards, his sword raised against Nik. I turned to guard his back and realized the battlefield was...empty.

All the soldiers that had flooded this part of the street had either been killed already or fled.

Nik quickly dispatched the soldier, and I bent over, my hands on my knees to catch my breath. I had no idea how long we had been fighting for, but every ounce of energy had been sapped from my body, leaving me exhausted through and through.

"We have to go find the others," Tess announced, joining us.

I nodded, swallowing. "Agreed."

We could still hear scuffling from further down the street, the clang of swords sounding further off in the distance. The view was obscured by the smoke that still rose from the rubble of the burning buildings. They had been reduced to ruins as Siraleth had, but my storm had stopped the fire from spreading further than this block and the next.

As we moved down the street, the sight of the bodies strewn about the rubble had bile rising in my throat. I recognized faces from our own resistance, mingled with those of the Nightshade army we had taken down.

We would need to sift through the dead—to give those of us who stood against Donika a proper burial. I would need to ensure Tyr was treated with the respect he deserved. Everyone had thought he turned on us, but he had given his life to save mine in the end, and I would never forget it. Guilt rose within me, so heavy it felt as if it was physically weighing down my every step.

I did my best to swallow back those emotions, though they threatened to destroy me. I reminded myself—not for the first time during this long night—that the time for grieving would come later. For now, we needed to find the others and count our numbers, determining who had survived this ambush and regroup.

Anger bubbled inside me that Donika hadn't even bothered to show up. I worried if her numbers were truly so large that the soldiers she sent here today were indispensable to her.

After a few minutes of walking, we found Isaac, Zion, and Puck in a group they could easily dispatch if we joined them. We jogged down the street, dodging the bodies and the fallen debris to engage in the fight with them.

It was almost over.

Almost.

I crept up behind the Shade that Puck fought with, easily sliding Stormslayer between his shoulder blades. He let out a shocked gasp, falling to his knees before he had a chance to turn and see who had come up behind him. I slid Stormslayer free as we moved onto the next Shade. A few of the Nightshades took one look at our group and took off, realizing the remainder of their army had either scattered or were slain in the battle.

Nik took on a Shade double his size, using his smaller frame and agility to evade him. Despite his size, the larger Shade was equally as fast. Puck joined him, and I turned my attention towards Isaac who was outnumbered, circled by three Shades at once.

An arrow sang through the air and hit the rubble a few feet from me, skittering against the rocks and missing its target. I turned, searching for the archer and where the arrow might have come from. Another arrow shot forwards, which Isaac dodged with his sword. His eyes narrowed.

My gaze scanned the buildings still standing in this part of the city. Was there an archer in one of these windows?

There, my sight snagged on a flash of light in the window of a fourth story town house.

"Isaac!" I called out, pointing Stormslayer. "There!"

"I've got it!" He called back.

That left Tess, Zion, and me to handle the rest.

Another arrow sang from the window, whispering through the air. This one didn't hit the rubble as the others had. There was no dull sound of the arrow burying itself in the rocks.

I heard a wet, fleshy sound that twisted my stomach into knots.

Cold dread settled over me as I turned, my mouth dry.

My eyes searched our group quickly. Tess and Zion had already taken care of the three Shades that had circled Isaac, and Isaac was climbing the stairs of the partially destroyed townhouse to dispatch the archer.

And Nik...Nik was still battling the larger Nightshade soldier.

But...something wasn't right.

Nik's face was chalky, a bright red spot blooming against the shoulder of his tunic. He glanced up at the soldier as he fell to his knees. The Nightshade raised his sword high as the realization dawned on me.

There was an arrow protruding from Nik's shoulder.

I abandoned Tess and Zion, running towards Nik as fast as I could. I pumped my arms hard at my sides, using a boulder to launch myself up to the height of the Nightshade, burying Stormslayer into the side of his neck before he could bring his sword down.

He pushed me off with a grunt, and I realized I hadn't buried it nearly deep enough to take him down. I fell to the ground beside him, my head cracking against a rock, my vision going dark for a moment.

But one moment was all it took.

All it took for the Shade to raise his sword.

And bury it in Nik's gut.

He slid his blade free and Nik doubled over. His hand immediately went to cover the wound, the arrow still protruding from his shoulder. Blood bubbled to his lips as our eyes met, and for a moment, all I thought was that *this* was what hell must feel like. *This* must have been how Nik felt earlier, when I was the one who had been injured. My heart still beat in my chest, but it was as if it had been cleaved in two.

But my injury...it wasn't...it didn't...

He fell to his side, his breathing shallow. I wanted to run to him, to heal him, but as I pulled on my magic, there was *nothing.*

My vision went red, and I swept Stormslayer out, slicing the Shade in the back of the knees hard enough for him to fall. I stepped up behind him and, without hesitation, ran Stormslayer across his throat.

I let his body slump to the ground and stepped over it, my heart beating so hard it felt as if it were in my throat. That it might beat right out of my chest.

"Nik!"

I could hear a struggle in the townhouse, and a moment later Isaac shoved the archer out the window, his body joining the others in a cloud of dust.

I ran to Nik's side, pulling his head into my lap. His eyes were closed, his breathing heavy and labored. The laceration in his abdomen bled through his fingers, making the wound from the arrow the least of our problems.

"Nik, open your eyes," I commanded, giving him a gentle shake. "Nik, can you hear me? Stay with me, Nik."

Hadn't he said the same thing to me mere hours ago? When Fletcher had wounded me? His eyelashes fluttered against his cheeks and when his eyes met mine, I had to swallow back my terror.

His eyes were a dull, lifeless blue.

"Poison," he whispered, blood trickling from the corners of his lips.

I shook my head violently, tears streaming down my face.

No.

If it weren't for that archer, the Shade never would have gotten the upper hand. Never would have had the opportunity to pierce him with his sword.

I couldn't lose Nik. *I couldn't.*

I blinked back the tears as they blurred my vision, wiping my face with my blood and dirt-stained shirt.

"Liss," I whispered back, searching frantically around us.

The only faces that met mine were that of Tess, Puck, and Zion, their expressions somber.

"Where is Liss?" I asked, my voice cracking.

"I haven't seen her," Zion's voice was sad as he crouched next to us.

"Isaac!" I screamed, gripping Nik's hand tightly in my own. I could not lose another person I loved. I wouldn't. "Isaac, I need you!"

I tried to focus, to dip into the well of my magic again. But again...I felt nothing.

"Dammit," I ground out through my teeth in frustration. I tried again and again.

There was nothing there. *Absolutely nothing.*

I could hear when Isaac joined us, cursing under his breath.

"He said it's poison," I told him, searching his gaze. "We need Liss. She is the most skilled healer."

"How did you heal your own wound before?" Isaac asked, his eyes searching mine.

"I used my storm magic...but there isn't any left. I depleted it. I can't feel *any* of my fucking magic. *Please*, you need to help him."

I could hear the panic in my own voice, and the calm soberness of those around me only made me want to scream at the top of my lungs.

Why wasn't anyone *doing* anything?

"I don't know where she is," Isaac replied, his hand covering Nik's over the wound on his abdomen. One of my hands was buried in his hair, the other gripping his shoulder tight. "We can't take the arrow out right now. He is too weak from the loss of blood as it is. We need to move him."

"To where?" I asked, my voice raw. "The safe house is gone. I don't have any supplies in the town house. *What do we do*?"

Isaac stood, searching the surrounding buildings until his gaze landed on one further down the street. He nodded to himself, turning to help Zion lift Nik.

"Where are we going?" I asked, stepping back so they could lift him, but reaching for Nik's hand.

His *cold* hand.

"I had a friend who lived in this district. She married a doctor. They should have some supplies in their house to stop this bleeding until we can find Liss," Isaac replied tightly.

I nodded, following them down the street through the smoke, away from the wreckage and into the darkness.

I swallowed back salty tears, my throat thick.

Where was Liss? Saanvi? Kenna? Warrick? I almost emptied the contents of my stomach when the thought hit me—that Liss might not have made it through the battle at all. That she might be dead.

Isaac shouldered open the doorway, and I had to let go of Nik's hand as we passed through. Tess and Puck were close on my heels. Isaac and Zion laid Nik across a table in the dining room, and I helped shove everything from the table onto the floor.

Nik grunted as he tried to sit up, and I took that as a good sign...that he had enough energy to even try. I remained at his side, his hand in mine as Isaac sent Zion and Puck to search for Liss. Tess clasped my shoulder with her hand, giving it a gentle squeeze.

My eyes met hers, and they were filled with unshed tears.

I shook my head, turning back towards Nik.

"He's going to be fine." I shook my head again. As if I could will it into existence. "He has to."

"Firecracker." His voice was hoarse, and as he coughed, he spat up more blood. "There's something I need to tell you."

"Whatever it is, it can wait. You need to save your strength right now," I told him, a faux smile gracing my lips as I glanced down at him.

I blinked, and a tear escaped my eye, landing on his cheek and rolling off. It left a trail through the dried blood in its wake.

"You don't understand," his voice was quiet as he struggled to keep his eyes open, trained on me.

"I don't need to. Shhh. You need to keep your strength." I pushed the hair back, out of his face.

"Diana—" His voice cut off as a coughing fit took him, his whole body racking with the effort.

The blood was seeping from his wound at an alarming rate and Tess had found towels for us to press against it in an attempt to slow or staunch the bleeding. He was pale, his pulse slow and thready.

I gave his hand a squeeze as he closed his eyes.

"Nik?"

Nothing.

"Nik, can you hear me?" My voice was fragile and broke as if it were glass as I tried to force it out.

Nothing.

"God dammit, Nikolai, squeeze my hand if you can hear me."

Nothing.

My eyes flew to Tess' and she had her hand on his wrist, her expression grim.

"No," I said, shaking my head. "No, he is going to be fine. I can't lose him. I won't. Nik? Nik, can you hear me?"

Nothing.

He couldn't be. He just couldn't be.

I wouldn't allow it.

I dipped into my magic again, *forcefully*. There was only a small ember. It was infinitesimal...but it was there. I dragged that scrap of magic to my core, bringing it through my fingertips as I placed my hands against his chest.

"Diana, what are you doing?" Tess asked, moving into my field of vision across the table from me. My eyes snapped open, meeting hers. "Diana, *no*. You've already depleted all your magic, there's nothing left. Your eyes..."

"We don't have another choice," I ground out, my teeth clenched.

"There's always another choice. Diana, there's nothing left but your life force. You can't do this." Tess' voice was panicked, but I could no longer see her. The only thing before my eyes was the swirling ember of magic as it flowed through my fingertips.

"Diana! Stop! If you give up your last ounce, it will be *your life* for his."

Her words sounded far away, as if I was under water and she was desperately trying to reach me from shore.

"Diana! Diana! Diana!"

There were other voices now, but I couldn't distinguish them. I felt hands clawing at mine, trying to scrape them away from Nik's chest, but I held fast.

If it was my life for his, I would give it. *I loved him.*

Didn't they understand?

Tears streamed down my cheeks in earnest, my hands glowing with amethyst magic where they connected with Nik's skin. His eyes were open now, the vibrant blue searching mine. His lips were moving, but I couldn't hear the words that were coming out of his mouth.

I smiled down at him, releasing one hand to run it through his blood-stained hair. He gripped my wrist tightly, and a surge of happiness swelled within me that he suddenly had the strength to do so.

It was working.

I would never recover if I didn't save him. The sight of his lifeless, dirt-stained, blood-soaked body with an arrow protruding from it would plague me forever. The feeling of his lips on mine, his fingers exploring my skin. I would never be able to let him go.

Never.

I would forever be *haunted* by the memory of him. By the loss of him. By all the what-ifs and could've beens. Even if he didn't feel the same.

I would *never* survive the loss of him.

Despite having pushed my feelings towards him *down* and *down* and *down* these past few months, they all came bubbling to the surface now. I loved him, and I wouldn't let him go.

I wasn't sure if the conscious part of me realized my strength was weakening as I pulled on that ember of magic, my knees buckling as I fell to the floor. My wrist was still tight in Nik's grip.

All I could hear was my name, *over and over again,* as my vision went dark.

28

Of two things I was certain. One: the darkness had swallowed me, and it had spit me back out. I had survived. Two: there truly *was* a limit to how much magic I could wield.

When the darkness engulfed me, I had no idea how long I had been down there. When I woke, I was in an infirmary of sorts, though different from the one at the safe house. In the end, I hadn't given my last ember of energy to Nik. I hadn't needed to. Liss had broken the connection between us before I had the chance and healed him.

Zion and Puck had found her.

My first words were for Nik, asking where he was. If Liss had made it in time. I couldn't describe the immense relief I felt when they told me she did. Nik was still weak, and I hadn't seen him, but he was *alive*. The dread I had felt in that moment, when he had stopped breathing, had threatened to consume me.

To tear my heart from my chest.

I hadn't even realized how strong my feelings were before that moment, before the threat of losing him had almost drowned me.

My second words were for my jacket, which had been taken from me when they had washed me and dressed me in a hospital gown. The key spell was still tucked away in the jacket pocket, and I would be damned if we almost lost that, too.

I was weak from pulling on the ember of my life and was in no position to travel yet, but one thing was certain: we needed to get out of Prins as soon as possible. Saanvi and Kenna had confirmed that the streets were flooded with Nightshade soldiers searching for us. They had collected our dead while I had been unconscious, and it made me sick to think I hadn't been awake to help.

To see how many had given their lives for our cause.

To defeat Donika once and for all.

I would never get those two days back that I laid motionless in the hospital bed, drained of energy and magic. Donika knew where we were now, and we needed to collect our dead and move on before she sent another force after us.

They had laid Tyr to rest, and I hadn't been there for that, either. I said a silent prayer that he would forgive me, if we ever met again. That the mother would protect him and watch over him. He was innocent, and he deserved his final rites. He had been only a boy, and his life had been needlessly snuffed out.

As had so many others.

It wasn't lost on me that I had killed our own when my storm had turned on me, controlling me and filling me with a bloodlust I had never known before. The grief from those events weighed on me each and every day I spent recovering in the hospital. That I was no better than Donika…that I had killed innocents, occupied my every thought.

We had lost a lot of lives during the battle, but Donika's army had lost more. We knew her numbers were much greater than those she sent to fight us, but the thought of her remaining soldiers returning with their tails tucked between their legs brought a small smile to my lips.

Liss had a place in Siraleth where we would be safe, and Donika wouldn't be searching for us there. We were splitting up, most of the resistance staying here in the city, and the council and a few other members traveling to Siraleth. Siraleth was still in ruins. There wasn't enough housing there for all of us.

Isaac's friend had secured several safe houses to split up the remainder of our numbers here in Prins, but we would need to keep a low profile. Liss' place in Siraleth was close to the portal, so we could use that to our advantage if need be. One thing we could be certain of after all of this was that Donika herself wasn't able to travel to the mortal realm.

Her soldiers could follow us there, *but she couldn't.*

We needed time to heal and regroup, and we couldn't do that under the watchful eyes of her spies. I was desperate to see Nik, but they hadn't let me leave my hospital bed in days. I still felt weak, my limbs heavy, and my magic was almost…*sore.* As if it hurt to pull on it, and it needed its own time to heal.

When I first awoke, I felt *nothing*, and I feared my magic would never come back to me. That it would rebuke me for trying to give it away in order to save Nik's life.

As it turns out...my magic had a soft spot for him, too.

Tess had returned to the town house with a heavy guard to retrieve the grimoire. It hadn't wanted to go with her at first, giving her quite the difficult time, but it eventually relented. It was safely tucked beneath my hospital pillow, and it was the only thing I truly needed when we traveled to Siraleth.

I had tucked the key spell back into the front of the book, and the next time I had gone to open it, the spell was right where it should have been all along. There was no longer a tear in the pages, as if it had never been missing at all. Liss had some knowledge about this particular spell, and I couldn't wait to get to Siraleth to pick her brain about it. I wasn't good at staying put and resting. I was anxious to get back to work. To regain my strength, master this key spell and find a loophole to bind my magic, and come up with a new plan of attack.

I wouldn't let Donika win.

I had killed Fletcher, and I hoped at least *that* had sent her a message.

I was not backing down.

The members of the resistance felt the same, their thirst for Donika's blood renewed by the blood she had spilled that night in Prins. I still needed to find more literature on dream walking, and how Corian was able to find us in the first place. Liss said there was a library left untouched in Siraleth, filled with old tomes, and I was anxious to get my hands on them.

Tess hadn't left my side in the hospital, and I was happy to see Isaac and Zion's faces when they had visited me. Liss had visited me as well, but most of her time had been spent by Nik's bedside, healing him. It had taken a lot of her energy, too. She had been healing everyone since the battle, and she needed to let her magic recuperate. We were all feeling weakened and worn down in the days that followed.

A part of me wondered why Donika hadn't sent any Noctani or Araneoch to do her bidding. With her monsters in tow, she easily could have wiped out our entire resistance. Had she sent this force of soldiers as a test? To see how many of us there were that would stand against her?

Word had spread about the resistance after the battle, and our numbers were growing by the day, more and more Shades joining our forces. Those that had lost a loved one in the battle had chosen to take up arms against her, and we were thankful for those that chose to step up.

"Aren't you supposed to be resting?" Tess asked, glancing at me over the top of her magazine. She had her long legs stretched out in front of her on the hospital bed across from mine.

"I'm not sure how I'm supposed to get any *rest* with these fluorescent lights beaming into my eyeballs," I told her, crossing my arms and glaring at the ceiling pointedly.

Tess laughed, tossing the magazine to the foot of the bed. "Have you found anything in the grimoire about the dream walking?" she asked.

I shook my head. "I searched all morning and came up with nothing. I'm hoping the books Liss has in the library in Siraleth will help."

Tess nodded. "I, for one, can't wait for you to get better so we can get out of here."

"It isn't only *me* that is still weak," I reminded her.

"I know," she replied, swallowing hard. "There are so many here that aren't strong enough to travel."

But we wouldn't have to wait on them, since there was only a small contingency of us traveling to Siraleth.

The others didn't know where we were going. We wanted to keep our location as secret as possible, which meant only those of us going knew the details.

"When do you think we will leave?" I asked.

Tess got up from the bed across from me and sat at the end of mine with a deep sigh.

"I guess that all depends on you," she pointed out.

"And Nik," I added resolutely.

"I overheard Liss and Isaac talking. They said maybe we should go ahead without him, he hasn't healed enough to travel yet."

"We can't leave him here unprotected. He betrayed Donika, she will be searching for him as much as she is searching for me," I replied, my chest tightening.

"I know, but we might not have a choice. His injuries were...grave. You should be ready to go in a few days...and the longer we wait, the higher chance of her finding us again. Her Nightshade soldiers are crawling all over this city, it's only a matter of time. We have to get you out of here," Tess replied, giving my leg a squeeze over the blanket.

"Will they at least let me see him before we leave?" I asked, my voice hopeful despite myself.

I hadn't been strong enough to leave the infirmary myself, but Nik also hadn't woken yet. Liss had him heavily sedated to accelerate the healing process.

"I'm not sure," Tess replied honestly. "You know he hasn't woken yet and hasn't spoken to anyone."

I nodded, swallowing back the emotion that threatened to choke me. Isaac and Liss hadn't left his bedside, and I knew he was in good hands, but I wanted to see him myself. I couldn't help the guilt I felt that I had been able to heal *myself* but not him. That I hadn't listened to them...and burned my magic out in anger over Tyr's death.

Tess could guess the thoughts behind my eyes, and she met my gaze with a serious expression.

"We have to talk about what happened out there, on the battlefield."

"I know," I replied, fidgeting with my fingers in my lap.

I pressed my nail into my thumb hard enough to distract me, to hold back the tears that threatened to fall.

"What was that?" she asked, her voice soft. "It was almost like you couldn't hear us, like you weren't yourself."

"I wasn't," I admitted, meeting her sympathetic gaze. "It was as if my magic had completely taken over me, I couldn't think of *anything* but revenge. I was *mad* with rage."

"Another wonderful side effect of using too much storm magic? Like the storm turning on you?" she asked.

"I guess so," I replied, shrugging my shoulders. "We don't know enough about my magic to be certain. All I know is...I was completely taken over."

Tess nodded in understanding. "You said Liss will be able to help decipher the key spell?"

"Yes, she said she has seen it before," I replied hopefully. "Let's hope she can also find a loophole to the whole bloodline thing."

"Maybe it only needs a witch's bloodline, not necessarily the witch being bound," Tess suggested. "If that's the case, Nik and Warrick would work. They are blood."

I nodded, "I hope so. But they are cousins, not technically a direct bloodline."

"True," she replied, "but neither you nor I are fluent in Latin, we can't be sure."

"Also true," I laughed, hoping she was right.

"The sooner we figure that spell out and bind your magic, the better. We can't afford any more incidents." She glared at me pointedly.

Incidents. As if that's all it was.

I had struck Shades down where they stood, with a mere thought.

I met her gaze. "The sooner the better, indeed."

In the end, they didn't let me see Nik before we traveled to Siraleth. Liss and Isaac insisted that he needed his rest, and promised to stay at his bedside until he was ready to join us. That left Zion, Puck, Warrick, Saanvi, and Kenna to escort us across The Shadow and to our new residence in Siraleth. The portal in Prins was still being watched—we would have to make the journey to Siraleth on foot.

Zion knew the place we were going.

After a week I was still drained from having expended so much magic, but I was strong enough to make it the distance to Siraleth. Zion knew his way through The Shadow as well as anybody else, and at this point we had spent so much time passing through it I was beginning to know the way on my own. I recognized the places we had gone searching for Phineas Wolfe as we passed them and desperately hoped we didn't run into him or anyone from his crew.

Luck was on our side today and we made it through The Shadow without incident. We picked up a few new items of clothing and added some food and water to our packs on the far side of Prins before crossing the border into Siraleth.

There would be no merchants where we were going.

I recognized the twisting cobblestone streets as we made our way through the abandoned city, curious which of the houses that still stood would become our new residence. I was surprised when we stopped in front of a familiar wooden door.

A door that had once haunted my dreams.

I initially dreamed of this door leading to the laboratory where I found the book of shadows, but in reality, it was the doorway to an old white cottage.

Zion shouldered the door open, leaving his packs by the entryway. If I remembered correctly, this house served as an exceptionally strong magical tether, and it only had one bedroom.

"You know this place?" I asked Zion as I stepped over the threshold, the wave of magic traveling from my toes all the way to the top of my head.

As it had the first time I had been here, I sensed the magic in this place deep in my bones. Zion turned to me with sad eyes, his expression full of an emotion I couldn't quite place.

"This is where I raised Donika."

"Where you *what*?!" Tess asked, immediately stepping back out onto the brick front steps. "You don't think she would ever come back here?"

"She can't," he replied with a shake of his head. "This place is heavily warded with magic. She is never welcome back here."

Tess' expression was as shocked as I felt, but there was no denying the magic that surged through this cottage. Through the back window, above the kitchen sink, I could see an old willow tree that still stood in the backyard. A broken swing made of wood swayed from its limbs in the soft breeze.

This was where Zion had raised Donika.

Where he and my mother must have built a life...before Osiris.

I had questions bubbling to my lips but I choked them back, reading the expression on Zion's face. This was difficult for him, but he knew we would be safe here.

Safe from his daughter.

They had all claimed she wasn't always like this. I tried to imagine a younger Donika, playing with toys on the hardwood floor of the tiny bedroom, or swinging from the old willow tree out back. No matter how hard I tried to picture it, I couldn't. I couldn't believe an untainted version of Donika had *ever* existed. Her soul was blackened beyond measure, and there was no coming back from that.

I wondered if I dreamed of this place because of the link it held to my mother. She had lived here, once. She had returned here with me, before she had hidden me in the human realm, with a human family, to keep me safe from the war that raged in Istmere.

Zion stood in the foyer, but his mind was elsewhere.

Tess and I took our packs to the small bedroom off the entryway and settled them onto the bed.

My eyes immediately traveled to the small closet where Nik and I had hidden from the soldiers in Donika's army.

Where we had kissed.

Where I had first admitted my feelings for him.

Tess followed my line of sight, and a knowing expression crossed her face, but she said nothing.

"Where will Warrick, Saanvi, and Kenna stay?" Tess asked, glancing around the tiny cottage as if another bedroom might appear out of thin air.

When Zion didn't respond she stood before him, waving her hand in front of his vacant eyes. "Hello?"

"My apologies," Zion replied, his hand on his chest as he snapped back to reality. He was likely thinking of my mother. This would have been one of the last places he ever saw her. "This way."

We followed Zion to the back of the house and out the door to a small wooden porch. Zion knelt, his hand on the wood as he whispered a spell I had never heard before. As he finished the words, a trap door appeared in the porch wood. He tugged on it, descending a small set of stone stairs.

The walls were cinder block, and at the bottom of the stairs was a wooden door identical to the one at the front of the house. My heart stopped in my chest as I watched it swing open beneath Zion's touch, leading to a long, dark, corridor.

This was the door I had dreamed of.

I knew where the staircase at the end of the hallway would lead, down, down, down to a laboratory. *My mother's laboratory*. Where she left the grimoire for me to find. A hot tear streaked across my cheek, and I hastily brushed it away with the back of my hand.

We followed Zion down into the darkness, down the spiral staircase. As I had dreamed, the laboratory door was built seamlessly into the masonry. What I *hadn't* dreamed was that there was more than one door here. There was a window at the top of the corridor that let light spill down, illuminating the space in the afternoon sunlight. Torches against the wall flickered to life as Zion walked onward down the corridor.

We passed a library which had my heart pounding rapidly in my chest. Was this the library that Liss had been talking about? The one that would have all the answers I was searching for?

We turned a corner and several bedrooms branched off from this corridor. They had thick red curtains pulled back to allow the sun to stream in. The beds were canopies, draped in rich fabric and accented with delicate woodwork that wove together as if they were serpents. It reminded me of the staff Donika had carried the last time I saw her.

"Was this always here?" I asked as we continued onward.

This hidden section of the cottage felt entirely different, and much more gothic.

Zion shook his head, but didn't glance back. "Most of it was, but we added to it after the war, as a haven for Shades remaining in Istmere. Came in handy when we started the resistance."

I was happy to hear Donika had never stayed here, never walked *these* halls.

Never slept in these beds.

"You can choose any room you'd like," Zion called over his shoulder.

We reached the end of the hallway and Zion held his hand to the stone. Without whispering a spell, the stone opened beneath his touch, revealing a circular opening that led to a narrow, dark tunnel.

"If there are any problems, you'll escape through this tunnel, do you understand?" His eyes were trained on me as he held his hand to the stone.

I nodded in response. I didn't relish the idea of running, but we would have small numbers here in Siraleth. It was smart to have a hidden escape route.

"Where does it lead?" Saanvi asked from behind me.

"Out," was all Zion replied as he removed his hand from the stone.

The rock moved back into place, and it was invisible once more.

Tess and I decided to let Zion take the bedroom in the upstairs cottage, not wanting to stay anywhere shadowed by the memory of Donika. We chose rooms next to each other in the downstairs wing.

The bedrooms were nicer than anything I had ever experienced before, similar to an expensive gothic hotel. Each room had a window that overlooked the backyard, which must have been a spell since we were certainly underground at this point. The canopied beds were accompanied with matching wooden dressers, night chests, and each room had its own washroom.

The claw-foot tub was black as well, with the curling feet of a creature I couldn't quite identify. There were ample towels and toiletries available, and plain tunics and riding pants in each dresser. I used my magic to light a fire in the grate, thankful for the warm sensation that coursed through me again.

It had taken so long for my magic to come back, I was scared for a moment that it wasn't going to come back at all. I had spent *days* in the infirmary without any magic.

I took a long soak in the claw-foot tub, wrapping myself in one of the luxurious robes hanging on the back of the door. I hadn't wanted to spend the night alone, so I had convinced Tess to spend the night with me in my chosen room.

She crawled into the bed beside me, her hair still wet from her bath and leaving streaks of water across the silk pillowcase.

"I finally have a room all to myself and you make me share...again," she laughed, turning the lamp off on the night chest.

"It's only for tonight," I promised her.

The room was thrust into darkness and I closed my eyes, willing sleep to take me. I tossed and turned for hours, unable to find the rest I so desperately sought.

My only thoughts were for Nik, and when he would wake up.

If he would wake up.

29

The two weeks after leaving Prins had been *agony* waiting for an update from Liss and Isaac. I hadn't waited for Liss to tear apart the library in the cottage underground, pulling out any tome from the stacks that I thought might help me with deciphering the key spell or learning more about dream walking.

So far, I had come up empty.

Tess hadn't left my side despite libraries 'not really being her scene' and she combed through the books with me day and night to pass the time. We studied the spells in the Kotova grimoire, searching for anything that might help us to stop Donika and eliminate her dark creatures.

Zion was in and out, and we weren't sure where he was spending his time when he wasn't in the cottage. It had to be difficult for him, returning to a place filled with so many memories, both good and bad. I felt closer to my mom spending time here, knowing that she had once slept in these rooms, pored over these books, and walked these halls.

Each day that passed left a pit in my stomach as we didn't come any closer to deciphering the binding spell. If we weren't able to bind my storm magic, it would be useless when we finally made our move against Donika. I would either burn out from using too much, my storms would turn on me and steal my magic, or I would become the bloodthirsty shell I had during the last battle.

None of those were options when I faced Donika. I needed to be ready. I was anxious that Donika would make a move against us soon, having seen our weakness in numbers during the battle at Prins.

Tess snuck off with Puck, leaving me alone in the library. The afternoon sun beamed in from the window high above me, warming the side of my face.

The library had vaulted ceilings three stories high, with ladders to access the books higher up. I sat at a table in the center, memorizing the siphoning spell from the Kotova grimoire. I read the words over and over. If I could understand this spell, maybe I could understand how to dismantle Donika's Noctani.

They wouldn't be easy to kill, and I dreaded the day we would face them in battle.

The heavy library door creaked open, but I didn't glance up from the book of shadows. It had to be Tess, returning to help me. Saanvi and Kenna hadn't spent much time with us since arriving at the cottage, and Warrick was nowhere to be found. He was taking the battle at the safe house particularly hard. I suspected he had lost a loved one in the melee, but he hadn't been around for me to inquire about it.

A hand grasped my shoulder, and I turned in surprise, my arm immediately moving to block and shield defensively.

"I guess I *did* train you well," Nik laughed, rubbing the arm that I had blocked.

My eyes met his, and warmth pooled in my core, an extraordinary weight lifting off my chest.

He was ok. He was alive. And he was *here.*

"I—I'm sorry, you surprised me is all. I didn't know you were on your way, I hadn't heard from Isaac or Liss..." I trailed off.

He let out a soft hiss, his hand moving to his abdomen.

"Are you ok? Here—" I moved to pull the chair out next to me.

"I'm ok, Diana," he replied as he took the seat I offered.

I swiveled to face him, and his knee bumped mine as he did the same. He moved his hand to my knee and gave it a squeeze. "I'm fine."

"You don't look fine," I replied.

"That's exactly what every guy wants to hear," he laughed, wincing when the movement caused him another surge of pain.

"Should you have traveled this far?" I asked, my brow furrowed. "You don't appear healed enough to have traveled at all."

"Isaac and I rode on horseback. Much faster," he replied, lifting his shirt to show me the bandage wrapped around his waist. There was a small spot where red bloomed across it, but otherwise the wound was much smaller than I had anticipated.

"And your shoulder?" I asked, raising an eyebrow.

"Good as new," he replied, moving the neck of his shirt down to show me the wound where the arrow had pierced him.

This one was almost healed, not even requiring a bandage. He held his shirt there, and my eyes drifted to the tattoos that peeked out from his chest. He removed his hand, letting the shirt pull back into place with a grin.

"You should be resting," I pointed out, "have you picked out a room yet?"

"Right across from yours," he replied, a smile in his eyes. "The one next to you was already taken."

I cocked my head to the side giving him a sarcastic look. "How can you be so glib? You almost *died.* You—you stopped breathing. I watched helplessly as you *stopped breathing* and there was nothing I could do about it."

"You *did* do something about it, Diana. *You saved me.* You almost gave up your life ember for mine, and that has got to be the dumbest thing you have ever done."

I reared back at his words.

"I couldn't stand by and do *nothing* as you bled out on the dining room table in front of us." I shook my head, willing the tears that stung the back of my eyes to retreat.

"This war cannot be won without *you.* You are the strongest witch we have and the best chance of defeating Donika. Alastir didn't envision me ending this war, he saw you. Istmere would go on without me...but without you? What would happen to the people here?"

"I wasn't worried about that in the moment," I replied, my gaze moving to my hands clasped together in my lap.

As a queen...I should have been thinking about that. My first thought should have been for the people of Istmere...but it wasn't. My first thought had been that I would give up *anything*, even my own life, for Nik.

He reached across us and grabbed one of my hands, pulling it against him. I could feel his heart beating furiously under my touch. "You were worried about me?"

My gaze met his and his mouth turned into a wicked grin. "Be serious, Nikolai."

"I am being serious," he replied, his eyes darkening.

I snatched my hand back and shot him a scolding glare, but his grin only deepened.

"You have no idea how scared I was, that I was going to lose you." My voice was barely above a whisper.

His eyes were smoldering as they held mine, so much passing between us that neither of us could put into words. I had loved him, then hated him, then loved him again, and the emotions were battling each other inside of me. I would give anything to know what he was thinking in this moment.

The library door burst open, Puck and Tess spilling inside. They were hunched over in a fit of laughter until they saw Nik and I sitting together at the table.

They both sobered quickly.

"Aren't you supposed to be in Prins, mate?" Puck asked, walking towards us.

Tess gave me an apologetic half-smile. At least she was able to realize when she was interrupting something now.

"Isaac and I traveled back today," Nik replied, bumping his knee against mine again as he turned towards Puck and Tess.

"And Liss?" Tess asked, grabbing a seat across from me.

"She will be here tomorrow, there was something else she needed to take care of," he replied.

"How's the studying going?" Puck asked, his eyes roving over the Kotova grimoire. I could have sworn I saw it shake, threatening to close out of the corner of my eye.

"I've found nothing of value," I admitted. "I need Liss' help to decode the key spell, and I haven't found anything in this library about dream walking. If I had the powers Corian had, we would have even more of an advantage against them. There are too many damn books in this library."

Nik glanced around, realizing for the first time precisely how large this library truly was. "Indeed."

"I've made some progress with the translation for the key, but not much. Latin was never my strong suit, and I don't think it translates word for word."

"What have you got so far?" Puck asked, craning his neck to see my handwritten scribbles in the notebook.

"We know it's a binding spell, and that it requires a bloodline to bind, but I think this also says you must bind yourself to another person. Another Shade. That's all I've got," I replied.

"That should be easy, there's no lack of Shades around here," Puck replied with a laugh.

Tess elbowed him in the side and shot him a glare that said he was certainly not as funny as he thought he was.

"We can help search for the dream walking books," Tess offered, pushing her chair back and moving towards the ladder.

"But this man needs some rest," Puck replied, pointing at Nik as he moved around the side of the table. "You are in no condition to pore over these books all night."

"I'm not sure that requires much physical effort...but the travel did take a lot out of me," Nik replied, moving to stand.

He cradled his abdomen with his hand as I caught him wince again.

"We'll fill you in on what we find," I assured him with a smile. "Go get some rest."

"I'll catch up with you later?" he asked, his eyebrow raised.

"Sure," I agreed, nodding.

Puck helped Nik to his room, though I was sure it was only so they could talk alone. Nik was more than capable of walking across the hall by himself. Tess climbed the ladder and began tossing down any books that had to do with dream magic.

This was going to take all night.

Luckily Zion popped by with coffee for us right before midnight and we drank it as if it were a lifeline. Saanvi and Kenna returned and went straight to bed, exhausted from patrolling. Warrick was still nowhere to be found.

"This is it!" Tess announced, jumping up from her chair.

It ground against the floor with a screech, the sound sending a chill up my spine.

"It's what?" I asked, peering at her from over my book.

My eyes were bleary, my entire body tired from sitting in the uncomfortable library chairs all night.

"A whole chapter on dream walking!" Tess pushed the book across the table towards me and joined me on the other side.

I blinked back my exhaustion and studied the paragraph she pointed at, running my finger along the words as they threatened to blur together. It was way past the time when I should have gone to bed.

Dream walking is a rare ability for Shades and is thought to be genetically linked. This trait usually manifests within bloodlines. Dream walkers are not only able to see the past, but they are able to see events currently happening, in another place.

My eyes met Tess'. We hadn't known that. How would I be able to see the past? I kept reading, Tess peering at the text over my shoulder.

Dream walkers can physically touch, remove, and alter physical objects and people when they are in a current *event. A dream walker can take an object or a person out of the dream with them.*

I could take *a person* with me? Like a portal? That could be immeasurably valuable, if only I knew how to do that. When I had taken the grimoire...I hadn't even realized I had done it.

A dream walker can determine the precise location of the event they walked into by leaving a token either in the location or on a person present, then channeling magic into *that token.*

To take objects or people out of a dream one would simply secure the object or person and wake up, but waking up is not always easy as dream walking is not always intentional. Often times a dream pulls you into an event on its own, but you can dream walk intentionally.

To wake up from a dream you have been pulled into you need to be self-aware that you are dream walking, or have someone on the outside wake your physical body.

To dream walk intentionally, one needs to draw on their ember of magic, think of the person or place they want to walk with, and recite the dream spell. The only caveat to this is that if another dream walker is present where you walk, they will be able to see you and know that you are there.

When you dream walk, those around you cannot see you except those with the same dream walking ability. If a dream walker is connected to a non-dream walking Shade, that is the only way a person without this ability might be able to see and touch the dream.

You cannot pull another person into the dream with you against their will...

"I'm going to assume the dream spell is somewhere in this text?" Tess asked, her brow furrowed.

"I hope so," I mused, shaking my head. "This has all the information we have been searching for, this is *amazing*, Tess."

Tess grinned down at me, happy to have finally found something useful to us. It had only taken us almost three weeks.

"I've got to study this, but I'm too tired to do it now. We need to keep it somewhere safe."

"Especially since it doesn't appear to have a mind of its own like the book of shadows," Tess pointed out.

I nodded. "Yes. In the wrong hands this could be dangerous. My only consolation is that I know Corian isn't watching us right now, or spying on our council meetings. If he were, I would know he was here."

"Agreed," Tess replied. "At least there's that."

"To track our location Corian must have left a token at the townhouse." I sighed, pinching the bridge of my nose.

Had I seen anything that appeared out of place when Corian had seen me at the town house? Anything that might have been a token he left behind? If Donika was able to speak with me in the dream, that meant she and Corian were connected somehow.

This book also confirmed Corian *hadn't* pulled me into the dream against my will after all, he was simply dream walking in the location that I was already physically in. They must have been searching for us and happened to get lucky.

"But the townhouse wasn't close to the new safe house, how would Fletcher have found it? He *did* say Corian sent him, right?" Tess asked.

"He did," I confirmed. "It must have been luck? Unless he somehow placed a token on my person, and I had no idea. Once he found out we were in Dragon's Hollow, maybe he sent soldiers to search for us. Maybe someone saw one of us going there. I'm not sure."

I pressed my pen into the spine of the book to hold my place and gently closed it, setting it atop the Kotova grimoire to bring it back to my room.

"There's too much to go through tonight, it'll have to wait until tomorrow." I grabbed the books and pressed them to my chest, making my way towards the library door as I stifled another yawn.

"What did I interrupt with Nik earlier?" Tess asked as she held the door open for me.

Our voices lowered now that we were in the hallway, only separated from Nik by the bedroom door.

"It was nothing, we haven't spoken since..." my voice trailed off as I met Tess' gaze.

"Since you almost sacrificed your life for his and destroyed any chance we had of defeating Donika?" Tess offered with a sarcastic smile.

"Yeah...that," I replied curtly. "But it was nothing."

"Whatever you say, witch," Tess replied with a wink.

I opened the door to my bedroom with my elbow and tucked the two books at the bottom of my underwear drawer. I lit the fire in the fireplace, took a long soak in the claw-foot tub. By the time I wrapped myself in my robe and prepared for bed I was restless.

It had to be past three in the morning at this point, but despite my better judgement I found myself sneaking across the hall, my hand poised to knock on the door across from mine.

I opened my mouth to say something, but I couldn't gather the courage. I dropped my hand back to my side and shuffled back across the hallway, my slippers scuffling against the stone floor.

I paused with my hand on the door handle, glancing back at Nik's door once more over my shoulder. There was no way he was awake at this hour, and whatever it is I wanted to say to him could wait until morning. I wasn't even sure what it was that had brought me here, had pulled me towards his door.

With a sigh I turned the knob and returned to bed.

Sleep didn't take me until close to five in the morning. When it did finally pull me under, I could only dream of black tourmaline eyes, lifeless and unending, with a shock of white-blue hair.

Liss had joined us in the cottage underground the next day, but she had been spending her nights in the single bedroom upstairs with Zion. Tess and I had speculated whether she was involved with Zion or Isaac, and I think we had our answer.

Tess and I had examined the dream walking book endlessly over the next week, learning everything we could to be prepared should we face Corian again. He was sneaky, and I didn't want to underestimate his place in this war. He was Donika's right hand now that Zion left her, and he was connected to Donika herself, making him a dangerous enemy.

Nik had healed rapidly over the last week, no longer requiring the bandages to cover the wound on his abdomen. His strength was returning, and he had even joined us in the sparring ring outside to watch and give us pointers. It was the only time we had spoken since being interrupted in the library, and we hadn't had any time alone.

Warrick had returned, but still hadn't spoken with anyone but Puck, who confirmed he had lost family in the battle. He had locked himself in his room and Zion had asked us to leave him be. I couldn't imagine what he might be going through and wanted him to know that he wasn't alone. He had friends that he could lean on.

We had been bringing him his meals and leaving him little notes, and each day the trays were returned empty. It gave me some solace that he was eating, at least.

He hadn't joined our sparring circles, which left Puck to lead the training on the days Nik wasn't well enough to join us. We had come a long way, but needed to keep up our strength. I was strong enough to take Saanvi on and *almost* win...but she was *fast.*

Nine lives and all.

That night when we left the training room Liss was in the library, studying and deciphering the key spell. Tess and I quickly bathed, changed, and joined her at the table where books were stacked high enough that you couldn't see the person sitting across from you.

"Any luck with the translation?" Tess asked as I followed her into the library, the heavy door swinging shut behind us.

I tossed my still wet auburn hair over my shoulder as I glanced at Liss' notebook, the translation almost complete.

"I'm not sure I'd call it luck," Liss replied with a smile, the wrinkles at the corner of her eyes crinkling as she peered up at us. "But I think I have everything we need to understand it."

"What did you find?" I asked, taking the seat next to her.

"I'm afraid I don't have the best news..." her voice trailed off as her gaze lingered on the page of the notebook before her.

I picked up the Kotova grimoire, flipping to the key spell and setting it down on the table before us. It felt as if the serpentine silver key was staring back at me from its place on the page.

"Have you found out how to remove the key from the book of shadows?" I asked, inclining my head.

"Yes," she replied curtly.

When she didn't expand, Tess cut in. "Well?" she asked, shaking her head with wide eyes.

Leave it to Tess to be impatient.

"As you already found out from Phineas Wolfe, the key to this spell, no pun intended, is binding. It requires a bloodline for the binding, two distinct generations. The blood must come from the one who will be bound, and the generation before or after her."

"The blood?" Tess asked, her eyebrows raised.

"This is blood magic?" I asked, resting my arm across the table.

Liss nodded. "I'm afraid so. Binding in and of itself is a dark magic."

I deflated with a sigh, resting my chin on the hand I'd propped on the table. We had figured as much but were hoping desperately for a loophole. There was no generation before or after me, and *creating* a generation after me certainly wasn't an option. Which meant we wouldn't be able to bind the spell, because both my mother and my father were dead.

What were we going to do with my storm magic being so unpredictable? With it threatening to turn on me, or take me over entirely?

"What options does that leave us?" Tess asked, her hand on the back of my chair.

"None, I'm afraid," Liss replied, her voice tight.

"Can I hear about the rest of the spell, anyway?" I asked, my voice soft.

It could still help someone else, at least.

Liss nodded, "I think the grimoire sent you the vision as a warning of sorts...about what was to come with your magic."

"Not much of a warning if I had no idea what it was trying to convey," I pointed out.

Liss let out a soft laugh. "The visions they send us don't always make sense in the moment, but they do in time. This spell is not particularly difficult to execute once you have the bloodline. The one who needs to be bound will delve into the grimoire and pick up the key. The bloodline and the one who will bind to the storm witch will pour their blood over the key as a sacrifice to the magic."

"Wait a second...it isn't only binding your magic, but binding it to another person?" I asked.

"Yes," Liss nodded, pointing out this line in her notebook. "The magic becomes a shared burden when the magic is bound. It is shared between two souls, two life embers. A binding of this nature can only be done willingly on both parts. Once bound, the magic will be shared between the two, a balance of sorts."

I pressed my fingers to the bridge of my nose as I took in everything she was saying. "Can it be any witch who agrees to be bound to you?"

Liss shook her head, moving her hand down to point to a passage further down the page. "The souls to be bound must have some kind of connection to each other. Not a blood connection necessarily, the bloodline is only required to perform the spell, but it can't be a perfect stranger either. One magic must recognize the other for the binding to take."

"Would a friend work?" Tess offered.

Liss nodded. "Yes, a friend would work. But the key is for the magic to be equally matched. If the Stormshade is so powerful that they need their magic to be bound in the first place, they would need to find another powerful witch willing to share the burden of the magic."

"So many conditions," Tess complained, plopping herself down into the chair across from me and moving the stack of books so she could see us clearly.

"This isn't easy magic, that's for sure. This is a complex spell with a lot of requirements, and unfortunately even if we had someone to bind you to, we don't have a bloodline." Liss didn't look up from her notebook, her eyes glued to the words on the page.

"Have you told Isaac and Zion yet?" I asked, suddenly exhausted.

"Not yet," Liss replied, "I haven't seen them yet today."

The sun had set during our conversation, the darkness visible from the window nestled among the vaulted ceiling. Liss must have been here all day deciphering this spell...all for nothing.

Until I had a child of my own, I wouldn't be able to perform this spell.

We needed to move against Donika soon, she was already escalating. Murdering innocents, experimenting on others, and turning them into monsters. Her control on this realm needed to cease, she had ruled with a dark and bloody hand for far too long.

"Do we have any other options?" I asked, only a small spark of hope still lit within my chest.

Liss shrugged, meeting my eyes. "I'm not sure. Where did you say you heard about this spell again?"

"Alastir, the seer. He told us the answers I was searching for would be with Phineas Wolfe. He had the spell from when he stole it from the grimoire, and the spell...well...it chose to come back with me. I found it in my jacket pocket after our meeting with Phineas."

"Phineas..." Liss mused, searching the recesses of her mind. "The name sounds familiar to me."

"You know him?" Tess asked.

"I'm not sure," Liss admitted. "But I know Alastir, he is one of the last seers left in Istmere. He must have sent you down this path for a reason."

"Maybe we can visit him again?" Tess offered hopefully.

"I'm not sure it's wise to return to Prins until things die down. We safely moved our numbers and scattered them across the city, but when I left, Donika's soldiers were still crawling all over the city."

“Maybe there is something else in one of these books, we can keep digging,” I replied, my eyes traveling to the tomes stacked stories high. “Do we have any other family grimoires we could consult?”

“We don’t have mine, but I do believe Zion has his. Maybe there is something to be found there,” Liss replied.

I nodded. “We should spend the next several days studying it. I’ve pored over the Kotova grimoire for hours and hours, I don’t think there’s anything else in there to help us at this point.”

Tess and Liss nodded in agreement.

“I’ll go ask him for it,” Liss offered, pushing back her chair to stand.

“Will it let us read it?” I asked, turning towards her as she made her way towards the door. “The Kotova grimoire is a bit picky, what about Zion’s?”

“His book of shadows is not...sentient...as yours is,” Liss assured me with a smile before shouldering open the library door and disappearing down the hallway.

I slumped down into my chair, my mind utterly exhausted and defeated. It felt as if every time we took a step forwards, we took three steps back.

“What now?” Tess asked, drumming her fingers against the table.

“I guess we tell Nik and Puck the news. Do you know where they are?” I asked.

“They both retired for the night. Nik is doing much better, but the sparring session took a lot out of him,” she replied.

"I'll loop Nik in, you'll tell Puck?" I asked, winking at her as I pushed my chair out to stand.

"You want a moment alone with lover boy," she teased, following me to the door.

"Or I'm simply being a good friend and giving you some time alone with your *boyfriend*," I pointed out.

"You are a good friend," she replied, forcefully planting a kiss on my cheek and shaking my shoulders in her tight grip. "I wouldn't trade you for anyone."

"I certainly hope not." I laughed, passing through the library door and into the hallway.

"Even if you did drag me into the middle of a decades old war against the dark queen who wants to see us dead," Tess threw over her shoulder as she made her way down to Puck's room.

"Yeah, because that's my fault," I called down to her, rolling my eyes.

She blew me a kiss, disappearing behind Puck's door without knocking. They had been inseparable these past few weeks, and things were getting serious between them. I was happy Tess had found someone she liked this much, I had never seen her settle down with one guy before Puck.

I paused before Nik's door.

As it had the other night, my panic rose within my throat, threatening to strangle me. My hand was poised to knock, but some buried piece of me couldn't bring myself to do it.

As I was about to turn, the door flew open before my raised hand, my mouth opening in surprise.

"Diana?" Nik asked, his hair shaggy as if he had recently gotten out of the shower and towel dried it.

"Obviously," I smirked, dropping my hand to my side.

"I was about to come to you," he replied, gesturing towards my door across the hall.

"I just finished with Liss and wanted to update you on the key spell."

"Sure," he replied with a nod, standing to the side to allow me to pass. "Come on in."

Nik's bedroom was set up much the same as mine was, a canopy bed draped in linens with a fireplace and a washroom. His sheets were black and made of silk, the bed unmade and rumpled. I perched on the edge of it as Nik knelt before the fire, stoking its flames.

"What did you find out with Liss?" he asked over his shoulder, not turning to meet my gaze.

Things had been...awkward and tense since our talk in the library. We hadn't spoken alone since then, and we hadn't addressed everything that had happened during the battle in Prins. It felt as if it was hanging in the empty air between us, a tangible, heavy weight.

I swallowed, fidgeting my fingers in my lap as I spoke. "We learned that it *does* require a bloodline from the Stormshade to be bound, either the generation before or after."

Nik turned his face so that I could see his profile, and his expression fell. He had been hoping there had been a loophole in that, too.

"What else?" he asked, pushing the poker back into the fire.

"She also said that the spell is blood magic, that most binding spells are. This spell doesn't simply bind one's magic, it binds your magic to another person. Another *willing* person, who also must be a powerful witch in their own right. It strikes a balance, and the two witches share the burden of the storm magic."

Nik nodded, standing from his crouched position, his back still turned towards me.

"Anything else?" he asked, his eyes on the flickering flames.

I squinted at his back, wondering why he wouldn't face me. Were things so irreparably broken between us? Did he feel...awkward that I had tried to save his life by offering mine? Guilty?

I shook my head, trying to focus on the conversation at hand.

"That's all, really. She told us Zion has his own book of shadows, so we are going to study that and see if there is anything there that might help us. But we might be shit out of luck."

My palms were beginning to sweat, and I rubbed them against my jeans to dry them.

"There's always another way," he replied, his mouth tight as he turned his face to the side.

"Is there?" I asked, my voice desperate. "Because I am starting to think you might have to win this war without me."

"That isn't an option," he replied, finally turning to face me.

His skin was flushed from facing the fire, his cheeks pink. His hands were stuffed into his jean pockets, his shoulders tight.

"It's not as if we have a choice, here. If we can't bind my magic, I can't use it. You saw what it did to me out on the battlefield, and while I was training with Isaac. It will either turn on me and hurt me, or take me over completely, turning me into someone else *entirely*."

"There has to be another option," he insisted, a muscle feathering in his jaw.

"I hate to break it to you, but we might need to come up with a plan B. Things aren't exactly looking up for plan A, and Donika is murdering innocents and experimenting on them by the dozen. Day after day. She needs to be stopped, and we are running out of time. Either we move against her, or she moves against us. Right now...we are weak."

"Nothing about you is weak," he replied, taking a step towards me.

I shook my head, standing from the bed. "I *am* weak if I cannot control my magic. We have nothing else in our arsenal that can take on Donika, and we need to seriously think about what we plan to do next."

"You are many things, firecracker, but *never* weak," his voice was low. Dangerous.

I took an involuntary step backwards, my knees hitting the back of the bed. Nik smirked, his head cocked to the side.

"Are we ever going to talk about it?" he asked, an eyebrow raised.

"Talk about what?" I replied cooly.

"About how you almost gave your life up for mine? About how you almost *died* saving me? About how you fought with more bravery than I have ever seen, even when you weren't raised to fight? About how you slayed your enemies without a second thought?"

I shook my head, biting back the frustration gnawing at my insides. "I did what you trained me to do."

"I trained you to sacrifice your life for mine?" he asked, his voice incredulous.

"I'm sorry if it makes you feel...awkward...or indebted to me in some way. I didn't do it to make you feel *uncomfortable*, I just couldn't stand to see one more person I care about die," I seethed.

"You think I feel *awkward*?" he asked, taking another step towards me. "*Uncomfortable*?"

"I don't know how you feel," I replied, my voice raised. "Just a few seconds ago you couldn't even look at me."

"Did it ever occur to you that I couldn't look at you because *I almost lost you, too?*" His voice was ragged. "That I held you in *my* arms as the life bled from you?"

"Why would that matter?" I asked, searching his crystal blue eyes.

He was so close to me that I could smell the cinnamon on his breath, the sweet smell of the bodywash he had used on his skin. His mouth turned up into a twisted smile, his eyes sparked with anger. I would have taken another step backwards, but my knees were pressed up to the edge of the bed as far as I could go.

"*Why would that matter?"* he shook his head, running a hand through his hair. "You seriously don't understand, do you?"

"Don't understand what?" I asked defensively.

"That *I'm in love with you*," he replied tightly, his jaw clenched. "That I would have *never* forgiven myself if you had died by Fletcher's blade, or given your life for mine. That I wouldn't want to live in this life without you."

I opened my mouth to reply, but words escaped me.

"You seriously didn't know?" he asked, his eyes burning with regret.

I shook my head back and forth, avoiding his gaze. His chest rose and fell with rapid breaths as I tried to gather my thoughts, to make sense of this.

I had pushed him away *so many times*, I never imagined he would feel the same way about me ever again. I had rebuked him time and time again, told him I hated him and would never trust him again. I never had a hope that things could be repaired between us.

I met his gaze again, my eyes gleaming with unshed tears. "I didn't know. That moment in the gym...at the safe house...I thought that was only a moment of lust and passion that we both gave in to."

Nik flinched back, his mouth tense. He paused, holding my gaze before he spoke. "I understand if you don't feel the same."

He turned to step away, but I caught him by the front of his t-shirt in a tight grip. His eyes traveled down to my hand, then back up to mine, but I didn't release my hold on him.

I swallowed hard, a thousand emotions battling for space within me.

Nik loved me.

We had been through hell and back, and Nik *still* loved me.

And I had come back to him. After everything.

And I loved him.

"It's *you* who doesn't understand," I told him, tightening my grip on his shirt.

I held his gaze as my own swam with tears. His usual sarcasm and bravado were nowhere to be found in his expression. The only thing left was raw, stripped, and full of emotion. I held his heart in the palm of my hand, and he had trusted me with it. A tear slid free, trailing down my cheek. Despite himself he reached out, palming my cheek to wipe the tear away gently with his thumb.

"Why do you think I was willing to give my life for yours? You think I would do that for anyone? I couldn't *stand* the thought of losing you. When you stopped breathing I—" my words cut off on a choked sob.

Nik's other hand moved to my neck, holding my face up to his.

"When you stopped breathing, I lost a piece of myself. I didn't want to be here without you, and I was *desperate* to give you any last ounce of magic I had left. To *save* you. To *heal* you."

"I thought you hated me." His voice was soft as his eyes roved over my face, a touch of disdain lacing his words.

"I did, you idiot. But not anymore." I shook my head, more tears wetting my cheeks. "Not anymore."

"Tell me how to fix this, Diana. Because I can't do this without you. I don't want to. I love you, and I *need* you. In this life and every after, mother save me. *It's only you.*"

An ugly laugh escaped me as I choked back another sob. Nik wiped away the tears as they fell.

"There's nothing to fix, Nik. I forgive you. I forgive you for *everything*, and I need you, too. I love you. *In this life and every after.*"

Nik let out a sigh of relief, the heavy weight between us lifting. I felt weightless for the first time in a long time, and the hungry expression in Nik's gaze told me he felt the same.

His touch alone was setting my skin aflame, and when he cocked his head to the side, his mouth curving into a wicked smile and his eyes darkening, warmth pooled low in my core.

All thoughts escaped me as desperate, unbridled, *want* replaced everything else.

And then his mouth was crashing into mine.

31

When Nik's lips met mine, my thoughts were consumed by him.

His mouth.

His skin.

His touch.

His presence was *everywhere.* He kissed me as if he was starving, devouring every inch of my skin with his mouth. My hands ran across his back and dipped under his t-shirt, exploring the hard planes of muscle there.

He pushed me back onto the bed, gasping as our mouths found each other's again. My auburn hair swirled behind me on the black silk sheets. They felt cool against my burning, flushed skin.

"I love you, Diana," Nik spoke into my mouth, "I love you."

His mouth moved to my neck as he tasted everything in his path.

"I love you, too." My voice was breathy, my hands buried in his hair.

Nik pulled back, meeting my gaze. "Tell me if you want me to stop."

I gripped his shirt and pulled him back down to me, my voice gruff in his ear. "Don't ever stop."

Nik needed no further encouragement, his mouth finding mine once again as I pulled at his T-shirt. We broke apart for only a moment, long enough for me to slip the white fabric over his head and toss it to the floor.

A soft gasp escaped me as I saw the scars left behind from the battle marring his tanned skin. I ran a finger along the mark where the arrow had pierced him, reaching up to kiss the spot that could easily have taken his life if it had been an inch to the left. My hands traveled down his torso, goosebumps raising on his skin at my feather light touch.

He watched me, eyes blazing.

My fingers found the linear scar on his lower abdomen, the one that had come inches from taking his life. He had stopped breathing, and the thought of almost having lost him had tears swimming in my eyes once more.

"Diana, I'm fine. I'm fine. *You saved me.*" His voice cracked as his hand gripped mine, placing a kiss in the center of my palm.

He pinned that hand to the bed while my other explored him, my fingers running over his taut muscles. I explored the hard planes of his chest, moving my fingers down to the rippled muscles of his abdomen before reaching his belt.

My fingers stilled as I glanced up at him, a playful smile on my lips.

"*Impatient*," he whispered.

His hand released mine, and I sat up halfway beneath him as he peeled my jacket and t-shirt off, tossing them to the floor. I laid back against the bed and his mouth found mine, his fingers exploring my skin.

His hand traveled from my neck down to my collarbone. It traced along my shoulder, over my breast and down to my navel. He parted my legs with his and slid his thigh between them, grinding against my core.

I let out a soft gasp and the corner of his mouth lifted into a smile.

"I want *all of you*, Diana."

"You have all of me," I told him. "Always."

His fingers found the buttons of my jeans and I helped him pull them off, tossing them out of the way, too. I reached for the buckle of his belt, and this time he let me. He watched as I pushed the jeans off him, holding his gaze. He kicked them off before bending over me again.

"Black?" he asked, raising an eyebrow as he ran a finger under my bra strap.

A blush rushed to my cheeks as he played with the material.

"Intoxicating," he whispered in my ear, placing a kiss against each flushed cheek.

His hips ground into mine, and I could feel the hard length of him between us. My hands moved to his back to pull him closer. The feel of his skin against mine set me on fire, and magic sparked to my fingertips of its own volition.

Nik's eyes turned molten as he felt the heat from my fingertips, the faint sparks stinging his skin.

"Naughty little witch," he crooned, his hand moving up my thigh, higher and higher. My core was liquid heat, his touch sending me into a frenzy.

He held my gaze as he dipped a finger under the rim of my underwear, exploring me for the first time. I let out a soft gasp as he immediately found the most sensitive place, his thumb working the bundle of nerves.

"Nik," I breathed as I ground against him, my voice raspy.

"Do you like that, firecracker?"

"Yes," I hissed, spreading my legs wider for him.

"That's my good little witch." His voice was soft in my ear as he kissed my jaw, his mouth moving to my neck.

He slipped a finger inside of me and I moved against him, wanting *more.* I was slick with desire, and Nik's mouth curved into a smile that I could feel against my skin at the effect he had on me.

"You have no idea how many times I have thought about this," he breathed against my skin.

"What else have you thought about?" I asked, my breathing rapid as he worked his fingers against me. Inside me.

He slipped another finger inside of me, and my hips bucked against him. I threw my head back, my eyes squeezing shut. I had *never* felt pleasure like this before.

"Eyes on me, firecracker, and I'll show you."

His reply was ragged as he lifted me, sliding the underwear off me. He sat back, taking his time pulling them down my legs. He planted a gentle kiss on my ankle before tossing the fabric to the floor.

His hand reached around my back to unhook my bra with one hand, and he tossed that to the floor as well.

I was left bare before him, and for a moment, a wave of self-consciousness rolled over me. I had never been entirely naked in front of anyone before. My eyes met his, and every trace of doubt was erased as I drank in his expression.

His mouth was parted as if on a sigh. He ran his tongue over his lips hungrily. His eyes were eager as they explored my body, traveling up to meet my gaze.

"*So* fucking beautiful," he breathed.

I reached for the band of his underwear to slide them off, but he shook his head. "Not yet."

His hands moved to my thighs where he gripped them, sliding me down on the bed closer to him. My legs were spread before him, and my breath caught in my throat as he planted a kiss on the inside of my knee, moving towards my center.

His eyes were on mine as he placed a final kiss on my thigh before kissing *between* my thighs. The feel of his tongue sent a shock through me, and I buried my hands in his hair. A soft moan escaped my lips as his tongue dipped inside of me, worked against me. He sucked on the most sensitive part of me, and I almost came undone, so close to the edge I was about to go rushing over.

"That feels so good," I cried, my head thrown back.

He chuckled against me, the sound sending a vibration through my core. He slid a finger inside of me and continued to work me with his tongue, the feeling sending a rush of heat across my skin.

I was so close to the edge, about to go soaring over. Nik's touch undid me, and I writhed beneath him.

"Nik I—" but my words were cut off as I went tumbling over the edge, my hands fisted in the sheets as I cried out, my head thrown back.

Wave after wave of pleasure pulled me under, and I bit my lip as his movements slowed. Nik lifted his head, licking his lips with a wicked smile. He licked each of his fingers, his eyes smoldering as they held mine.

"My turn," I replied, sitting up and pushing him back against the bed.

His smile deepened as I straddled him, the center of me grinding into him. I kissed his neck, biting him gently as I moved down to his shoulder. My hardened nipples grazed against his chest as I ran my fingers along his abdomen, planting soft kisses in a trail towards his navel, my lips lingering on the scar that almost took his life.

My fingers hooked under the lip of his underwear, and I slid them off. He sprang free, and my mouth parted in surprise. He was bigger than I expected. I licked my hand before grabbing the length of him, my eyes on his.

At the first touch, his hips bucked against me, and he let out a soft moan, his head propped on his bent arm as he watched me. I slid my hand from base to tip, smearing the bead of liquid there with a grin.

"Wicked little witch," he hissed, his eyes darkening.

My hand slid back and forth over him as I lowered my mouth to his skin, planting a trail of kisses across his stomach. My eyes were on his as my mouth found him, my tongue flicking over the tip of him, tasting him.

"*Diana,*" he growled, his hand in my hair.

"Do you like that?" I asked, my eyes blazing with desire.

"There is *nothing* I could love more," he replied, his voice raspy as he watched me.

"Nothing?" my smile was sinful as I closed my mouth around him, taking more of him.

I used my hand to work him simultaneously, and Nik ran a hand through his hair before he fisted it in the sheets, his eyes never leaving mine.

I savored the salty taste of him and closed my eyes as I moved my mouth over him, taking as much of him as I could. Nik's hand moved from the sheets to my hair, where he held firmly but gently as he guided my head over him.

I lifted my head, my eyes on his as I licked my lips, just as he had.

"You are going to *undo me,*" he growled as he grabbed me and flipped me over to lie on my back.

"I like the taste of you," I whispered, digging my fingernails into his back as he pressed against me.

I could feel his hard length against my thigh, and I reached between us to grab hold of it again. I moaned as he thrust his hips against me, sliding his length over my core and the wetness there.

"So wet for me," he crooned, his forehead against mine.

I lined him up with my center and my wide eyes met his.

"Are you sure, Diana?" he asked, his voice gentle, his breath smelling of cinnamon as it fanned across my face.

I nodded, my other hand moving to cup his cheek. "I'm sure. I want *all of you*, Nikolai."

His eyes gleamed as he looked down at me. "I love you, Diana."

"I'm yours," I replied, releasing my hand from his length as he slowly pushed into me.

There was a pressure, then a sharp pain, my thighs gripping against him, my nails on his back. He stayed like that without moving, filling me, waiting for me to adjust to the feel of him inside of me. I ran my hands through his hair as I held his gaze. A calmness settled over me, as if there was nothing more *right* in the world.

Nik and I together.

I nodded softly, and he began to move, the pain becoming a dull ache, then disappearing entirely as I became accustomed to the feel of him. His strokes were gentle at first, but as I began to moan against him and dig my nails into his back, he quickened his pace. His hands were planted on either side of me, his face buried in my shoulder as he tasted my skin.

I squeezed my thighs against him as his movements turned to pleasure, the feel of him inside of me sending a hot wave coursing through me. I buried my hands in his hair as he kissed my neck, my jaw, my ear, my cheek. His mouth found mine again, and he kissed me ravenously, biting at my lips as I cried out.

With each thrust, it felt as though he was deeper and deeper within me. I couldn't tell where I ended, and he began. We were moving together as one. It felt as if I could read his mind and he could read mine, each of us anticipating what the other wanted. *Needed.*

His hand found mine, and he interlaced our fingers, pinning my hand to the bed beside us. His other hand buried in my hair as he claimed my mouth with his. My cries turned to whimpers as my pleasure crested, a wicked grin across Nik's face as he devoured my moans with his own mouth.

His breath quickened as did his pace, hitting a place within me that had me seeing stars behind my eyes before I fell over the cliff, grasping him tighter against me. My nails left scratches along his back as I caught my breath, giving his bottom lip a soft bite.

"You are so Goddamn perfect," he growled in my ear, his hand releasing mine against the bed.

His hand found my ample breast, and he swirled the nipple between his fingers before his mouth found it, sucking gently.

My back arched off the bed as he thrust into me. His other hand moved to cup my rear, pressing me against him tighter and tighter as he chased his own release.

His body contracted, spasming as he cried out, and my mouth devoured *his* cries this time, wanting *every* part of him.

All of him.

The good and the bad.

Nik was complicated, but I wouldn't ask for anything different. He was stubborn and arrogant, protective, and gentle.

And he was *mine.*

He bent over me, kissing the scar on my shoulder where the lightning had struck me. His lips lingered on my skin, his eyes meeting mine with a soft smile. He fell to the side of me, curling against me, his head propped on his arm against the pillow.

"I can't believe you're mine," he whispered against my cheek, his arm around my shoulders as I pressed my back into him.

"I'm yours," I promised softly, turning to place a light kiss on the tip of his nose.

Something was different in his eyes, as if they sparked with hope for the first time. Nobody had ever accepted *all* of Nik. There was always some piece out of place, something that felt as if it didn't belong. His upbringing was complicated, he was always told he was never good enough.

But he was good enough for me.

More than good enough.

I curled into him, his legs sliding between mine as we tangled together in the sheets. A feeling of true, unadulterated peace settled over me, and I wanted to grasp it and hold on to it as long as I possibly could.

I wasn't sure how much time had passed, or how many rounds we had gone by the time the sun ascended in the sky, draping the room in the soft glow of dawn.

A beam of sunlight crossed the room and fell across Nik's face, illuminating his blond hair in its orange glow. His lashes were closed, softly fanning against his cheek, a soft smile across his lips.

Even in sleep, he appeared so peaceful.

I sighed deeply, wrapping myself into him before I finally let sleep take me.

32

I woke with the sun high in the sky, streaming in through the open windows. Nik was still wrapped around me, a sleepy smile on his face. A part of me still couldn't believe that last night was real, that this was truly happening. I leaned in and placed a gentle kiss on Nik's lips before turning to get up, trailing the bed sheet along with me.

"Where do you think you're going, firecracker?" he asked, rubbing sleep from his eyes and stretching.

I took a moment to admire his bare abdomen in the afternoon sun, his tattoos curling around his taut muscles.

"See something you like?" he asked as my gaze lingered.

"Lots, in fact. But we promised to meet the others in the library," I reminded him.

He let out a soft groan before rolling out of the bed, the view of his bare behind causing me to pause even further. The bedsheet curled around my body was tight in my fist as I bit my lip. He turned to me with a raised eyebrow, and I turned away quickly, a flush rushing to my face.

"You can look all you'd like, firecracker," he told me, reluctantly pulling on his briefs and crossing the room to me.

His hand caught at the sheet wrapped around me and gave a playful tug, but my hands held.

"You know I love that blush."

I shook my head with a smile. "We will have plenty of time for a...replay...later. I don't want to keep them waiting."

With a reluctant nod we dressed, taking our time to stop for kisses and gentle touches to the point that at least twenty minutes had to have passed by the time we finally made our way over to the library.

To my surprise, Tess and Puck were nowhere to be found. Had we slept that late? There was a handwritten note in what appeared to be Liss' handwriting taped to the stack of books on the table asking us to meet her in Zion's office.

We traveled down the hallway hand in hand, towards the last room on the right, right before the hidden tunnels. I raised my hand to knock, but the door swung open of its own accord.

They were expecting us.

Zion sat in the cushy leather chair at the desk. Liss was across from him with her hands buried in her lap.

"What's wrong?" I asked, sensing the tension in the room before either of them had a chance to speak.

"Come sit," Zion smiled softly, indicating the chairs across from him.

I took the one next to Liss, Nik settling into the chair on my other side.

"What's going on?"

"Liss told me about the key spell," Zion replied simply, leveling me with a gaze I couldn't quite read.

"And?" I asked in confusion. "We don't have a bloodline...so we have to find another way."

"There may *be* another way," he replied, his gaze cutting to Liss.

"What did you find?" I asked, moving to the edge of my seat.

I could feel the anxiety bubbling up within me where it had been nothing but serenity only moments ago. Was there a chance Zion had found another way for me to control my storm magic? If he had...this would change everything.

It wouldn't matter how many we lost in the battle in Prins, we would be able to move against Donika much sooner than we had expected. If I could bind my magic and use it against Donika, it would change the tides of this war.

"It isn't a workaround. Not exactly," he replied, his mouth tight.

"What does that mean?" I asked, my brow raised.

My eyes cut to Liss, but she was silent in the chair beside me.

"We have a bloodline."

My hand flew to my throat in confusion. My gaze fell on Nik, but he appeared equally as confused as I was. I had told him last night about how we would need to find another way, because the bloodline needed to come from the witch who would be bound. A *direct* bloodline.

"Zion, what are you talking about? Everyone in my immediate bloodline is dead." I shook my head in confusion.

"Not everyone," he replied softly.

"*What are you talking about?*" I asked, my eyes once again flicking towards Liss.

My pulse had ratcheted up, my heart beating painfully fast in my chest. As my gaze traveled from Liss back to Zion, a wave of vertigo hit me, my vision blurring.

One moment I was there in Zion's office, my eyes flashing back and forth between Zion and Liss. The next, I was pulled into a vision, one I recognized as having been sent by the book of shadows.

Once again, I was seeing through the eyes of someone else, the same someone holding the intricate silver key. Their hands rested above the grimoire, their fingers tracing the elaborate serpentine designs and the teardrop crystal. The hands delicately placed the key atop the tattered pages of the book, and exactly as it had before, the Kotova grimoire was engulfed in flames.

When the smoke cleared, the key was drawn onto the page, no longer a physical object. My vision traveled up the hands, the arms, the shoulders, until I could see the vision of the person clearly before me.

It was my mother.

Her strawberry blonde hair fell in soft curls around her shoulders, a soft smile on her lips as she tore the page from the grimoire.

Why was she removing the spell? What was she doing?

She carefully tucked the page into the breast pocket of her vest before closing the book. It snapped shut, the leather straps swirling around its binding to seal it closed.

My mother turned her back on the grimoire, leaving the room and closing the door behind her. Without the protection of the Kotova grimoire, the spell could be taken by anyone. *Was this how it found its way into the hands of Phineas Wolfe? Had he stolen it from my mother? But why had she ripped it out of the book in the first place?*

My vision snapped back to the present, Liss watching me carefully. My eyes snapped to Zion's, my brow creasing in confusion.

"I don't understand...the grimoire...it showed me a vision. My mother, she stole the spell out of the Kotova grimoire all those years ago. But...why? That's all I saw, all it showed me. As usual...I have more questions than answers."

"She was trying to help a friend," Zion replied softly, his eyes on me.

"A Stormshade friend? Only a Kotova would be able to access it in the grimoire, and only a Stormshade would have need of the spell."

Zion nodded.

"And Phineas stole it from her?"

Zion nodded again.

"But I don't understand...how do you know all this, and why did the grimoire show me *this* vision? Alastir had said the grimoire, the key, explained that Stormshades weren't endlessly powerful. That the spell would allow me to control my storm magic, and that the grimoire was sending me a warning by showing me this vision. But what does all that have to do with my mother?"

It felt as if there were a pair of hands around my neck, threatening to strangle the breath from my lungs. I was on the precipice of something, but I wasn't sure what, and I didn't know why Zion wouldn't spit it out.

If they had found a bloodline for me to use for the spell...did that mean there was someone else alive in my mother's bloodline? But that still wouldn't be a *direct* bloodline...I wasn't sure if that would work.

I shook my head, meeting Zion's gaze from across the desk.

"What are you getting on about?" I asked, frustration lacing my tone.

"Liss," his voice was gentle as he turned to her. "It's time."

"Time for what?" I asked, my gaze meeting hers.

There was a sadness there, one I hadn't seen in her before. Was she related to me? Related to my mother? What were they keeping from me?

"Anna...it's time."

"Anna?" The name left my chest as if it had been clawed out, scratching my throat on the way up.

I paled as Liss shook her head back and forth, tears sliding down her cheeks. "I didn't want it to happen this way."

"For what to happen this way?" I asked, my hand reaching across the space between us to rest on her knee. "I'm sure if you explain, we can clear all of this up—"But as the words left my mouth, Liss began to change before me.

Her nose became smaller, more rounded. Her eyes were bigger, *bluer*. Her skin was paler, more freckled. Her strawberry blonde hair a rosier shade.

"Wha—" My words cut off as she raised her chin to face me.

I had seen my mother in visions, the visions the grimoire had sent me.

I would have recognized her. How would I not have recognized her?

"It's a glamour," Zion explained, as if plucking the question directly from my thoughts. "She has been wearing a glamour since you met her."

"No—" I shook my head back and forth viciously, pushing back in the chair. "Who are you?"

I rose to my feet and Nik followed, silent at my back. I could feel his hand reaching out for me, but he stopped just shy of touching me.

My voice was brittle as it left me.

Weak.

Breakable.

"How could you?" My voice was raw. "Why?"

I didn't think there would be *anything* that could break me after everything that had happened in the Stormvault.

Everything Donika had put me through.

I had been wrong.

Across from me sat my mother, Annelise Kotova.

And she was *alive*.

33

My emotions were battling for space within me, pushing me in every direction at once. My storm magic swirled in my core as I broke apart, but I tried my hardest to push it back down.

I wasn't bound.

Not yet.

But I could be.

Because my mother...she was alive.

And she had been here with me this *whole time.* She had hidden her identity and broken me out of the Stormvault. Donika thought she was dead, but she had snuck into The Stone Palace right under her nose to free me.

Each revelation had more questions bubbling to my lips, but none of them would come free.

Tears streamed down my face, and I hastily wiped them away with the back of my sleeve, my eyes on Zion and Annelise.

Why did this feel more like a betrayal than a homecoming?

Why had they kept this from me?

"I can't imagine what you are thinking right now—" Zion started, cutting off when he registered my bewildered expression.

"That's right, you can't," I bit out, the backs of my eyes stinging with fresh tears.

"But we can explain everything," Annelise finished for him, standing.

She held her palms out to me, as if calming a scared animal.

I backed away towards the door, my vision flooded by my tears. Nik's jaw was set, his shoulders tense.

He hadn't known, either.

I thought she was *dead*. That Donika had killed her in The War of Siraleth. Had she been merciful? Had she not been able to bring herself to kill her own mother? Had Annelise been in hiding all this time, only to come out when I needed her help? Surely she hadn't been in the castle this whole time, right under Donika's nose...

Zion had known her true identity this entire time, and he had kept it from me. Isaac had to have known, too. Betrayal stung freshly in my gut as I shook my head back and forth.

A choked sob escaped me as I turned, reaching for the door handle.

"Diana, wait—"

But her words were lost behind me as I escaped into the hallway, greedily drinking in deep breaths of fresh air. I continued on, up and up the spiral staircase and out of the cottage underground.

I needed air.

It was Nik's voice at my back now, calling out my name, but I didn't stop.

I couldn't.

I didn't stop until my feet were tired and I didn't know where I was.

I blinked back my tears and realized I stood in the remains of an old bookshop somewhere in Siraleth, the rubble surrounding me. I glanced up to the sky as thunder cracked overhead, and I bit my lip as I tried to push my storm magic back down. I didn't want to hurt anyone, but I didn't know how to process these emotions without them swallowing me alive.

My mother was alive.

She was alive.

Why hadn't she told me earlier?

Nik gave me my space, respecting that I needed time alone to process. He kept a safe distance, watching over me from a crested hill in the distance.

His eyes were on me always, but I felt so *alone.*

I desperately wanted Tess, but I didn't know where she was.

I had never known my mother. This is the woman who stashed me with a human family in the mortal realm until my storm magic awakened. She had spell bound me, hoping I would never find out I was a witch at all.

She had left me with strangers, never knowing my birth family. Never knowing my true lineage. Never knowing I was a witch of the Kotova bloodline, and that I was the key to ending the war in Istmere.

And she had never come back for me.

Betrayal was fresh in my gut when I finally sank to my knees, a cloud of dust rising around me. The sun was setting over the horizon as Nik picked his way down the hill, careful not to loosen any of the rocks on the ledge. He found me on my hands and knees, pulling me into a tight embrace.

"I'm so sorry, Diana. I'm so sorry." His hand stroked my hair in a soothing motion as he held me tight, his other swirling across my back.

A humorless laugh bubbled to my lips as I recognized the harsh contrast between this and the last time I had been betrayed. Nik was the one comforting me now, and I fell into him. I clung to his shirt with my fists, leaving streaks of wet tears across it.

And he held me that way until I finally stopped.

At some point all the tears had escaped me, and I was left dry and numb, kneeling in the rubble of Siraleth.

Nik wordlessly picked me up, carrying me back to the cottage underground in his arms. The last thing I wanted to see was Annelise and Zion right now, but there was nowhere else to go. He tucked me wordlessly into my bed and immediately went for Tess.

He must have explained to her what had happened, because she quietly crawled into bed with me and wrapped herself around me. She held me tightly and rubbed circles on my back until I was able to fall asleep from sheer exhaustion.

She was with me when I woke, still wrapped around me, her chocolate brown hair cascading across the pillow.

I still felt numb.

I had cried myself empty last night, and I knew that the numbness would soon retreat in favor of *anger.*

And I welcomed it.

I would rather feel anger than nothing at all.

I couldn't wrap my head around Annelise having been with us this entire time, hiding her identity. To what end? Would she never have revealed herself if we hadn't needed the bloodline to complete the binding spell? Would she have gone on as 'Liss,' the member of the council who had helped rescue me from Akra—forever?

I didn't know why she hadn't told me who she was in the first place. I understood needing to keep her identity a secret when she snuck into The Stone Palace right under Donika's nose, but after that? And Zion knew her true identity this entire time. Isaac, too. It was clear Nik, Tess, and Puck were as in the dark as I was. She had done a remarkable job of keeping her identity a secret with the help of the glamour potions.

My entire life she had still been alive…*and she had never come back for me.*

She let me think that the mortal family she placed me with was my blood, and she never looked back. She had sent me there to keep me safe, but why hadn't she returned?

I tear slid down my cheek as Tess stirred next to me. I wiped it away with the back of my sleeve and stifled a sob as it rose in my throat.

Even if Annelise *had* wanted to wait for Istmere to be safe again, she had to have known that I was the key. Alastir, the seer, knew as much. The amount of magic I had was prophesied, and she would have known exactly who they were talking about when they heard only a powerful Stormshade witch with too much magic could end this war.

She could see how much I was struggling with controlling my magic and chasing down empty leads about the Kotova grimoire. She could have confessed at *any* point. That she, too, was a powerful Stormshade, and that the grimoire had once been hers before it was mine.

Things felt clearer now, knowing the truth. The way she had looked at me when she had come to the Stormvault. The way she had been protective over me and adamant about my healing when my storm had turned on me.

But she wasn't only *my* mother...she was Donika's, too.

And Donika hadn't had the strength to kill her.

Somehow, my mother had made it out alive.

Tess stirred again, and I shuffled slightly to encourage her to wake. She wiped sleep from her eyes as she stretched, letting out a groan.

"What time is it?" she asked, throwing an arm across my stomach.

"I've got no idea," I replied, my eyes trained on the ceiling.

"Has Nik been back?" she asked, searching my face.

We hadn't even gotten to have the mandatory best friend breakdown after I'd had sex for the first time. I had been thrust right back into more betrayal and lies. A humorless laugh escaped me at the thought. I could see on Tess' face that she could tell something had changed between us, but I hadn't been able to talk to her about it yet.

"I don't know, I just woke up," I replied, turning to face her.

I rest my head on the silk pillowcase as another tear escaped, staining it with a wet droplet.

"I know you might not want to hear this, but it could be good news," she offered with a shrug.

I pinned her with a glare that had her laughing, grasping my hand in hers. "Nobody knows Donika like your mother. Nobody. And now you can bind your magic and we can finally move against Donika. Plus, we have had some trouble deciphering some of the spells in the Kotova grimoire. She will know them."

"That's all true," I replied, my lips thin. "So why didn't she tell me earlier?"

"I don't know, Diana. She must have her reasons. Maybe she was afraid of how you would react. Or that too much had passed for there to ever be a future between you two."

I shook my head, another tear slipping free. "I would have welcomed her back if she hadn't kept it from me."

"Would you have?" Tess asked with a raised brow. "I've known you for a long time and...it might not be one of your best qualities, but you internalize *everything*. You hold everything inside and let it fester until it turns to anger and hate. You are the worst grudge holder I know."

"I forgave Nik," I pointed out as I wiped away the tears. "And he betrayed me."

"He did, but he hadn't meant to," Tess mused. Her head snapped back towards me, her mouth open. "What do you mean you forgave him?"

She gave me a gentle nudge that had a soft laugh escaping my lips. "I forgave him for everything."

She raised her brow at me, and I couldn't help but laugh. Tess never failed to put a smile on my face.

"You naughty little witch! We will have to unpack that later," she told me as she moved to sit up.

I joined her, my chest sore from all the crying I had done in the past twenty-four hours. I nodded in agreement. "Yes, later. First, we need to bind my magic."

"Agreed. That is our number one priority. Are you ready to see her again?" she asked.

I shook my head. "Not at all, but I don't have a choice. I need her blood for the spell, and her magic. The sooner I bind my magic, the better."

"Who will you bind to?" she asked, throwing the blankets off to stand. "You know I would bind to you in a heartbeat, but I don't know if I am a strong enough witch to tether your magic."

I had thought about that, too. "I was planning to ask Nik."

"Even before your reconciliation?" Tess moved to the window and pulled the blinds open, letting the sun stream in. I squinted against it, but moved to join her. There would be plenty of time to wallow in my self-pity later.

Today, we would bind my magic.

Today, I would become the fierce storm witch that Donika had no hope of defeating.

"Yes, even before our reconciliation," I replied.

"I think you forgave him before you even realized you had," Tess pointed out. "Binding your magic to his? That's serious."

I nodded. "He is quite possibly the strongest witch I know."

"He is *definitely* the strongest witch we know. Other than you, of course."

"Of course," I replied with a laugh.

I changed out of yesterday's clothes and splashed water on my face to help wake me up. I avoided my reflection in the mirror, pulling my hair back away from my face into a ponytail. I wasn't ready to face Annelise and Zion, but as Tess had said, I had no other choice.

We found Puck and Nik in their rooms, and they joined us in the hallway. Without a word Nik wrapped me into a tight embrace and I let myself sink into him.

Things had changed between us, but I still had an important question to ask him. If he didn't agree to bind his magic to mine, I wasn't sure who I would turn to. He had every right to deny me, holding half of my storm magic would be no easy feat, and it would change both of our lives forever.

"Can we get a minute alone?" I asked Tess over Nik's shoulder.

He still held me tightly against him."Of course. Meet you in Zion's office in ten?" she asked as she moved towards the spiral staircase that would bring them up out of the cottage underground.

I nodded in response, and Tess and Puck left us alone in the hallway. I dipped into the library and Nik followed, wanting more privacy. I moved towards the table in the center that still had our books stacked atop it and shuffled onto the desk, resting my feet on the chair.

"There's something I want to ask you," I told him, meeting his gaze. He stood across from me, leaning over the chair I rested my feet on.

"Anything, firecracker." His eyes were a soft blue in the dim lighting of the library, and for a moment I was almost lost in them.

"You can say no, if you want to. I don't want you to feel any pressure to say yes or feel obligated in any way." I was rambling, fidgeting with the hem of my shirtsleeves.

If he said no, I would have to turn to Zion or even Warrick. I wasn't sure I wanted my magic bound to either of them for an eternity.

"I understand." He smiled softly, reaching across to rest a hand on my knee. "You can ask me anything, Diana."

"I'll just get it over with then. Will you bind to me? I need a powerful witch to bind my magic to, and there isn't anyone else I would rather share this burden with and—"

"Yes," he cut me off with his simple reply, as if he had already known exactly what I was going to ask.

"Yes?" I asked, holding his gaze.

"Yes, Diana. I would do *anything* for you. You still doubt that?"

"No. I don't doubt that I just—" I shook my head back and forth, unsure what I had been thinking, exactly.

He moved closer, his hands resting on my knees as he leaned over me. The scent of his body wash wafted off him, and it took everything in me to keep my eyes on his.

"I would happily bind to you, Diana. It's you and me. In this life and the next."

"In this life and the next," I whispered against him as my hands found his neck, bringing his mouth down to mine.

He kissed me softly at first, tentatively. He knew I was fragile at the moment, the news of my mother being alive still had me reeling. I kissed him back hungrily, and he quickly matched my intensity.

He pulled the chair away and my legs fell back against the table before his hands found the inside of both of my knees, spreading them apart. He stood between them and I wrapped my legs around him, pulling him closer. My hands moved to his back and up his shirt, running over the taut muscle there. I wanted nothing more than to forget everything else, to melt into him.

He nipped at my bottom lip hard enough to draw blood and I arched into him, my fingernails digging into his tanned skin as I groaned into his mouth. One of his hands was buried in my hair, the other on my hip, holding me against him. His mouth moved to my cheek, my jaw, my neck, and further down under the collar of my shirt. His hand moved from my hip to dip under the hem of my shirt, traveling over the bare expanse of skin on my stomach.

His hand moved higher, the shirt coming with it as he cupped my breast, letting out a low groan himself. The library door opening had us springing apart, but to my relief it was only Puck.

"Ten minutes?" Puck laughed, pointing at his watch with a grin.

"I'm coming," Nik groaned, turning back towards me.

"I wish," I whispered, my voice ragged as I caught my breath.

Nik turned to me with a wicked grin, his eyebrow raised as Puck slipped back out the door so we could gather ourselves.

"Naughty little thing," he crooned, running a hand through his hair with a laugh.

Despite everything that had happened yesterday, I found myself smiling. I rose from the table and adjusted my clothing, making sure my hair was still pulled back and wasn't mussed or out of place.

"Let's do this," I said, my voice holding more resolve than I felt.

Nik turned towards the door, holding his hand out to me as he said, "Are you ready to bind yourself to me, forever?"

34

We met Tess and Puck in Zion's office, where Zion and Annelise were already waiting. She fumbled with her hands in her lap as we joined them. Without a word she beckoned us to follow her, and we made our way down the hallway, up the spiral staircase and out of the cottage.

The grimoire was safely tucked under my arm as we walked.

"Where are we going?" Tess called from behind as we made our way through the winding cobblestone streets of Siraleth.

"We need a place of immense power to complete the binding," Annelise explained, not glancing over her shoulder.

Zion was quiet beside her.

I knew where we were going...I had seen it. The grimoire had shown me. We were going to the place Osiris, my father, was slain.

The place Donika killed him and almost killed her.

We crested a hill, and I could see the rubble mound before me. This ground was marked by an immense amount of magic, and you could feel it running up through your feet and into your bones. My magic responded in kind, and was at the tips of my fingers, waiting.

We found a level place among the rubble and Zion and Nik helped to clear a space free of the stray cinderblocks and rocks.

Annelise wasted no time on explanations and began right away. The others stood back as Nik, Annelise and I stood in the center. Annelise circled us, salt dripping from her hand as she went. The salt would keep the magic *inside* the circle, and with a spell of this magnitude it was of the utmost importance.

Once we were enclosed in the circle Annelise held her hand out for the grimoire, and after a moment of reluctance I complied. My hand felt empty without it, and I had the sense that the grimoire felt the same.

It *wanted* to come back to me.

Annelise flipped to the page with the key spell, running her fingers delicately across the parchment. She recited the words I had heard in the vision, the words that had allowed her hand to reach into the page. She turned the book towards me, her expression expectant.

"*Hac voce te voco, clavem. Prodeunt,*" I chanted as my hand spilled into the page, disappearing at the wrist.

When I pulled my hand back out of the book, the key was within my grasp, as if it had been a physical thing all along. The crystal caught the light of the sun high in the afternoon sky, blinding me for a moment. When my vision cleared a shock of energy ran up my arm, stinging the scar on my shoulder where the lightning had struck me. I almost dropped the key from the shock of pain, and I had to concentrate to keep it held within my grasp.

My magic surged forth hungrily, anxious to feed into the key. It was as if it recognized this ancient magic on its own, and knew what would happen next.

Annelise closed the grimoire and set it on the ground before us.

"Nik, would you like to do the honors?" she asked.

Before I could ask what, exactly, he was about to do, he waved his hand and a small black cauldron appeared before us with a single glass goblet sitting atop a pedestal.

I raised an eyebrow at him, but he only laughed.

"Shapeshifter magic," he explained with a shrug.

I would never get over how he could simply conjure things out of thin air like that. They had to come from *somewhere,* and I recognized these items from the laboratory in the cottage underground.

Annelise bent to lift the cauldron, humming a spell under her breath until the cauldron began to smoke. She placed it on the pedestal, reaching into her jacket to extract a dagger she had hidden there.

She cut the dagger across her palm, letting the blood flow into the cauldron. She passed the dagger to Nik who did the same. When it was my turn, I handed the key to Nik and raked the dagger across my palm, hissing at the pain as I let my blood trickle into the cauldron to join theirs.

Annelise covered the cauldron with her hand, another spell spilling forth from her lips. I met Nik's eyes across the circle and the corner of his mouth lifted into a reassuring smile.

We were about to be bound for eternity, and the thought had my heart in my throat. When Annelise finished the spell she turned to Nik, then me, her gaze hard.

"There is one more thing I need you to understand about this spell before we do it."

"Ok," I replied warily, my heart racing in my chest.

"This spell will not only bind your *magic,* but your *lives.*"

I swallowed hard, meeting Nik's burning gaze across the circle as understanding dawned on us.

"If you die, so does he. If he dies, so do you," Annelise's voice was firm, but gentle.

She didn't want us to blindly bind ourselves together to win this war, she wanted us to have all the information so we could decide for ourselves the best course of action. A wave of emotion rolled over me as I met her gaze, her eyes glistening with unshed tears.

"This isn't a complication we discussed," Zion called from outside the circle, his hard gaze settled on Annelise.

"It isn't your choice, Zion," Annelise replied, her voice ragged. "The choice is *theirs.*"

"But if he dies—" Zion shook his head, his eyes sparked with anger.

"Then she dies," Annelise finished for him. "There is a price to this kind of magic, Zion. *This is the price.*"

"It's a chance we have to take," Nik spoke, his voice gentle.

His eyes held mine across the circle and they blazed with emotion. He was willing to tie not only his magic to me for an eternity, but his *life.*

"That is, if you agree," Nik continued. "The decision is yours, Diana."

Tears pricked the back of my eyes and I tilted my head back, willing them away. I had cried entirely too much lately. I clenched my fist around the wound from the dagger, the movement stinging and bringing clarity to my thoughts.

If Nik died, I would die.

If I died, so would Nik.

"And the spell is permanent?" I asked, my gaze traveling to Annelise.

Her eyes were soft as they met mine. Gentle. Understanding.

"As far as I know, yes."

I swallowed hard, my eyes moving back to Nik's. All I found there was warmth. Love. Empathy. He was willing to live with me or die with me, whatever fate had in store for us. If I died in this war, if that was the price of killing Donika, then he would die beside me.

And he was willing to pay that price.

For me.

A choked sob left me as I crossed the circle and fell into his arms. They came around me and held me up as I clung to him. The thought of losing him was devastating. Overwhelming. But this spell meant I would never have to live without him.

"If you agree, I agree," I told him, pulling back only enough to look into his eyes. "This changes things. If it changes your answer, I understand."

"Nothing has changed for me, Diana. In this life and the next, I'm yours."

I fell into him as another sob tore free from my throat, tears wetting my cheeks as they fell in earnest. A million emotions were swirling inside of me, and I didn't have time to process any of them. Annelise and the cauldron were patiently waiting, as was my magic.

We reluctantly released each other, and I crossed the circle again to stand by Annelise.

I nodded, meeting Zion's gaze, then hers. "I'm ready. Let's do this."

"My strong, magnificent, daughter." Annelise's voice was strangled as she turned to me, pride in her eyes.

Another wave of emotion rolled over me and I bit my lip *hard* to push it back. If I let it, the emotions and the consequences of the last few weeks threatened to drown me.

Annelise instructed me to drop the key into the cauldron. As soon as I did and the key mingled with our blood, it began to sizzle. A sweet-smelling smoke wafted into the air.

Annelise filled the single glass goblet with the blood, her eyes turning black, swirling with blood magic. She handed the goblet to me, and my hands trembled as I took it from her. The black eyes staring back at me were familiar, and I felt a pang in my stomach at the thought.

She knelt to retrieve the grimoire once more and opened to the page where the key spell was written.

"Hold the goblet and recite with me," she instructed.

I moved to read over her shoulder, the grimoire giving an involuntary shudder as we spoke.

"Hoc sacrificium alligabo."

"Hoc sacrificium alligabo."

"Hoc sacrificium alligabo."

The goblet was suddenly warm within my grasp, the spell having heated its contents.

"Now drink," Annelise instructed.

At first I balked at the thought of consuming the blood, but her black eyes met mine and there was something encouraging in them. These were not the black, lifeless eyes of someone lost to dark magic. I brought the goblet to my lips. I had expected the salty, metallic taste of blood but what I found in the goblet was both sweet and tangy.

"Now, Nik," she instructed.

I passed the goblet to him as I licked my lips clean, the blood staining my teeth. He brought the goblet to his mouth, his eyes on mine as he drank.

I felt a pull deep within me, the ember in my core surging forth as he swallowed. He passed the goblet to Annelise, but she did not drink, she simply placed it on the ground before us.

"Clasp your hands together, the next part requires a physical connection."

We did as she asked, our hands lacing together as we faced each other. He gave me a reassuring half-smile, and I was glad I couldn't see the blood that I'm sure stained his teeth as well. As our hands connected my magic surged forth again, pressing against me so intensely it almost swept me off my feet.

This was blood magic, and my magic both reveled in it and rebelled against it at the same time. It wasn't dark magic, but it was unmistakably powerful and intense. For a moment I could picture how Donika could get drunk on this feeling, addicted to the power I sensed rushing through my veins as we recited the spell and my magic responded.

But no feeling in the world could excuse the lengths she went to. The lives she took. The sacrifices she made.

Annelise placed her hand over ours, reciting the last part of the spell.

"*With this power I bind. Hac potestate teneor.*" Her voice took on a melody as she repeated the words, over and over, blood red swirling in her black eyes.

My head was thrown back as magic surged up within me, running down my arms and through my fingertips towards Nik. He staggered back as the magic hit him, but he held on tightly.

The power surged within me so powerfully I ground my teeth against it, rearing back unintentionally.

"Hold fast!" Annelise called out, her hands grasping ours.

The rocks and sand kicked up around us inside the circle, my hair pulling free of its ties to swirl around me. The circle had become a tornado, the wind powerful enough that it threatened to sweep us off our feet.

But we held fast.

As my magic passed through my fingertips, I could sense another magic filling me, a magic I had never felt before. I dug my feet into the ground, determined to remain standing as the amount of power and magic rushing through my core threatened to bring me to my knees.

"Almost there!" Annelise called over the whipping winds.

My hair blew across my face, only allowing me to see bits and pieces of the magic flowing around us. Violet threads of magic encircled my hands, holding mine to Nik's. In kind, crimson magic encircled his.

My breaths quickened as my brow furrowed, the amount of power filling me threatening to shatter me as if I were made of glass. My eyes found Nik's through the dirt and sand, and they were wide as they held my gaze, Irises flashing violet as my magic filled him.

My knees threatened to buckle beneath me but Nik's grip on me held me upright, and with one final word Annelise released us, and we sprang apart.

I hit the invisible shield of the salt circle with a crash, falling to my knees in the dirt. My vision swam for a moment as I realized we were finished. The spell was finished.

We were bound.

Nik's eyes darkened as they met mine across the circle where he had been thrown back, too. He must have been feeling exactly what I was.

I felt *everything.*

I could feel Nik as if he were a piece of me, deep within the ember in my core. His energy was distinct, not as if it mixed with my own. I reached my hand out to him, and shadows snaked towards him from my fingertips. I pulled my hand back, my eyes flying to Annelise's in alarm.

"This is a normal part of the binding. Each of you will have magic from the other, though not at the same strength or power as the one born to it."

Nik nodded as he stood, coming to my side and helping me stand. Tears swam in my eyes as I glanced up at him, and his eyes sparked with something hungry. Despite the others being present, he brought his mouth down to mine, consuming me in a fiery kiss.

When we broke apart, Annelise was waiting patiently beside us with the goblet in her hands. She dipped her thumb into it and swiped the blood across my forehead, then Nik's.

"May the mother witness, they are bound."

"May the mother witness, we are bound," we replied in unison.

As we spoke the words, the salt circle broke apart, Annelise's eyes returning to their oceanic blue. The residual power in the circle spilled outwards, and as if it were a vortex we were pulled apart once more. Despite the rush of magic, we quickly found our bearings.

Tess and Puck were smiling as they moved towards us.

I reached into my core and pulled on my storm magic, and it answered willingly. Eagerly. The sky darkened and cracked with thunder overhead. A bolt of lightning streaked across the sky. I waved my hand, and at once the clouds began to dissipate.

"Can I do that?" Nik asked with a smirk as he wound his arms around me.

"Not to that extent," Annelise replied, leaning against the pedestal in the circle, "but some storm magic, yes."

The spell had clearly taken a lot out of Annelise, and Zion went to her, holding her upright in his embrace.

With a wave of Nik's hand the cauldron and goblet returned to the cottage laboratory.

"Can I do that?" I asked, raising my eyebrow at him.

"We will just have to see, firecracker," he replied with a smile.

We had done it. We had the power between us to defeat Donika and bring peace to Istmere once more.

I could use my storm magic at will now, and I felt *powerful.* I could sense the magic sizzling right under my skin, warming me. The magic was singing right below the surface, never fully returning to my core as it had once before.

My storm magic and I were one.

And Nik...I could feel him as if he were a part of me. As if his soul resided in mine, and mine in his.

In this life and the next, we were bound.

Forever.

35

We hadn't been able to find Isaac when we returned to the cottage, the following days consumed with plans of how to move against Akra. We would have to fill Isaac in once he returned—whenever that was. We assumed he was connecting with our resistance forces in Prins.

The library had turned into a full-on war room, complete with parchment maps strewn across the tables and little figurines signifying our forces, and Donika's.

We didn't have an exact number of how big Donika's numbers were, but with the help of Zion's intel, we knew that they crushed ours in comparison. But with my storm magic being bound, we were banking on not needing as many men. We had to consider that we wouldn't have the element of surprise, after she sent her forces to attack us in Prins, she was expecting our retaliation.

We hovered around the table in the newly appointed war room, the pieces moving about the board as we tested different strategies.

"If we can get someone to open the gate from the inside, we can use the secret passages we escaped through to access the castle," Zion pointed out, moving a piece towards the back of the mountain.

"You think it will come to that?" Annelise asked, pointing towards her pieces on the battlefield at the base of the mountain. "You don't think she will want to meet us out here with her forces?"

"I think she will," Zion agreed, "but I think Donika herself won't show her face. I believe a smaller contingent of us will need to breach the castle walls to bring her down."

I nodded in agreement. I didn't see Donika facing us on the battlefield herself, she would send her soldiers, Araneoch, and Noctani to do her bidding, but she would certainly take all the glory if she was victorious.

"I think our fastest and most powerful soldiers should breach the castle through the secret passageways. They are narrow, only allowing for soldiers to pass through single file."

"Agreed," Nik replied, moving his own piece towards the back of the mountain. "But how many soldiers will she keep in her immediate guard to protect her?"

"Knowing Donika?" Zion laughed humorlessly as he ran a hand down his face. "Not many. She might be egotistical, but she is proud. She will have Noctani, and Corian most certainly."

"And how do we handle the Araneoch and Noctani?" Tess asked, her arms folded across her chest. "We haven't battled them yet. We had a difficult time taking down the Araneoch as it was on the training field that day, but the Noctani? We have no idea if they will fall in battle the same way, if our weapons will even work against them."

Zion nodded thoughtfully. "There's no reason to think they won't, the Araneoch weren't immune to our weapons. It is a chance we are going to have to take and pray that she hasn't had that much success with them. When I left The Stone Palace, there were only a few. Just short of ten if I had to hazard a guess."

Nik turned towards me, his brow furrowed. "Have you had any more visions about Donika or her Noctani?"

I shook my head. "No, I haven't had a vision about her in a concerningly long time. I haven't dream walked in weeks. It makes me think Corian is actively blocking me."

"We might need to dream walk intentionally to see what they are up to," Tess replied with a nod. "It's dangerous if she runs into Corian, but otherwise it would give us the upper hand...which would be invaluable."

"I have to agree," Nik replied with a nod. "We should plan to try to spy on her at least once or twice before we make any moves. And I still would want Isaac's input when he returns from Prins."

My eyes moved back and forth between Nik and Tess, shocked they were getting along so well and agreeing on something for once. Nik wasn't the biggest fan of Tess when they had first met, but it appeared they had moved past that.

Plotting war strategies had kept me busy, not allowing me any spare time to overthink my relationship with Annelise. We hadn't spoken since the binding ceremony. I was still angry with her, but I didn't want to unpack those emotions yet. I wanted to plot against Donika, and deal with everything else later.

"How many are we thinking for the castle attack, ten men or so?" Zion asked, studying the map.

"Give or take." I shrugged. "I'll be going, obviously, but I think Nik should stay back."

"What?" He turned towards me, an expression of hurt crossing his features. "I'm one of the strongest witches, and I wield shadows. You'll need me there."

"I wield shadows now too, remember?" I asked, a dark shadow snaking out from my raised palm to prove my point. "Have you forgotten that if you die, I die? And vice versa. We can't risk one of us being taken out before we even get to her. Only those of us in this room know that we are bound, but it's still a risk we can't take."

Nik appeared as if he was about to argue, but he bit his lip, his gaze falling to the map. He knew I was right, whether he wanted to admit it or not.

"Annelise and I will be with you," Zion confirmed as he met my gaze.

"Is that wise?" I asked, my brow raised. "Does she know Annelise is alive?"

"We must assume she knows I'm out there...somewhere. She let me live that day on the battlefield, but she hasn't seen me since. I've stayed out of her way, but I will stand by no longer. If my presence can help in any way, I need to be there," Annelise replied, her mouth tight.

"And can you do it?" I asked, my jaw set.

"Do what?" she asked, her stern gaze holding mine.

"Watch me kill Donika. She is your daughter, after all. I can't have you second guessing at the last moment and getting in the way."

"I won't get in the way," she protested, slamming her fist down on the table and rattling the figurines.

"You wouldn't do it intentionally, but *she is your daughter*," I replied, my voice tight.

"As are you," she countered, raising her chin. "I understand what needs to be done. I will not let her continue to terrorize this realm, or the ones I love any longer."

I nodded, holding her gaze. I could see where I got my stubbornness from.

"Then it's decided, you'll join us. But make no mistake, I am breaching the castle to kill Donika, not capture her."

"I understand," she replied, her voice cold.

"The same goes for you," I told Zion, turning my gaze on him. "If you are a hinderance in any way, if you stop me from taking her down—"

"I won't," he replied, his eyes sad as they held mine. "I have seen firsthand what Donika has done. I have already turned my back on her. The little girl I raised has been dead for a long, long time. I am ready for what is to come."

I gave a curt nod and turned my attention back towards the map.

"So we will have five to ten of our fastest, strongest, witches breach the castle with me. The remainder of our forces will meet hers out on the battlefield here." I pointed towards the open plains at the bottom of the hill The Stone Palace resided on. "What do you think our final numbers are?" I asked.

"It's hard to say without confirmation from Isaac, but I would have to say we are just shy of twenty-five hundred men and women ready and willing to fight. We lost close to a third of our forces in the battle at Prins."

I swallowed hard, bile rising in my throat. We had estimated Donika had at least five thousand men, maybe more.

"So, the tide of this battle will depend on me," I replied with a deep sigh, pinching the bridge of my nose with my fingers.

If I could infiltrate the castle and kill Donika before we lost too many of our soldiers on the battlefield, we could take Akra. If the battle raged on between our forces, we would lose.

"No pressure." Tess laughed, giving me a gentle nudge.

Puck came into the library then with a tray of food and drinks, and we swarmed him as if we hadn't eaten in days. It had been almost a week since we had been bound, but the feeling of Nik's ember in my core was still something to get used to.

As he moved towards the door, further away from me, I could feel it in my bones. I knew exactly where he was without even glancing up from the map. It was as if we were magnets, always aware of where the other is, but pulled together no matter what.

I raised my eyes to him, and he shot me a knowing glance over his shoulder, as if he, too, felt the distance between us now. When we had bound ourselves...I had no idea the effect it would have on us.

I could study the map until my eyes glazed over and my face turned blue, but the odds were not in our favor. If a group of us couldn't breach the castle and kill Donika, we would lose this battle. It would be years and years before we could rebuild a force big and powerful enough to move against her again, and most of us would likely need to retreat to the mortal realm to escape her.

I threw my head back, shaking my hair out behind me. Staring at the map for so long was beginning to give me a headache. Or maybe it was the fact that we were walking into certain death.

I still had a knot in my stomach about our forces facing down Donika's creatures born of dark magic. We had faced the Araneoch before and had seen what a force they were. I had only seen the Noctani in my dream walking, and a chill ran down my spine at the thought of their fangs and their black, lifeless eyes.

She was sure to surround herself with Noctani to protect her, and they could siphon my magic if they got too close. They would need to be dealt with first, they were the biggest threat to us.

My hand moved involuntarily to touch Stormslayer tucked against my thigh, and I closed my eyes against the feel of cold steel. I would need to carry throwing knives and a sword as well, which meant Nik and I had a lot of training to do.

We hadn't set a date to move against her yet, we had to wait for Isaac to return. He had been gone just over a week and he hadn't left a note, we had no idea when to expect him back.

I wanted to move against her sooner rather than later. The anxiety building up to this would threaten to undo me, and I didn't want to lose my nerve. I had killed Shades in the battle at Prins, but this was different.

This was my *sister*.

I had been imprisoned by her, tortured by her, and still a pit formed in my stomach at the thought of what I had to do. What I *must* do. Not only for myself, but for all the Shades in Istmere.

As long as she lived, she would never stop killing innocents. Murdering Stormshades. Controlling people and mutilating them with her black magic. She needed to be stopped once and for all.

Nik returned to my side with a slice of something that appeared to be pizza, which he offered me. I shook my head, the taste of bile still raw in my mouth.

"No thanks, I can't stomach anything at the moment."

"I know you, Diana. When the time comes, you won't hesitate."

"I know," I replied, my gaze falling to the sharp iron peaks of the castle on the map. "But what does that say about me? That I would kill my own sister without hesitation?"

"It says that you care about the people of this realm," he replied, his eyes soft as he placed a hand on my shoulder, turning me towards him. "That you wouldn't subject them to another fifteen years of suffering under a tyrant. That you recognize Shades of any kind should be safe in their own homeland, not hunted for the magic they were born with. Or experimented on or sacrificed on the whims of a mad woman. Donika is the Black Heart, and you are incredibly brave for going up against her. You are the queen Istmere needs."

"Incredibly brave?" I asked, a humorless laugh escaping me. "Or incredibly stupid."

"Brave," he replied, his eyes darkening. "You are the bravest woman I know."

"You must not know that many women," I teased, nudging his side.

He choked on his pizza with a snort and wrapped his arm around me.

"You'd better watch yourself, Firecracker."

"Or what?" I asked with a devious grin. "You'll punish me?"

"I just might have to," he replied, swallowing hard.

He held my heated gaze, his presence tangible in my core. I had to admit, the sex had been good the first time, but now that we were bound?

Mind blowing.

It was as if he could read my mind and I could read his. I couldn't wait until our meeting ended for the night and we could crawl back into bed together. It had taken Tess and Puck a lot of convincing to get us here in the first place, we had been tangled together in the sheets all week.

I had never believed in soulmates before, but that is exactly what this binding felt like.

Soulmates.

Puck came up behind Nik and grabbed him in a headlock, breaking our trance. He gave me an apologetic smile as Puck shuffled him away to eat at one of the tables with him. Tess joined me, but I couldn't stomach anything tonight with thoughts of war heavy on my mind. She ate while we stared at the map thoughtfully.

I had never planned a battle before, and I hoped we were making the right decisions. I knew that Zion and Annelise were experienced in the art of warfare, but I couldn't help wanting Isaac's opinion on our plan, too.

As they always did when left unoccupied, my thoughts wandered to my troubles. I still wasn't ready to speak with Annelise yet, but I knew it was inevitable.

I loved my mortal mother with my whole heart, and it almost felt like a betrayal to be so relieved that Annelise was alive and well. I was still bitter she hadn't revealed her identity to me sooner, and there was still a lot we needed to unpack between us when the time came.

I needed to pick off one problem at a time, and right now our biggest problem was Donika.

Once we had eaten dinner and hammered out our plans with Saanvi and Kenna, we decided to turn in for the night. Tess couldn't help but wiggle her eyebrows at me when she saw I was retiring to Nik's room and not my own.

I had been spending every night there.

I slipped inside and took a long, warm soak in the tub while I waited for Nik. I sank into the claw-foot tub and lathered myself with the decadent soaps he had never made use of.

"Diana?" I could hear him calling from the bedroom.

"In here!" I called back.

Nik rounded the corner to the washroom with an eyebrow raised.

"You're ready for me, are you?" He leaned over the tub, placing a gentle kiss against my mouth.

"I'm ready for bed," I teased, splashing him with the water.

My hair was pulled back so it wouldn't get wet, and Nik ran his hands into it, grasping it and tilting my head back towards his.

"Have I told you that I love you?" he asked, his tone wistful.

"A time or two." I smiled against his mouth as he lowered his lips to mine.

Kissing Nik felt like the first time *every* time. I could feel the butterflies in my stomach, the heat in my core, a tickle running up my back and the urge to giggle. His magic and mine swirled right under our skin, mingling. Our magic was one and the same now.

We each still had our affinities, but they were bound to one another. It was both incredible and terrifying at the same time.

"Are you ok?" he asked, pulling away and sitting on the stool beside the tub.

He dipped his hand into the warm water, running it up and down my leg in a soothing motion.

I leaned back and closed my eyes, groaning at the sensation. Every touch felt like *heaven* with him. He grasped my ankle in his hand and my eyes popped open to meet his, a devious grin across his lips.

"I'm fine," I replied, cocking my head to the side and daring him to stop.

He resumed his soothing motions, stopping at my knee and making his way back down.

"I want you to know I understand what a hard thing it is that we are about to do." He held my gaze as he spoke, his voice soft.

"I know you understand," I replied gently.

"You are not alone in this, Diana. Whatever you need from me, I'm here for you. Tell me what I can do to make this easier for you."

"I wish you could be there with me," I replied, running the water over my shoulders.

My breasts were hidden beneath the bubbles but as I stretched back the peaks of them appeared as they crested the water, and Nik's gaze immediately heated.

"I'm trying to have a serious conversation here," Nik admonished, peeking at me from under his eyelashes.

"I know." I laughed, leaning back again so that my breasts crested the surface of the water once more.

"Diana..." his voice was both teasing and laced with desire. "Is this your way of trying to change the subject?"

"Maybe," I admitted, rubbing the loofa over the skin of my abdomen.

"There's nothing you have to hide from me. I want all of you, always. Every piece of you, even the parts you try to hide away. I know you are strong, but you don't have to be strong all the time. You're allowed to feel emotions other than anger."

I leaned my head back against the tub and closed my eyes, biting my lip. How could he read my mind so completely? I know the bond didn't offer that much, as his thoughts were still a mystery to me.

"I'm scared," I admitted, sinking further into the tub.

He gave my knee a squeeze beneath the water. "I know."

"I'm scared what kind of person this will make me. I know that she's evil, I know what she's done, but I also know I will be changed when all of this is said and done. What is the price I will have to pay for this? What piece of my soul will die when I do this?" I shook my head. "I'm scared I won't be able to do it when it truly comes down to it. I'm scared that if I do, I'll never come back from it. That I'll never be the same. I'm scared you'll look at me differently—"

Nik cut off my words as he stood, pulling the t-shirt over his head and revealing the tattoos that swirled along his chest and neck, down his bicep. He held my eyes as his hands moved to his belt buckle.

"I will *never* look at you differently."

He slid his pants off, then his briefs, climbing into the tub with me. He sat facing me, our legs twined together.

"You say that now, but you might," I told him, raising my chin in defiance.

"I won't. Diana Kotova, I have been in love with you since the moment I met you. I fell first. How could I not when you are so strong, and fierce, and kind? You *will* be changed by the time the war is over. We all will. But know that no matter what happens, I will be by your side."

A tear escaped, running down my cheek and falling into the water before us with a soft plop. Nik leaned forwards to rub the tear from my cheek, but all he managed to do was rub soap onto my skin.

I choked out a laugh as I grabbed his shoulders, pulling him towards me. His hands were on my legs beneath the water as our mouths met, and a jolt of electricity ran up my spine. He captured my mouth with his, his hands finding my ankles and tugging me forwards and against him. I slid into his lap easily.

"What would I do without you?" I asked against his mouth.

"What would *I* do without *you?*" he asked back.

I wrapped my legs around him, bringing him closer. I could feel the hard length of him between us and I nipped at his bottom lip.

"Oh, who's trying to be serious now?" I teased, grinding against him.

"Fuck being serious," he growled against my mouth.

His hands ran up and down my back, pressing me tightly against him. No matter how much of Nik I had, I always craved more. My mouth moved to his shoulder, and I bit down, eliciting a hiss from him.

"Wicked witch," he chided as he dug his fingers into my back.

"Would you have me any other way?" I asked against his skin.

"*Never.*"

He lifted me then, lining himself up to my entrance. When he pulled me back down, I let out a groan as he filled me, the water sloshing over the sides of the tub. I braced my hands on the rim behind him as I threw my head back in pleasure, moving up and down in agonizing slowness.

Nik dug his fingers into my hips, and I reveled in the thought of the bruises they would leave behind tomorrow. I loved to wear him on my skin.

Nik's hands moved around my back up to my shoulders where he pulled me down with each thrust. I leaned back, glancing down at him as I rest my hands against his shoulders and rode him. His eyes were pure liquid flames as he watched me, my full breasts bouncing before him. He took one into his mouth and bit down, eliciting another groan from me. My hands moved to his hair where I buried them in it.

He felt *so damn good.*

His hands on my shoulders increased our tempo, and the water sloshed to the floor in big splashes, eliciting a soft giggle from me. I would be the one having to clean that up later. He moved his hips to meet mine, both of us chasing the pleasure that was fast approaching.

I cried his name as I came, over and over against him. His mouth captured mine again as he found his own release, pumping into me so hard the breath left my lungs.

I fell into him, completely sated and spent.

My breasts were pressed against his chest, my legs still straddling him. My head fell to his shoulder where I placed a gentle kiss.

"I love you, Nikolai." My voice sounded like a prayer as I leaned back only enough to meet his gaze.

"I love you, Diana. I am the luckiest bastard alive to have the privilege of being bound to you."

Nik helped me wash off a second time, and we toweled dry, stealing kisses while laying towels across the floor to soak up the spilled water from the bath.

Nik had successfully distracted me and washed away the anxiety of the oncoming battle...for now. I knew that it would come back to me in the darkest hours of the night, haunting my dreams. I wasn't prepared for what was to come, but I also wasn't sure there was anything I could do to relieve that anxiety.

We both fell into bed naked. We were still damp, wrapped in each other's arms. I pressed into Nik's chest, and he wrapped his arms around me, quickly finding sleep. I lay awake in his arms for hours until sleep finally took me.

Nik had chased away the nightmares for now, but they would come back.

If not tonight, then tomorrow.

If there was one thing I could rely on, it was that they always did.

36

I had slept without nightmares for the first time in what felt like weeks. Despite my anxiety, I was more rested than I had been since coming to Istmere. The sun was streaming in through the window across from the bed, and Nik's arms were wrapped around me, his soft breaths in my ear.

The serene sounds of his sleeping were interrupted by a fierce knock on the door, and he woke with a start.

"Can we have one moment without being interrupted?" he groaned, hanging over the bed to grab his pants.

"I think we had several uninterrupted moments last night," I reminded him with a mischievous grin.

"Well, I'd like a few more," he teased, shrugging his pants on and heading for the door.

I tucked the bedsheets around me to cover myself. He opened the door, his hair disheveled and his zipper undone.

"What can I help you with on this fine morning, Puck?"

"I'd like to inform you that not only is it actually *late* afternoon, but Warrick is back. He wants us to meet him upstairs, he made it sound urgent," Puck said.

I could picture the smile on his face, though I couldn't see him past Nik's frame in the doorway.

Late afternoon? How long had we slept?

"We'll be up soon," Nik replied, shutting the door mercilessly in Puck's face.

"That wasn't very nice," I chided, sitting up and taking the white bedsheet with me.

"Well, I don't think it's very nice of him and Tess to be interrupting us every five seconds," his tone was sarcastic, but I knew he was also being a bit serious.

I rolled my eyes at him. "They are our best friends, and we do all share this house with them."

"I don't care," he replied, leaning over the bed to place a kiss on my cheek. "I want alone time with you."

"I do too," I sighed, getting up and searching the dresser for an outfit. "But alas, Istmere needs saving and all that."

"What a needy realm," he teased, coming up behind me and turning me towards him. He captured my mouth with his. "We should just get rid of it entirely."

"Now you sound like Donika," I replied with a raised eyebrow.

Nik laughed, releasing me to search the floor for his favorite t-shirt to pull on.

We had dressed, and the sun was high in the sky indicating it was, indeed, *late* afternoon. I couldn't wait for this battle with Donika to be over with so I could have a million lazy days like this, spending hours in bed with Nik. He grasped my hand in his as we made our way down the hallway and up the spiral staircase that led to the backyard of Zion's cottage.

We made our way through the main floor of the cottage and out to the street in front, Tess and Puck following closely behind. Zion and Annelise were already waiting, an agitated looking Warrick standing in the middle of the cobblestone street.

"Will you tell us what is going on now?" Zion asked, his arms crossed over his chest.

"I had to wait for the others," Warrick sputtered, his eyes darting towards us. "It's Isaac—"

"What about Isaac?" Annelise cut in, moving towards Warrick. "Why had you waited to tell us? Is he alright?"

"He needs our help, *all* of us. Donika's forces have him cornered in Prins. We need to go. Now." His words were strangled.

Is that why Isaac hadn't returned yet?

"Were you with him? How did you escape?" Puck asked.

My hand subconsciously moved to make sure Stormslayer was secured to my thigh, my throwing knives securely tucked into my boot. Nik had luckily strapped his sword to his back as well before we left the room.

This wasn't the way we wanted to face Donika, it wasn't on our terms, and there was no way to prepare.

Warrick shook his head, his expression unreadable. "No, I wasn't with him, but I saw them. They're going to capture him and take him back to Akra, and there will be no way for us to break him out again until we move against Donika."

We all nodded in agreement. This isn't the way we planned it, but we needed to save Isaac. We needed to move, *now*.

Warrick turned and started down the cobblestone path at a fast pace and we followed. I thanked the mother I had been training, otherwise I never would have been able to run from Siraleth to Prins. I *still* wasn't much of a runner to be quite honest, but to save Isaac, I would need to push myself.

The sky was darkened up ahead, the clouds dark and angry. They swirled together in a mixture of black and grey, the wind moving them across the sky at an alarming pace. As we ran, the sun was hidden behind the shadow of the oncoming storm, casting Siraleth in a blanket of darkness.

Tess ran beside me, pumping our arms to keep up with the others. Warrick was fast, but so were Puck and Nik. They didn't hold themselves back to keep pace with us. Isaac was in trouble, and we couldn't leave him in Donika's clutches.

He was a Stormshade. She would never let him live.

As we passed between two columns that were once an archway composed of stone and mortar, I could feel the spell lift. The one that had concealed us from Donika, here in Siraleth.

The one that kept her *out*.

My stomach twisted as my magic pressed at my fingertips, an uneasy feeling washing over me. Warrick turned to ensure we were following on his heels, his eyes wild.

As Warrick rounded a corner and disappeared from sight, a creature came bounding towards us from the same direction. Puck and Nik skidded to a stop, Tess and I almost crashing into them.

I would recognize those spindly spider-like legs and horrifying human head anywhere.

Araneoch.

Donika's dark creatures bounded towards us, and I barely had the chance to slide my dagger free as I was pushed down, Nik standing over me with his sword drawn. The Araneoch moved quickly, knocking Nik sideways with one of its long, hairy legs and its horrific empty face met mine. Despite it having no visible eyes, it could see me. Its head moved side to side, tracking my movements as I tried to evade it.

I scrambled for Stormslayer, gripping it in my fist as I quickly rolled out of the way. A sharp, poisonous pincer hit the dirt right where I had just been standing. I spun to my feet and lashed out, slicing the leg but not severing it entirely.

The Araneoch hissed and reared back, and I advanced again. I cut forwards with my dagger once more, entirely severing the leg and the poisonous pincer from its body. I only prayed they had *one* pincer, and not one for each leg.

Nik leaped from behind, driving his sword into the plump body and pulling it free. Black blood spattered across us and I choked, gagging at the wretched smell. As the Araneoch crumpled we turned, moving on to the next creature.

My heart stopped in my chest as I took in the scene before me.

How many were there?

The streets were filled with them. Everywhere I looked there were spindly spider-like legs. We were outnumbered beyond belief, and bile rose in my throat as I hesitated. Puck, Tess, Nik, Zion, Annelise, Warrick...we were outnumbered.

Where was Warrick?

I searched the streets, my head whipping back and forth, but there was no sign of him. My stomach curdled as the realization hit me.

It had been a trap.

To lure us out of the spelled area of Siraleth where Donika could not enter.

But why? *Why would Warrick do this?*

Tess' scream had me lurching back into action, running towards her as fast as I could. Just as Nik had, I leaped into the air, driving Stormslayer into the body of the creature and watching it crumple beneath me.

The key to killing the Araneoch was to sever their heads or stab their bodies, the trick was making it past their long, poisonous legs.

My jacket was covered in the slick, black ichor. I reached a hand down to Tess to help her up, her face splattered with the dark liquid. She wiped it away hastily as she made her way back to her feet.

There were too many of them, and not enough of us.

As we dispatched one, another came rushing forwards. The streets were slick with their tainted blood as we fought, my breathing rapid.

Why would Warrick have led us into a trap? To what end?

Nik and Puck were counting aloud, and we had dispatched four Araneoch at this point. We were having more luck teaming up than trying to take them down alone. They were fast, but not particularly smart. I used my magic to strike them as I moved towards the next with my dagger.

The binding allowed me much more precision with my magic, and lightning shot out, striking the Araneoch dead where they stood.

But even bound, I wasn't endlessly powerful as the histories foretold. I tried to create a storm to pull from, but every time I dipped into my well of magic, I was interrupted by one of these creatures. Each time I had to focus on dispatching them with Stormslayer versus pulling more magic from the sky.

The clouds were swirling angrily, but it wasn't my magic that had stirred them into a frenzy. Siraleth was enveloped in a blanket of night, the streets stained black with Araneoch blood. I was pushed to the ground from behind by another creature, Stormslayer sliding from my grip and skittering against the cobblestones out of my reach.

I tried to crawl towards it, but a spindly leg moved into my vision, halting me. There were two of them, and one of them stood between me and my dagger. It wasn't ideal, but I reached for one of my throwing knives as the creature bent down over me.

Its wretched saliva dripped onto me as it studied me with its eyeless face, its head cocking to the side. It pressed me against the cobblestone with one of its legs on my shoulder. The pincer was pressed directly over my shoulder, far too close to my heart. I wouldn't survive a poisonous sting like that.

For a moment, time stopped as I waited to see if it would strike, but it only peered down at me with an unreadable expression, its mouth turned down, hiding its fangs. I reached into my core of magic to pull lightning from the sky, but as I grabbed the magic above me, I felt it cut off sharply, as if with a blade.

“That’s enough,” a chilling voice spoke as the sound of boots rounded the corner of the building Warrick had disappeared behind.

My head hit the cobblestones as I lay back, my blood running cold. My palms were sweating, my mouth dry. Stormslayer still lay a few feet away from me, but I couldn’t reach it with the Araneoch standing in the way.

What had cut off my connection to the magic in the sky? I dipped into my core again...but was met with a sizzling energy that I recognized from training with Isaac.

There was another Stormshade here. Was it Isaac?

“I wouldn’t do that if I were you,” the silky voice chided, crouching to get a better look at me splayed beneath the dark creature.

I set my jaw, biting the inside of my cheek. I wouldn’t let her see me afraid. A tall, blond man stood over Donika’s shoulder, his expression tight.

“Donika. I should have known.” When I spoke my voice was cold, no trace of the unease I felt lacing my words.

“Yes, you should have,” she snickered, lifting a lock of my blood-stained hair with the edge of her serpent staff. Her other hand held her onyx blade. “You’ve looked better, little Stormshade.”

“I could say the same about you,” I replied, making a show of looking her up and down slowly.

Her black eyes squinted in anger as she stood, nodding towards the blond man behind her and the Araneoch. The creatures retreated, allowing me to scramble to my feet before her. My gaze moved towards my dagger, but I knew I wouldn't be able to grasp it before Donika ran me through with her own blade.

My mouth was tight as I met her searching gaze. I was surprised to see she hadn't brought Corian with her, and I didn't recognize the blond man that stood behind her. Had she replaced her second in command?

"So, you found us. Congratulations," I seethed through my teeth.

"It wasn't terribly difficult." She shrugged, examining her perfectly manicured nails as I stood before her, covered in dirt and blood. "Your little Warrick made for an easy target."

"Leave Warrick alone," I ground out, my jaw tight.

"You defend him still?" she asked with a raised eyebrow. My eyes darted over her shoulder where Warrick stood, head down. He wouldn't meet my gaze. "He all but *jumped* at the chance to bring me to you when he found out his family had been captured in our little raid on your safe house in Prins. Blood comes first, after all."

We hadn't known any of his family had been captured. He hadn't said anything. He had only spoken with Puck since holing himself up in the cottage. We knew he had told Puck he had lost family in the battle...but we had assumed that meant they were dead.

If Warrick had told us that members of his family had been captured and used as collateral, we could have come up with a plan. We could have raided the castle and *saved* them. Instead, he took Donika's deal.

He betrayed us.

He hung his head in shame, avoiding our glares.

I knew he had bad blood with Nik, but I never imagined he would choose Donika's deal and turn his back on the council. He had been with the resistance and on the council for *years*, why hadn't he come to us for help? Had he truly thought the only way to save his family was to sacrifice us to Donika?

Donika's word couldn't be trusted, he was a fool for thinking otherwise. All he accomplished was ensuring that *all of us* would suffer now.

Nik spit in the dirt, lunging against the hold Donika's soldiers had around him, his gaze focused on the man over Donika's shoulder.

"How dare you show your face," Nik seethed, his jaw tight.

The man turned towards him, his expression blank. Almost bored.

"How lovely to see you too, son."

Son? This *was Nik's father?*

This man abused him and abandoned him, only to join Donika's army. My stomach turned as my gaze darted between them.

"Blood means *nothing*," I spat at her, holding her piercing gaze.

Nik hadn't seen his father in *years*, and he hadn't known where he disappeared to. Had he been in The Stone Palace all this time? And did Warrick truly think Donika would give his family back after he led her to us? That they were safe now?

"Blood means nothing? Is that so, mother dearest?" Donika asked, her gaze darting towards where Annelise was restrained on her knees. "I knew it was only a matter of time before you showed your face again. And you haven't learned your lesson, it seems. You are still on the wrong side of this war. I should have slit your throat when I had the chance."

Annelise flinched back at Donika's words, a tear falling from her cheek into the dirt. All this talk about moving against Donika, but the truth was, she hadn't been ready to face her. At least, not like this.

On her knees before her. Again.

"What do you want?" I asked through my teeth.

"The same thing I wanted last time, little sister. I want the grimoire, and I want you dead," she replied with a wicked smile.

My eyes met Nik's and the expression in his gaze threatened to unravel me. We had to make it out of this. We *had* to. If we could convince her to capture us instead of kill us, we could find a way to escape the Stormvault.

We had done it once, we could do it again.

"And daddy dearest?" Donika turned towards Zion with a laugh. "You...now you surprised me. You had me fooled. You stood by my side all these years, pretending to back my claim to the throne. But you turned on me, too. Just like everyone else." Donika shot a glance towards Nik's father before turning back to us. "My, my, the family drama."

"I did not want to turn on you, Donika, but I cannot stand by as I watch you murder innocents," he pleaded.

"*None of them are innocent,*" she spat, her temper rising.

While her attention was focused on Zion, I reached into the core of my magic and fueled it through my fingertips, thunder rolling overhead, and a lightning strike poised to crack right before me. As the bolt of energy shot from the air Donika raised her staff and the magic dissipated.

Her smile deepened as she met my gaze, my stomach lurching.

Had Donika just...no. She couldn't.

Had Donika just used storm magic?

She threw her head back, her white and blue hair cascading around her as the wind whipped in a vortex between us. I did as she had, reaching my magic out and leaching the energy from her gale.

Her laughing continued as she slid her onyx blade back into the holster on her hip.

A deadly silence spread around us, and no one spoke. The only sound was my rapid breathing as I gathered magic in my core, preparing to strike.

"Little sister, if you dare lash out at me with your storm magic again...my soldiers will slit Nik's throat before my body even hits the ground," she warned, her eyes hardening.

My eyes darted towards Nik whose jaw was set, his head held back against the chest of one of the soldiers.

A blade at his throat.

"May the mother damn you, Donika." The words ground out through my clenched teeth.

"The mother damned me a long, long time ago. Now give me the grimoire," she crooned.

"It's not like I have it on me," I replied tightly. "And what do you need it for, anyway? You don't need the siphoning spell anymore."

"I might not *need* it anymore, but I still want it," she replied, snapping her fingers at her side.

A soldier moved forwards then, a slumped body in his arms. Even without seeing his face, I recognized Isaac. He was curled in on himself, a keening cry escaping his lips.

"What have you done to him?" I demanded, taking a step forwards.

Donika's serpent staff lashed out faster than I could blink, landing against my stomach. "Not another step," she cautioned, "or he dies."

I swallowed hard, pressing my eyes closed tightly.

"What do you want with him?" I asked, meeting her gaze once more.

"Weren't you curious where I got this storm magic from?" She cackled.

She held her palm out, a blazing flame licking against the skin of her hand, but never burning her. The gem set in the bezel of her staff was glowing, ablaze with flickering flames that glowed within.

She *had* used storm magic.

And it had been Isaac's.

The magic held within her staff must be the magic she stole from others, to use for herself. It was no wonder my magic had recognized it as something dark, and powerful.

"Donika, what have you done?" My voice was cold dread as I pushed my magic back down. If she killed Nik, I would die, too.

"I've only leveled the playing field, little Stormshade. Who says you get to have all the fun?" she asked.

Her eyes fell on the soldier who held Isaac, and he yanked Isaac's head back by his hair. Isaac's eyes were endless and black, his teeth sharpened into fine white points that protruded from his mouth in a painful way.

Bile rose in my throat once more, my magic surging forwards violently, begging to be released.

Isaac was one of Donika's Noctani.

She had used those dark, magic siphoning creatures to steal his storm magic and leave him like this. A monster. But she *hated* Stormshades...why would she do this? Why would she want his magic?

"How could you do this?!" Annelise cried, pushing against the restraints of her captor.

Her cheeks were wet with tears, a choked sob escaping her throat as she met Donika's gaze.

"Ah, I had a feeling there was something going on between the two of you. I wanted to hit where it hurts, so to speak," Donika replied, her eyes burning with hatred as she gazed from Isaac to Annelise. "Zion never was good enough for you, was he?"

"Donika, stop this." Zion's voice was sad as he hung his head, unable to look at her.

"Don't you understand?" she asked, moving towards him. She pulled her sword free of its scabbard once more, using it to turn his face towards her. "I will *never* stop. Not until every single soul that stands against me is vanquished from this realm. Hell, this *planet*. You, included."

She had hesitated to kill our mother once, but I doubted she would hesitate again. We were as good as dead.

Donika somehow had this sick sense of betrayal, as if any of us were going to stand by her side as she murdered innocents. As if we were in the wrong, not her. Her view was so *twisted* beyond reason, I feared there would be no way to manipulate ourselves out of this.

If I tried to strike her down with magic, she would kill Nik. But could I live with the fact that Nik and I would be dead, as long as Donika was, too?

I met Nik's gaze across the cobblestone street and could see the resolve in his eyes. He gave a soft nod, his neck cutting against the blade held to his throat. A small trickle of blood ran down his neck, escaping under his white shirt. He was willing to sacrifice his life if it meant Donika was gone, too.

I knew I was willing, I had known this war might end in my own death. I had come to terms with that a long time ago. If it meant the people of Istmere would be safe from this tyrant, it was a price I was willing to pay. A true queen would give anything for her people. Donika had stolen everything from me, including my crown, and I wasn't going to let her get away with it.

I met Tess' gaze, and she lunged against the hold of the guards, tears streaming down her cheeks as the storm clapped above us. Thunder shook the ground we stood on.

Tears blurred my vision as I pulled on my magic, the corner of my mouth curving into a sad smile as I held her gaze. I didn't know our story would end here, and the thought felt as if it were a knife in my heart as my fingers sparked with magic.

Her eyes blazed, sobs wracking her body as she fell to her knees. The rain above us began slowly, kissing our cheeks and mixing with our salty tears. Within moments the rain had become a deluge, soaking us through.

A soft laugh escaped me as I turned to Donika.

"Little Stormshade..." Donika warned, moving her sword to point at my throat.

I smiled, leaning into the blade, my chest warming as blood pooled there.

"Diana, *please.*" I could hear Annelise's voice begging, but it sounded as if she was very, very far away.

My gaze turned towards my mother, and I met her eyes through the tears glistening in my own. I hadn't even gotten a chance to know her.

I pushed the thought aside as I pulled my magic from the sky, letting it well within me to the point of pain. Donika's eyes flashed with what I could only assume was fear before everything moved all at once.

Donika reached out with the butt of her sword, knocking me to the ground as my feet came out from under me. As I registered that she hadn't struck me down with her blade, Puck kicked a throwing knife towards Nik. He leaned forwards, the knife at his throat cutting into his skin as he grabbed the knife from the dirt, turning to plunge it into the soldier's neck.

Isaac rose to his feet, his expression cold and dark. He moved forwards, his fangs protruding from his mouth as he smiled wickedly, approaching Nik. More Noctani were coming forth now, appearing from around the corner of the building where the Araneoch had appeared.

I flattened to the dirt as I scrambled for Stormslayer, finding the handle and gripping it tight. My core was still filled with the storm magic I had pulled from the sky, and I lashed out. As I did, Donika raised her hand against my attack, the storm magic bouncing off her own. The rain was falling in such a thick torrent it was difficult to see what was happening as I raised my dagger against Donika, and she parried, taking a step back.

Tess was still being held by the soldier whose arms were wrapped around her, but Puck had broken free. The Noctani approached me and Donika stepped back, a sinister grin on her lips.

She hadn't struck me down...because she didn't truly want to kill me. She wanted my magic, and the Noctani was the way she was going to get it.

I lunged forwards, but the Noctani were *fast*. In a blur of motion the Noctani before me had moved out of the way of my blade, and was behind me, their hands on either side of my head. I bucked, knocking the Noctani in the face with the back of my head. My skull throbbed as I moved out of their reach.

"Diana!" Tess screamed as another Noctani approached.

I turned towards them, slicing out without hesitation. I was fast enough this time, and my blade sliced through the abdomen of the Noctani easily. The Noctani fell, slumping over as I pulled Stormslayer free and whipped around.

They appeared to be susceptible to our blades just as they would have been when they were Shades. That was good news, at least.

I could see out of the corner of my eye Tess struggling to break free as the soldier held her tightly, Puck coming up behind him and running him through with his Katana. Tess fell to her knees as the hold of the soldier released.

Nik was moving across the battlefield with incredible speed, his sword swinging true with each strike.

How many of them were there? When I had seen Donika last, she had only recently started having success in creating them. I hadn't imagined she could have created so many in such a short period.

I wasn't sure how, *exactly*, they stole magic, but I had to assume it was through their fangs and hands as the Noctani kept descending. Their goal appeared to be placing their hands against our skin instead of striking us down, maybe to get a better vantage point to sink their fangs into us.

My eyes searched for Donika, but she had disappeared in the melee.

That bitch.

Warrick was gone, too. As was Nik's father. Had he only made an appearance here to torture us? To weaken Nik?

I ran forwards, burying my dagger in the chest of another Noctani as I heard a blood-curdling scream from behind me.

Before I had time to turn, before I could register what was happening, I felt something deep within my core shift. The piece that I had become accustomed to over the last week, the piece that had been added during the binding ceremony...that piece was...broken.

I fell to my knees, Stormslayer clattering to the ground before me as my hand clasped my chest. My breaths were coming in short, rapid pants as I turned, unsure of what I would find.

Everything moved slowly as I slid into a puddle of rain, my heart constricting and causing my lungs to sputter.

I couldn't breathe.

Couldn't see.

Couldn't speak.

Tess was kneeling on the ground, her hand clasped over her mouth, sobs racking her body as she grasped tightly to Puck's jacket with her other hand.

Annelise was sprawled out on the stone, a dagger protruding from her leg. Zion hovered over her, trying to form a tourniquet to pull the blade free.

The bodies of Noctani were strewn about, not having disappeared as the Araneoch did when they were dispatched from this realm.

And Nik...Nik was on his knees. His head hung so I couldn't see his face, a Noctani standing behind him with a sickening smile, blood trickling down its chin.

I could feel, without knowing, that something was impossibly, horribly wrong. The piece of Nik that resided in me after the binding ceremony felt...fragmented.

Shattered.

Broken.

My other hand flew to my chest as I tried to suck in a breath, but I only managed a small amount of air.

I felt as if I was breaking apart.

My heart was torn in two as my magic filled me, pressing against my skin so forcefully that I felt as if I could hover over the ground with only the storm energy itself.

A sob wracked my body as that small piece of Nik from the binding ceremony became smaller and smaller inside of me until I couldn't feel it at all anymore. Tears streamed down my cheeks as I fell towards the cobblestone, my hands out before me to break my fall. My nails dug into the cobblestones so hard that they bled. A cry escaped me as the Noctani above him turned, retreating down the street.

I wanted to run after it, to run it through with my blade, but I couldn't move.

Couldn't breathe.

I could feel my heart shattering into a million fragmented pieces as Nik set his shoulders, cracking his neck. He moved to his feet, his head still hung before him, his face obscured. The rain stung my skin violently, each drop a knife against my skin.

We had only had *one week.*

For one week, we were *bound.*

For one week, we were *happy.*

For one week, I had pictured a life for us...*together.* After all of this.

And it only took *one moment* for all of those hopes and dreams to be *shattered.* Torn apart.

My magic was no longer under control, spiraling wildly as the storm above us raged with immense power.

The binding was broken.

I had no hope of controlling this storm now. The storm raged overhead, but it wasn't mine any longer. The storm magic filled me to the brim, my vision going white as I tried to hold it in. I didn't want to hurt anyone else. I couldn't. I wasn't in control.

Nik's lips curved into a sinister smile as he lifted his head. My heart was in my throat, the overwhelming need to retch filling my every thought.

Nik's skin was a glass-like milky white, chalky and colorless. His lips were turned into a smile around his sharp white fangs, his gaze finding mine.

A gasp escaped me as I realized the striking blue color was gone.

In its place was endless, lifeless black.

My nails were scratched bloody, my heart shattered and fragmented. I was covered in ichor, the storm around us raging without mercy.

Nik was Noctani.

As the rain fell violently around us, a sob tore through me.

My magic detonated, and the last thing I saw was Nik's black, lifeless eyes as the world went white.

Acknowledgements

Writing this book felt like a fever dream. As you may know, the first book of the series was a work in progress for almost 14 years, but this book came together in just over one. Diana and Nik guided me and told me where the story would go, and I never thought it would come so easily!

I could never have finished this book without the support of my friends and family, and their understanding of my hermit-like tendencies and not being heard from for months.

A special thanks to my Mom and Dad who helped me complete a laundry room renovation smack dab in the middle of writing and editing this book. A thank you to Grammy Frohman who is my #1 cheerleader and is always proud of me no matter what I do, but also pushes me to be proud of myself and my own accomplishments.

A thank you to my sister Jennifer, and my brother Eric, for understanding why I've spent all my nights buried in books (including those nights spent on a Caribbean cruise). To my nieces Layla and Lexi who recognize my book when they see it, and can't wait to read it when they are old enough.

A special thanks to my friends without whom I would be eternally lost. Jenn, Lisa, Laura, Brian, I hope you enjoy this story as much as you did the first.

I also need to thank my incredible book team, without whom this wouldn't have been possible. Emma Jane at EJL Editing for her amazing editing skills (I'm sorry about all the improper dialogue tags...again. I am definitely getting better!), Fran at MerryBookRound for this incredible cover that is quite possibly the most gorgeous thing I have ever seen, and Hillary Bardin, Rachael at Cartography Bird Maps, and Alice Maria Power for bringing my characters and the realm of Istmere to life in their amazing artwork.

And lastly to you, the readers. Thank you for taking a chance on this series. None of this would be possible without you, and I am forever thankful for your support. I am looking forward to the final chapter in Diana & Nik's story, and to finally writing a book that doesn't end on a whopping cliffhanger.

Maybe.

ABOUT THE AUTHOR

Michelle Frohman is an avid reader, writer, and animal lover. She writes young adult and new adult fantasy and paranormal romance and has a B.S. in Animal Science and an M.B.A. Michelle resides in Connecticut with her three cats Kasha (the spicy one), Kiwi (the sensitive one), and Peach (the fluffy one). When she's not reading or writing you can find her obsessing over her cats, drinking unhealthy amounts of peach tea, working on her interior design blog, or riding horses.

instagram.com/michellefrohmanauthor

tiktok.com/michellefrohmanauthor

facebook.com/profile.php?id=100094541655815

www.ingramcontent.com/pod-product-compliance
Lightning Source LLC
Chambersburg PA
CBHW031824310726
48972CB00005B/1149

9798988304548